THE SCENE CLUB

Andy Mellett Brown

This book is dedicated to the stylish
young men and women who attended
The Scene Club in Soho, London,
1963-66.

Acknowledgements

Thanks must firstly go to my wonderful wife Patricia, supplier of endless cups of tea and, when my imagination failed me, the occasional plot line. Also to John Steel, for an interview that he will doubtlessly have forgotten but which made a lasting impression on me, to Craig Sams, for getting me into the basement below Ham Yard, to those members of *Original Modernists 1959-1966,* who talked to me about their experiences at The Scene Club, and to Marie Marshall, Jacqueline Izzard, and Christina Davison, my merry band of proof readers, without whom there would be a great many more typos in *The Scene Club* than I hope there are. Thank you all.

CHAPTER ONE

Holly Holgate slipped the cassette out from its case, wondering as she turned it over in her hand about the last time she'd handled an audio cassette. They were redundant technology. The kind of thing, she supposed, that almost everyone possessed back in the day but next to no-one possessed now. Replaced by Spotify and the Apple Store.

Sourcing a cassette player had been only marginally less challenging than locating the recording. As soon as she'd realised that the recording was on audio cassette she'd begun asking around, drawn a blank and had finally resorted to eBay. Fifteen quid plus postage and packing on a *buy it now*, from someone called "retroelectro", all lower case, with an address in Putney and 99.8% positive feedback.

She reached out, pressed the button marked "OPEN" and slid the cassette into the player. The lid closed with a satisfyingly plastic clack. She pressed the "PLAY" button, sat back in her chair and waited.

'Spencer Milburn, welcome to the programme.'

The audio sounded tinny but the recording was clear enough. She reached for the volume control and nudged it up a notch.

'Thank you. It's a pleasure to be here.'

His accent was unmistakable.

'Can we start by talking about the early days?'
'Sure we can.'

The accent surprised her for no particular reason. After all, he was from the North East. They all were. Though Micky, the more famous or infamous of the Milburn brothers, had long since abandoned his home town. She wondered where Spencer and the others lived these days. Assuming they were still alive. She made a mental note to try to trace them.

'You were a founder member of The Monks.'
'Yes, that's right. Pete and I first met when we were fifteen. Peter Lumley, that is. We formed our first band in 1958. Then in fifty-nine we met up with Trevor Fenwick, persuaded him to join us and that became the nucleus of The Monks.'

The Fifties. Spencer Milburn had formed his first band sixty years ago, more than twenty years before she was born. It was almost a lifetime ago. To listen to him speak, you'd have thought it was yesterday.

'How did you know Pete? Did you meet him at school?'
'Yeah, we were school drop outs, actually.'
'Really?'
'Sure. We both dropped out of school when we were fifteen. We were hopeless academically, at A levels and all that, you know? So we both dropped out and enrolled at the Newcastle College of Art. Which is what you did in those days if you didn't want to work for a living.'

The interviewer had laughed wryly. Like he wanted to give the impression that he knew what you'd done in those days if you didn't want to work for a living. Which she sincerely doubted. *Pretentious twat.*

'So we had three and a half years at art school and that's when we formed our first band.'

His accent might be broad but his voice was soft and rounded. Comfortable. Like this was familiar territory. Like he was sitting by the fire telling his grandchildren about what he'd done during The War.

'Why the drums, Spence?'

Except that Spencer Milburn didn't have any grandchildren. She knew that. He'd never married. Never fathered any children, as far as she knew. Unlike his brother, who had reportedly fathered only marginally fewer illegitimate bastards than Genghis Khan.

'Well, you know, that's an old story. Because when we first got together, in fifty-eight, rock and roll was taking off in a big way. Until then the dance music for kids had been jazz. Mostly traditional jazz, as a matter of fact. I wanted to play trumpet. That was my first instrument. When Pete and I formed our first band it was a little jazz combo. But Pete very quickly realised that rock and roll was where he wanted to go, you know. Rock and roll, and blues. So we did an about change. The drummer switched to bass guitar…'

'That was Richard Lambton, right?'

'Yes, that's right. Ricky switched to bass guitar. Electric. They were just coming out then. Pete, who had been playing banjo, switched to lead guitar. I dropped the trumpet and picked up the drums.'

Just coming out then. They'd been playing in a band before electric instruments had become available. To the likes of working class kids, at least. It seemed impossible to imagine it, in these days of digital recording, when just about anyone could make music, upload it to YouTube and broadcast it to the world.

'And, of course, your brother Micky took lead vocals.'
'No, that was later. Pete did the vocals in those early days. Micky didn't join us until sixty-one. Prior to that he'd fancied himself as a trombone player. But he was hopeless at it. I mean really hopeless. It was only when the band started to take off and Micky hit his sixteenth birthday that we convinced him to take the vocals. He had one hell of a voice, even then.'

Sixteen. It was hard to imagine Micky Milburn ever being sixteen. Though she'd seen pictures of the band when they first made it big. Even at that stage Micky Milburn's craggy features had made him look at least ten years older than he was. *Christ, he must look positively ancient now. He must be positively ancient now.*

'And the band, I mean The Monks, took off quite quickly and had some enormous hits in the early sixties didn't it? It must have been an exciting time for you, as a young man new to the big time?'
'It was. It was phenomenal. By late 1963, when The Beatles had already hit the charts in a big way, it was time to get out of Newcastle, head south and get into the London scene. That's what you had to do. Simple as that. I mean, we were as big as we were going to get in Newcastle. What we didn't realise was that it was happening all over the country. People in Glasgow and Liverpool and Sheffield and wherever, were finding the music.'
'Rhythm and blues, you mean?'

'Sure. But there were two distinct streams, you know. There was The Beatles in Liverpool…'

'The Mersey sound, you mean?'

'Yes. And then there was Alexis Korner and The Rolling Stones. They started a whole movement, you know. Of rhythm and blues-based bands. The Stones were the big ones. That was where we saw ourselves going. That was what took us to London.'

She reached for her mug. She'd balanced it precariously on a pile of magazines towards the middle of her crowded desk. She took a mouthful of tea. It was lukewarm. She thought about pausing the recording to make a fresh cup and then thought better of it. She rebalanced the tea cup on the pile of magazines and sat back in her chair.

'Were The Monks heavily influenced by rhythm and blues, right from the start?'

'Sure we were.'

'What sort of music were you listening to?'

'We were very taken with Ray Charles, you know? His early stuff. It was absolutely sensational. Also more obscure stuff like Jimmy Reed, John Lee Hooker, Fats Domino and the great rock and rollers.'

'Of course, Micky was always into rock and roll, wasn't he?'

'Yes, that's right. Micky fancied himself as a bit of an Elvis Presley. He was more into that, you know. The James Dean thing. Leather jackets and motor bikes.'

She smiled. She'd read about the London scene at the beginning of the sixties. Emerging, mainly from the modern jazz clubs of the late fifties, the early trendsetters had come from various sub-groups of sharp, fashion-conscious young men. They'd been into the newly discovered music of African America, and the clothes and shoes they saw illustrated in Italian magazines they picked up

5

from the newsstands on Oxford Street. Drawn to the clubs and coffee bars around Soho, the last thing these forward thinking boys, with their near obsession with the latest nip and tuck to their tailored suits, would have been seen dead in was a biker's leather jacket.

'Whereas the rest of you were more blues oriented. Did that cause tension between you, even then?'

'Yes, I guess so. So we tried to compromise by playing Little Richard stuff. Chuck Berry. But always Pete and I would try to pull us back to the blues. You know, that Kansas City style of blues. Big Joe Turner. Joe Williams. That kind of urban blues that needed a big, rolling piano. That's what Trevor Fenwick provided for us.'

'So you came to London.'

'Sure.'

'Did you find a big rhythm and blues scene waiting for you?'

'Well, you know, as in any decade, there was everything waiting for you in London. You could go to The Flamingo in Wardour Street and see some of the best live blues and jazz based blues in the world. You had Georgie Fame and The Blue Flames resident. Chris Farlowe and The Thunderbirds. Zoot Money's Big Roll Band, with a fifteen year old Andy Summers on guitar. That was really world class stuff going on down there. You had every would-be pop star and rock and roll player in the country trying to get laid, you know?'

The interviewer had laughed, slightly awkwardly. Which seemed curious until she remembered that he was interviewing a seventy year old man. The thought of someone who was old enough to be your grandfather getting laid was a bit like imagining The Queen on the toilet. It might happen but you didn't really want to think about it.

'As you know, the station has a big mod audience. We tend to think of The Monks as first and foremost a mod band. But did you think of yourselves as a mod band at the time?'

'Well, no we didn't. But funnily enough, I played a gig just last year and some guy came up to me and bought me a pint. A guy who had hung out at The Scene Club in Ham Yard just off Great Windmill Street, which is where we first started to play when we arrived in London. He was one of the early mods and he said "The Monks were our band." He said, "I know people think of The Who when they think of the mods but for those of us at The Scene Club it was The Monks", you know?'

The Scene Club. Another of those vanished 60's dance clubs that had been dotted about London's West End like confetti. Usually upstairs in a pub. Or, as in the case of The Scene Club, in a sweaty basement long since requisitioned for some other purpose. She wondered, briefly, what had become of the place. Did anyone know? Did anyone care? The world had moved on and the kids with it.

'But you didn't see yourself as mods at the time?'

'No. Well, the thing is, we were just a bunch of northern rockers. Especially Micky. I mean, he still had the greased back hair when we arrived in London. He got rid of that pretty damn quick.'

I bet he did. The clean cut, fashion conscious London mods would have despised anyone with grease under their finger nails, or worse, in their hair.

'The fact is that we didn't even know what a mod was until we arrived at The Scene Club. It was purely a London phenomenon at that time. That look. The clothes they wore. The Italian scooters lined up in Ham Yard when we arrived there for our first gig. Lambrettas and Vespas, covered in chrome and lights, with foxtails on long aerials fixed to the back. We'd never seen anything like it. And the attitude of those guys. The way they stood. The way they talked and danced. It just wasn't anywhere else in the country at that time. I'm talking early sixty-four, you know?'

'They took to you, though. Despite Micky's greased back hair?'

Micky Milburn had been a fraud from the start. He'd only ever been interested in one thing. *No two*, she corrected herself. The Monks and their music had only ever been a vehicle to get him there. Money was the first and women was the second and, by all accounts, he'd set about acquiring as much as possible of both with considerable gusto from the start.

'They loved our raw edged blues sound. Which surprised us. Because the DJ, a fella called Guy Stevens who was a very early importer of American music, was playing mostly soul and soul-based rhythm and blues. Tamla Motown. I mean, he was one of the first guys to play Motown, you know. They were listening to Mary Wells and Martha and The Vandellas down at The Scene Club long before Motown got anywhere near the charts.'

'What was the fashion like? Amongst the mods at that time, I mean.'

'As I remember it, there were two distinct kinds. The guys with the suits and the scooters, you know. They were the faces. The guys that set the standard. But there was another kind of mod. They had very short hair and wore little trilby hats with half inch brims. And the drugs. Man. I mean, we'd come across drugs before. But the mods at The Scene Club popped Purple Hearts like confectionery. If the place got raided, everyone would stand in a circle and empty their pockets onto the floor. It would be covered in them. Those guys got blocked, the whole time, you know?'

Blocked. She smiled. It seemed like such an old fashioned term. Each generation had their word for it, she supposed. *Wasted* was what she'd heard some kids calling it on the bus the other day. With that ridiculous street accent that always sounded so implausible coming from working class, English white boys. Trying to sound like they were riding the New York subway. Rather than a Number 14 to Putney. God, it was painful.

'There was a drug scene in London, as early as sixty-four?'

Stupid question. There'd been opium dens in London, a century before. Even she knew that.

'Sure there were. It was the only way you could dance all night. Maintain that energy. The ones with short hair started to wear baggy trousers and very lightweight, flexible dancing shoes. They did this amazing, athletic kind of dancing. Mostly to the DJ's stuff. I mean, people go on about Northern Soul now, which was much later. These guys were doing exactly that down at The Scene Club in early sixty-four. The kind of dancing style that became associated with Northern Soul and the Wigan thing, you know? Those kids were way ahead of their time.'

'Did you have any idea then, that twenty years later you'd still be playing?'

'No, man. Never. I thought it might be great for a couple of years and then we'd have to work for a living, you know. Get a proper job.'

She couldn't help warming to him a little, as much as she didn't want to. She'd built a picture of the Milburn brothers in her head. Mostly from the stuff that she'd read about them. Or from scratchy black and white film converted to video. Interviews with some plummy accented BBC interviewer like this one, pretending to be 'hip' but sounding like a right cock. Mostly with Micky Milburn, it had to be said. Micky had been the main event from the start.

'But when The Monks were at their height, you must have thought that something big was happening. Something that was going to last?'

'Well, to be honest, we didn't get much time to think about it. The pressure became intense. I mean we left Newcastle at the end of 1963 and within a few months, by the summer of 1964, we were topping the charts all over the world. We were jetting off to New York and playing a week at the Paramount Theatre in Times Square. Appearing on The Ed Sullivan Show and stuff like that.'

'It must have been an incredible experience. Five working class lads from Newcastle, travelling down to London in, what was it, an old Commer van?'

'It was a Standard Atlas actually.'

(Interviewer laughs) 'It must have been one hell of an experience?'

'Well, precisely. I mean in those days Geordie lads like us went into the factories and were lucky if they got a holiday in Blackpool, you know? They didn't jet off to America the way that people do now. The only people who got to The States were very rich or business people. Arriving in America was like landing on a different planet. I mean all our influences had been from there. Rock and roll, blues, jazz, the movies, the books. Everything that had influenced us had come from across the water. And suddenly there we were. For us to fly out there and arrive with a Number One single, you know? To drive into Manhattan from the airport with police outriders. It was just the most fantastic experience.'

She was warming to him because, perhaps for the first time, she was thinking about what it must have been like to have been there. To have been him. A gangly lad from Newcastle. One minute, gigging around endless, shitty little North East working mens clubs in a battered old Standard Atlas. The next, flying into JFK with hoards of girls screaming your name and offering to jump into your bed and shag you stupid. Like you were one of The Beatles or something. It was hardly surprising that half of them had gone off the rails. Ended up throwing television sets from hotel windows and snorting themselves into oblivion. She was warming to him, in spite of herself, because unlike his brother Micky, who by all accounts considered himself to be God Almighty, Spencer Milburn sounded like he had survived it all with something approaching humility.

'You left The Monks in 1966, didn't you?'
'Yes, that's right.'
'Why was that?'

If her attention had been beginning to wander, with those three words her thoughts had snapped back into focus. *Why. Was. That.*

'I'd just had enough, you know? We were on a treadmill. We had no time to stop and think. It was just too much.'

The usual bullshit. The same lame response every ex-sixties pop star relied on to explain why they'd burned up, dropped out and shuffled off back to obscurity. Except that in the case of the Monks, that hadn't been it at all.

'The other thing was the money. It had just disappeared. I mean, we should have been well off. Kids nowadays make fortunes in just a few months and we'd been on the treadmill for over two years and weren't getting any money. We were on a fixed retainer. And when we asked what was going on, we were told that the money had been put in a tax free haven in The Bahamas and that kind of crap? Well, if it was, the account didn't have our names on it, that's for damn sure. We were screwed. You know. Royally screwed.'

'By Marty Phelps, your manager, you mean?'

He had hesitated. Just for a second. She noticed it.

'Well, you know, I don't want to name any names. And to be fair, it wasn't just Marty. It was the record label. The promoters. The hangers-on. They all screwed us. So I thought, well I've had enough of this. That was practically the end of the band anyway. We'd been pulling against each other for a while. Maybe all along.'

He was avoiding the real cause of the tension between them. Deflecting. Or maybe he had told the story so many times that he actually believed it. But whether he'd convinced himself of it or not, the story he was peddling was still bullshit.

'Since Micky joined, you mean?'
'No, not just Micky.'
'But Micky was part of the problem wasn't he? You're on record as having said at the time that it was Micky who caused the split.'

Micky had been the problem, sure enough. He'd been the problem all along.

'There were, I suppose, what you might call artistic differences between us.'

Artistic differences, my arse.

'About your music? The material?'
'Partly that, yes.'
'And what else?'

She was holding her breath. She realised it and exhaled. There was no way he was going to spill the beans. That was way too much to hope for.

'Micky bought into the hype. Thought he'd outgrown us. Read the newspapers and believed all that shit. It's difficult not to when you've got people whispering in your ear the whole time. Feeding your ego. You've got to remember that we were all young men and Micky was the youngest of all of us.'
'He saw himself as bigger than The Monks?'

Bigger than The Monks. Of course Micky Milburn had seen himself as bigger than The Monks. He had always been bigger than The Monks. But that had nothing to do with it. Not directly, anyway. When was the interviewer going to get to the point?

'I think so, yes. People were telling him that without him The Monks were nothing. Just another backing band. And then there was all the drugs and the... Well, you know.'

Now she had stopped breathing altogether. This was why she'd hunted down the tape. She focussed. She wanted to hear it.

'You mean the girls.'
'Well... I suppose so.'

He hadn't meant to go there. She could hear the reluctance in his tone. He'd got carried away. Told the story so many times that he hadn't seen it coming. The shutters were already coming down. The interviewer needed to move quickly.

'Like the girl who went missing. What was her name? Gina wasn't it?'

Gina Lawrence. He knew perfectly well. This was where he'd been headed all along. If Spencer Milburn hadn't seen it coming he was certainly seeing it now.

'No. No, that was all just rubbish. Newspaper talk, you know.'

Newspaper talk. She reached across her desk and picked up a yellowing newspaper from the pile beside her tea cup. The headline on the front page was clear enough. "THE MONKS AND THE MISSING TEEN", with a hastily snapped picture of Micky Milburn being bundled into the back of a car by Marty Phelps, the band's manager.

'But when that story broke it must have had an impact. The reports that she'd been hanging around with you and Micky. That must have got to you, surely?'
'Well, of course, it was very sad. I mean the poor girl's family…'

He was stalling. Trying, desperately, to re-write his script. The words were empty. Hollow. To his credit, the interviewer was having none of it.

'People have said that it tarnished both your subsequent careers. What do you say to that?'
'Say to it? I don't say anything to it. Like I said, it was rubbish then and it is rubbish now. We barely even knew the girl, to be honest and…'
(Interviewer interrupts again) 'Really? But there was a lot of talk at the time. Persistent rumours that the two of you were an item.'
'Rubbish, man.'
'That Micky had muscled in.'
'You'd have to ask Micky about that.'
'That it had led to a serious rift between the two of you.'

And there it was. Spencer Milburn had hesitated for a moment longer than was comfortable. For a moment she thought that he might be about to break the silence that he and Micky Milburn had maintained for the last fifty years. She waited.

'I've got nothing to say about that. I thought you invited me on to the show to discuss the band.'

'Yes, of course. But before we move on, you're saying, categorically, that you had absolutely nothing to do with Gina Lawrence's disappearance?'

'Of course I had nothing to do with it. Look, what is this?'

'Hey, I'm just trying to give you an opportunity to set the record straight. But we can move on to your later career if you…'

'I don't think so.'

(The sound of scraping chair legs. Muffled, heated voices. Then silence).

She pressed the cassette player's stop button, sat back in her chair and let out a long breath. Spencer Milburn might be softly spoken but he wasn't your typical cuddly grandad and this wasn't a fireside children's story. He was a bloody liar. He had lied at the time of her disappearance. He was lying on the tape recording. It had been obvious to the interviewer and it was obvious to her. Both the Milburn brothers had lied all along. The question was why? Nothing that she'd heard had altered her view of the likely answer. They were lying about Gina Lawrence because Micky Milburn had killed her and Spencer Milburn knew it.

CHAPTER TWO

Thursday, 5 May 2016

Harry Stammers undid the chin strap, removed the crash helmet from his head and ruffled his hair with his free hand. He'd thought about catching the train but he'd missed the 08:32 and Ellen had needed the Alpha for a meeting with a supplier in Watford. Maybe it was time they got another car. They had talked about it. Ellen's business was doing well and his promotion meant that they could afford it. But another car was going to make it more difficult to justify holding on to the Spitfire. Even though the little sports car spent most of its life under a tarp in Mike's garage, three cars and a scooter between two drivers would be an extravagance, however you looked at it. Getting rid of the Spitfire was simply out of the question. They'd been through too much together, him and that car. They were all emotionally attached to it, though Jane, of course, pretended otherwise. The last time he'd asked her about the car, she'd threatened to get it towed away "if you don't do something about that big green bogey in my garage." But that was just Jane.

The public car park had already been half full as he rode up from the main gate. Fortunately, his new position at The Park meant that he'd been assigned a private parking space in front of the bungalow that housed the museum's offices. It had seriously pissed off Jane. She'd called him a "pretentious wanker" for having his name painted on the tarmac. He'd had it done just to wind her up.

Thinking about her reaction always made him smile. It scandalised her entirely when he left the scooter there. But that was just Jane too. He smiled inwardly, bent down, turned the scooter's fuel tap to the "OFF" position, straightened himself and walked the dozen or so yards to the bungalow. She was waiting for him in the doorway.

She growled. 'You're late.'

He glanced at his watch, as if only vaguely interested. 'Not really.'

She folded her arms and stared at him.

He held out the helmet.

She carried on staring at him.

He shrugged, stepped past her, hung the helmet on a coat hook by the door, removed his parka and hung it on the hook next to the helmet. 'By a few minutes, maybe.'

She glanced at the clock on the wall. 'By forty-five minutes. And by the way, we've got three hours until she arrives. The security people have been here since eight. The caterers are up at the mansion. The gates open to the press in forty minutes and to the public thirty minutes after that. In case you'd forgotten.'

He had known Jane ever since he'd started working at the former code breaking centre. He'd applied for his first job at The Park after he and Mikel Eglund, now Jane's husband, had paid G-block an unofficial visit by climbing in through a broken window at the back of one of the derelict prefabs attached to the main building, after dark one April Sunday evening. Whereas the brick and concrete buildings that comprised G-block had been built to withstand whatever Nazi Germany cared to throw at them, the prefabs had been a later and less substantial addition. By the time that he and Mike had explored them, they'd been falling down. Making their way along their crumbling corridors had been hazardous in the extreme.

While the deplorable state of such an important site in the nation's history had appalled him and left him feeling that something should be done to halt the decline, there had been something else that had prompted him to apply for the curator's job when he saw it advertised in The Guardian a few weeks later. The decaying buildings of unrestored Bletchley Park had an atmosphere. Like an echo, left behind by the thousands of men and predominantly women who had worked there during The War. He'd found it both magnetic and impossible to explain to anyone except Ellen, his wife for the last ten years. She had given his sensitivity to buildings and places a name. She called it "intuition". He'd have dismissed any other label as mumbo jumbo but the word "intuition" seemed to at least imply a measure of normality. The term "intuition" he could live with.

He'd never really tried to explain it to Jane. Though he had often wondered what had motivated her to take a job at The Park. Given the pittance she was paid, it was unlikely to have been her salary. He'd asked her once. She'd replied "It's a job, isn't it?" and that was all he'd ever got from her on the subject.

He had, though, liked Jane Eglund, or Jane Mears as she had been then, from the start. It had understandably mystified his other colleagues because to say that she had an acid tongue would have been an understatement. Cutting and rude to just about everyone she encountered, Jane had managed to turn sarcasm into an art form. She rarely smiled and was, as far as Harry was concerned, just plain scary when she did. She certainly wasn't physically attractive. Her short black hair and sharp bird like features gave her a severe appearance that scared anyone with even a modicum of common sense. He'd liked her nonetheless. Because she was clever and exceptionally good at her job. Because she was about as direct as it was possible to be. With Jane, he had always known exactly where he stood. There was never any bullshit. Never any padding. She didn't speak in riddles or offer platitudes. She never told him what he wanted to hear. Not ever. She was honest to the point of brutality. Most of all she was staunchly loyal. Knowing that Jane Eglund had your back was like having a personal life guard. She had, quite literally, saved his on more than one occasion and he had absolutely no doubt at all that she would, if called upon to do so, save it again.

He flashed her a smile. 'Well, we'd better get on with it then. However,' he interrupted himself, 'first things first.'

She raised an eyebrow.

'Coffee. Strong. Black. No sugar.'

'Fuck off.'

'It was worth a try.'

'You know where the kettle is.'

He knew exactly where the kettle was.

He was standing on the steps of the mansion, watching the Royal car pull away. It was a black four-by-four. A Range Rover with tinted windows. Bullet proof, he supposed. Top of the range but not quite the Bentley he'd been hoping for. Preceded by a police outrider and flanked by a black Jaguar without plates. An SO14 car apparently. Occupied by men in dark grey suits with bulges where their Glock 17s were stashed. Or so he'd been told by the police officer who had earlier seemed to take such pleasure in searching his office. What the hell PC 7417 had thought he was going to find under the Chief Officer's desk God alone knew.

The driveway in front of the mansion was lined on one side with cheering school children waving plastic union jacks and, on the other, with park veterans, many perched on electric mobility scooters, trustees who mostly looked like they soon would be, and invited members of the public. At the far end of the drive was a cordon for the press and other media. The BBC had a camera crew on a small scaffold tower, recording a piece for the regional evening news.

His eyes were fixed on the huddle of reporters and photographers lined up along the cordon's edge. His one-time celebrity status had earned him several run-ins with the press pack, though in recent years they had thankfully mostly lost interest. He had more than sufficient reason to thoroughly distrust the lot of them. And distrust them he did. As far as Harry Stammers was concerned, the sooner they were off The Park the better.

He watched the photographers straining to catch a last minute picture as the Range Rover sped by. No doubt hoping for a parting shot of Her Royal Highness, lulled into a sense of false security by the tinted glass, picking her nose or more likely, taking a well earned slug from the Royal hip flask. It was, after all, well past gin-o'clock.

All faces turned as the car sped by. All, that is, except one. A young black, or possibly mixed race, woman with big hair. Harry had the distinct feeling that she was watching him, though the sun behind the trees to the rear of the press cordon made it difficult to make out her face. He held up his hand to shield his eyes from the glare.

'Well, Stammers, I'd say that was something of a success, wouldn't you?'

He half turned, his eyes still straining to make out the woman's features. There was something about her. Something odd. Out of place. Like she had been photoshopped into position. He felt the hair on his arms prickle. 'Sorry?' He glanced over his shoulder at the balding man who had approached him from behind. 'Oh, Major, sorry. Yes, it was…' His voice trailed away as his attention was drawn back towards the press cordon. His view of the woman had been obscured by another reporter who had stepped into his field of vision and who had also now turned to face him. She was older perhaps. Probably not by much. White. Short dark hair. Wearing a tan-coloured jacket. Her face was clearer. She was staring at him. Or so he thought. He looked away, not wishing to attract her attention any more than he thought he already had.

'It's a relief, isn't it? Visiting royalty and the television coverage will no doubt do wonders for our visitor figures and of course Underground Bletchley is going to be an absolute triumph. But it has been something of a strain, hosting Her Royal Highness and all that.'

Major Sir John Huntley-Gordon was the Trust's Chairman. Now twice retired. First, from a reputedly unremarkable career in the Royal Signals and subsequently from his position as The Park's Chief Operating Officer. It had, by all accounts, been the Major's personal recommendation and his casting vote on the board of trustees that had led to Harry's appointment as The Park's new Chief Officer. It had been a surprise appointment. To Harry as much as to everybody else.

'I mean, jolly well done Stammers. Not just for pulling it off today but with the whole Underground Bletchley project. It's a tremendous personal achievement. You're a credit to The Park.'

'Thank you, Major.' It had been a long time coming. A very long time. Two years for the clearance from English Heritage. Best part of five to secure funding for the tunnel restoration and visitors' centre. Another three for the actual building work. They'd delayed the opening by six months, just to fit in with the Princess Royal's timetable.

'No need to thank me, Stammers. Without you, none of this would have happened,' the Major said, holding out his hand.

Harry shook it willingly but his attention had once again returned to the press cordon. It was emptying rapidly, the reporters and photographers drifting away, some of them across the lawn towards the lake and others towards the car park. He tried to make out the two women and for a moment thought he had lost them. Then the woman with the tan-coloured jacket had reappeared at the cordon's edge, the younger woman behind her and the two had begun walking towards him.

There was no question in his mind that they were reporters. He could see the camera around the older woman's neck. 'No, not at all. Thank you for all your support and, of course, please do pass on my thanks to the trustees. Underground Bletchley has been a team effort,' he said, shaking the other man's hand a little too vigorously. He realised he was doing it and stopped. 'Excuse me, Major. Would you mind?' He released the man's hand. 'I'm rather afraid that I am needed back at the office,' he added hastily. Without waiting for a reply, he turned and walked purposefully away. The lie was plausible. The truth was that he'd done all the interviews he was going to do for one day.

'Mr Stammers?'

He heard her hurried footsteps coming up behind him. He picked up his pace.

'Mr Stammers?'

She had gained on him. He ignored her.

'Sorry. Mr Stammers?'

He looked over his right shoulder, expecting to see both women but saw only the elder of the two.

'Mr Stammers, I'm sorry,' the woman said, puffing slightly. 'Have you got a few minutes?'

Harry glanced to his left. 'No,' he said without slowing. 'I've given all the interviews I'm going to give today.'

'Please? Just a few minutes?'

He felt her hand on his upper arm. He stopped and turned, making no effort at all to mask his irritation. She was pretty and slightly red faced. She released his arm awkwardly. Like she knew that she'd overstepped the mark.

'I told you, I'm not doing any more interviews today. You and your colleague can contact the Press Office.'

'My colleague?' She looked puzzled.

He hesitated. 'The woman with you,' he said, feeling slightly foolish.

She looked at him blankly.

'Well, anyway,' he said. 'If you'd like to contact our press officer, I'm sure she'll give you what you need.'

'You don't understand. Sorry. Look, I don't want an interview.'

He glanced at the camera around her neck. It was a Nikon. Expensive. The kind of expensive that only a professional could afford.

She followed his eyes. 'I'm not paparazzi, if that is what you're thinking.'

He grunted, turned and began walking away. 'Sorry. Not today,' he mumbled over his shoulder.

She followed him. 'I just want to talk to you.'

'Why?' he asked, keeping his eyes firmly on the pathway. 'What do you want?'

She was dancing along beside him. 'I…'

He had no intention of helping her to find the words she was clearly having trouble finding.

'Look, can we just stop? Please? For a moment?'

It took him less than a moment to consider and then dismiss the request. 'No, I'm sorry. Call my office. Maybe another time.' He kept walking.

'I need your help.'

He had turned left onto the pathway up to the bungalow. If he couldn't shake her off, Jane sure as hell would. 'My help? With what?' But he wasn't about to wait for an answer. 'No. Don't even go there. You're a reporter. You want a story. We've given you your story. Princess Anne. Underground Bletchley. Opens to fee paying visitors at nine-thirty tomorrow morning. Special rates for groups. Thank you and goodbye.'

'Yes, I am a reporter. But I didn't come here to see Underground Bletchley. Or Princess bloody Anne. I came to see you.'

'Well, I'm sorry you've wasted your time.'

'Mr Stammers. Harry, please.'

He ignored her.

'You find people, right?' she said breathlessly.

He flinched. He had been half expecting it.

'You found your mother and your wife, after they were kidnapped. Twice. Once in the tunnels below Belsize Park and again in the New Forest.'

So she'd done her homework.

'You found Martha Watts.'

They were approaching the relative safety of the bungalow.

'Against all the odds. Despite some very powerful people trying to stop you.'

She was audibly panting now.

'Look, who are you?' he said, turning to face her.

'My name is Holly Holgate. I need your help to find someone. Like you found Martha Watts.'

So she'd done her homework well. He shrugged. 'Martha Watts was dead when we found her.' He could see images of the Bletchley Park log reader's mummified body in his mind's eye. Along with the message to her mother she'd scrawled on the wall of the cell in which she'd been incarcerated. One hundred feet below Belsize Park Underground Station. "TELL MUM I LOVE HER".

'I know,' she said quietly. 'I know she was.' She was still panting. 'The woman I'm looking for. Her name was Gina Lawrence.'

The name rang a vague bell but he couldn't quite place it.

'She's dead too, Harry. I'm sure of it. Murdered.' She took a long breath. 'I need to find out what happened to her.'

She was staring at him. He met her eyes. They were deep green. 'Then go to the police,' he said firmly.

'It's not that simple.'

It never was. He snorted. 'Why not?'

'Because I don't have enough evidence. Yet.'

'Then find it. You're a reporter, aren't you? An investigative journalist? So go and investigate.'

She faltered.

He broke eye contact and reached for the door handle.

'There are people trying to stop me,' she blurted. 'Powerful people, Harry. Influential people. There's serious money behind them. Here and in the States. They've threatened me. I already know too much.'

Her reference to the States had rung another vague bell but her final sentence was ringing a louder one. 'Look, I'm sorry but what has this got to do with me? I run a museum, not a bloody detective agency. Whatever you've read about me, whatever you've heard. It's all just media bollocks.'

She opened her mouth to speak.

He held up his free hand. 'Look, if you know anything about me at all, you'll know that I'm certainly no kind of bodyguard.' He was thinking of the friends who had tried to help him in the search for Martha Watts. Friends who were either dead or still suffering from their injuries because of the choices he had made. It wasn't something that he liked to think too much about. 'If you are in trouble, save yourself a whole lot more and go to the police.'

'I can't.'

He sighed. 'Then do yourself a favour and forget about it. Whoever this Gina Lawrence is to you. Take a tip from me. Drop it. It's not worth it.' But as he said it his eyes strayed over her shoulder to a horse chestnut tree in the middle distance and to the young woman who had stepped out from behind its trunk. She was holding the hand of a small child. A little girl. Their features were blurred. Like they were there but not there. He felt a sudden and overwhelming sense of sadness. It washed over him like a wave. For a moment he felt light-headed. 'I'm sorry. I can't...' he stammered. 'I really can't.' Struggling to tear his eyes from the vision behind the reporter, he hauled open the door, staggered into the bungalow and slammed the door shut behind him.

CHAPTER THREE

Saturday, 1 February 1964

'Who's the bird?'

'What?'

'I said, who's the bird?'

Spencer Milburn had heard him the first time. Feigning deafness, he stared at his brother blankly.

Micky Milburn put his glass down on the bar behind them and leaned sideways towards him, his eyes on the girl. 'Don't make out like you haven't noticed her,' he shouted over the music from the stage speaker to their left. 'You've had your eyes on her all night, man.'

Spencer had noticed her all right. Straining to see her from his position at the rear of the small stage. With the lights down, the rest of the band out front and the club's dance floor packed, he'd caught only brief glimpses of her, darting in and out of view between the predominantly male dancers in their three-buttoned suits and Italian leather shoes. She was wearing skin tight ski pants and a polka-dotted blouse.

'Look at her. Now, that's what you call a mover. Sure beats the birds back home, eh?' Micky added, nudging him in the ribs with an elbow.

They'd been on stage for the best part of two hours. Belting out pretty much the whole of their repertoire with hardly a pause and finishing with a barn-storming version of James Brown's *Night Train*. Dear God though, Spencer Milburn reflected, it had been hot. The band had played some sweaty dives in their time. Countless pokey little pubs and working mens' clubs around the North East of England. None of them as hot as this. He'd been sweating like a pig behind the drum kit.

The club was in the basement of a Soho block. Most of its interior had been painted black. Walls, corrugated iron ceiling, even the doors to the cloakroom. All except the corridors at the rear and the booths arranged along one side of the dance floor. At first it had struck him as odd, given that people retreated to the booths for privacy, that their walls were the only walls in the whole place to have been painted white. The flashing dance floor lights periodically illuminating their startled occupants in various snapshot poses. Until it dawned on him that the effect was very probably deliberate and aimed at disrupting both the petting and pill dealing, which seemed to be the preferred activities. They'd come across drugs back home, of course, but in nothing like the quantity or variety that he had encountered at The Scene. The place was awash with them.

It was airless too. There were no windows at all. The only source of ventilation being a doorway through to a narrow concrete stairway, leading up and out into Ham Yard. With the doors closed, the whole place packed with dancers and the PA and lights pumping out heat, playing The Scene Club was like playing a sauna. Spencer Milburn stared at his brother. 'Behave yourself,' he mouthed. Attempting speech, at that particular moment, would have been pointless. The DJ had just spun Major Lance's *Hey Little Girl* and the whole place had erupted.

Not that telling Micky to behave himself was likely to have the desired effect, Spencer reflected. His brother was a cocky bugger. He always had been. His junior by just two years, still their mother had expected Spencer, as the older of the two, to look out for him. It had been difficult enough at school. Micky was mouthy even then and not at all averse to thumping kids two or three years his senior and twice his size. Within three months of Spencer leaving the school and term starting, there had been an altercation between Micky and the older brother of some girl he had taken a shine to and Micky had been expelled.

Recruiting him to the band had seemed to Spencer to be the logical thing to do. The only way to bring Micky back under his wing, and ultimately to keep him out of prison, which is where everyone reckoned he was headed unless steps were taken. Still, Rick and Pete, the band's guitarists, had been none too keen. Micky already had a reputation for trouble. It followed him around like a bad odour.

Ultimately it had been his voice that had swung it in Micky's favour. Even at sixteen years of age, Micky Milburn had possessed one of the finest male singing voices that didn't belong to an African American that Spencer had ever heard. Where it had come from, how some hacky lad from Monkchester whose speaking voice was pure Geordie was able to sing like he came from downtown Detroit, was anybody's guess. But sing, Micky undoubtedly could and in the end they had all reluctantly agreed that Micky and The Monks were made for each other.

Micky grinned. 'Well, if you're not interested, I'm gonna pull it,' he shouted into Micky's ear. 'All that fanny bouncing up and down. Fuck me. Just imagine that.'

'Leave it out Micky,' Spencer shouted back, making his irritation obvious.

'I bet she'd blow like a train, man. Like a *Night Train*.'

Spencer's eye had been drawn to a couple of mods who were leaning against the wall to Micky's right. One of them had his thumb in his trouser pocket. The other took a draw on a cigarette, his movements so tightly controlled that they appeared choreographed. Spencer wondered whether they'd been practising the look in their bedroom mirrors. Together, probably. They had exchanged smiles at Micky's last comment, sung as it was at the top of his voice and in his best imitation of James Brown. Spencer turned and stared at his brother. 'Look. Leave-it-out,' he said, jabbing a finger into his brother's chest.

If he had been hoping that Micky was going to do as he was told, he'd been mistaken. His brother had simply stared back at him, grinning like an idiot, daring him to take it further but knowing that he wouldn't. Spencer had been tempted to smack the little fucker, right between the eyes. That would have wiped the grin off his face.

'You two want another drink?'

Trevor Fenwick had materialised beside them, like a genie from a lamp. Spencer held Micky's stare for a moment longer and then turned towards the pianist. Trev was a big bloke. Six foot four with hands like Henry Cooper. Spencer would never cease to be amazed at how he managed to play the piano so well with hands the size of dinner plates.

'They're on Marty's tab,' the keyboard player added. 'We might as well make the most of it.'

Micky held up his glass. 'What, more of this? I'd rather drink my own piss.'

Micky did have a point. The Scene Club had a bar but bizarrely, given all the drugs, not an alcohol license. It was strictly soft drinks only. A choice of powdered cola or something that tasted vaguely like lemon squash and probably was. 'No, you're all right,' Spencer replied. 'I said I'd meet Pete in that pub on the corner for a pint of something half drinkable. I should be going.'

'Except that he couldn't tear himself away from the bird,' Micky said, gesturing toward the dance floor. 'What do you reckon, Trev?'

'What bird?' the pianist said, turning and peering out into the crowd.

'Her with the arse.'

Trevor Fenwick nodded. 'Who, Gina? Forget it. She's a no-go.'

They both stared at him.

'How the hell do you know her name?' Spencer voiced the question he assumed Micky was thinking.

The keyboard player ordered a drink. 'Stick it on Mr Phelps's tab, would you pal?'

The barman nodded.

'Why's she a no-go?' Micky asked with renewed interest.

Spencer groaned inwardly.

'The guy on the door told me. She's one of Marty's girls. Strictly off limits.' The pianist reached out and took the drink from the barman. 'So keep your hands to yourself, hacky lad.' He turned away but said over his shoulder, 'Piss Phelps off and we'll be in the van back to Newcastle quicker than you can say "left without a record deal".'

Spencer watched him weave his way back across the dance floor. He was wondering what being one of Marty's girls meant. He didn't much like the sound of it.

'Jesus, I swear she's not wearing any knickers,' Micky whistled.

Spencer had just about had enough. He faced his brother. 'For fuck's sake, Micky. You heard him. She's a no-go. Got it?'

'Sure,' Micky replied, holding up his hands in mock surrender but still grinning broadly.

Spencer stared at his brother like he meant it.

Micky slipped his hand into his trouser pocket. 'Chill out, man,' he said holding out a clenched fist.

Spencer eyed his brother with undisguised suspicion. 'What?'

'Take it.'

'Take what?'

Micky looked over each of his shoulders. 'Just take it and keep your bloody voice down, would you?'

Spencer saw the mods leaning against the wall behind Micky exchange knowing glances. He held out his hand.

Micky dropped two bluish coloured pills into his palm.

Spencer closed his hand hurriedly and snatched it away.

Micky put his hand to his mouth and swallowed.

'What the fuck are you doing?' Spencer hissed.

'Purple Hearts, man. They score them like sweets down here.'

He'd had enough. Babysitting Micky was bad enough on home territory. Down here, with all the temptations that London had to offer, he was on a hiding to nothing. 'Here,' he said, taking hold of his brother's arm and thrusting the pills back into his hand. 'Find some other pill head to share them with. Those two over there look like nice boys,' he said gesturing over Micky's shoulder. 'I'm away, man.'

But it hadn't just been the pills that had pissed him off. It had been the attention Micky was paying the dancer and the expression on his face. Spencer Milburn knew exactly what that look meant. He knew it only too well.

He emerged from the door at the top of the stair well and stepped out into Ham Yard. Micky could be such a dickhead. He'd lost count of the times he'd had to dig him out of some scrape or other. While he could handle himself well enough if push came to shove, which it invariably did wherever Micky was involved, the plain fact was that he just wasn't cut out for physical confrontation. He didn't like it, he didn't need it and the more it had happened, the more resentful he had become. He'd told Micky that he'd had enough on more than one occasion. That he'd bloody well have to look out for himself. Fuck all difference that had made. If anything, knowing how he felt seemed to provoke Micky to new extremes.

Spencer pulled a packet of Cadets and a box of matches out from his trouser pocket and lit a cigarette. As well as the trouble, there was the constant competition. Micky always had to get one up on him. Go one step further. Bigger. Bolder. Louder. If Spencer had a mate, Micky had to muscle in. If he bought some new threads, Micky bought better. If he liked the look of a girl, Micky made a point of chatting her up and shagging her if he possibly could. Just to show him that he could. The truth, Spencer reflected, was that the older Micky got, the more intolerable it was becoming and the more resentful he had begun to feel about it. It wasn't as if Micky was some spotty kid, competing for his big brother's attention. In a couple of months Micky would be twenty.

Then there was the band. They were on the verge of making it big. Marty Phelps had already managed to book them studio time and they'd recorded some cracking demos. Phelps had promised them a recording contract and told them it was imminent. All they needed was the right song. They could not afford to screw it. They all knew that. All except Micky. Micky seemed to think that screwing it came with the territory. Well, if Micky screwed this one for them he'd be out on his arse, voice or no voice. Spencer took another draw, exhaled through his nose and flicked the ash from his cigarette onto the patch of ground to his side.

It was refreshingly cooler in the yard above the night club. Oddly peaceful too, given all the hullabaloo below. The only other people in the yard were a young couple loading up their scooter, ready for the ride home. Spence wondered how far they had come. Londoners, he guessed. Like most of The Scene Club's regulars. From their reaction whenever he spoke, it was evident that most of them had never heard a Geordie accent. Several of them had mistaken him for a Scouser. He had, he supposed, The Beatles and Cilla bloody Black to thank for that.

The scooter started after three or four kicks, the putt-putt of its two-stroke engine echoing around the yard. It was one of a couple of dozen or so, lined up around the yard's perimeter. He watched them push the scooter off its stand, mount up and they were gone, leaving a cloud of exhaust smoke billowing behind them.

Maybe he should have a word with Phelps. Marty wasn't stupid. He knew the score. It had been Marty who had spotted them in a working mens' club in Newcastle. He'd seen how they operated.

Seen their potential. Maybe he'd be able to talk some sense into Micky. Tell him to lay off.

Somebody had pulled open the door down to the club. The sound of Georgie Fame's *Yeh Yeh* had floated up the staircase and drifted out into the yard. It faded away again, presumably as the door had swung closed. Spencer had walked a couple of paces down the row of scooters and was looking at a Vespa GS with striped side panels.

'Nice scooter. I was hoping I'd find you out here.'

It was a female voice. He turned. The dancer in the ski pants.

'Yeah?' he said, flushing slightly. He hoped she couldn't tell in the dark. There was an awkward pause.

'Is it yours?' she said casually, following his eyes. She had a broad London accent.

'Nah. We've only been down here a couple of weeks, like. Living out of the van, you know. Or kipping on somebody's floor.'

She smiled. 'You're the drummer, right?'

It wasn't really a question.

'I mean, with The Monks.'

'Sure.' He was trying to sound cool. Like he didn't really care that she knew he was the drummer, or that she'd been hoping to find him out here. She was wearing a short fur jacket over her blouse. He thought she looked pretty damned fine.

'Gina,' she said, holding out her hand.

He shook it. 'Spence. Spencer Milburn,' he added, as an afterthought.

'Oh,' she said, grinning. 'Gina Lawrence. Pleased to meet you, I'm sure.'

He let her hand slip from his. 'Only, well, you can call me Spence if you want. Only m' mam calls me Spencer.'

'What does your Dad call you?'

He thought about it. 'Marra if I'm in his good books.'

'Marra?'

'It's Geordie for mate.'

He remembered that he was smoking. 'Cigarette?'

'Please.'

He slipped one from the pack, offered her a light and sheltered the match with his hand while she lit the cigarette. He caught her perfume. It was sweet.

'You're from Newcastle aren't you?'

'Born and bred. You from round here?'

'Edmonton Green.'

He looked at her blankly.

'North London. The other side of Tottenham.'

'Oh, right.' He dropped his cigarette butt and stubbed it out with the toe of his shoe.

'But I've got rooms upstairs,' she added.

'Upstairs? Upstairs where?'

She pointed to the block behind them.

'You live in rooms above the club?'

'Yeah. For now anyway. It's a bit of a shit hole to be honest. I can't wait to get out. To make something of myself, you know? There was an agent down here last week who reckons he can get me on to Ready Steady Go. You know, as a dancer?'

'Yeah?' The TV show was required viewing for every wannabe dancer at The Scene Club.

'They've got Martha Reeves on in a couple of weeks time. I wouldn't mind dancing on television to The Vandellas.'

'An agent? I heard you were with Marty?'

She took a draw on her cigarette. 'Yeah? Who told you that?'

He shrugged. 'I dunno. I just heard.'

'Yeah? Well things between me and Marty are a bit...' She hesitated. 'Awkward at the moment, you know?'

He didn't know. He had no idea.

'Well, anyway, there's a private party later. At Guy's place in Wardour Street.'

'Guy?'

'Guy Stevens. The DJ?'

He looked at her blankly.

'You must have heard of him? Everybody knows Guy.'

'Sure,' he lied. He had never heard of Guy Stevens.

'Moonie is coming over. You know, from The High Numbers. Maybe Ronnie from The Birds. And Chris Farlowe is already here. He came over especially to hear you play. Did you see him?'

Spence shook his head. He hadn't and right now he didn't much care. She was gorgeous. Up close her mixed descent was more obvious. She had straightened her long black hair. It fell from a half-beehive and cascaded across her shoulders. Her dark eyes were lined with penciled black eye liner. 'Keith Moon? That drummer that everyone is on about, right? The crazy guy?'

She smiled. 'You can swap notes or whatever you drummers do.'

He thought about it. 'Well, I don't know,' he said, looking at his watch. 'I was supposed to be meeting Pete in The Lyric for a pint,' he said, gesturing toward the pub on the corner, away to their right. 'And then I think we were planning on heading back.'

'Guy has got an incredible record collection,' she said, obviously trying to tempt him. 'Ships them over from the States. You might even find some material. You know? Stuff you might want to cover?'

It was tempting. They were always on the look out for new material. More to the point, she was tempting, whatever Trev had said. He was giving it some serious thought. Until the inevitable happened.

'Besides, Micky's coming,' she added, casually. 'He asked me just now. He's a bit of a lad, your brother ain't he? Pinched my bum, the cheeky sod.'

CHAPTER FOUR

Thursday, 5 May 2016

'What the hell is wrong with you?' Jane was staring at him. 'You look like you've just seen a ghost.'

Harry flinched. 'There is nothing wrong with me,' he snapped, trying to avoid her eyes.

She said nothing.

'There was a reporter outside,' he added, with reluctance. 'Holgate or something. If she's still out there give her thirty seconds to leave and then call the gate. Have her escorted off The Park. Call the Police if you have to. Is that clear?'

Jane got to her feet and stepped out from behind her desk.

He brushed past her. 'I said, is that clear?' he barked over his shoulder. He couldn't remember the last time he'd risked barking an instruction at Jane and he wasn't going to wait around now to discover her reaction. Having made it past her desk, he carried on going. Down the corridor to his office. He entered, closed the door behind him and walked across to the window. He took a deliberate breath, separated the wooden blinds with his right hand and peered out into the courtyard. There was no sign of the reporter. Or of anyone or anything out of the ordinary. He let go of the blinds, walked across to his desk, slumped down into the black leather office chair and closed his eyes. But with his eyes closed he could still see the two figures beside the tree in the courtyard, their outlines burned onto his retinas like he'd been staring at them against the sun.

It wasn't the first time something like this had happened. He'd once imagined the face of long dead Martha Watts, staring at him through a tube train window at Belsize Park Station. And there had been unexpected emotional responses to objects too. Like the sense of foreboding he had felt when he'd grasped the door handle to the room, in the tunnels below the station, from which the missing Bletchley Park log reader had been dragged to a lonely death.

Intuition. That's what Ellen had called it. Intuition he understood. Intuition he could deal with. The ability to know or to suspect something instinctively. Not through reasoning or logical thought but from some innate or unconscious knowledge. Like a hunch. A gut feeling. These were normal. They could be tested and either ratified or dismissed. By men of facts. Men like him. Seeing people who were not there, on the other hand, was for awkward, chewing-gum kids in Hollywood movies and frumpy spiritualists in half-full village halls.

But if the vision of the woman and child had been intuition, it was a different kind altogether. He'd seen them in broad daylight for one thing. That had never happened before. And the image of them, standing there beside the tree. There but somehow not there. That intense sense of sadness. He rubbed his face, opened his eyes and tried to focus on the world inside his office. The books on the shelves. The research papers on his desk. The world of facts. His world.

They had not been there. Obviously. Therefore he had imagined them. These were facts. Beyond any reasonable doubt. Why he had imagined them, he couldn't say. He wasn't particularly tired or under pressure. Things were fine at home. Things were great at home. The more he thought about Ellen and Martha, their daughter, the more absurd the whole thing seemed to become.

The missing girl, Gina Lawrence, had nothing to do with him. Holgate was just another bloody reporter on the trail of a story. So she'd done her homework. So what? It wasn't difficult to find him on Google. He'd been the little guy who had toppled Max Banks MP. Hotly tipped to be the country's next prime minister, the story of the MP's downfall had propelled Harry to the front page of just about every national newspaper in Britain. He'd been propelled back there again, for another five minutes of fame, when he'd rescued his mother, his future wife and her Great Aunt Elsie from the clutches of Günther Möller, the crazed son of a Nazi U-boat captain, with a secret. They'd buried it with Elsie when, free of the threat that Möller had posed, she had finally passed away.

Holgate certainly wasn't the only woman with a sob story to have been prompted by the newspaper headlines to seek him out. For a while there had been a string of them. Mostly begging him to find missing husbands or sons. And especially from The War, as Martha Watts had been. Pilots or air crew who had disappeared in a Lancaster or a Spitfire over some Scandinavian fjord. Or agents dropped into occupied France, never to be seen again. He'd refused them all. He was done with it. Done with the trouble that it had bought him and worse, his friends. Done with chasing other people's bloody… The thought pulled him up short. There was a knock on his office door.

He'd imagined it. Holgate had planted the thought and, for whatever the reason, his unconscious mind had filled in the blanks. It had been an aberration. Nothing more.

The door opened and Jane stepped into the room. She had a face like thunder. 'What, so you can't answer your bloody door now?' She was carrying a cup and saucer. She marched across to his desk. 'Here,' she said, all but throwing the cup and saucer down in front of him with a clatter.

'Thank you.'

She took a step backwards and folded her arms.

'So. Did you speak to the reporter?' he asked, trying to keep his voice level. Like he was in control.

'Yes.'

'What did she say?'

'Not much. I didn't give her much of an opportunity to say anything. I gave her thirty seconds to leave. Exactly as you instructed. As you *made clear*,' she added, so icily he imagined he could see ice crystals forming on her lips.

He cleared his throat. 'Look, I'm sorry,' he said after a moment.

She said nothing.

'I didn't mean to…'

'Stop blabbering and tell me what Holgate said to you that put you in such a bloody spin.'

He said nothing.

'Don't even think of palming me off with your usual bullshit. What did she want, exactly?'

'She wanted me to help her look for somebody,' he said, surrendering to the inevitable.

She was watching him.

'For a missing, presumed dead somebody.'

She said nothing.

'All right. For a murdered somebody.'

'Why?'

'Why? Because she thinks I'm Sherlock bloody Holmes. How the hell should I know?'

Jane snorted. 'So she's not the first and she probably won't be the last. What's the big deal?'

'Big deal?' he parroted, with little hope that she was going to let the thing drop. 'Did I say there was a big deal?'

She stared at him, her arms still folded. 'Did she give a name to this somebody?'

'Forget it Jane. It's not happening. And that's final,' he added for emphasis.

'I asked for her name.'

Harry sighed. He knew Jane. Give her the name and she'd have the victim's life story within 24 hours. Which was tempting. Something about that name was familiar. He decided that he might as well go with the flow. 'Gina Lawrence. Ring any bells?'

'No. Should it?'

Harry shrugged. 'Maybe.'

'So if Holgate wasn't the issue this Gina Lawrence is?'

Harry reached across his desk and picked up the coffee cup. He took a hesitant mouthful. He wouldn't have put it past her to have added ground glass. 'There was no issue. I just had a feeling, that's all.'

'A feeling,' she said, watching him carefully. 'What kind of a feeling?'

He put down the cup, got up from his chair, walked across to the window, hauled up the blinds with the pull string and scanned the courtyard again. 'Something about the name Gina Lawrence is familiar. I can't quite place it. It just unsettled me, that's all.' He turned to face her. 'No big deal. No drama. Okay?'

'Ah, so now we get to it. You mean *that* kind of a feeling.'

He'd never directly discussed it with Jane. Any of it. But Ellen and Jane had been close friends, ever since the day that Ellen had first come to Bletchley Park and Jane had gate crashed their lunch together in the Hut Four canteen. To be fair to Ellen, there'd been several times since when his behaviour had meant that she had needed a friend to confide in. Especially in the period leading up to the death of Ted Stammers, the man with whom he had grown up but who had turned out not to be his biological father. In the years since, the two women had become ever closer and, while it sometimes grated that she knew just about as much about him as his wife, Jane had come to both their rescue more than once. Without Jane's friendship and guidance he wasn't sure that Ellen would have coped. He turned to face her. 'It's really no big deal, Jane. Forget it. I said I'm sorry, okay?'

'Tell me.'

He stared at her.

'I said, tell me.'

He let out a long sigh. 'I don't know what triggered it. It's been a long day. Maybe I was tired. Maybe the sun was in my face. Maybe she got to me.'

'Harry…'

He stared at her. 'While I was talking to Holgate, I thought I saw something. Over there,' he said pointing back toward the window. 'Beside the tree in front of the car park.'

'What did you see?'

'Well, I didn't see it, obviously,' he tried to back track.

'What did you see?' she insisted.

He started to object.

'Oh for God's sake, man. What in God's name did you see?'

'I thought I saw her,' he blurted. 'Gina Lawrence.'

'The dead woman?'

'Yes. The dead woman.'

Jane stared at him.

Her expression left him guessing. 'This is the bit where you ask me how I knew it was Gina Lawrence,' he said, at last.

'How did you know it was Gina Lawrence?'

'I don't know how I knew. I just did. Call it intuition if you like. Ellen does.'

A restrained smile broke the corner of her mouth.

'Well, I'm glad you find it funny.' But in truth, the hint of her smile had released some of his tension.

'Funny? I find you fucking hilarious. A man so concerned with establishing historical facts that he's made a career out of it. Reduced to a jabbering wreck by a vision in the car park. And in broad day light too.'

'Fuck off.'

'Well, all right. But even you must see the funny side.'

'Yeah? Well, it gets worse.'

Her face softened.

He hated the rare occasions when she looked like she was feeling something approaching compassion. It was downright unnerving.

'Go on.'

'She was not alone.'

'Not alone?' she repeated. 'Who was with her, for God's sake. Don't tell me it was a hooded figure with a black cape and a dirty great scythe?'

'Are you going to take this at all seriously or are you just going to take the piss?'

'Oh, come on. You can hardly blame me.'

Harry sighed again. He couldn't blame her at all. It was crazy. Sensing stuff was one thing but seeing things in broad daylight that simply could not be there was something else entirely.

Jane stared at him. 'This really got to you, didn't it?' she said suddenly.

'Yes, it did,' Harry replied, honestly. It really had.

She unfolded her arms and walked across to him. Taking hold of his shoulders she said gently 'Tell me.'

'It was a child, okay?' he replied, trying to avoid her eyes. 'A little girl. Six, maybe seven years old. It was difficult to tell.'

'Why was it difficult to tell?'

'Because their faces were obscured,' he said quietly. He was picturing them again in his mind.

Jane hesitated. 'They had no faces?'

He pulled away. 'I didn't say that,' he replied, failing to mask his embarrassment.

'What then?'

'I said their faces were obscured. As in indistinct. Out of focus.'

Jane was silent.

He turned. She was watching him intently.

'You are going to talk to Ellen about this,' she said eventually.

He hesitated.

'Harry…' she growled.

'Yes, I am going to talk to Ellen about it,' he interrupted. 'Of course I'm going to talk to her.' He knew that if he didn't, Jane would.

'Good. You must.'

'I will. But then that's an end to it, Jane. Whatever I saw. Whatever I imagined I saw,' he corrected himself, 'whatever the reason for it, I am not going there again.'

Jane said nothing.

'Holgate. Lawrence. I don't care. I am not interested. I've done with all that. I've found all the people I need to find. Ellen, Martha, my mother, you, Mike. I don't need to find anyone else. It's not happening. And I don't want you looking into it. I don't want to know. Is that clear?' But this time he said it with a softer tone. This time it was a request, not an instruction.

'Yes, it's clear.'

'Well, all right then' he said, making a conscious effort to relax.

She smiled. 'Now finish your coffee.'

'I will. And for God's sake stop smiling,' he added. 'You're making me nervous.'

Harry pulled the scooter up on to its stand and took off his helmet. Ellen's red Alpha was parked on the street in front of the house. He'd been wondering whether they'd be at home. Friday was Guides night. He looked at his watch. Ten to seven. He stepped around the scooter, sheltered his eyes with a hand and peered into the house through the bay window. The television was on but the living room was empty. He tapped on the glass.

The little two-and-a-half bedroomed terraced house had been their first place together. Harry couldn't really imagine them living anywhere else. Martha Rose had been born there. Ellen had insisted on a home birth. 'I'm not ill, I'm pregnant. I don't need an operation and I'm not giving birth to our child in a hospital,' she'd vowed. While he'd seen where she was coming from, he'd worried endlessly about some complication or other. But in the end, the birth had been straightforward and Martha Rose had entered the world without any major issue. Although a certain amount of screaming had been involved, that was for damn sure. Half the population of Leighton Buzzard had probably heard it.

The house was plenty big enough for the three of them. But in recent months Ellen had started making noises about moving. The house was on the main road into the Bedfordshire town from the south, which made it noisy from the traffic that choked the road in the mornings and evenings. It often backed all the way up the hill as far as the local park and sometimes as far as the bypass that ran around the expanding town's southern perimeter.

It could be noisy late at night too, especially at the weekends when half the town's drunks seemed to stagger past the house, singing and shouting obscenities at the tops of their voices on their way home to the housing estate that had grown up on the other side of the park. On occasion they'd relieve themselves or throw up in the front garden on their way past, just for good measure. In the early days it hadn't bothered them so much but with Martha now ten years old it had dawned on them both that there were probably better places for their daughter to be a teenager. He caught sight of movement and made his way around the scooter to the front door. Ellen was waiting for him. 'Hello love,' he smiled.

She kissed him on the cheek. 'How did it go?' she smiled back. 'Sorry I didn't call. The meeting went on for ages and then I was driving and well, you know, it was one thing after another.'

'That's all right.' He followed her through the little hall that always smelled slightly of damp. They'd had the floor boards up twice but had never traced the source. 'It all went pretty much to plan,' he said, removing his coat and hanging it in the cupboard under the stairs. 'Princess Anne was nicer than I thought she was going to be. Really quite normal, apart from that haircut and the ridiculously plummy accent.'

'Pretty much?'

'Dad?' He heard Martha's feet on the open plan stairs, before he saw her. When he did, he saw that she was wearing her new blue, Guides polo shirt with a bright red collar.

'I'll tell you later,' he mouthed, bracing himself.

Martha flew down the stairs and threw herself into his arms as she usually did. It was one of their rituals. He tried to kiss her but her long blonde hair got in the way. Not for the first time, he wondered how much longer he had before she'd be too old to throw herself into her dad's arms.

'Kettle's on,' Ellen said over her shoulder, disappearing into the kitchen. 'Martha, get your shoes on. We're late.'

'Good day?' Harry said, lowering his daughter to the floor.

'It was okay. Except that Emily was crying at assembly.'

'Emily? Why was she crying?'

Martha pulled a face. 'Her cat died.'

'Oh no. You mean Smudger?'

Martha shook her head. 'No, idiot. Smudger is Haley's cat. Emily's cat was called Morris The Loris.'

Martha loved cats. Harry pretended to, mostly for her sake, but in truth he was about as big a fan of them as they were of him, which wasn't much. 'Oi, who are you calling an idiot,' he said, catching hold of her.

She giggled.

'Martha hurry up and get ready now. We'll be late.' Ellen had come back into the room clutching Martha's coat.

'Well, that's awful. How did Morris die?'

'He got run over,' Martha replied, pushing her feet into the shoes that Harry had retrieved for her from the cupboard. 'Emily said he was squashed as flat as a pancake in the road.'

'Poor Emily. Did she see it happen?'

'I don't know,' Martha said, wrinkling her nose. 'I don't think so.'

'Come on,' Ellen said, holding out her coat. 'Here.'

'I don't need a coat.'

'Yes, you do. It'll be chilly when you come out.'

'Oh, mum,' Martha complained.

'Won't be long.' Ellen swept Martha out of the room and they were gone.

Moving house wasn't going to be easy for Martha, especially if, as Ellen had hinted was her preference, they moved to another area entirely. Martha's world revolved around her friends and their cats. But if they were going to move, now was probably the right time. Martha was ten years old. She'd be changing schools next year. After that and with Martha settled into secondary school, it was only going to become more disruptive. Then, of course, there was Lizzie. His mother had moved to a nearby village to be close to them. Telling her that they were contemplating moving away was likely to go down like a lead balloon.

He had walked into the kitchen at the back of the house and was stirring his tea.

They'd talked about Oxfordshire. His salary had risen significantly with his promotion and Ellen's business was doing so well that she was thinking, in any case, of opening another branch. She'd looked at a vacant shop in Burford, on the edge of the Cotswolds. Harry had baulked at property prices when they'd checked them out on *Rightmove*. Still, he supposed that they could afford it. Just about.

He picked up his tea cup and stepped out into the office. They'd built it where the lean-to used to be. He sat down in front of the computer screen and hit the space bar, fully intending to take another look at properties on *Rightmove*. Instead he found himself opening Google and typing a woman's name into the search bar.

CHAPTER FIVE

Saturday, 1 February 1964

'Do you want a drink?'

'What?'

'I said, do you want a drink?'

'Oh, sure.' Spencer Milburn could barely hear her above the music.

Gina put a hand on his arm and moved closer. 'They're in the kitchen.'

The DJ's first floor flat in Wardour Street was huge. Far bigger than he'd been expecting. The living room was vast, with painted walls and a high ceiling, at the centre of which was the biggest crystal chandelier he had ever seen.

'Come on.' She tugged at his jacket sleeve.

While it was big, it certainly wasn't grandly furnished or decorated. The room had no floor covering. Just bare floor boards and little by way of furniture. Or possibly the DJ had moved it out for the party. The place was packed with people and the air was thick with tobacco smoke. He caught a glimpse of his brother, his arm around a young woman in a white mini dress. With short, boyish blonde hair and big round, painted eyes, she was stunningly good looking and scarily thin. Even from a distance, she looked spaced out. As the crowd parted briefly he saw Micky's hand slide down her back to the top of her thigh. Spencer rolled his eyes. He turned and followed Gina Lawrence out, through a doorway, into the hall that ran the length of the flat. There were half a dozen or more snogging couples dotted along its length and at least one group of three. Two men taking it in turns with a girl who was evidently drunk, stoned or both. She looked half their age.

Gina led him along the hallway, nodding and speaking occasionally to people as they passed them and once pausing to shove away the advances of a drunken man who had emerged from a room to their left, doing up his flies. When he glanced into the room from which the man had emerged, Spencer caught sight of two half naked girls, one on top of the other with a bottle raised to her mouth.

He'd been to some pretty wild gigs in his time but this was on another scale. This was where it was happening. Where they needed to be if they wanted to make it. The band had built an enthusiastic following in and around the North East, but the dingy northern clubs they'd played had been exactly that. Dingy northern clubs. The same clubs that his father and grandfather had frequented before him. That they still frequented. Boozy working mens clubs, where old men in cloth caps sat in huddles after a day's work, talking politics over a pint of Newkie Brown. Brown clothes, brown beer and drab decor, stained by the tobacco smoke from the old mens' pipes. Newcastle was about the past. It seeped from the walls into the people. Weighing them down. Keeping them in check. The music the band played might be new but the history of the venues where they played it had held them back. Had they remained in the North East, it would always have held them back.

London might as well be on a different planet. Here, they were at the centre of something new. Something different. There was nothing old or brown about it. The London scene wasn't about the past at all. The kids here didn't think or behave like their parents. This wasn't about looking backwards. These mods were living in and for the present. They took their inspiration from Europe and

America. The clothes; the music; the buzz. It was impossible not to feel it. They were at the beginning of something that was going to sweep away the old order.

'Name your poison?'

They had entered the kitchen, at the centre of which was a table covered in bottles. It was surrounded by people, helping themselves to drinks.

'My what?' He had no idea.

She smiled. 'What are you drinking, dumbo?'

'Oh, I dunno. Wine maybe?' he said, flushing slightly.

'Wine,' she said doubtfully. 'Is that what you Geordie lads drink then?'

It wasn't. In fact he rarely drank the stuff. But it sounded more sophisticated than beer. He shrugged. 'No, not really,'

She took hold of his hand and led him toward the table.

'Gina, darling. Who is this splendid specimen?'

A middle aged man had stepped out of the crowd around the table and turned towards them. He was wearing a bow tie, a tweed sports jacket with a matching waistcoat.

She leant towards the man and allowed him to kiss her on the cheek. 'Dougie, this is Spencer Milburn, from The Monks.'

Dougie held out his hand 'Douglas Marwood.'

Spencer shook it.

'I was at The Scene earlier. It was a great set, Spencer. In fact the best set I have heard this year. I rather think that Marty might just have done it again.'

Spencer smiled awkwardly. 'Thanks. You know Marty?'

Dougie laughed. 'Oh, we know Marty, don't we darling?' he said, turning towards Gina.

Spencer caught her pained expression. It was surprisingly bleak. Like a deep shadow had passed across her face. But she said nothing and quickly masked it with a forced smile.

'Marty and I go back a long way,' Dougie added, returning his attention to Spencer. 'In fact Marty tells me that you have recorded a demo for us.'

Spencer looked from Dougie to Gina and back again. 'Us?'

'Decca Records.'

'Decca? Isn't that the company that turned down The Beatles?' He regretted it as soon as he had said it. The Beatles had gone on to chart for Parlophone with six hit singles, four of them number ones, and two top selling albums. Everybody reckoned they were going to be the biggest thing since Elvis.

Dougie Marwood looked to Spencer like he'd been slapped in the face with a wet fish. 'The Beatles,' he said, indignantly, 'are a flash in the pan. They won't last.' He turned away with a flourish and added over his shoulder, 'Pop music for twelve year olds.'

Spencer watched him leave. He swallowed awkwardly and turned back towards Gina, who was staring at him slack jawed, the beginning of a smile creasing the corners of her mouth. 'I'm sorry. I didn't mean to.' He hesitated. 'I mean, I didn't think…'

She reached out and put a finger to his lips. 'Spencer Milburn,' she said, her eyes sparkling so brightly that it was like there were stars behind them. 'That was, without the doubt, the best put down I have heard in years.'

'No, I…' he stammered.

But his words were silenced. She had leant forward and kissed him full on the lips. Then she reached behind him, took a bottle from the table and said, 'Come with me.'

They had found what was probably the only empty room in the flat. Once he had realised her intentions, it didn't matter to Spencer Milburn in the slightest that it was the bathroom. Gina had dragged him there, closed and bolted the door, unscrewed the top from the bottle she'd taken from the table in the kitchen, took a long swig, handed it to him and watched him drink. Whatever it was, it was strong. When he had finished, she had taken the bottle from him, refitted the cap and put the bottle down on the floor behind her.

He'd watched her undress, as if transfixed. She had kicked off her shoes and slid out of her ski pants. Naked, except for a silver St Christopher, which she wore on a chain around her neck, she had stepped forward and kissed him again.

It was the first time that he'd ever made love to a woman while standing. It had been awkward and fumbling at first. But then he'd shoved her against a body length mirror, fitted to the bathroom wall, and lost himself to the passion of it. When they were done and as he was struggling to get back into his trousers with something approaching dignity, he'd noticed the print of her bottom in the mirror glass.

'What's so funny?' she said, her self consciousness plain.

He pointed and soon they were both laughing out loud.

Now they were sitting on the floor beside the bath in silence, sharing a cigarette.

'Can I ask you something?' he said at last.

'That sounds serious.'

He hesitated. He'd already committed one faux pas. He knew that this might be another.

'Oh God, it is serious.'

'I just want to know. About you. I mean, everything about you.'

She took a drag on the cigarette and handed it to him. 'You can ask me anything, Spencer.'

He swallowed. 'Those marks.' They ran vertically down her stomach, either side of her navel. He'd noticed them while she was dressing. They were, as far he'd been able to see without staring, her only blemish. Her light brown skin was otherwise perfect. Her slender body, perfectly proportioned and about as beautiful, he reflected, as it was possible for a body to be. That's what he should have said. That's what he ought to be saying right now. But her smile had faded and she had looked away in silence. 'I'm sorry. I shouldn't have,' he stammered. 'I mean, you're absolutely gorgeous. They're just marks. They don't bother me at all. I mean why should they? It's just that…' He hesitated. *Oh God.* He was digging a hole and he needed to stop.

'They're stretch marks,' she said suddenly, looking off into the middle distance.

He had thought they might be. His mother had some, the same. She was always complaining that they were his fault. He'd been such an enormous baby. 'I'm sorry,' he apologised awkwardly. 'I shouldn't have asked. It's none of my business.'

'From the birth of my daughter,' she continued, her eyes filling with tears. They were soon running down her cheeks. He reached across and took her hand. She let him.

'She'll be two years old next Saturday. February 8th. That's her birthday.'

He waited. There was more to come.

She faced him. 'I gave her up.'

She was searching his face. Watching his expression. Trying to gauge his reaction. Hers was a picture of undisguised anguish. It was contorting her features. He reached out and cupped her face in his hand. 'It's all right,' he said, staring into her eyes. 'I'm sorry. I shouldn't have asked.'

She shook her head vigorously, pulling away from his hands. 'No. No it's not all right. It was never all right. I should never have let her go. I should never have agreed to it. I was wrong. It was all wrong. But…' Her voice trailed away.

She had stopped herself from saying more. He could see the effort of it in her jawline. He reached for the bottle that they'd left on the floor beside him and examined the label. It was gin. He unscrewed the lid, took a swig to steady his nerves and held it out to her. 'Here. It'll make you feel better.' He'd been trying to think of something more comforting to say. Thinking, hard. Trying to work out what it meant. About her. She was not the only young woman ever to have given up an unplanned child for adoption, if that was what had happened.

'Thanks,' she said, raising the bottle to her mouth and swallowing. She lowered the bottle. 'You're wondering who the father was, aren't you?'

He thought about it. 'No, not really.' But he was. She'd given birth, just two years before. Nine months before that there had been someone special. Special enough to have fathered her child. And there it was. A tinge of jealousy. Which was crazy. He'd only just met her. So they'd screwed. So what? Sex counted for nothing these days. Everybody did it. Was he any different? Was she? 'It doesn't matter. It's you and the present that I'm interested in, Gina. Not your past.' And then an afterthought struck him and he spoke it. 'Unless he's not in your past,' he said quietly.

She laughed but there was no joy in it.

'What?'

'That's just it, isn't it? He'll never be in my past. He's got my daughter. That's never going to leave me is it? I'll never be free of it. Every time I see him. Every time I close my eyes, she's there. Reminding me of what I've done.'

He was trying to work out what to say that might offer her some comfort, but what the hell did he know? He'd never thought about it before. The reality was that he had no idea how it felt to have a child, let alone, to give one up. 'You've got your whole life in front of you Gina. Think of the future and where it could take you.'

'Take me? Where am I going to go, when that bastard has the only thing that matters to me? He's got it all. Money, a career, a massive great house in Hertfordshire, and now he's got a fucking family. My family. What have I got?'

He was trying to piece it together when something struck him. The look on her face when Dougie Marwood had mentioned Marty Phelps. Her response when he'd mentioned Marty earlier, in Ham Yard. Trev's warning. What had he said? That she was one of Marty's girls? But Phelps was married. Spencer knew that. If Gina and Phelps had embarked on an affair, how comes Phelps had the child? Had he fought her for custody? Spencer didn't know much about the law. Perhaps it was a possibility. If not an affair then what? If Phelps had forced himself on her, then even Spencer knew that he'd never have got custody. This was heavy stuff. Did he really want to get any more involved than he already was? Phelps was the band's manager. If he blew it with Phelps, they'd be finished. *Jesus*. Trev hadn't been joking when he'd said that Gina Lawrence was a no-go. He needed time to think. Maybe he was putting two and two together and making five.

Quite without warning there was a thud on the door and a muffled voice. 'Hey, are you going to be much longer? There's a queue forming out here.'

'Sorry,' Spencer called back. 'Give me a minute.' He turned to Gina who was already getting to her feet. 'Come, on,' he said, sliding an arm around her waist and smiling weakly.

'You know who the father is, don't you?'

'Later. We can talk about this later. Let's just get out of here,' he said, tugging her gently.

She held back. 'You know who, but you don't know what I've done.'

Did he want to know? He reached out for the lock and opened the door. 'Come on. Let's get out of here.'

CHAPTER SIX

Friday, 6 May 2016

'Well?'

'Well, what?' Harry replied, trying to look as disinterested as possible.

Jane stared at him. 'Don't give me that. You know full well.'

They had seated themselves at a table in the Hut Four canteen. Decorated and laid out to mimic The Park's wartime canteen, it was a standing joke among the canteen staff that so many American tourists found it "awesome" to be eating where Alan Turing had eaten, because he hadn't. The Park's wartime canteen had been elsewhere.

Harry had opted for bacon and eggs. He allowed himself a cooked breakfast once, maybe twice a week at most. He didn't want his arteries clogging any more than they probably already were. Jane was peeling the top off a yoghurt pot. She had chosen orange juice. He had gone for coffee. Which had improved markedly since he'd insisted on the installation of a proper espresso machine. After the parking space with his name painted in big letters, the coffee machine had been one of his first actions on taking up his post and, for once, Jane had actually agreed with him. Though why, he had no idea. She never drank the stuff.

'All right. So I googled the name,' Harry said, casually.

'I knew it,' she crowed with a satisfied smirk.

He took a casual swig from his coffee cup and smiled at her acidly.

'And?'

'And I knew I'd heard the name. I was right. That's all.'

'That's all,' Jane mimicked.

He ignored her, glancing toward the main door as a couple of contractors with hard hats entered. First thing in the morning the canteen was rarely busy, catering mainly for staff, until the coach loads began to arrive, usually after 10am. At lunch time and especially if the weather was good, it would be heaving.

'Not remotely interested,' she said, eventually.

'Nope,' Harry agreed, chewing on a piece of bacon.

'You didn't find it at all interesting, for example,' she continued, 'that Gina Lawrence was a dancer at The Scene Club in Soho.'

Jane knew about his interest in the sixties mod scene. Anyone who had known him for longer than five minutes did. The Lambretta and parka were the giveaway. 'Not remotely,' Harry said, avoiding her eyes.

'Or that she was reportedly shagging both the Milburn brothers at more or less the same time.'

Harry grunted. 'Newspaper talk.'

'That is Micky and Spencer Milburn. From The Monks.'

'Tittle-tattle.'

Jane laughed. 'Tittle-tattle? Have you been reading P.G. Wodehouse again?'

He scowled.

'Do you know something, Harry?'

'No. But I'm sure that you're going to tell me.'

'You are such a colossal bullshitter.'

Harry smiled inwardly. She was right, of course. He'd spent almost two hours reading everything he'd been able to find on Gina Lawrence and The Scene Club, before Ellen had returned from Guides with Martha. He put down his coffee cup. 'Okay. So I looked her up.'

Jane began to speak.

Harry held up his hand. 'All right, her links to The Monks and The Scene Club make her disappearance moderately interesting. But she disappeared. Nothing and no-one says that she was murdered.'

'Err.. That's not quite right.'

'What do you mean that's not quite right?'

'Well, Holly Holgate says she was murdered, for one.'

Harry shook his head. 'And how does she know that?'

'Well, maybe if you'd listened to her, we might have found out.'

He snorted. He was not about to admit that she had a point.

'In fact, she's quite insistent. Don't you at least want to know why?'

'No. I don't. She's a reporter after a story.' He thought about it. 'What do you mean, she's insistent?'

'You haven't read your email this morning, I take it?'

'No. That's what we pay you for.'

Jane glowered. 'Oi. Watch it, Sunshine. I don't have to work here you know.'

He'd gone too far. 'I'm sorry.' He waited.

'Apology accepted.'

Harry put down his knife and fork and pushed his plate away.

'She's emailed you. Twice, as a matter of fact.'

'So delete them. And empty my recycle bin. I don't want to know.'

The contractors with hard hats had seated themselves at the next table. They had both double ordered and had set about demolishing the most enormous breakfasts Harry thought he'd ever seen.

'Did you know that Gina Lawrence was just eighteen when she went missing? She was just a kid.'

He tore his eyes away from the carnage that was happening on their neighbouring table. 'So what? Teenagers go missing all the time. They did then and they do now. Doesn't mean I want to go looking for them. Besides, what's it got to do with me?'

'Hey, stop right there,' Jane said, holding up her hand. 'You're beginning to sound like a callous bastard.'

He rolled his eyes.

'Did you talk to Ellen about what you saw?' Jane asked, apparently changing tack.

'You mean what I imagined I saw.'

Jane looked at him like she intended to throttle him at any moment.

He sat back in his seat as a precautionary measure. 'Yes, I talked to Ellen. You know I did.' He knew it because he'd heard Ellen on the phone to Jane, about an hour after their conversation.

'What did she say?'

'I'd like to be able to say that it's none of your business. But you know what Ellen said, because she told you.'

'I'd rather hear it from the horse's mouth. So what did she say?' Jane repeated.

Harry sighed. 'She said that stuff like this usually happens for a reason. That she understands how it unsettles me but that I should trust my intuition.'

'And?'

'She said I should have given Holgate a fair hearing.'

'Well, amen to that. That's exactly what you should have done.'

He folded his arms. She was beginning to annoy him. 'Why? What's it got to do with me? I don't need it Jane. It's not my problem.'

'Listening costs nothing, Harry. You could have heard her out.'

'Yeah? To what end?' he said, a little more loudly than he had intended. The contractors on the next table looked up from their overly full, but rapidly shrinking Full English. Harry lowered his voice to a whisper. 'You, of all people, know where it got us the last time I listened to my bloody intuition. It damn well nearly got us all killed, that's where.'

'That was different.'

'Tell that to Tomas Dabrowski.' The young Pole had been blackmailed and then murdered during their search for Martha Watts.

When Jane didn't answer, he continued. 'Whose fault was it, eh? That your husband still walks with a limp? That Marcus will never walk again? Whose fault was it that Tom had his face blown off by a racist nutter who, when he was done, threw his body in Aldenham reservoir with nothing but a couple of bricks for company? I'll tell you whose. It was mine. All because I listened to my bloody intuition. Because of the decisions I made. Not you. Me.'

'Oh, get over yourself Harry. You made a decision to help somebody. An elderly woman who was in no position to help herself. She asked for your assistance and you agreed. Which was the right thing to do. You had no idea where it would take you. How could you? How could any of us? That's life. Unless you're going to live it in a box, too scared of your own shadow to take any risks. And please don't patronise the rest of us. We were perfectly capable of making our own choices. You didn't shoot Mike in the foot, or throw Marcus down a lift shaft. If you want to assign fault, then assign it where it's due.'

'Yeah? Well I'll tell you this,' he said, raising his voice again and this time not caring who heard him. 'It is not going to happen again. Full stop. The end.'

Jane was staring at him.

'Delete her emails,' he continued. 'Forget about Gina Lawrence. Tell Holgate, if she calls, that she can fuck right off. Is that clear enough for you?' And with that he got up, pushed his chair back and stomped away toward the canteen door.

When he was gone, Jane finished her yoghurt, drank the remainder of her orange juice, cleared the table and, as she got to her feet, said under her breath 'bullshit.'

***

After the conversation with Jane over breakfast, Harry had retreated to his office and stayed there, working on a report for The Department for Media, Culture and Sport on a set of proposals for future building renovations at The Park and an article for the Evening Standard on Underground Bletchley. He had avoided checking his inbox until mid-morning, by which time Jane had, as instructed, deleted the emails from Holly Holgate. The reporter had since twice called by phone. The first call had been intercepted by Jane. The second, received while Jane was at lunch, had been put through, under duress, by Jess, the office trainee. Harry had subsequently reprimanded her, much to Jane's annoyance when she returned from lunch. Harry had hung up as soon as the reporter gave her name. Fortunately, he was out of the office all afternoon, lecturing a group of visiting Japanese students from Kyoto University in the mansion library. He'd left early, without any further discussion with Jane.

'You look bushed.'

They'd not long finished supper. Martha was upstairs doing her homework and he and Ellen were seated on the sofa, watching nothing in particular on television. 'I am. Completely.'

Thankfully, Ellen had not mentioned the subject of Holly Holgate. He really didn't want to go there again. He'd said his piece to Jane and he didn't much fancy a repeat performance for Ellen's benefit. There was nothing more to say about it. Although he had little doubt that Ellen and Jane had discussed their conversation. Why else would Ellen have so studiously avoided the subject?

'Have you spoken to your mum?' Ellen asked, out of the blue. 'We said we'd go and see her tomorrow afternoon.'

'Oh God, yes. I had completely forgotten.' They hadn't seen Lizzie for a fortnight, even though she lived less then ten miles away. 'I'll give her a ring in the morning.'

'You better had. Martha's been looking forward to it all week. I can't believe she hasn't nagged you about it. She's certainly been nagging me.'

'Well, she might have said something about it, now that you come to mention it. It had just slipped my mind with everything going on at BP.'

Ellen said nothing.

He yawned.

'Do you fancy an early night, once Martha is in bed?'

He grinned.

Ellen shook her head. 'You can forget that, soldier. I've got to be on parade in the morning. I said I'd do a couple of hours in the shop, first thing. We've got a big order coming in.'

'Really? I can be quick.' He flashed her what he hoped was an inviting grin.

Ellen leaned across and kissed him. 'Tempting,' she said, sliding her hand under his shirt. There were footsteps on the stairs. She kissed him again.

'Yuk. Do you have to?' Martha said, peering around the double doorway that divided the dining from the lounge.

There was a knock on the front door.

'I'll get it,' Martha called out.

'Damn it. I've told her not to answer the door after dark,' Ellen said, getting to her feet.

'Dad, there's a lady here to see you,' Martha called out again.

Ellen had already made it into the hall, with Harry not far behind. Martha was staring past their visitor as if transfixed. But Harry barely noticed.

'Mrs Stammers? Harry...' the visitor said, peering over Ellen's shoulder. 'I'm sorry to call on you like this, but I really need to speak to you.'

Ellen had half-turned and was looking at him, a question forming on her lips.

'What the hell are you doing here? How did you get my home address?' Harry barked.

'I'm sorry. Give me just ten minutes of your time. Please. That is all I need...'

'I don't want to hear it,' Harry cut her off. 'I told you. I'm not interested.' He was vaguely aware that Martha was still staring. He glanced down at her. 'Martha, go inside.' He took hold of her arm but she was rooted to the spot.

'Mrs Stammers. My name is Holly Holgate.'

Ellen had turned back towards their uninvited guest.

'Martha, I said go inside. Now,' Harry instructed. He pulled her backwards and shoved her behind him. As he turned to face the reporter he saw that she had taken hold of Ellen's hand.

'I need Harry's help, Mrs Stammers. To find someone. Like he found Martha Watts. Like he found you. Please.'

Ellen removed her hand slowly.

'I've had enough of this,' Harry barked again, pushing past Ellen. 'Leave now. If you come back, I will call the police. Do you hear me? If you ever...' But as his eyes adjusted to the darkness outside, he saw them. Two hazy figures standing on the pavement behind the reporter, hand-in-hand. A dark skinned young woman, her hair in a beehive and beside her, a small girl. A little younger than Martha perhaps. Wearing a pink bathrobe. He felt the hair on the back of his neck prickling and the same sense of intense sadness that he had felt when he saw them at The Park. It swept over him. He stepped back, reached for the edge of the door and slammed it in the reporter's face.

'Harry? Are you all right?' Ellen said, looking shocked.

He was leaning against the hallway wall. The sense of sadness, which had been so strong with the door open, had been extinguished immediately the door was closed. Like a light being switched off. Still, it took him a moment to regain his composure.

'Harry?' Ellen had stepped forward and placed a hand on his arm.

He nodded. 'Yes. I'm… fine.'

They turned.

Martha was standing at the foot of the stairs, staring at them. And then she spoke. 'Daddy, who were those people? Why was the little girl in her dressing gown? The lady looked sad. I think they wanted our help.'

CHAPTER SEVEN

Saturday, 7 May 2016

Their short journey to Ivinghoe had been a joyous, if somewhat noisy affair. When Ellen had fished out a Madness CD from the compartment beside her seat and Harry had slid it into the player, Martha had begun to sing at the top of her voice, as she often did when they travelled even moderate distances in the car.

If she had been troubled at all by the events of the evening before, Martha, at least, had given little indication of it. She had apparently accepted his offered explanation that the woman and the little girl on the pavement behind the reporter had been passers by, their attention drawn by his raised voice. Although he'd struggled to explain why she'd been wearing a bathrobe. Still, Martha had gone to bed without further comment and, as far as he knew, slept soundly through to the morning. She'd certainly bounced out of bed in good spirits and, with Ellen working at the shop, had spent the morning playing in the garden.

Martha's cheeriness during the journey had been infectious despite the atmosphere between them. In the hour or so between her return from the shop and their departure, Harry had successfully avoided further discussion with Ellen, but it had been obvious that it was still on her mind. And with good reason. Try as he might, and he had been trying all night and most of the morning, there was simply no way that he could explain how he and Martha had both seen the same two figures standing in the street. The same two figures he had seen at The Park. Figures that Ellen had not seen.

After Holgate's departure and as soon as he settled Martha into bed, Ellen had set about quizzing him. The trouble was that he could offer her no answer. Had they been there, Ellen would have seen them. Had they been conjured by his imagination then Martha could not have seen them. Except that she had. Which was impossible. And round and around their conversation had gone. Unable to answer her questions or to offer her any kind of explanation that made any sense at all, he had resorted to avoidance and then to brooding silence. Ellen had been close to tears by the time that she had gone to bed. He had sat with his head in his hands for at least an hour, before sheepishly climbing the stairs and joining her.

Still, as he had pulled into Vicarage Lane, with its terrace of tidy brick cottages, they'd all been singing loudly and the unspoken tension between them had begun to dissipate.

'Hooray!' Martha yelled, as Harry reversed the car into a parking space. 'We're here. Can I ring the bell? Can I?'

Harry regarded the fact that Martha had lived the whole of her life knowing her grandmother on the Stammers side of the family, as little short of miraculous, when from the age of seven he had grown up entirely without her. While they had been told by their father that she had left home, he and his younger sister Kate had known nothing about her reason for leaving, nor where she was or even if she was still alive. Worse still, for the duration of their childhood and on into adulthood, Ted Stammers had refused to acknowledge her existence, banning them as children from even speaking her name. It was only shortly before his death that he had offered Harry any clue that she might still be alive, and only when he and Jane had rescued her from her burning cottage in the New Forest, that Harry and Elizabeth Stammers had been re-united.

'Go on then,' Ellen replied, reaching for Harry's hand. Ellen knew, more than anyone, what Martha's relationship with her grandmother meant to him. 'Come on,' she said, flashing him a weary smile. He squeezed her hand. They had been through a lot together and, no doubt, there would be further challenges to come. They'd survived it all with love and at that moment, he was very glad indeed that they had.

Lizzie Stammers had opened the door and was struggling to remain on her feet as she grappled with her granddaughter. Martha had thrown herself into her arms, much as she liked to do with Harry. The difference being that Lizzie Stammers was five feet six, seventy-eight years old and a good deal less steady on her feet.

'Martha, for heaven's sake be careful,' Ellen called out, but to little evident effect.

'Hello you two,' Lizzie said, once she had disentangled herself from their daughter. 'Come in. Come in,' she laughed. 'Guess what I have baked for you, Martha?'

'Carrot cake!' Martha beamed.

The interior of his mother's cottage in Ivinghoe was much as Harry recalled her house in the New Forest, albeit that he'd only seen the hallway and lounge before the whole place had been engulfed in flames. Lizzie Stammers had started the fire herself when she'd thrown a burning oil lamp at her captor, setting him ablaze along with the house. She'd lost everything, bar the clothes she'd been wearing when Ellen had dragged her from the blaze.

Lizzie had initially rented the Ivinghoe cottage and then bought it outright from the landlord once the house in Hordle had been rebuilt and sold. From the outset, she had set about recreating her former home in the New Forest, sourcing suitable furniture from an auction house in nearby Tring and decorating and furnishing the cottage in the same country cottage style. That she should want to do so had, at first, seemed odd to Harry. He'd imagined that she might have preferred to forget the horrors that had happened there.

But when she'd explained that for more than thirty years the cottage had been her refuge from the madman who had hunted and almost killed her, and that she was determined that he would not prevail, Harry had at least understood her logic. He was watching her and Ellen from the kitchen window, taking turns at pushing Martha on a swing in the garden.

Building a relationship with his mother had been a good deal easier than Harry had imagined that it might be, given that she'd been absent from so much of his life. They'd talked frankly and at some length about the circumstances that had led her to accept a new identity away from her children and, although there were matters, and one in particular, that she preferred to avoid, Harry had long since decided that it was better to look to the future than to be embittered by the past. That had been Ted Stammers' mistake. While he'd had every reason to feel betrayed by his wife, because she had certainly betrayed him, Harry had no doubt that she had loved him. Hating her, to the extent that Ted had tried to erase her from their lives entirely, as well as from his own, had ultimately done him no good; it had made Ted Stammers an embittered and hateful man.

The issue that she had difficulty discussing more than any other, and which they had learned to avoid so far as they could and to skirt around when they couldn't, concerned Peter Owen, former leader of the far-right Nationalist Union of Great Britain and Harry's unacknowledged biological father. It was evident, both from his mother's reaction when Owen's name was mentioned, and from the bouts of depression from which she still suffered periodically, that her relationship with Owen still haunted her. Harry had concluded, from what little conversation they had managed on the subject, that their serial affair had been utterly ruinous to her, as well as to her family. Ultimately it had caused the rift between her and Ted, who she'd married after the first phase of her relationship with Owen, and had been Ted's reason for refusing to go with her when she'd been offered a new identity.

Harry caught his mother's eye through the kitchen window and smiled. She returned the gesture and began walking back towards the house. He watched her approach. To see her now; a short, unremarkable looking woman in her late seventies, sleight of figure and with greying blonde hair, it was difficult to picture her as the undercover MI5 agent she had been, let alone to imagine that she had, single handedly, hijacked and driven a Semtex laden Post Office van out into the Hertfordshire countryside where it had exploded harmlessly, foiling Peter Owen's plan to explode it beneath the Palace of Westminster.

It had always seemed to him unfair that she had never received any acknowledgement from her former paymasters, let alone any public recognition, for this extreme act of bravery. Her continued silence and the personal sacrifices she had made, had seemed to him an injustice of gross proportions. Although, had recognition been offered, Harry could see no circumstances in which she would have accepted it. Lizzie had insisted on anonymity. Indeed, when news of their rescue from the New Forest had broken, she had begged Harry and Ellen to help keep her name and whereabouts out of the newspapers and they had gone to some lengths to do so. Harry had often wondered why, until sitting in her garden a few years later, she had revealed to him her fear that publicity might reveal her relationship with Owen and worse, prompt contact from him. Harry had no desire to meet his biological father; he felt no affinity with a man of Owen's political persuasion and who had played no positive part in their lives. But Lizzie had revealed the possibility of contact from Owen as her greatest fear. Harry had speculated that she feared the power that he had exerted over her and might still exert. Her disastrous obsession with Owen had taken her to the edge of ruin. It was as though, watching her walk towards him, Harry could see the shadow of it still, lurking like a demon a few feet behind her, waiting to pounce. Harry shook his head. He'd had enough of demons for one weekend.

'I thought I'd make us a fresh pot of coffee,' Lizzie said, as she came into the kitchen.

'That's all right. I can make it,' Harry offered.

'Do you want to?'

Harry nodded.

'I'd better sort out the carrot cake. Martha will never forgive me if I forget.'

'Oh, I don't think there's much chance of that, do you?' Harry laughed, opening a kitchen cupboard and reaching for the coffee tin.

'Is everything all right between the two of you?' Lizzie asked casually, while she arranged the cake on a plate and began slicing it into segments.

'The two of us? You mean Ellen and me?'

Lizzie nodded.

'Yes, of course. Why do you ask?'

'Oh, I don't know,' Lizzie said, vaguely. 'She seems a bit quiet, that's all. Like she's worrying about something.'

Harry hesitated. 'We had a reporter come to the house last night, that's all. She's been making a bit of a nuisance of herself actually. She turned up to the opening of Underground Bletchley. Wouldn't take no for an answer.'

Lizzie had stopped what she was doing and was staring at him. 'A reporter? What did she want?'

Harry noticed her worried expression. 'Oh, no it's nothing to worry about. Honestly. She's got some sob story she wants me to look into. You know, the usual nonsense. People seem to think I'm Sherlock bloody Holmes.'

Lizzie resumed slicing the cake. 'So she turned up at the house?' she continued, casually.

'Yes, at about half past eight last night. Unfortunately, Martha got to the door before we did. The reporter was bang out of order. I was bloody furious.'

'What was the sob story?'

'She wants me to help her to discover what happened to a young woman who went missing from a London dance club in 1964. There were rumours at the time, linking her disappearance to The Monks. Remember them?'

'Remember them? I saw them play.'

'You what?' He stared at his mother, opened mouthed.

'At a jazz and blues festival in Richmond in...' she hesitated, '1965 or possibly sixty-six.'

'You're kidding?'

His mother smiled. 'The girl who went missing was called Lawrence, or something, wasn't she?'

Harry shook his head in disbelief. 'Yes. Gina Lawrence.'

'That's right. The rumours were that she'd been involved with both the Milburn brothers. It followed them around for years afterwards.'

'Jesus, are you sure you wouldn't like me to put you in touch with the reporter?' Harry joked.

Lizzie Stammers laughed. 'Yes, I'm quite sure. So what's the reporter's angle?'

'She believes that Lawrence was murdered.'

'By?'

'We didn't get that far.'

'Intriguing.'

'I guess.'

'So why doesn't she go to the police?'

Harry shrugged. 'Why do you think? Because she wants the story, I expect. Though she made up some cock and bull about being threatened.'

'You didn't believe her?'

Harry considered the question. 'I didn't give it a great deal of thought. Either way, it's not my problem. You know how I feel about getting involved, and especially about the press.'

'You and me too. I meant to tell you, actually,' Lizzie said, changing the subject. 'I had a call last week from Liaison at Millbank.'

'Millbank?' He had always known that The Security Service had maintained a residual link with her after the fire and her relocation to Ivinghoe. She had told him that it was their standard practice to keep track of former intelligence officers long after retirement; indeed, permanently. But he had assumed that they had long since ceased to have any active interest in her.

'Apparently, someone has been talking to the press. She was a young undercover police officer.'

She had paused then, as if uncertain about whether to say more. Harry decided to tread carefully. 'And this is relevant to you because?'

'We were both undercover at the same time, although for different masters. The point is that she may have revealed certain details about my service. Millbank wanted to warn me, in case I am approached.'

It crossed his mind to ask which details but he decided not to go there. 'Have you been approached?'

'Thankfully, not and it'll probably come to nothing. Millbank are usually...' she hesitated, 'careful to clean up following a leak. They have a reputation to maintain,' she said, with apparent disdain. 'But I thought that you should know. In case anyone approaches you or Ellen, or you notice anything unusual.'

'Like reporters appearing out of nowhere, wanting my help with a story,' he said, considering the possibility that this might have been Holgate's motive and then dismissing it.

'Yes, exactly. Although it may be entirely coincidental that this reporter has approached you about the Lawrence story. Let's face it, there is no obvious connection.'

'Oh don't you worry about that. I have absolutely no intention of finding out. I intend to have nothing more to do with the bloody woman.'

His mother raised an eyebrow.

'What?'

She smiled. 'Harry Stammers. You know, I might have missed out on thirty odd years of your life but I've spent the last ten years doing my best to catch up. I think I know you pretty well. I can tell when something or someone has got you hooked.'

Harry held up a hand, while pouring coffee with the other. 'No way. Absolutely no way.'

'Just be careful, that's all,' she said, her expression suddenly serious. 'This reporter could be entirely genuine. But a lot of them aren't, let's face it.'

She was damn right about that.

At which point Martha came bowling into the kitchen. 'Yes! Carrot cake. I love carrot cake. Can I have an extra large slice please Nana?'

CHAPTER EIGHT

Sunday, 8 May 2016

Ellen Stammers pulled onto the gravelled drive, turned off the Alpha's ignition, reached for her bag and got out of the car. She adjusted her jacket and clicked her key fob. The car doors locked with a reassuring clunk. She walked the short distance to the house, her shoes crunching on the pea-sized gravel. The door opened as she reached for the bell.

'Ellen.' Jane stepped forward, placed a hand on her upper arm and kissed her on the cheek. 'How are you?'

She smiled. 'I'm fine.' Which they both knew was a half-truth at best.

'Come in.'

It would have been more accurate to have said that she was still as nonplussed by events as she had been on Friday evening. But there would be time for that. Besides, Jane already knew it from their earlier telephone conversation. She stepped into the tiled hallway.

'How was Lizzie?'

She thought about it. 'Lizzie was fine,' she said, deciding against mentioning the call from Millbank. 'Where's Mike? Is he well?' she asked, following Jane into the kitchen.

'He's out, doing amateur radio. You know, sitting in the middle of a field on Dunstable Downs, talking bollocks over the radio to other geeky old blokes. Mostly called Dave, I expect.'

'Dave?'

Jane rolled her eyes. 'It's Mike's little standing joke. Apparently, if you ever meet a radio amateur for the first time, call him Dave and you'll have at least an eighty percent chance of being right.'

Ellen smiled. 'I'll remember that, if I ever do.'

Jane shrugged. 'Well, Mike thinks it's funny.'

'Hey, this looks fab,' Ellen lied, scanning the room. It was the first time she'd seen their new kitchen.

'Thanks. I'm really not sure about the Scandinavian look. It was Mike's choice.'

Ellen wasn't sure about it either. 'You let Mike choose it?'

Jane nodded.

'That was brave of you. I wouldn't trust Harry with a paint brush, let alone let him loose with the Ikea catalogue.'

Jane smiled. 'Coffee? Or would you prefer a glass of wine?' She looked at her watch. 'You're all right. It's after midday.'

'I'd better not. I'm driving.' She hesitated. 'Oh, to hell with it, I can have one. I should have brought a bottle. Sorry. I've been a bit all over the place.' She took off her jacket, hung it over the back of a chair and sat down.

Jane had taken a bottle from the fridge and two glasses from a wall cupboard. She arranged them on the table in front of them. 'I'm not surprised. So. Tell me about it,' she said, filling both glasses.

Ellen picked up her drink, waited for Jane to do the same and said, 'Cheers.'

They clanked their glasses.

'I don't know where to begin. I just can't get my head around it.'

'You're absolutely certain that Holgate was alone?'

'I've asked myself the same question. Over and over.' She had. She'd thought of little else. 'But there was nobody there, Jane. Had there been, I would have seen them. I would,' she said, still trying to convince herself that there might be any other possibility. 'It just doesn't make any sense.'

Jane said nothing.

'It's one thing that Harry has these experiences. He always has. Well, ever since I've known him. But how can Martha possibly have seen the same two figures that Harry saw?' she said, shaking her head. 'It's just not possible. Is it?'

'You're sure that Harry saw them?'

She grimaced. 'You know Harry. Getting him to acknowledge it at all was hard enough, let alone describe what he actually saw. But, take it from me, he saw them. The same two figures that he saw at The Park. You should have seen his face.'

'You're forgetting, I saw it the first time. Shock, followed by confusion, followed by denial?'

'Yup. That sounds about right.'

Ellen didn't and couldn't blame him. It was one thing trying to convince him, as she had, that seeing and sensing things that were not there was an extension of the kind of intuition that everyone experiences at some time or other in their lives. But seeing them in broad daylight. Opening your front door to them. That was something else entirely.

'What about Martha?' Jane asked, after a short pause. 'You have talked to her about it, I take it?'

'Yes, of course. Although we didn't want to make a big deal of it. You know, scare her? We both played it down, to be honest.'

'Was she scared?'

Ellen shook her head. 'That's the irony of it. The one person who seems completely unbothered by the whole episode is Martha. She seems to have taken it entirely in her stride.'

'Well, that's good.'

'Is it? I'd have been completely terrified at that age. I'd probably be completed terrified now.'

Jane tipped her head in agreement. 'How did she describe what she saw, exactly?'

'She said that there was a dark lady and a little girl.'

'A dark lady? Did she mean that the woman was black?'

'I think so.' Ellen took a mouthful of wine. 'I just don't know. I really don't.'

'And the child?'

Ellen shrugged. 'She described her as a little girl. Smaller than her. She was wearing a pink dressing gown, apparently.'

'A dressing gown?'

'Yup. Don't ask me, Jane. I have no idea.'

Jane was thoughtful. 'But the two figures; a black woman and a young child, are consistent with what Harry said he saw at The Park on Thursday. What are the chances of that being coincidental?'

She shrugged again. 'Nil? But what's the alternative? That they really did see the same two figures? How can that possibly be?'

'Is there no possibility that Martha might have overheard your conversation on Thursday evening, when you and Harry discussed it? No possibility that having overheard you talking about it, her imagination got the better of her?'

She began a reply but Jane interrupted.

'I mean no possibility at all?'

She thought about it some more. 'No. None. Martha was in bed and we were in the office at the back of the house.'

'Could she have come down? Could she have been on the stairs and overheard you?'

'No. We'd been in the office most of the evening and the lights in the dining room and on the stairs were off. Martha would never have come down the stairs in the dark. Besides, I checked on her when I went up to get ready for bed and she was fast asleep.'

Jane stared at her. 'In which case I reckon you're just going to have to take them both at their word. I don't know where else you can go. You've always said that Harry has a sensitivity. Both of us have either witnessed it or experienced the aftermath. I know that I give him a hard time about it, but I was there on Thursday. He was genuinely rattled. He was telling the truth. I certainly believed him.'

'I know. I believe him too. I always have. But...' Ellen's voice trailed away.

'Martha?'

She nodded.

'If Harry has some kind of sensitivity. If that's what it is. Then maybe Martha has inherited the same sensitivity.'

Ellen began to object.

'I know,' Jane interrupted. 'I know. But you're trying to rationalise the irrational. Harry sees what he sees. He senses what he senses. If you accept that then it becomes plausible that Martha might have inherited this same ability from her father. I mean we inherit our physical features from our parents. Why not our minds?'

Ellen drained her glass.

'If we accept it then we can move to the next question. Why are they seeing these two figures? What are they sensing exactly?'

Ellen rolled her eyes. 'Harry won't even go there.'

Jane smiled. 'Bloody men. Why can't they ever discuss the way they feel, for God's sake? The world would be a whole lot better place if they did.'

'Amen to that,' Ellen agreed.

'The thing is, there has to be a reason, doesn't there? Otherwise it's just random.'

Ellen thought about it. 'It's never just random. Whenever Harry senses something, it's always for a reason. It leads him somewhere.'

'Exactly. So where is this leading him?'

Ellen grimaced. 'I wish I knew.'

Both women stared into their glasses.

It was Jane who spoke first. 'What about Martha? Has anything like this ever happened before?'

Ellen shook her head. 'No, never.'

'She's never had an imaginary friend?'

'No.'

'So, why now? What triggered it?'

Both women were silent again.

'Maybe it's not a what. Maybe it's a who,' Jane said suddenly.

Ellen had been thinking the same thing. She looked up from her glass. 'You mean the reporter. Holly Holgate?'

Jane nodded. 'It was contact with Holgate that triggered it for Harry. Holgate who was present on Friday evening, when Harry and Martha shared the experience. Holgate's the common factor here.'

She was right. There was only one person who might be able to tell them where this was heading and that person was Holly Holgate. 'Do you think we should talk to her?'

Jane had poured herself another glass of wine. She held out the bottle.

'No, I'd better not.'

'Yes,' Jane said, after a short pause. 'I can't really see any other way.'

'Harry will have a fit.'

'Do you think so?'

'I know so.' He had been adamant. There was no way he was going to talk to Holgate.

'We don't have to tell him,' Jane added, as if reading her thoughts.

'I don't know. I've given him a hard time in the past about keeping stuff to himself. I'm really not sure that I want to go there.'

'Look, Harry is stuck,' Jane argued.

Ellen laughed. 'He's not the only one.'

'Yes, but Harry is a rationalist, through and through. He experiences something for which there is no explanation and he freezes. Like a rabbit caught in headlights.'

'It's not just that, Jane. I know Harry. He's afraid. And when he's afraid, he shuts out the threat, puts his head down and carries on regardless.'

'Exactly. So don't you think that by seizing the initiative and talking to Holgate we might be doing him a favour?'

'Perhaps. But I bet he won't see it that way.'

'Which is another reason to keep it to ourselves.'

She said nothing. But she was thinking.

'Look, my bet is that this isn't going away. I reckon it's only a matter of time before he sees them again and this thing escalates. Until you both have no choice but to face up to it. So rather than wait for the crisis, maybe we can make it easier for him. Talk to Holgate and move this forward. Once we know what we're dealing with, we can give him something more logical to work with. Besides…'

Ellen knew what was coming. She braced herself.

'This time, it isn't just about Harry, is it?'

She flinched.

'What are you and Harry going to say to Martha the next time she senses something? And the time after that?'

'I don't know. I don't have the faintest idea.'

'Tell me to mind my own business Ellen. Seriously. But Martha is your daughter as well as Harry's. Sometimes we women have to step up to the mark. All joking aside, Harry is doing his best. I've no doubt about that. He's a good man and a great father. You know how fond of him I am. But men have their limits, let's face it.'

Ellen said nothing, but she was thinking that Jane had a point.

'I've got Holgate's email address. I kept her emails to Harry.'

Ellen smiled weakly. 'I can do better than that.' She reached for her bag. 'I've got her mobile number.'

Jane grinned.

She held out a business card. 'She slipped it to me on Friday. Harry didn't notice.'

Jane gave her a knowing wink.

'Let's get this done as soon as we can. I really don't want to keep it from Harry any longer than I absolutely have to.'

'Agreed.'

CHAPTER NINE

Tuesday, 10 May 2016

It was an opportunity too good to miss. That's what he'd been telling himself all morning. That's what he was telling himself now, looking up at the street sign fixed to the wall of the pub on the corner of Great Windmill Street and Ham Yard.

He'd attended a meeting in London to discuss a new museums initiative at the Department for Media, Culture and Sport. The DMCS's offices in Parliament Street were little more than fifteen minutes walk from Ham Yard. He'd found himself checking the location on Google Maps and arguing with himself on the train going in, finally deciding against. But when the meeting was over, instead of heading for the tube station at Westminster, he'd found himself walking along Whitehall and via Cockspur Street and Haymarket, across Shaftesberry Avenue, to Ham Yard. He was standing there now, at the Yard's threshold, telling himself that his decision to take a look around the location of the former Scene Club had nothing whatever to do with Holly Holgate or Gina Lawrence. That he was simply recalling his youth, when having seen Quadrophenia on a dodgy VHS video cassette he'd borrowed from a mate at school, he'd bought his first parka and a pair of black and white bowling shoes from Melanddi's in nearby Carnaby Street and started calling himself a mod. Half the kids he'd hung out with at the time had done the same.

The Scene Club had been long gone by then. But, like the former Flamingo Club, around the corner in Wardour Street, The Scene had near-legendary status for just about every mod-revivalist Harry had ever come across. Maybe because so many original mods had been regulars. Maybe because the club had vanished so suddenly, once they'd moved on and modernism had become mainstream, diluting much of its early appeal. Whatever the cause, and while he would have hesitated to admit it to anyone who wasn't in-the-know, stepping into Ham Yard felt like a pilgrimage. That was why he had come, he told himself again. Nothing remotely to do with Holly Holgate or Gina Lawrence.

The few surviving pictures he'd found on the internet of the club's 60's exterior showed a grimy backstreet London yard, surrounded on three sides by tall, equally grimy looking, turn of the century buildings. Probably warehouses; storage for the many shops and businesses that lined Great Windmill Street. But as he entered Ham Yard, with The Lyric public house to his left, he was confronted not by grime but by an impressive modern hotel, its yellow brick and white concrete walls towering above him. He stopped and stared upwards. Bizarrely, the hotel was crowned by a fringe of foliage; presumably a roof garden for customers to enjoy the sunshine, away from the hustle and bustle of the London traffic. Or perhaps, he reasoned, they were growing vegetables and herbs up there for the hotel's restaurant.

Harry let his gaze return to street level. To his right, a uniformed doorman was ushering a number of suited passengers from a black Bentley Mulsanne into the hotel. He caught the doorman's eye and nodded. The doorman blanked him, reminding him that he had no real business in the yard.

Harry felt suddenly self-conscious. As though every pair of eyes in the yard were not only trained on him but could see his true purpose, whatever that was. Either he was re-living his youth, which was embarrassing. Or he was there chasing ghosts, which was embarrassing. He repressed a sudden urge to yell "Bell-boy" at the top of his voice, re-enacting the scene from Quadrophenia when the character, Jimmy Cooper discovers that his hero isn't what he has been pretending to be. Instead, Harry made for an expensive looking boutique on the far side of the courtyard, trying to give the impression that something in the boutique's window had caught his eye and that he was wealthy enough to afford it. Until he realised that the boutique sold particularly expensive ladies underwear.

The truth, no matter how reluctant Harry was to admit it, was that he wouldn't have been there had Holly Holgate not nudged his interest. At least her messages had subsided. He'd been in the office when she'd made another telephone call into The Park. Jane had insisted on taking the call in private and had been evasive, when later he'd asked her about their conversation. But whatever had been said, Harry was content that it had done the trick. He'd heard nothing from Holgate since. Neither had Martha said anything more about the incident at their door and, in truth, he was more than happy to let it lie. Because no matter how hard he had tried, he could not explain how his daughter had seen the same two figures he had seen. He could make no sense of it at all. As far as Harry was concerned the sooner they all forgot the whole thing, the better. Yet here he was. And since he was here, he resolved, he might as well make the most of the opportunity.

He'd already worked out the rough location of the club's original entrance from the few remaining exterior pictures he'd found on the internet. Toward the front of the yard, between The Lyric and a modern building in the same style as the hotel, Ham Yard narrowed and culminated in a dead end. Here, the modern build gave way to the earlier, grimy buildings that had once enclosed the yard on three sides. The doorway down to The Scene Club had been on the right, in one corner of the dead end. As he approached it, he felt a flutter of anticipation and then a surge of recognition. Gone was the illuminated sign announcing "The Scene" with an arrow pointing downwards, high up on the wall above the doorway. But otherwise, the entranceway looked exactly as it had in the pictures. There was absolutely no doubt about it. This was the same doorway through which countless young people had passed on the way down to the venue below. He stopped, removed his smartphone from his pocket and took several photographs.

Though he had tried on several occasions, Harry had never been able to adequately convey to Ellen the response that physical places such as this triggered for him. It was more than a sense of history, although that was certainly part of it. This place; the very spot on which he was standing, along with the venue below, had been one of the birth places of a cultural revolution that had re-shaped Britain and was still shaping it. In this place, the Britain that had fought and suffered the privations of the Second World War; an austere, black and white Britain of bomb shelters and ration books, had given way to the technicolour Britain of the swinging sixties. In many ways, he reflected, this place was as much a part of British heritage as Bletchley Park, albeit for very different reasons. While it was a thought that would undoubtedly have scandalised his colleagues back at The Park, it was nonetheless true.

But it was more than just the history of places such as this. It was their ability to take him there; as though the walls of a building or the space between them could somehow hold a memory. Sometimes, walking into a building or a place, it was as though he could hear the echoes of the voices of the people who had once filled the space, or see their shadows, or sense their emotions. Perhaps he'd been unable to adequately explain these sensations to Ellen because he'd never felt wholly at ease with them. But whether at ease with them or not, as he approached the green painted doors that had once opened onto a stairway down to The Scene Club, he was certainly feeling them. The hair on the back of his neck was standing on end and his hands were trembling slightly. He returned his smartphone to his jacket pocket.

The doors were closed. They had no handle or lock on the outside, presumably being push bar operated from the inside and providing a means of escape to whoever now used the basement space below, if anybody did. There was no obvious sign that the doors were still in regular use and no indication of what lay behind them. Harry was about to turn away, satisfied as he was that he got all that he was going to get, when he felt a compulsion to reach out.

He was telling himself not to do it as he raised his arm and placed the palm of his hand flat on the door. The moment his hand came into contact with the cold metal surface, he felt the ground beneath his feet give way. It was as though he had crested the top of a roller coaster run and had dropped suddenly. As he went down, he felt an intense wave of anxiety, accompanied by paralysis that made it impossible to move his limbs and then his vision blurred and went black.

The first thing he saw as he began to surface was a figure looming over him, in silhouette against the light. A woman. Her hands coming towards him. He was convinced that she meant to smother him.

'Get off me,' he croaked.

'Are you all right, Love?'

'I said, get off.' He shoved her hands away.

'Take it easy. I reckon you must have fainted.'

He struggled to bring his vision properly into focus. He was slumped against the door. A woman in a bright green high vis jacket was kneeling beside him.

'I'd better call an ambulance.' She reached for a radio clipped to her collar.

'No. No, I'm fine.'

'Well, you don't look it.'

He was already attempting to clamber to his feet. 'I said I'm fine.'

'Are you sure?' She eyed him doubtfully.

He had managed to stand. 'Yes. I just lost my footing, that's all,' he said, brushing dust from the arms of his jacket. 'It was nothing.'

'What were you doing down here anyway?'

'What?' He stared at her.

'What were you doing down here?'

'I was...' He hesitated. 'I took a wrong turn, that's all.'

It was entirely obvious that she didn't believe him.

'Look, I'm fine. Now, if you don't mind, I'd like to go and get a coffee or something.'

'Well, as long as you're sure.'

'Yes. Thank you.'

She reached down to retrieve his bag. 'Here,' she said, handing it to him.

'Thanks,' he said awkwardly.

'You're sure you're all right?' she repeated.

'Yes, absolutely sure. Thank you.'

She stared at him for a moment longer, shook her head and then turned and walked away, still shaking it.

He put his bag over his shoulder and followed her. Before the doorway was completely out of sight he turned to take a final look. There, standing in the space in front of the doors where he had fallen, was the woman with the bee hive hair, wearing ski pants and a short fur jacket and the child, incongruously, in a bright pink, all-in-one, swimsuit. They were motionless and both staring at him.

'For fuck's sake,' he muttered under his breath.

A car horn blared suddenly. The Bentley was reversing. He stepped out of the way. When he turned back towards the doorway, the woman and girl were gone.

CHAPTER TEN

Sunday, 26 April 1964

Spencer Milburn was sitting behind his drum kit, tapping the edge of a snare drum irritably. He was only vaguely aware of the other band members on stage: Rick and Pete off to his left, tuning their guitars; Trevor Fenwick to his right, arranging sheet music on the stand above his keyboard. Trev was the only one of them who read music, but then he was the only one who was a classically trained musician. Spencer, like Rick and Pete, had learned his instrument by ear, having switched from the trumpet to percussion when the band had dumped jazz, in favour of rhythm and blues.

Spencer was doing his best to ignore Micky who was, as usual, off-stage, waiting for their performance to begin. Micky had taken to bounding on to the stage as the band played the opening few bars of their first number. He reckoned that it added impact to their stage presence. It irritated Spencer beyond words, but at least it meant that he didn't need to engage in any pre-gig banter with his brother. The two had barely been on speaking terms. The main cause of that, as far as Spencer was concerned, was once again being played out in front of him. Micky was leaning against the bar, surrounded by a gaggle of young girls, one of whom was Gina Lawrence.

Spencer had tried to distance himself from the dancer after their liaison at the DJ's flat. It had been easy enough, at first. The band had been busy. There were regular gigs at The Scene and several sessions in the recording studio, arranged by Marty Phelps. Within a fortnight of the party they had signed a record deal at Columbia Records and their first single had been scheduled for release. Three weeks later, the single had been released, entered the charts at number 34 and promptly bombed. They had all been desolate, but Phelps had chosen another song and a week later they'd been back in the studio. The single had been released at the beginning of the week and tonight its chart entry position was due to be announced. The word was that it had done well but thus far Marty Phelps had failed to put in an appearance. Which could be good or bad news depending on how you looked at it.

While it had initially been easy enough to focus on the band, the truth was that Spencer had felt increasingly torn over the dancer. There had been other girls back home. Gigging around Newcastle, it had not been difficult to find a girl willing to spend the night in his bed and Spencer had not exactly been immune to their advances. But the truth was that they had been nothing special and moving from one to the other as the band toured the clubs of the North East and ultimately, leaving them behind in Tyneside, had come at little or no personal cost.

Gina Lawrence was different. They had connected, in more ways than the purely physical. Latterly, he'd found himself watching her dancing from behind his drum kit at the back of the stage. They had hardly exchanged a word since the party. They didn't need to. There was a link between them, like an invisible thread. He knew it and, he was sure, so did Gina. When she danced, as she did whenever the band appeared, he was in no doubt at all that she was dancing for him.

Watching her dancing was both bewitching and tortuous. Bewitching, because as she floated around the dance floor, weaving her way between the packed dancers with delicate, flowing movements, he would catch her staring at him and feel the thread pulling tighter. Tortuous because he could see the gathering turmoil behind her eyes.

Spencer had tried to rationalise his feelings for the dancer. It was her vulnerability, he reasoned. Knowing what he knew about her. About the child she had given up. Whatever the circumstances and whether or not she had done wrong, she was suffering. That much was plain and knowing it; watching it displayed on the dance floor in front of him each night they played, tugged at his conscience. But that wasn't all. He was increasingly worried about her. As he watched her popping pills like most of the dancers did, watched the young faces who supplied them, buzzing around her like bees around a honey pot, he had seen her spirits fade. It was as though the lights that had so dazzled him, twinkling behind her eyes, were being slowly extinguished, one-by-one. It was painful to watch.

The more he had watched her, the more he was sure that he was right about the source of her turmoil. Phelps came to the club only occasionally but, whenever he did, he was always the centre of attention, especially among the club's female dancers. As well as managing The Monks and a number of other bands, Phelps was known as an agent with connections across the entertainment industry. The talk at The Scene had it that making it as one of Marty's Girls gave you a golden ticket to fame and fortune and all of the club's female dancers lavished him with attention. All, that is, except Gina.

If she was dancing when he arrived, she would stop on sight, usually disappearing to the bathroom or into one of the booths, arranged along one side of the dance floor's perimeter. Spencer would catch glimpses of her, briefly illuminated by the dance floor lights, sitting alone and disconsolate. If Phelps remained at the club for longer than half an hour or so, she would leave. On one such occasion he had witnessed her stumble into Phelps as she emerged from the corridor leading to the cloakroom. While Spencer had caught nothing of their conversation, their body language had laid bare the gathering enmity between them.

While witnessing her gradual decline had made it increasingly difficult to ignore his feelings for her, his growing conviction that Marty Phelps was the cause had served only to emphasise his dilemma. The record deal, first promised and then duly delivered by Phelps, and the release of their second, make-or-break single, had if anything increased their dependence on Phelps. Spencer knew that he could not afford to blow it by becoming involved in a dispute between Gina and Phelps, especially given that this particular dispute had the potential for public scandal. He had suspected that whoever had fathered Gina's child, might have slept with her when she was underage and he had confirmed it one evening, when he had snuck into the tiny office at the back of the venue and checked the club's membership records. Gina's membership application, completed in what he assumed was her crude handwriting, gave her date of birth as August 5, 1945. If the child's second birthday had been on February 8 as she had told him, then assuming that the pregnancy went anything like full term, it didn't take a rocket scientist to work out that the child had, in all likelihood, been conceived in May 1961, several months before her sixteenth birthday.

While he had been able to maintain an increasingly agonising distance from her, Spencer had been wholly unable to stop himself from intervening, without her knowledge as far as he knew, to protect her from some of the excesses, at least, that were on offer at The Scene Club. He had remonstrated, angrily, on more than one occasion, with a couple of faces who he'd seen supplying her with Drinamyl, or 'Purple Hearts' as they were known, due to their bluish colour and triangular shape. He'd put it about that Gina was off limits to their drug dealing and even gone as far as enlisting Rick, the band's bass player and hard nut, to back up his threats. Rick's kid sister had overdosed on amphetamines one night in 1963 in a club in Middlesborough. She'd recovered but Rick was anti-drugs as a result and had been sympathetic when Spencer had told him about his fears, minus most of the detail, for Gina Lawrence.

Spencer looked across at Micky standing at the bar. If Rick had been amenable to Spencer's desire to watch out for the dancer, his brother had not. He had taken it as something of a personal challenge. Micky's ego, already inflated way beyond its worth, as far as Spencer was concerned, had expanded along with the band's growing popularity among the mods who frequented The Scene and beyond. Spencer had all but given up trying to control his consumption of pills and alcohol, which had itself led to several heated, public arguments between the two of them. But latterly, Micky had taken to holding wild, after gig parties, sometimes at the band's new digs in Waterloo, occasionally at the flats of the many girls who seemed so keen to secure his favours and once or twice at the houses of their parents while they were away for the weekend. Spencer had himself witnessed Micky, off his head on drugs, with half a dozen semi-naked girls, back at the Waterloo digs. Pete, the band's rhythm guitarist had even bragged that he'd joined them. When word had got back to Micky that Spencer had gone soft on Gina Lawrence, Micky had immediately begun to mock him at every possible opportunity and then to make his own moves on the dancer. It had infuriated Spencer to the point that, as the release of the band's second single had approached, the two brothers were barely able exchange a civil word.

Spencer watched now, as Micky slipped an arm behind Gina's back and the two exchanged knowing smiles. Resisting the temptation to kick his drum set across the stage, he caught Trevor Fenwick's eye, nodded vigorously at Pete and Rick and rapped out the timing for their opening number on the rim of his snare. He did it with considerably more force than was strictly necessary.

CHAPTER ELEVEN

Wednesday, 11 May 2016

The morning after his journey into London, Harry had posted the pictures from Ham Yard on '*Original Modernists 1959-1966*', one of the Facebook groups of which he was a member, along with a description of the Yard and the doorway down to the former club. His closing comments had been: -

"I've no idea what is down there now or whether any sign of the former club still exists. It has, after all, been fifty years since The Scene closed its doors for the last time. But I'd very much like to find out. It is probably not going to be possible to get a butcher's inside. Unless, of course, someone knows who owns the building now and can pull a few strings for me. There might be a pint in it!"

Within an hour or so, there was a string of enthusiastic comments from the group's other members. Harry was sitting at his office desk now, reading them. The reply that caught his eye was from someone called Des Munroe. It read: -

"If you're serious about going in for a look, get in touch. If it is connected to the hotel then I can probably get us in. You're not the only one who fancies a peep inside. I'll drop you a PM."

Harry immediately checked his messages and found that Des Munroe had sent him his email address. Harry opened Outlook and sent: -

"Hi Des. Thanks for getting in touch. I would definitely be interested in taking a look if that were possible. I've no idea what the place is used for now. Do you? Anything you can do to make it happen would be very much appreciated. Do let me know if you have any success. Regards, HS."

By the end of the day, Des Munroe had replied: -

"We are on for next Tuesday 17 at 6pm if you are available? I happen to know Millie Travers, whose family owns the hotel in Ham Yard. Her daughter, Jet, has offered to show us around the hotel's basement which apparently spans the entire yard, so very likely is where the doorway leads. The V&A are filming an interview with me on Tuesday at my flat at the other end of Great Windmill Street for an exhibition that opens in September. Why don't you come along to the flat and, once the V&A have finished, we can proceed together. We should be done by 6pm but if the filming overruns Jet Travers says she's cool until 8pm. I'm at Number 8. Ring the top bell when you arrive."

Harry read the email with incredulity. It was amazing where Facebook could get you, he reflected. As far as he was aware, nobody who knew anything about The Scene Club had managed to locate it precisely, let alone visit the former venue, since the club had closed its doors for the last time, reportedly in 1966. There wasn't a single picture of the modern interior on the internet and only conjecture about what the space was used for now, if indeed it even existed in any identifiable form. Yet, within just a few hours, he had seemingly achieved the impossible. Gone were the days when you had to climb in through an open window in the middle of the night, or abseil down a lift shaft to gain access to the world's hidden places. Here was somebody he didn't know, inviting him to his flat in Central London, to meet somebody else he didn't know, who was going to show them around the basement of the hotel owned by a family he also didn't know, apparently for no other reason than that they could. The whole thing seemed unreal. Which led him to wonder about Des Munroe. He googled the name and discovered that Munroe was the retired managing director of a well known pharmaceuticals company, in respect of which he had retained a considerable share holding, which would undoubtedly make him a wealthy man. Quite why a man like Munroe had offered Harry the chance to explore the basement below Ham Yard Hotel, rather than simply explore it himself was anybody's guess. But offer it, he had. Harry typed and sent a reply:

"That's fantastic news and yes, I'm available. See you at your flat at 6pm. With many thanks, HS."

Then, as an afterthought, he went back onto *Original Modernists* and re-read the The Scene Club thread, at the end of which was a new message from somebody called Lester Pilkington: -

"Does anyone else remember Gina Lawrence? The dancer who went missing from The Scene in April 1964? She and her best friend Lynette Bell were mates of mine. Until all that stuff with the Milburn brothers. Dead dodgy if you ask me."

Harry stared at the text. Gina Lawrence and The Scene Club. Try as he might to explain away his interest in the venue as purely historical, it was clear that the two were inexorably linked, whether he had cared to acknowledge it or not. The truth was by allowing one into his thoughts, he had admitted the other. Whatever source his mind was tapping in to in order to produce the visions and sensations he'd now experienced on three separate occasions, there would be a reason for it. There always was. As unwelcome as his intuition might be, it was never wrong. It might have got him into a whole heap of trouble but it had led him to the truth. In the end.

Harry sat back in his office chair, still staring at his computer screen. That was just it. What end would there be this time, if he allowed them all to become embroiled again in a story to which he didn't even know the beginning, let alone where it might take them? That was how the search for Martha Watts had begun. With a vision of the missing log reader in a tube train window and a feeling, each time he passed through Belsize Park Station that the log reader was there. It had been his choice to look for Martha Watts but his friends who had suffered the consequences. The people he loved. And if that wasn't bad enough, this time there was something else. Something he had been avoiding. Something that he was sure that Ellen had also recognised but they had both left unsaid. He could not escape the conclusion that this time, Martha was involved.

Her vision of the two figures was no accident or coincidence. It didn't work like that. Martha had seen what she had seen. Which meant there was a reason for her also. If she hadn't already, she would almost certainly go on seeing them until it was discovered. Harry had been afraid that there might be no way to stop it; no way to protect her. But it struck him now that by his continued denial he would be leaving her to face it alone. That was something that he could not allow to happen.

But if they were going to face it together; if there was really no alternative, then he needed to be certain that she had seen the same figure that he was sure was Gina Lawrence. He reached for the keyboard and typed a reply: -

"Hi Lester, I don't suppose you or anyone else have any photographs of Gina Lawrence, do you?"

***

The drive to Friern Barnet from the shop in Hadley had taken Ellen no more than twenty minutes. She had found the pub, parked the car and found them a table in a quiet corner, away from the bar. Jane had showed up within minutes of her arrival and had bought them both drinks.

'You managed to get away then,' Ellen said when Jane had seated herself. 'Cheers,' she added.

They clanked their glasses.

'Of course. I told them that I had an afternoon appointment with the doctor.'

'How did Harry take it?'

Jane rolled her eyes. 'How does Harry usually take it when I take time off?'

She shrugged. 'Badly?'

'Do you know, he had the bloody cheek to ask me what was wrong with me?'

She shook her head. 'Really?'

'I told him to mind his own business. Then I thought better of it and told him that I have period problems. That shut him up.'

Ellen smiled. 'I bet it did. He gets squeamish at the mere sight of a Tampax.'

They both laughed. But Ellen's laughter was short lived. 'You are sure we're doing the right thing?' she said, frowning.

'Of course.'

'I just don't like doing this behind Harry's back, that's all.'

'I know you don't. Believe it or not, neither do I. But it's the only way, Ellen. You said yourself that Harry would have had a fit.'

She was right, of course, but keeping their meeting with Holgate from Harry had brought back some unhappy memories. 'Did I ever tell you that the first time they went into the shelter at Belsize Park, Harry was going to do it without my knowledge?'

Jane frowned. 'You didn't. But Harry told Mike and Mike told me.'

'I was so hurt.'

'Why?'

She thought about it. 'Because the search for Martha Watts was about us. Harry and me. It was what brought us together. By cutting me out, it felt like he was telling me that he didn't need me.' She'd been absolutely furious with him. It had been their first serious argument, albeit that it had lasted all of about twenty minutes.

'He was trying to protect you.'

'Do you think so?'

'I know so. That's the trouble with men. They seem to think we need protecting. It gives meaning to their otherwise sorry existence,' Jane said, smiling. 'Take that away from them and they don't know where they are.'

Which might have been funny in other circumstances but Ellen was in no mood for humour. 'Which sounds just a bit like a case of pot calling kettle black,' she said, staring down into her wine glass.

Jane hesitated. 'Look, you said yourself that Harry just can't handle it right now. Which means that we either sit on our hands while he contemplates his navel, or...'

'That's not fair,' Ellen said, flushing. 'Harry's doing his best.'

Jane sighed. 'All right. I know he is. But right now, he's burying his head in the sand. All we're doing is giving Holgate a hearing. If Harry had done that in the first place, then this would not have been necessary.'

Ellen smiled weakly. 'I guess so.'

'If it will make you feel better, then tell him as soon as you get back tonight. If Holgate has any hard evidence, anything at all, then that'll give him something to work with. If not and she turns out to be a fruit cake, then it might not have resolved the issue but at least we'll know where we are. OK?'

Ellen nodded.

'The point is we're trying to move this on because Harry can't,' Jane said, nodding toward the front of the pub.

The reporter had entered the bar.

Jane stood up.

Holgate spotted them.

Ellen watched her approach. She was prettier than she remembered, with short, dark hair, pixie-like features and wide set eyes.

'Holly,' Jane said, holding out a hand.

The reporter shook it.

'You've met Ellen?'

Ellen had got to her feet and held out her hand.

'Mrs Stammers,' the reporter said, tentatively taking her hand.

She was well spoken, with hardly any hint of an accent. Ellen smiled. 'Call me Ellen. Please.'

'Can I get you a drink?' Jane offered.

'Thank you. A half a lager would be great.'

Jane nodded and headed off towards the bar.

They both sat.

'Thank you so much for offering to see me, Ellen,' the reporter began. 'I really wasn't expecting Jane's call.'

'You didn't really leave us with much choice.' She hadn't meant it to sound as confrontational as it did.

The reported flinched. 'I'm so sorry for turning up at your house the other night. It's just that…'

'It's all right,' Ellen interrupted. 'Harry should have listened to you when you approached him at Bletchley. I'm afraid he has a bit of an aversion to journalists.'

Holgate smiled. 'I did try to explain that I wasn't looking for an interview.'

'He is aware of that. In his defence, he's had some…' she hesitated, searching for the right words, 'issues with the press. And he gets a lot of requests from people wanting his help. If it's any consolation, he has declined them all. Please don't take it personally.'

'Does he? Get a lot of requests for help, I mean?' The reporter seemed surprised.

'Yes. They have tailed off a bit over the last couple of years but he still gets them.'

'He has refused them all?'

'Every one,' Ellen agreed. 'You have to understand Holly, that the search for Martha Watts and everything that followed came at considerable cost. Not just to Harry but to all of us.'

'I know that.'

'Harry blames himself. He always has and I expect he always will. You will, I hope, understand his reluctance to go there again, no matter how apparently worthy the cause.'

The reported shifted uncomfortably in her seat. 'In hindsight, door stepping him was probably not my finest moment. Perhaps, if I'd been more circumspect?'

Ellen thought about it. 'No. I know my husband. He would have rejected you in any case.'

Jane had returned with Holly's beer.

'Thanks and thank you again for agreeing to see me.'

Jane took her seat. 'Shall we get straight to the point?'

The reporter nodded.

'Tell us about Gina Lawrence,' Jane continued. 'What is your interest in her and why do you need Harry's help?'

Holgate glanced first at Ellen, then at Jane. 'Well, the middle part of your question is straight forward, at least. So maybe that is where I should start?'

Ellen nodded.

'Gina Lawrence was my aunt. Or more accurately, my grandmother's illegitimate daughter. The half-sister my father never knew.'

CHAPTER TWELVE

Wednesday, 11 May 2016

Harry had waited up. He hadn't been expecting Ellen to be so late. She often worked into the evening and sometimes she and Nicky, her business partner, went out after work for something to eat. On such occasions, they had an arrangement with a couple with a daughter in Martha's class. They'd collected her from school and given her supper. Harry had picked her up from their place just after seven.

Martha had been quiet in the car and unusually, had done her homework and gone to bed on the stroke of nine, without complaint. It was after eleven when Ellen had finally appeared.

'Good night?' he asked, as she flopped down on the sofa beside him.

'Interesting night.'

'Interesting?'

Ellen hesitated. 'I'll tell you in a minute. How was Martha?'

'She was fine. A bit quiet. I haven't heard a peep from her since she went up,' he said, noting the shadow of concern that passed across Ellen's features like a rain cloud. 'She was fine,' he added with what he hoped was a reassuring smile. 'I think she was just tired.'

He held her eyes, aware that she was searching his face for any sign of even a half truth. It was a skill that she had honed to something approaching perfection. God help him if he ever needed to keep a secret.

Apparently satisfied, she said 'How about you? What have you been up to?'

He had contemplated not telling her. He wasn't sure how she was going to take it. But if he had learned one thing from their eleven years together, it was that attempting secrecy was always counter productive. They had encountered many challenges, since the day when he'd first clapped eyes on her, emerging from her car outside the butcher's shop in Southwold. Things had generally gone a whole lot better when they had faced them together. 'You're not going to believe this.'

Ellen cocked her head to one side. 'Try me,' she said, as though she was not only likely to believe it, but, impossibly, knew what he was about to say.

He took a breath and then recounted his on-line discussion with Des Munroe.

Ellen listened in silence.

By the time he had finished, there was an odd half-smile creasing the corner of her mouth. It wasn't the reaction he'd been expecting. 'Are you going to tell me why you're smiling?'

'No. I'm going to tell you what was interesting about my evening. And I want you to hear me out. OK?'

He wasn't sure that he liked the sound of that.

'I said, OK?' Ellen repeated, her smile fading.

This was serious. 'OK.'

'Good. Jane doesn't have a problem with her periods and she didn't have a doctor's appointment this afternoon.'

'How do you know about...'

'Just hear me out,' Ellen interrupted.

He hesitated and nodded.

'She didn't have an appointment with her doctor. Jane and I spent the evening in a pub in Friern Barnet, with Holly Holgate.'

He was momentarily lost for words. 'You saw Holly Holgate?' he managed.

'Yes,' Ellen said simply.

'With Jane.'

'Yes.'

He was stunned.

'I'm sorry that I didn't tell you. If it's any consolation, I agonised over it. Ask Jane, if you're in any doubt about that.'

He felt a flash of anger. 'Jane. Oh, I get it...'

'Stop it.'

'That bloody woman...'

'Harry, I said stop it.'

She had raised her voice. He stared at her.

'It wasn't Jane's decision. It was mine. Will you hear me out?' She met and held his eyes. 'Please?' she added, her tone softer.

He nodded.

'I agreed to see Holly Holgate because I decided that we needed to hear what she has to say.'

'You decided,' he said, letting his anger show again.

'Yes. When Martha saw them on Friday, Harry, it changed everything. We both know it. But you didn't want to go there. In fact, you've gone out of your way to avoid discussing it. So yes, I decided.'

She was right, but he wasn't ready to concede the point. Not yet. He said nothing.

She stared at him. 'Look, I understand why it's difficult for you. I didn't want to try to force you to do something you were clearly not ready to do. But Martha saw what she saw. We both know how this works. Sooner or later it is going to happen again. Burying our heads in the sand is not going to help her. It is not going to help us. We need to know what we're dealing with here. Then perhaps, we can tackle it together.'

The irony was that he had reached much the same conclusion. If she'd waited another 24 hours, he'd have come around. 'I know you think that I bury my head in the sand. But I don't.' He'd recognised the absurdity of his last statement as the words had left his lips.

She stared at him like only she could.

'All right, sometimes I do. But mostly it just takes me a little longer to get there. You could have told me, that's all. We could have discussed it.'

She held his eyes. 'I know. But I thought that seeing Holgate might help us to move this forward. Give us something more tangible to work with. I'm sorry that I didn't discuss it with you. Perhaps I should have. But Harry, you don't always make that easy.'

He started to object.

'I'm not blaming you. I know this is difficult. But you've got to admit it, the way you reacted to Holgate and what happened on Friday made discussion very difficult. I did try.'

To be fair, she had tried but she'd been asking the impossible. 'What could I say, Ellen? What is there to say? I don't have the faintest idea how Martha could possibly have seen the same two figures I saw. It's been doing my head in.'

'I know it has. It's been doing mine in too. But you won't solve anything by shutting it out. You'll just leave us to deal with it on our own.'

He could see that. 'I take your point. I'm sorry. I just don't know what to do for the best.'

She smiled and took hold of his hand. 'I know that you're trying to protect us. But this isn't all on your shoulders, Harry. I'd rather we faced this together.'

He nodded.

Her expression hardened. 'But if there are times when you can't or won't, then be assured that I will. When it comes to Martha's wellbeing, I'm not prepared to be passive.'

He recoiled. 'I don't want you to be passive. Jesus, you're hardly passive.'

'I know, but sometimes you've got to let me make the decisions and respect them when I do, especially when it comes to Martha. When Holly turned up at The Park and asked for your help, that was your issue. Your refusal to have anything to do with her was your decision and I respected that, even though, to be honest, I didn't agree. But when she came here and Martha saw what she saw, it became our issue. By denying it you made it mine. So I made a decision.'

'I respect your right to make decisions. Of course I do.'

'Well that's good. Now hold that thought, because there's more.'

'More?'

'Yes, but we'll get to that. So long as we're all right. I'm sorry that I saw Holgate without telling you. Really I am. It felt like I had no alternative.'

Harry thought about it. She was right. He had backed her into a corner. 'Apology accepted.'

'Are you sure?'

'I'm sure. This whole business confuses the hell out of me,' he said, honestly. 'You know it does. But, believe it or not, I was coming round to the idea that we needed to confront it together, for Martha's sake. I can hardly blame you for getting there first. Now are you going to tell me what Holgate had to say for herself?'

'Yes, but let's make some coffee first. I'm parched and I've got a lot to tell you.' She stood up. 'For one thing, seeing Holy Holgate wasn't the only decision I made today,' she said over her shoulder.

'Dear God, is there to be no end to my torment?'

'I'm afraid not,' Ellen called out from the kitchen. 'Brace yourself, soldier.'

'So, it turns out that Gina Lawrence is, or was, Holly Holgate's aunt,' Ellen said, her coffee cup raised to her lips.

They had seated themselves on the sofa.

He was genuinely surprised. 'They're related?'

Ellen nodded. 'Gina was her father's half-sister, of whom he knew nothing and which Holly only discovered last year, when her grandmother told her, shortly before she died, that she'd had an illegitimate child to an American airman in 1945.'

Harry swallowed a mouthful of coffee. 'Well, I didn't see that coming.'

'She gave the child up for adoption and wanted Holly to find her. It was her dying wish. She wanted Gina to know that she had given her up, not because she didn't love her but because she did. She wanted her to know that she had regretted it every day since.'

Ellen didn't have to ask him whether that rang any personal bells. When Lizzie had left him, his sister Kate, and Ted Stammers, she'd believed it to be in their best interests. Whether she'd been right, of course, was debatable. But like Gina's mother, Lizzie hadn't abandoned her children because she didn't care about them but precisely because she did.

'That was why Holly set out to find Gina Lawrence. She didn't succeed. What she found was Gina's adoptive mother, still mourning Gina's disappearance. An elderly woman called June Lawrence. Mrs Lawrence told Holly that Gina had been a particularly troubled and difficult child. She had run away from home several times during her early teens.' Ellen paused. When Harry said nothing, she continued. 'In 1961, Gina had said that she was going to stay with friends. She wouldn't say which friends and she never revealed where she had been staying. While there was occasional telephone contact, Mrs Lawrence didn't see her daughter again for some months. She finally reappeared and Mrs Lawrence was able to visit her in May 1962. Gina was living in a poky little flat above a Jazz club in Soho called Cy Laurie's.'

Harry knew the name. 'Which later became The Scene Club.'

Ellen nodded. 'Apparently so. During the investigation that followed her disappearance from her flat above The Scene Club in

1964, rumours were being circulated that Gina had a drug problem and that she'd worked from the flat as a prostitute to fund it.'

'Could be,' Harry reflected.

'Holly doesn't think so. She says that the source of these rumours was an interview Micky Milburn did with the Daily Express a few days after Gina went missing. June Lawrence was also adamant that they were false.'

'How could she know?' An unwillingness to believe the worst about your daughter was understandable, even admirable, but that didn't make it untrue.

'She couldn't, of course. Not with absolute certainty. But when June and Donald Lawrence, Gina's now deceased father, had asked the street girls in Soho, and to their credit they left no stone unturned looking for her, not one of them said Gina had been working the circuit.'

'What about the regulars at The Scene? Did the Lawrences speak to them?'

Ellen nodded. 'Yes, they did. They were told that Gina had earned a living waitressing at several Central London restaurants, but that her first love had always been dancing. She'd hoped to be selected for Ready Steady Go. Apparently the Scene Club was regularly attended by the show's talent spotters.'

'It was,' Harry interjected. 'That's where Twiggy got her first break.'

'Was it?'

Harry nodded. He'd seen a documentary featuring the former model.

'Gina first came across the Milburn brothers and their band,' Ellen continued, 'in early 1964.'

'The Monks. It was their first residency when they came down to London from Newcastle.'

'Several of the regulars at The Scene told the Lawrences that Spencer Milburn had taken a shine to Gina. They might not have been an item but he certainly took her under his wing. He was, by all accounts, very protective of her.'

'Protective? About what?'

'There was a big drug thing going on at The Scene and, by all accounts, some fairly wild parties. Spencer was very anti drugs. There were reports of several arguments between Spencer and Micky Milburn, both about the drugs and about Gina Lawrence. The story goes that Micky Milburn was not averse, after a gig, to a night in bed with half a dozen willing girls.'

'Like a lot of them did. Like a lot of them probably still do,' he observed.

'That's as maybe, but Holly says that there was a darker side to Micky Milburn. If he selected a girl who was unwilling at the beginning of the evening, Micky plied them with enough drugs to make them more than willing by the end of it.'

Harry knew about the rumours concerning Micky Milburn. 'Nothing was ever proven about that and the Milburns always denied it.'

'Well, of course they did. I mean, they were hardly going to admit it. But did you know that in 1987, Micky Milburn was arrested in Florida for the violent rape of a girl half his age?'

'Vaguely.' He recalled the story. 'He was found not guilty wasn't he?'

'He was. But the allegation was that he had drugged her. And you must know about his reputation for misogyny?'

'Everybody knows about it. That doesn't make him guilty and it doesn't prove that he had anything to do with Gina Lawrence's disappearance.'

'Perhaps not,' Ellen agreed. 'But Holly says that she has found a new witness. Somebody who wasn't interviewed by the police during the original investigation, such as there was one. It was a bit of a farce, apparently.'

Which was hardly surprising. As far as he knew, unless the missing person was a child, or there was any direct evidence of foul play, missing persons were rarely investigated particularly thoroughly. 'A witness to what?'

'A witness who says that she was in Gina's flat, *with* Gina and Micky Milburn on the night Gina went missing.'

Her meaning was pretty obvious. 'You're saying that the three of them slept together?'

Ellen nodded. 'That was certainly the implication. There was a party. To celebrate the band's first number one.'

'I'll Be Seeing You.'

'Eh?'

'The name of the song. I've got a copy of it on 45 somewhere.' In fact he probably had all of The Monks singles somewhere. 'Did she say what happened?'

'Not exactly. She told Holly that she was too stoned to remember.'

'Convenient,' he said, not even trying to mask his scepticism.

'But she did tell Holly that Milburn had been feeding them pills like Smarties. Holly got the distinct impression that there was a lot more the witness could have said.'

Harry was thoughtful. If the three of them got it together, then he could well understand her reluctance. 'This witness. What's her name?' he said suddenly.

'Lynette..'

'Bell,' he finished the name for her.

Ellen stared at him.

'Lynette Bell was Gina's best friend at the time. According to some bloke on one of the Facebook groups I'm on. So how did Holgate find out about her?'

'Richard Lambton told her.'

'You're kidding,' Harry said, surprised. 'I thought Lambton was dead. I thought that apart from the Milburn brothers, they all were.'

Ellen shook her head. 'Not so, apparently. Lambton is still alive. When she saw him he was in a pretty sorry state. Living in sheltered housing in Newcastle and suffering from dementia by the sound of it. Holly said that he kept repeating himself.'

'Not exactly reliable then,' Harry said, a little more dismissively than he intended.

Ellen raised an eyebrow. 'No. But the fact that your Facebook source named Lynette Bell is consistent with what Lambton told Holly, at least.'

'So far as it goes.'

Ellen nodded.

'So has Holly spoken to the police?'

'No, she hasn't.'

'Why not?'

'Because Lynette Bell begged her not to, for one thing.'

'Why?'

'Because she's afraid.'

'After all this time? Of what?'

'You mean, of who. Micky Milburn. Bell would say very little over the phone but she was terrified of Micky Milburn discovering that she'd been found, let alone that she'd been talking.'

Harry thought about it for a moment and then shook his head. 'It's not exactly convincing, is it? I mean, Micky Milburn lives in the States. As far as I know, he's been over there since the late sixties. What risk could he possibly pose to Lynette Bell?'

'I've no idea. But Holly is convinced that there's a lot more to Lynette Bell then she has so far discovered.'

'Like what?'

'Like what she is she doing in the Highlands of Scotland? According to Lambton, Bell left London shortly after Gina's disappearance and dropped out of circulation. It turns out that she's been living up there ever since under an assumed name. Why would you do that if you had nothing to hide?'

Which was a fair point. It did seem unlikely to have been purely coincidental. 'But if Bell was using an assumed name, then how did Holly track her down?'

'For the last few years she's been using her real name to draw benefits and her state pension. Holly has a contact at the Benefits Agency. Bell freaked when Holly first made contact.'

'I bet she did.'

'She begged Holly not to reveal her whereabouts to anyone.'

Harry rolled his eyes. 'Like us, you mean.'

Ellen said nothing.

'That's reporters for you. It's intriguing. I'll give you that.'

Ellen smiled. 'That it is.'

'So what does Holly want from us? When she spoke to me at Bletchley…'

Ellen raised an eyebrow.

'All right, when she *tried* to speak to me at Bletchley, she said that she'd been threatened. What's all that about?'

'Holly has been doing a lot of digging for quite some time. Pretty much from the get go, odd things started happening. She works as a freelance journalist, right?'

Harry nodded.

'Well, almost immediately, the work started drying up. First, her long standing contacts started declining her work. One by one.'

He was dubious, which must have shown in his expression because Ellen held up a hand.

'I know. But her Twitter and Facebook accounts were hacked. Somebody posed as Holly on line. Journalists rely on their contacts, right? By the time Holly had regained control of her social media accounts, most of her regular contacts had pulled the plug and want nothing more to do with her.'

He was still unconvinced.

'Then six weeks ago, she got hold of Micky Milburn.'

'Micky Milburn spoke to her? How did she manage that?'

'By posing as a Radio Two DJ. She asked for an interview.'

'He agreed?'

'Yup. He fell for it pretty readily, apparently. She spoke to him at his home in Florida. The call lasted all of ten minutes. The moment he got wind of her interest in Gina Lawrence he became abusive and ended the call. Since then, she has received a string of anonymous and threatening phone calls.'

'Threatening?'

'The caller knows where she lives. Threats of rape, if she doesn't drop it. That kind of thing.'

'Jesus.'

'Then two weeks ago her flat was broken into and ransacked. They stole her laptop, all her papers on the Lawrence case and a tape she had of the interview from a few years back with Spencer Milburn. Since then, she has been followed. Nothing too intrusive. Just enough to let her know that they are watching her.'

'Did they take anything not connected with the Lawrence story?'

Ellen hesitated. 'I don't know. I didn't think to ask.'

'Does she take these threats seriously?'

'Oh come on, Harry,' Ellen said, shaking her head. 'Put yourself in Holly's shoes for a moment. She is a woman who lives alone. Since all her contacts backed out, she's been dealing with this entirely on her own.'

'So why doesn't she just drop it?'

Ellen stared at him.

Harry shrugged. It was, as far as he was concerned, a perfectly reasonable question.

'She's doing it for the same reason we did it eleven years ago.'

'Are you certain about that? It's hardly the same,' he said dismissively.

'Isn't it? We did it for Elsie. We did it because it was right to do it. The more we were threatened, the more we were determined to see it through.'

'Yes and look where that got us, Ellen. Remember where it got you.'

Her expression dropped.

He knew that he'd gone too far. Ellen had been imprisoned in a tiny room, one hundred feet below Belsize Park tube station, with nothing but the mummified corpse of Martha Watts to keep her company. Later, she'd been kidnapped and held captive by Günther Möller who had threatened to butcher them all in cold blood. 'I'm sorry. I didn't mean to…'

'You're right,' Ellen interrupted. 'We put our lives on the line. More than once. We all did. I regret what happened to Marcus and the others. You know I do. But I don't regret what we achieved. And do you know what?'

'What?'

'I am proud that we had the courage to see it through.'

Ellen had been to hell and back. If anything, it had made her stronger. He leaned forward and kissed her. 'And I am proud of you Ellen. Prouder than you'll ever know. But this time, we've got our own Martha to worry about.'

'I know we have,' she said, quietly. 'Don't think that doesn't worry me, Harry. Martha seeing those two figures on Friday freaked me out. Just like it freaked you out.'

'Not quite like it.' It was, perhaps a little churlish to point out that Ellen's experience could never be the same as his. That she would never understand precisely how it felt to see and sense things that were not there. That could not be there.

'Do you know, I wish I could see them?' Ellen said, an edge of anger in her tone. 'Can you imagine what it feels like to know that I'll never be able to share what you and now Martha experience?'

'I'm sorry. I didn't mean to…'

'You're right,' Ellen cut in. 'I can't know what it's really like. But I do know that what you sense; whatever it is, wherever it comes from, never lies. It leads you to the truth in the end.'

'In the end.' he echoed, frowning.

'It never lets you go and now, what scares me more than anything, is that it'll never let Martha go. Unless we follow your instinct and see it through. That's why I went to see Holly Holgate.'

He ran his hand through his hair.

Ellen smiled, weakly.

'What?'

'You haven't done that in a while.'

'What?'

'That thing with your hair. You used to do it all the time. Whenever you were stressed.'

'Maybe I haven't been stressed in a while.'

Ellen reached for his hand and grasped it tightly. 'We're in the same place aren't we? We both know what we need to do. You've already made your decision and I've made mine.'

He smelled a rat. 'Hang on. What decision have I made?'

Ellen smiled.

He knew that smile.

'You've decided to go to Ham Yard next week. You're not thinking about it. You didn't ask for my opinion or permission. You said that you had agreed to meet Des Munroe at his flat. Decision made. Just as a matter of interest, what would you have done had I said that I didn't want you to go?'

He thought about it. 'But you didn't. You never do. You always respect my...' He hesitated. He could feel the jaws of the trap that she had laid for him closing. He shook his head. He had to hand it to her.

'Exactly. I always respect your decisions. And I hope you're going to respect mine.'

He stared at her.

'Jane and I are going to Scotland on Saturday morning, with Holly.'

'You're what?' It was the second time that she had stunned him in one evening.

'We'll be back on Monday. We're going to see Lynette Bell.'

'You can't be serious,' he protested. 'You said yourself that Holgate is being followed.'

'Harry...'

'It's not safe. I'll go with her, if one of us must.'

'No. You won't. You're going to respect my decision.'

He stared at her. He had been well and truly out manoeuvred. Done up like a kipper. A highland kipper.

'Lynette Bell is a frightened woman, Harry. Getting her to talk requires a feminine touch. You turn up with Holly and Bell will run a mile.'

'But..'

'But nothing,' Ellen was adamant. 'I know you want to protect me, Harry. I wouldn't have it, or you, any other way. But I have thought about this and made a decision. Besides, I'll have Jane with me. Who would you most want by your side at the first sign of trouble?'

She had a point. The two of them would be a force to be reckoned with.

'Well, exactly.'

But he was not convinced that she was doing the right thing.

CHAPTER THIRTEEN

Sunday, 26 April 1964

Two thirds of the way through the set, Marty Phelps and his wife had arrived. A buzz had immediately swept around the basement venue. The band had been in the middle of Lew Herman's "*Night Time is The Right Time*" and finished it to thunderous applause. Phelps had come straight to the stage and, once the closing bars of the song had played out, stepped up to the microphone.

'Ladies and gentlemen,' he began, in the forced Oxbridge accent that had begun to grate on Spencer, 'on Monday, as you will all no doubt be aware, Columbia Records released *I'll Be Seeing You*, a little number penned by a certain Mr. Trevor Fenwick...' he said, gesturing toward the keyboard player. Trevor Fenwick duly bowed. Applause broke out, cheers rippling around the audience.

Phelps waited for the sound to subside. 'The second forty-five from our very own, no,' Phelps corrected himself 'your very own, The Monks.'

More cheering and fevered applause.

'Tonight, I'm delighted to able to tell you that *I'll Be Seeing You* has not only charted, but went straight into the chart at...' he hesitated dramatically, 'Number One!'

The crowd erupted. Several girls leapt forward to embrace Micky, Pete and Rick. Trevor turned, reached across to Spencer and shook his hand.

Spencer, who had been seated behind his drums had clambered, shakily to his feet. He couldn't quite believe it. He'd been optimistic about the single's chances. It was a great song and the band had put everything they had into the recording. Even Spencer had been forced to admit that Micky's vocals on the track had been outstanding. Moody, even aggressive at times but lyrical where the song required it, the studio sound engineer had proclaimed his "smoking vocals", a phrase subsequently picked up by the record company's PR people for use on the record's picture sleeve. But the most that Spencer had been hoping for was a place in the Top 20. 'Straight into the chart at Number One,' he said out loud, as much for his own benefit, than for anybody else's.

Trevor Fenwick grinned. 'Number Fucking One,' he repeated. 'Yes,' he said, punching the air with his fist.

Spencer swallowed hard. It was crazy. Just a few months before they'd been playing the likes of The Monkchester British Legion. Now they were Number One across the country. Up there with The Beatles, The Rolling Stones, Elvis Presley and all the others. Not just up there, but topping them. It was unreal. It was going to change everything.

It had taken a full ten minutes for order to be restored, at which point Phelps had taken the mic once again and proclaimed, 'Ladies and Gentleman, I give you Britain's Number One, The Monks!'

They had played out the remainder of the set and ended it with a thumping rendition of "I'll Be Seeing You". But Spencer had been in a daze. It was the one and only time that he saw Gina Lawrence dance in Marty Phelps's presence. She had come forward and danced in front of the band. But when they had finished, it had been Micky who had leapt from the stage and swept her off her feet. Spencer had caught her eyes, as the singer spun her around. There was no look of joy. Only surrender.

CHAPTER FOURTEEN

Sunday, 15 May 2016

Their journey to Balnakeil, on the north-west coast of Scotland, was an arduous one and would have been more arduous still had they not broken the journey by staying overnight at a small but comfortable hotel in Inverness. They had travelled up on the 09:00 from London Kings Cross, changed at Edinburgh and caught the local train, arriving in the highland town a few minutes after 5pm on Saturday afternoon. They'd had dinner at the hotel, spent an hour chatting about nothing in particular in the bar, before Ellen had given her apologies and returned to her room. She had called Harry and Martha, who had both seemed fine, and gone straight to bed. She'd slept solidly until 8am.

Holly had booked a hire car over the internet, along with their travel tickets, the day after their meeting in Friern Barnet. After breakfast, they'd collected the keys from the hotel's reception and found the car, a silver Audi A4, waiting for them in the hotel car park.

Balnakeil was a three hour drive through the rugged highland countryside, first to Lairg, then along the road beside Loch Shin, turning northeastwards at Laxford Bridge toward the village of Durness. They'd left Inverness in bright sunshine and good spirits, with Holly at the wheel of the Audi, but as they'd neared Durness, the weather had taken a distinct turn for the worse. Ominous dark grey clouds had rolled in from the sea to the north and a blanket of drizzle had descended over the treeless landscape, gradually obscuring the distant mountains ahead of them.

They'd driven the last few miles towards Durness in silence, Ellen's thoughts returning to the woman they had travelled almost the length of the country to see. Lynette Bell. She'd be in her seventies now, Ellen reflected, having spent her early years in London and the rest of them in this remote place. What was it that had driven her from London, to spend the remainder of her adult life about as far away from her former home as it was possible to spend it without leaving the country altogether? Surely Holly was mistaken in her assumption that Micky Milburn, an ageing rock star who had made his home some 4000 miles away in Florida, could possibly wield the kind of influence necessary to explain Lynette Bell's self-imposed isolation. Somehow, Ellen concluded, there had to be more to it than that.

The satnav announced 'Left turn ahead', snapping Ellen's thoughts back to the present.

Once they were out of Durness itself, the village's scattered single storey houses gave way to open grasslands, a well maintained drystone wall running along both sides of the road as it snaked its way toward Balnakeil. Ellen was glad that Holly was at the wheel. The driving conditions were deteriorating rapidly. 'What a place for a hippy commune. Not exactly idyllic is it?' she observed.

'Depends on your idea of idyllic,' Holly replied. 'It's quiet, I'll give it that.'

'It wasn't exactly a hippy commune,' Jane added. 'It was a craft village. A cooperative. It still is, apparently. When the first settlers came out here, there was no plumbing and no electricity. Can you imagine how cold it must have been in the winter, before they got those,' she said, pointing at a series of wooden poles supporting heavy electric cables that criss-crossed the road.

Up ahead of them a cluster of single storey, squat, rectangular buildings gradually materialised from out of the drizzle. They looked to Ellen a little like buildings she'd seen at Bletchley Park. Their utilitarian design and steel window frames gave them a distinctly military appearance. 'What was this place? Before the settlers came, I mean?'

'It was an early warning station during the Cold War,' Jane replied. 'Part of our defences against nuclear attack,' she added.

'Can you defend against nuclear attack?' Ellen wondered out loud.

Holly smiled. 'Probably not. But if you know they're coming you can at least take the time to kiss your ass goodbye.'

'A cheery thought,' Jane replied.

Holly had pulled the Audi over, into a lay-by beside the concrete buildings, then she'd turned left onto a single lane track that ran gently downhill, into the main site. The first few buildings they encountered didn't look to Ellen as though they had been occupied since the abandonment of the station but, as they drove down the track, the dereliction gave way to a row of neatly painted buildings, several with makeshift front gardens. 'Lynette's place should be down here, just before the track turns left.'

They pulled over.

'I'll call her,' Holly said, reaching into her pocket and taking out her mobile phone.

'No need,' Jane observed, nodding towards the building on their left.

A woman had emerged and was sheltering in the door way, leaning on a walking stick. She had long grey-blonde hair, Ellen observed, and was wearing what looked like a hand knitted, knee length woollen cardigan over an even longer pink dress.

'Dear God, is that a maxi?' Holly said. 'She either reads *Vogue* or she's been wearing that for longer than I've been alive.'

They got out of the car.

Ellen caught the woman's eye, smiled and raised her hand in assumed recognition. The woman did not return the gesture. Instead, she stared at them for a moment, before turning away and disappearing back into the building, leaving the door open behind her.

Had Ellen or either of her companions glanced over their shoulders, back up the track toward the road, they might have caught a glimpse of the grey Freelander that had briefly pulled up beside the entrance to the track and then pulled away again, disappearing out of sight. But they didn't. They each followed Lynette Bell into the little green and white painted building that had been her home, ever since the day in 1964 when she had arrived in Balnakeil, having left her former life in London behind her.

***

Harry and Martha were eating supper at the dining room table. She had again been unusually quiet. Harry had put it down to Ellen's absence. She'd seemed happy enough when Ellen had gone off and they'd twice since spoken on the phone, Martha apparently keen to hear about Ellen's journey. But she'd spent most of the day in her room and she'd said practically nothing since coming down for supper.

'What are you going to do tonight?' he asked, trying to make conversation. '*The X-Factor* is on later. We can watch it together if you like?'

Martha nodded. 'If you want.'

'I tell you what. We've got some ice cream in the freezer,' he added, trying to sound as cheerful as he could. 'I know Mum doesn't really like us eating on the sofa but I don't think she'd mind, just this once. I'll clear the table when we've finished and then how about we eat it in front of the telly?'

Martha nodded again but said nothing.

They continued eating in silence.

That she had something on her mind was self-evident and Harry was pretty sure that he knew what it was. He'd been avoiding it. Putting off the inevitable. Hoping that if Martha raised it, Ellen would be there to handle it because he wasn't at all certain that he knew how.

He glanced across the table. It struck him that she looked suddenly older. He'd always thought of her as his little girl. A child whose life revolved around childish things. Cats, mostly. But understanding this would have been beyond most children. She would be struggling to make sense of her experience; an experience he had struggled with, even as a mature adult, and still did. It had been Ellen who had helped him and now, somehow, he needed to help his daughter. It was a responsibility that weighed heavily on him. He couldn't let her down. Not now. Not ever. He needed to find an opener. He took a breath. 'Is everything all right, Love?' It was a pretty lame attempt but at that moment it was the best that he could do.

Martha put down her knife and fork and stared at her plate.

Had she cried he would have rushed to her side and thrown his arms around her. He wanted to. But she didn't. Her expression was thoughtful.

'What's up?' he prompted again.

'I've been thinking,' she said, looking up from her plate and staring at him. 'About ghosts.'

They both knew how loaded that word was. He could see it in her expression. 'Have you?' he said, trying his damnedest to keep his voice level.

Martha nodded.

'You mean, like the ghosts in films and stories?'

'No, not the ones in films. They're just stupid.'

He smiled, in spite of her seriousness. 'Yes, they are.'

Martha was struggling for words.

'What have you been thinking? About ghosts, I mean,' he offered.

She considered the question. 'I think,' she said carefully 'that real ghosts are different.'

He needed to think quickly. He didn't believe that they were ghosts. Not in the sense that were the spirits of dead people. He certainly didn't want her to think that. But neither did he want to make her feel silly and, least of all, to shut her down. What she had seen; what they had both seen, was real in the sense that they had both seen it, although he still couldn't rationalise how. 'Different? What do you mean?' he said, still searching for the right approach. Then she surprised him.

'Well,' she said slowly, 'for one thing, I don't think they are really dead people. Like they are in films.'

'Don't you?' he said, feeling thrown. The statement showed considerable insight. More insight than he'd been expecting.

She shook her head. 'No, I don't.'

He needed to create a space. 'Look, why don't we clear the table. We can leave the washing up. I'll get us some ice cream and then maybe we can talk about this some more?'

Martha nodded.

They cleared the table together in silence. He could tell that she was thinking. It was as though having opened a bag neither of them really knew the name of the cat that was going to come climbing out. He knew that if he was dismissive, as many parents might have been; like perhaps he was supposed to be, he was going to create a barrier between them or worse, leave her to deal with her feelings on her own. Dealing with these *ghosts*, whether dead or not, would be hard enough for an adult. It could easily become too much for a ten year old child. How was he going to explain it in a way that she was going to be able to handle? What explanation did he have? What explanation was there? As he filled two dessert bowls with the Green and Black's he'd located in the freezer, he was wishing fervently that Ellen had not gone to Scotland. Which got him thinking about how Ellen might have handled it had she been at home. As they made their way into the living room, ice-cream bowls in hand and seated themselves on the sofa, he'd begun to form a plan.

'Do you know what I think, Love?' he said, spooning ice-cream into his mouth and swallowing too quickly, which made his throat ache and his eyes water.

Martha was trying not to react but the smile leaked out of the corners of her mouth. She shook her head. 'No,' she replied, giggling.

'I think that you're right. I don't think ghosts are dead people either. In fact, I don't think they really exist at all.'

Martha's expression became serious. 'But if they're not real, how come I've seen them?' She hesitated. 'I have you know,' she added. 'I'm not lying.'

'Martha, Love, I know you are not lying. I would never think that. Not for a minute. OK?'

She nodded.

This was good. He was on the right track but he needed to get something straight. 'These *ghosts* that you have seen. I don't think they are really ghosts at all, not like the ghosts in stories anyway, but let's just call them that for now. OK?' The truth was that he couldn't immediately think of another word for them.

She nodded again.

'How often have you seen them? I mean how many times?'

Martha thought about it. 'Three times.'

Three times. He put his ice-cream bowl down on the little coffee table in front of them, making a conscious effort to remain calm. 'Tell me about those three times. When was the first time?'

'When that lady came to the door the other night.'

'But she wasn't a ghost. She was a reporter.'

'No, not her. They were standing behind her. A lady and a little girl.'

He needed to make sure that she hadn't just picked up on his own reaction. 'How did you know that they were ghosts and not real people?'

She thought about it. 'Because they were kind of fuzzy.'

'Fuzzy?' He knew exactly what she meant but he wanted her to describe it. 'What do you mean, fuzzy?'

'I don't know. Like when you're taking a video on your phone and your hand shakes.'

Which was a pretty accurate description. 'Okay. I know exactly what you mean. When was the second time?'

'Yesterday. Just after mum went.'

'After mum went?' He was making a poor job of masking the sudden stab of anxiety that he had felt in the pit of his stomach. 'Where did you see them?'

'They were standing outside in the street. I saw them from my bedroom window.'

'The same two people? The lady and the girl?'

Martha nodded.

'What were they doing?'

'Nothing really. They were just standing there. Looking up at me.'

'Okay. Did you see them again? A third time?'

Martha took a mouthful of ice-cream.

He waited. He really didn't want to hear what he suspected might be coming next.

'Yes. In my bedroom.'

The thought of it: of his little girl seeing ghosts in her bedroom, was twisting his guts. 'You saw them, in your bedroom?'

'Yes. Kind of.'

'What do you mean, kind of?'

'Well, I only saw the little girl. Her mum wasn't there.'

Her mum. Was she guessing? 'How do you know that the lady is the girl's mum?'

Martha shrugged.

Wrong question. He tried again. 'This was the same girl, you saw outside when the reporter came to the door?'

'Yes. But that's what I was trying to tell you. The little girl is different.'

'It was a different little girl?'

'No. It was the same girl. But she is different.'

'How is she different?'

'I don't know. But she is. She isn't like the lady. She's just not the same.'

He had no idea what she meant. He wasn't entirely sure that Martha did, either. But he didn't want to press her too hard. 'Did she do anything? Did she say anything?' He needed to keep it simple.

Martha frowned. 'No. But,' she hesitated, obviously struggling for words again, 'it felt different. Kind of.' Martha had finished her ice-cream and put her bowl down on the coffee table, beside his.

'Here,' he said, patting his thigh with his hand.

She climbed onto his lap and they held each other.

'How did it make you feel when you saw the girl in your room this morning?' he asked, breaking the silence.

'I don't know. I wasn't scared or anything.'

Wasn't scared? Jesus. He was damn sure that he would have been at 10 years old. He was pretty sure he still would be had the girl appeared at the foot of his bed. 'Well, that's good.' He kissed the top of her head.

'It made me feel,' she again hesitated, 'sort of *worried.*'

Harry felt a sudden wave of emotion. This just wasn't fair on Martha. It was too much for her. 'I know, Love. I know.' He wanted to tell her that there was nothing to be worried about. But that would have implied that he knew what the hell was going on. The truth was that he was just as troubled as Martha. Maybe more so.

'Something isn't right, Dad. I know they're not real. They can't be. But I know that something is wrong with them. I don't know how I know. I just do.'

He was stroking her hair, struggling to keep his emotions in check. He was trying to work out what he was feeling. And then it dawned on him that the emotion he was feeling was pride. He was incredibly proud of her. Any other kid would have freaked. Ten years old and she was calmer than he had been. She was thinking. Trying to rationalise it. Just like he had tried to rationalise it. He'd been trying for a very long time. She was making a better job of it than he ever had.

'How come I can see them?' Martha continued. 'If they are not really there?'

This was the question he needed to answer. If Martha was going to be able to cope with these visions and feelings, she needed an explanation to hold on to and he needed to supply it. Right now.

He needed to lay any thought that these were ghosts, at least in the conventional sense, to rest. He needed to do this for Martha as Ellen had done it for him. 'It's our brains working, Martha,' he began, thinking on his feet. 'You know like when you imagine something. When you think about something?'

'Yes.'

'Well, it's like that. Our brains are thinking all the time. They are so clever. Even when you're asleep, your brain is busy thinking and feeling things that are not really there.'

'But this wasn't like a dream. Well, not exactly. And I wasn't asleep.'

'I think that you have an especially clever brain, Martha. Everybody's brain is amazing. But our brains are all different. Some of us can play football better than anybody else. Or play musical instruments. Or do amazing maths. We can all get better at these things through practice but some of us will just never be as good at them as others are. Your brain is extra special. It helps you to see and feel things, that other people don't.'

Martha was quiet for a moment. 'You can see them as well, can't you? You've got an extra special brain like mine.'

He smiled. 'Yes, sweetheart. I see them too sometimes. I think that you and I are alike, Martha.'

'What about Mum?'

'Mum's brain is clever in different ways. In fact your mum is one of the cleverest people I have ever met. But her brain is different.'

'She can't see them?'

'No, Love, she can't.'

Martha fell silent.

He felt her regret. He and Ellen had both regretted that she couldn't share their experiences. Ellen had said as much. 'I want you to promise me something, Martha. It is very important. I want you to tell me and Mum whenever you see or feel things that are not there. Do you promise?'

'Yes, I promise.'

'And I don't want you to tell anybody else. Not your friends or teachers. Just Mum and me.'

'What about Nana Lizzie?'

He hesitated. 'Yes you can tell Nana Lizzie. But nobody else.'

'Why not?'

'Because their brains are clever but not special like yours and they don't love you like we love you. If you tell them, they might think you're telling lies.'

'Or that I am just being weird.'

He laughed. 'Yes, they might think that. But you are not being weird, Martha. Don't ever think that. There's nothing weird about your brain. Our brains are just different. Most people, who don't have brains like ours, just don't get it. They'll probably never get it. So it's best if we keep it to ourselves.'

'But Mum understands, doesn't she? Why can't other people?'

'Mum understands because she knows us. She knows that we are not making it up. Do you promise that you won't tell anyone else?'

'I promise.'

'Good.'

'Can I tell you something else?'

'Always. You can always tell me and your mum. There is nothing that you cannot tell us. Got it?'

'Yes.'

'Good. So tell me.'

Martha hesitated. 'I think that the lady is lost and she is very sad. I don't think she likes being lost.'

It was the second time that Martha's insight had surprised him. He had sensed their sadness, though he hadn't attached the emotion to one or other of them and he'd had no sense of its cause. 'What about the girl? Is she lost too?'

Martha screwed up her face. 'I don't know. I don't think so. I don't think she is with her mummy. Not in real life.'

'Why do you think that?'

Martha was thoughtful. 'My brain told me,' she said, cheerily. 'Can we watch X-Factor now?'

'Yes, Sweetheart,' he said, laughing more out of relief than anything else. She was amazing. The discussion, had it been between adults, would probably have lasted hours. Not only was Martha clever enough to know her own limits but she was wise enough to close the conversation down once her limit had been reached. 'Yes, we can watch X-Factor now.'

His relief, however, was short lived. As he sank back into the sofa it suddenly dawned on him that he was going to have to relay the last twenty minutes to Ellen. That was not going to be easy.

CHAPTER FIFTEEN

Sunday, 15 May 2016

Ellen reckoned the room into which they had followed Lynette Bell to be no more than twelve feet square. An iron beam ran across the concrete ceiling, from left to right. The walls, the ceiling and the iron beam had all been painted pale yellow. A tatty Aztec-patterned rug covered almost the whole of the floor. The room's contents comprised of a battered velvet two seater sofa, a leather arm chair that had clearly seen better days, an old fashioned electric heater attached to the wall and a TV in one corner on a little cupboard made from drift wood.

Lynette Bell had gone into an adjoining room and returned, after a few moments, with an additional wooden chair which she held out to Ellen. Then she seated herself on the arm chair which they all took as their invitation to sit. She had not offered them a drink, nor did she make any comment. Instead, she stared at them each in turn. Ellen shifted uncomfortably.

It was Holly who broke the silence. 'Lynette, I'm Holly Holgate.' She had taken a business card from her bag. She stood up and handed it to the former Scene Club dancer. 'These are my friends' she added, retaking her seat. 'Ellen Stammers.'

Ellen nodded. 'Hello Lynette.'

'And Jane Eglund.'

Jane nodded.

Lynette Bell ignored them.

Holly had removed a note pad and pen from her bag. 'Thank you again for agreeing to see us.'

Bell eyed the notepad with suspicion.

'We're hoping that you can tell us about Gina Lawrence.'

'I told you,' Bell said suddenly, 'I'm saying nothing on the record. It was fifty years ago. I left it all behind when I came up here.'

Holly hesitated and then put the notepad and pen back in her bag. 'I'm sorry. This is strictly off the record. You have my word.'

The former Scene Club dancer stared at her. 'Why should I trust you? How do I know you're not going to take everything I tell you to…' She hesitated.

'Lynette,' Ellen broke in. 'We're not going to take anything you tell us to the police, we've…'

'I didn't say anything about the police. Why would the police be interested in someone who went missing fifty years ago?'

The word "police" had obviously struck a nerve but there was no point in pursuing it. 'We just want to find out what happened to Gina,' Ellen replied. 'She was Holly's Aunt. Holly wants to find her. That's all. We're really not interested in anything or anybody else.' Which wasn't exactly the truth but they needed to gain her confidence.

Bell laughed but there was a slightly manic edge to her laughter that made Ellen recoil. 'How are you going to find her after all this time?'

'We probably won't,' Holly said flatly.

They all turned to face her.

'If the people who knew Gina won't speak to us then we've got very little chance. You knew Gina. You can choose to help us or you can send us away with nothing.'

Bell said nothing.

'But if you do that, then we're not going to just give up. We will have to look elsewhere.'

Ellen could see where Holly was heading. It was the same thinly veiled threat that she had used to persuade Bell to see them.

Bell was stuck between a rock and a hard place. If she sent them away without explanation, then that would imply that she had something to hide. If it resulted, as Holly was implying that it would, in them digging further, then who knew what they might find? But if she told them anything that implicated Micky Milburn, she ran the risk that they might reveal her to him as their source, whether intentionally or not. If she was as afraid of him as Holly had surmised, then that was going to be just as unpalatable. Damned if she did and damned if she didn't. Ellen watched her squirm.

'What do you mean, look elsewhere?' the former dancer said, her eyes darting between them.

'I mean that you'll leave us with no alternative but to speak to Micky Milburn,' Holly pressed.

It was a high risk strategy and, of course, something of a bluff. Holly was banking on her not knowing that she had already approached and been rebuffed by Milburn. It crossed Ellen's mind that if the bluff failed and Bell revealed that she did know, then that in itself might be something of a revelation.

Ellen was not expecting her reaction when it came. Lynette Bell began to cry. 'You don't know what you've done by coming here. How hard it's been all these years,' she spluttered. 'Gina was my friend. You don't know the half of it.'

Ellen got up and knelt in front of the former dancer. 'Then tell us, Lynette,' she said softly, taking hold of her hand.

'I can't. I can't,' she sobbed. 'You don't understand.'

Ellen glanced at Holly who nodded. 'I can see that you're afraid. What I don't understand is why. What are you afraid of?' Ellen continued.

'They sent me away,' Bell wailed. 'When Gina went, they sent me away.'

'Who did?'

The former dancer continued to sob.

'Lynette,' Ellen said, holding on to the dancer's hand. 'Who sent you away?' she pressed.

'Mr Phelps,' the former dancer spluttered, looking up suddenly and staring at her.

Ellen glanced at Holly and then back to the former dancer. 'Why did Marty Phelps send you away, Lynette?'

'I can't,' she said, shaking her head. 'He made me swear. When I came up here.'

Ellen let go of Bell's hand and sat back on her haunches, glancing first at Holly and then at Jane.

'When I spoke to you last week, you told me that there had been some kind of party. In Gina's flat,' Holly pressed. 'The night she went missing. But you wouldn't tell me any more. Why?'

'I thought you'd go to them. I thought you'd tell them that you'd found me. You mustn't do that. Please,' she begged.

Ellen felt the tug of her conscience. Was it fair to put Bell under such pressure? Unless she was a very good actress, the distress that it was causing her was plain. 'Them?'

'Phelps and that bastard, Milburn. If he finds out I've been talking to you....' She left the sentence unfinished. 'Please.'

'Who attended this party?' Holly broke in.

Bell hesitated. 'They all did,' she said, suddenly. 'The band, Phelps and all the others. But Micky got Gina to invite us both up to her flat. She didn't really want to. She didn't even like him. She was in love with his brother.'

'Gina was in love with Spencer Milburn?' Ellen asked. They knew that Spencer Milburn had taken a shine to Gina Lawrence but evidently there had been more to it than that.

'Yes, she was only stringing Micky along to make Spencer jealous. But we had all been drinking and Micky was feeding us pills. Especially Gina. By the time we got up there, we were both off our heads.'

'Did anyone else go up to the flat with Micky, you and Gina?' Holly asked.

'No. But Spencer found out and there was an argument between him and Micky on the stairs. He tried to stop it but Micky just laughed at him.'

Ellen tried to imagine the scene. To do that to your brother. If Bell was telling the truth and there was no reason to think that she wasn't, she'd been right to call Micky Milburn a bastard. 'What happened when you got upstairs?'

'It all got out of hand. I can't remember,' the former dancer said evasively, tears rolling down her cheeks. 'I was off my head. We both were,' she said, shaking her head like she was trying to convince herself as much as her audience. 'I can't remember.'

Ellen didn't believe her. Bell had remembered the argument on the stairs. She could remember what happened when they got to the top of them. 'You say that it got out of hand? What do you mean?'

'What do you want me to say?' Bell said, as if cornered. 'Micky was a bastard like that, okay? He liked to have several girls in bed with him at once,' she blurted. 'He'd get them high and then he'd get them to...' She hesitated.

'He'd get them to what?' Ellen pressed.

'Perform for him,' she spat, her expression a mixture of anger and disgust. 'He liked to watch girls...' She hesitated again. 'And he liked it rough,' she continued, smiling crazily. 'The rougher the better.'

'You mean violent?'

'Yes, I mean violent. He liked it that way.'

This was important. It wasn't difficult to imagine that Micky's violence might have gone too far, fuelled as it evidently had been by drugs and alcohol. She glanced at Holly.

Holly nodded.

'Lynette, this is important. When you say that Micky was violent, we need to know whether he was violent towards Gina and, if he was, what exactly he did to her.'

The former dancer refused to meet her eyes.

'Did he, at any time, hold Gina by the throat or cover her mouth?'

Bell said nothing.

'Lynette, please.'

'I can't remember. I can't. We were off our heads. I must have passed out. All I remember is waking up and everybody shouting.'

She had side stepped the question. To a point, Ellen could hardly blame her for avoiding the sordid details. 'Everybody?'

'Milburn and Phelps.'

Ellen glanced at Jane. 'Marty Phelps was there, in the room with you?'

'Yes. He was shouting. They both were.'

Ellen was trying to work out how Phelps had come to be there. 'But you said that nobody else went upstairs with you to Gina's flat. When did Phelps join you?'

'I don't know. It must have been while I was unconscious.'

Ellen was thinking. Had Phelps joined them by chance or had he been summoned?

'Where was Gina exactly, when you woke up?' Jane broke in.

'On the floor. Micky and Phelps were both yelling at me. I was confused.'

'Was she conscious?' Jane continued.

The former dancer had hesitated. Ellen had noticed it and from the look on her face, so had Jane.

'I don't know. I just don't know. It was chaos. I didn't know what the hell was happening.'

'You said they were shouting. Yelling at you. What were they yelling?' Jane asked.

'Phelps was saying that the press were downstairs. That one whiff of what had happened and the band would be finished. He was threatening to dump them if Micky didn't get his act together. All I remember is Micky threatening me and Phelps shoving me out of the door.'

'How did Micky threaten you? What did he say?' Jane pressed.

'He said that if I breathed a word of it to to anyone, he'd kill me.'

'So you left?'

'Yes, I left. I didn't want to. I was worried about Gina. But I was confused. From all the drugs. And Micky was scaring me.'

Ellen was trying to imagine what she would have done had she been in Lynette Bell's shoes. She was damn sure that, however scared she might have been, she would not have left the room without checking on her friend. 'Was that the last time you saw Gina?'

'Yes. I tried calling her,' she added hastily, 'the following day and the day after that. But there was no reply. I went to her flat but she wasn't there. Nobody had seen her. Then a few days later, Phelps came to see me.'

'What did he want?'

'He said that Gina had gone. That nobody knew where she was. That the police had been to the club and that the press were sniffing around. He told me to leave.'

'What do you mean, he told you to leave?'

'He said that they wanted me out of the way. That they couldn't take the risk of me talking to the police or the press about what had happened. That they'd keep my name out of it. But I had to go. I swore that I wouldn't say anything but he wasn't having it. All he was concerned about was the band. He gave me no choice.'

'Go where?' Holly cut in.

'Phelps said he had some contacts up here in Scotland. He offered to set me up, up here.'

'He offered you money?'

'Yes.'

'And you agreed?'

'Yes. I didn't have any family down in London and I was out of work. He said that so long as I kept my mouth shut, he'd see me all right.'

'Phelps offered to pay you off in return for your silence and you agreed?' Holly asked.

Ellen heard the contempt in Holly's question and from her reaction it was evident that so had Lynette Bell. She leapt to her feet. 'Yes, I agreed,' the former dancer yelled. 'I told everyone that I'd got a job up North and a few days later, I packed my bags, caught a train and I never went back. What was I supposed to do? I was eighteen years old. I was scared.'

Ellen had clambered to her feet. 'What about Gina?'

'Do you think I don't feel guilty about that?' the former dancer yelled, rounding on her. 'I've regretted the events of that night every day since. If I hadn't taken those drugs. If I'd tried to talk her out of inviting Micky up to her flat, like Spencer wanted. None of this would have happened. Don't you think I know that?'

They were all on their feet.

It still didn't make sense to Ellen that she had left without making any real effort to satisfy herself about her friend's safety. 'Didn't you want to know whether she was at least safe?'

'I had no choice,' the former dancer repeated.

There was an edge of aggression to her tone that made Ellen take several steps backwards.

'Maybe they paid her off, like they paid me off,' the former dancer spat in Holly's direction. 'Maybe they sent her away too. I don't know. I'll never know, will I?'

Jane stepped forwards. 'Don't you think you should calm down?'

'I don't think,' the former dancer returned, between gritted teeth. 'I've made a life for myself up here. I don't have much but it's a good life. Or it was, until you found me. If you don't stop poking your noses into this, it won't just be me that lives to regret it. Phelps is one thing. At least he kept his word. But Micky Milburn is an evil bastard. Do you think he's going to swallow you raking this all up again? The moment he finds out that you're making trouble, you'll find out just how evil he can be,' she added wagging her finger towards Ellen.

'I said calm down,' Jane said, stepping between them.

Lynette Bell stood her ground. 'I've told you everything I know. Given you what you wanted, for all the good that it will do you. Now get out.'

None of them moved.

'I said, get out. Get in your bloody car, drive all the way back to London and stay there.'

With that their audience with Lynette Bell was over. She hustled them out of the door and slammed it behind them. They got into the silver Audi, reversed up the track and drove back towards Durness in silence.

Once they were out of sight, a grey Freelander pulled into the lay-by at the top of the track from which they'd emerged, seconds before. Two men got out of the car, glanced over their shoulders and made their way down the track toward the little green and white building that had been Lynette Bell's home for the last 52 years.

It was the morning after their meeting with Lynette Bell. They'd chosen to break their return journey to London by staying a second night at the hotel in Inverness. After breakfast, Ellen had returned to her room, packed her bag and was now sitting in the hotel's reception, waiting for Holly and Jane.

They'd talked at length about Lynette Bell during the journey back to the hotel and again over dinner. Ellen had agreed that, so far as it went, the former dancer's account of events at the Scene Club had been plausible. They'd also agreed that the gaps in Bell's account were less so. Especially, when it came to the period between the row involving Micky and Spencer Milburn on the stairs up to Gina Lawrence's flat and the point at which the former dancer had claimed to have woken up, to find Micky Milburn and Marty Phelps yelling at each other. Although she had made reference both to Micky's sexual preferences and his propensity for violence, and Ellen could understand why she had not wanted to recount the actual events in detail, the gaps in her account, had been anything but plausible. A great deal more had obviously happened between the three of them and Bell's unwillingness to share the detail was unlikely to have been down to her embarrassment alone.

Ellen had her doubts too, about the plausibility of her explanation for Marty Phelps' reaction in effectively exiling her to Balnakeil, solely on the grounds that he didn't want her being interviewed by the police or the press about Micky Milburn's sexual improprieties and a young woman who, at that point, had been missing for no more than a few days. Plenty of people would have known about his after gig parties, not least the young women who had attended them.

She had also been wondering whether it would really have been all that remarkable or scandalous, even in 1964, that here was a pop star who liked to bed multiple young women at once. Other bands were busily building a reputation for womanising, drug taking and throwing televisions from hotel windows. Some of them went on to positively court such notoriety. It certainly hadn't done their record sales any harm.

Which had led them all to the conclusion that there had to be more to Phelps' claimed reaction and Lynette Bell's exile than that. The question which had been buzzing around Ellen's head half the night, was how much more. It was possible that Gina Lawrence had died on the floor in her room from an overdose of drugs and alcohol or perhaps Milburn's propensity for rough sex had gone too far. Holly had held to her theory that Micky might have a tendency to violent rape, citing the later allegations in Florida that did, they had all been forced to acknowledge, bear certain similarities. But Ellen couldn't imagine how they were ever going to be able to prove either of these scenarios. The central problem was that no body had ever been found. While that remained the case, Gina Lawrence, was sadly, but simply, just another missing person. They could not and should not, Ellen reasoned, rule out the possibility that, as Lynette Bell had postulated, Gina Lawrence had been alive and been made an offer, like Bell, that she could not refuse.

'Hi Ellen.'

She had momentarily closed her eyes. She opened them again at the sound of Holly's voice. 'Oh, hi. Sorry. I almost nodded off.'

Holly smiled. 'No sign of Jane yet?'

Ellen shook her head, her attention drawn to two police officers, wearing high-visibility jackets, who had entered the hotel and who were standing at reception, talking to the receptionist. Holly had followed her eyes, just as the receptionist had pointed towards them.

The two police officers walked purposefully towards them. Ellen stood up.

'Which one of you is Holly Holgate?' the first of them said, when they were within earshot.

Ellen hesitated.

'I am,' Holly replied.

'Is there a problem?' Ellen asked, looking from one police officer to the other.

'And you are?'

She flushed. 'Sorry. Ellen Stammers.'

'Miss Holgate, can you confirm your address please?'

Holly gave them the address of her flat in London.

'Can you confirm your whereabouts yesterday afternoon, between approximately 12 noon and 3pm?'

Holly glanced at Ellen. 'We were in Balnakeil, in the Highlands.'

'Where exactly in Balnakeil?'

'At the craft village.'

'What was the nature of your visit to the craft village at Balnakeil?'

'I'm a freelance journalist. We were interviewing someone for a story.'

Jane had appeared, with her overnight bag. 'What's going on?'

The second policeman held up his hand.

'Miss Holgate, what was the name of the person you interviewed?'

The three women exchanged glances.

'Rachel Walsh,' Holly said cautiously.

Ellen was momentarily confused and then she remembered that this was Lynette Bell's assumed name.

'Were you all present during this interview?'

'Yes,' Ellen replied honestly.

Jane followed suit.

'In that case, I must ask you all to accompany us to Inverness Police Station.'

'Why, what's happened?' Ellen asked.

'You will be told about that when we get to the station.'

'Hang on a minute,' Jane broke in. 'We've got a train to catch. Are we under arrest?'

'No, Miss?'

'Mrs, Jane Eglund. If we're not under arrest, then I'd like to know what you need talk to us about.'

'We'd prefer to do that at the station.'

'Well, you might, but I wouldn't. Before I accompany you anywhere, I'd like to know what this is all about.'

'Very well, Mrs Eglund. At seven-thirty this morning, Rachel Walsh was found hanging in her flat. She was later declared dead at the scene.'

CHAPTER SIXTEEN

Sunday 26th April 1964

The after gig party to celebrate their new Number One single had continued, unabated, late into the evening. Spencer Milburn had tolerated, rather than enjoyed it, torn as he was between a feeling of jubilation at the band's success, fury at his brother's behaviour and mounting concern for Gina who, by the look of her, had already taken enough Purple Hearts and God knew what else, to make her eyes widen and her pupils dilate alarmingly. She had either been drifting among the dancers, staring at them semi-vacantly, or as she was now, draped over his brother's shoulder, the two of them surrounded, as Micky usually was, by a gaggle of girls. Spencer was watching them from the back of the stage, to which he had retreated on the pretext of packing up his drum kit. Micky was sitting on a stool in front of the bar, smoking a cigarette. Marty Phelps had arranged for the delivery of half a dozen cases of Champagne. The bottles were lined up along the bar behind Micky. He was lording it over them, occasionally reaching across to fill the glasses of his admirers, or popping the cork of a fresh bottle and spraying them with Champagne to bouts of excited laughter. Gina, whose glass Micky had kept constantly refreshed, was looking increasingly oblivious to her surroundings.

'You all right Spence?'

He tore himself away from the sight of them. 'Yeah, great Trev. Couldn't be better, man' he said, unable to mask his gloom.

'Have you had enough of this too, for one night?'

Spencer shrugged. 'Just about.'

'I was planning on calling it a night soon, if you want to come back with me. I reckon we can afford a taxi, eh?' The keyboard player grinned. 'No more riding The Tube. Not now that we've hit the big time.'

'I don't know,' Spencer replied, glancing back towards the bar.

The keyboard player had followed his eyes. 'Come on, give it up man. What will be will be, eh?'

Spencer stared at him.

The keyboard player clasped his shoulder. 'You've done what you can. She's a big girl. Give it up.'

Spencer felt suddenly defeated. Trev was right. There was nothing more he could do. Micky was uncontrollable. In fact the more he had tried to control him, the more Micky seemed inclined to want to rub his nose in the fact that he couldn't. One of these days it was going to come to a head. One of these days he was going to lose it entirely. But not tonight. Tonight was about the band. He nodded. 'I'll just go and take a leak and then do you know what? I'm done.'

He passed Ricky and Pete with a small group of Scene Club faces on the way to the bathroom. 'I'm getting off in a minute, with Trev. We've had enough for one night. You want a lift back?' he said to Pete Lumley.

The guitarist pulled a face. 'Nah. Me and Ricky are going over The Lyric before it closes. There's only so much of this shit I can take,' he added, holding up his champagne glass. 'We fancy a beer before we pack it in.'

Spencer nodded. 'See you back at the house then.'

He made it to the bathroom and stood next to a young mod at the urinals. He was holding a cigarette with one hand and his dick with the other. 'All right, pal? Top set tonight and congratulations on the single.' He had transferred the cigarette to his mouth and had reached down to zip up his flies.

'Thanks, man.'

The bathroom was at one end of a short corridor. Being below street level, there were no windows, the corridor being lit by a series of fluorescent tubes. Half way along the corridor, to his left, were a set of doors through which a wide concrete staircase led to the building's upper floors. At the corridor's opposite end were doors that opened back out onto the dance floor. He was about to haul them open when they were suddenly flung inwards, almost knocking him over.

A young woman had crashed through the doors backwards. She was wearing a lilac coloured mini dress and was holding a bottle of Champagne in one hand and a handbag in the other. She turned and grinned at him.

'Lynette? Jesus.'

She looked drunk. Or pilled up. Or both.

'Spencer? Sorry,' she giggled. 'Hey, isn't it amazing about the single? I can't wait to see you and Micky on Ready Steady Go.' She lurched onwards.

'Thanks.' He reached for the doors, stopped and turned. 'Lynette?' he called out.

The girl stopped and turned.

He walked back along the corridor towards her. 'You're a friend of Gina's aren't you?'

'Sure,' she smiled.

He hesitated. 'Only, by the look of her, I think she might have had enough.'

The dancer looked at him blankly. 'Well, I..'

'Look,' he interrupted. 'Any chance you could have a word with her? Maybe, help her up to her flat? See her into bed? Make sure she's all right?'

Her smile had turned to a grin. 'Oh. I think they're already on their way up.' She nodded toward the doors to the stairs. 'Micky asked me to fetch some more Champagne,' she said, holding up the bottle. 'But shhh…' she added, trying to put a finger to her lips but remembering that she didn't have a free hand. 'It's a private party. Strictly invitation only. Know what I mean?' She tried to wink.

He didn't wait for her to complete the gesture. He knew exactly what she meant. He ran down the corridor, turned right and crashed through the doors to the staircase. He flew up the first three flights, rounded a bend and saw Micky and Gina on the landing above him. Micky was holding a bottle in one hand and had his other arm around the dancer.

'Gina. Stop,' he called out breathlessly.

They both turned.

'What are you doing?' he croaked.

'Spencer?' Gina's voice was thin and uncertain.

'Gina, please,' he said, gathering himself for Micky's retort, which he knew was going to come.

Micky held out his arm expansively, the wine bottle still in his hand, 'Spence, man' he grinned. 'We were planning on just the three of us, you know what I'm saying? But I'm sure that Gina and Lynette will be happy to fit you in, won't you girls?' he added, glancing first at the girl to his right and then over Spencer's shoulder, back down the stair case.

Lynette Bell, who had followed Spencer up the stairs, pushed past him holding up the champagne bottle. 'Sure. The more the merrier,' she slurred, finally making it to the landing.

Spencer had followed her up. 'Shut the fuck up, Micky. Just shut the fuck up,' he said, stepping onto the landing.

'Hey, man. No need to get so uptight. We're just gonna have some fun. You do still know how to have fun don't you?'

'Yeah, I know. But my kind of fun doesn't involve feeding girls pills to get them into bed. Look at the state of them.'

Spencer was now facing his brother who had stepped forward, leaving the two girls holding onto each other behind him.

Micky stared at him, still grinning. 'Oh that's right,' he said, his expression becoming thoughtful. 'I hear you prefer to do them standing up, shoved up against a bathroom wall,' he mocked. 'That's right, isn't it Gina?' he added, glancing over his shoulder toward the two girls.

Gina said nothing.

Spencer recoiled. He felt like he'd been punched in the guts. He bowed his head.

'So she shagged you in the DJ's bathroom. Big fucking deal. Now she fancies the real deal. Get over it.'

'Get out of my way, Micky' he said woodenly. He brought up his eyes and stared squarely at his brother.

Micky didn't move.

'I said, get out of my fucking way,' he yelled, reaching out, planting his hand squarely on his brother chest and shoving him backwards.

Micky held his ground and then stepped aside, with a slow sweeping bow. 'Be my guest.'

The two girls had retreated to the back of the landing.

Spencer took a step towards them. 'Gina. You don't need to do this.'

The dancer stared at him, wide eyed.

'Think about it. Please. You don't need to do this. We can talk. We can work it out. When you've got your head straight.'

'My head?' It was as though she could barely hear him. Like she was somewhere else. Talking through a haze.

'Think, Gina. You've taken a lot of pills. You're off your head. You don't want this. I know you don't.'

She stared at him blankly.

'Lynette?' he said, switching his attention to the second girl. 'You can see that she's in no fit state. Take her upstairs. Stay with her. Tell her we'll talk in the morning.'

Lynette hesitated.

'For God's sake Lynette, she's your friend.'

'Oh yeah? And who made you her keeper?' the second dancer slurred. 'You don't own her. You don't own me. What's your fucking problem?'

Micky had put the bottle down and had lit a cigarette. He placed a hand on his brother's shoulder. Spencer whirled around. Micky blew smoke in his brother's face. 'You're bang out of order, man. Who Gina chooses to invite up to her flat is Gina's business. Not yours. Get over yourself, Spence.'

Spencer ignored him and turned back toward the two girls. 'Gina?'

The dancer had taken a shaky step towards him. He reached out and placed a hand on each of her shoulders. 'Gina?' For a moment he thought that she was going to embrace him. But she didn't embrace him. 'Get over yourself, Spence,' she said, her voice suddenly clear. And then she laughed at him.

It was too much. Spencer Milburn turned, ashen faced, pushed past his brother and fled back down the stairs.

CHAPTER SEVENTEEN

Monday, 16 May 2016

Harry had been sitting at his desk when the call from Scotland had come through. Ellen had sounded surprisingly calm in the circumstances but then she'd had time to come to terms with the news. He was still sitting there, reeling from it, an hour after Ellen's ten minute call from Inverness Police Station.

He'd been replaying her words in his head. While Lynette Bell, or Rachel Walsh as she had been known in Balnakeil, had been angry when they had left, nothing about her behaviour had suggested to Ellen that she'd been sufficiently disturbed by the interview to commit suicide. But it was suicide that had nonetheless been the avenue that the police were pursuing, though they'd told Ellen that they were ruling nothing out until the Procurator Fiscal's report.

Ellen had told him that she'd played her interview straight and answered their questions honestly. It was the only thing she could do, given that the three women had been unable to swap notes. While the detectives who had interviewed her had wanted to explore the extent to which anything that the three women had said that might have triggered the reaction, they'd shown only moderate interest in the Gina Lawrence story, which, on reflection, was hardly surprising. It was difficult to imagine them getting terribly excited about someone who had gone missing in London over fifty years previously. The police rarely seemed to show much interest in missing persons, unless they were children, let alone cases that had gone as cold as Gina's had. Doubtlessly and to be fair, Harry reflected, they would have plenty of other cases to keep them occupied.

So far as Ellen had been able to surmise, Lynette Bell had been found hanging from a rope tied around an iron beam that ran across the ceiling in her living room. If Bell's place was, as Ellen had suggested, similar to the generator houses at Bletchley Park, then there was probably a gap between the beam and the ceiling, enabling a rope to be slung over the top. He knew that because he'd helped Mike Eglund and the resident radio society at Bletchley to restore one of The Park's former generator houses. There had been the same kind of cast iron beam, originally used to suspend pulleys and heavy lifting gear to service the generators.

Ellen had also said that according to the police officers who had interviewed her, there'd been no sign of forced entry and, at this stage anyway, no indication that anyone else had entered the building since the three of them had left it. While they were not under arrest, Ellen, Jane and Holly had been asked to remain in Scotland for at least another 24 hours, by which time the police hoped to have the Procurator's initial report.

Harry had gone over and over the facts, so far as he knew them, trying to decide whether there was any credible threat to Ellen and the others. Not that there was a great deal he could do about it from Bletchley. He had a sudden urge to talk. He reached for the phone on his desk and dialled a number.

Mikel Eglund was Harry's oldest and, after Jane, his closest friend. He'd had known him since their days together at university. Harry had studied social history and Mike, engineering. Originally from Norway, Mike had been instrumental in their search for Martha Watts, the missing Bletchley Park log reader. Tragically, he had earned himself two gunshot wounds for the privilege. One through the shoulder and the other making a mess of his left foot. Somehow, he'd survived and miraculously his surgeons had managed not just to repair his shoulder but, even more miraculously, to put the shattered remnants of his foot back together. There were several steel rods inserted and, ten years after the event, he still walked with a limp.

One of the other miracles that Harry had witnessed ten years previously was Mike's burgeoning relationship with Jane. He still marvelled at it. Quite how the two of them had ever got it together he'd never been able to imagine. They were completely unlike each other and Jane had hardly seemed to Harry to be the marrying kind. He'd been confounded by their relationship then and it still confounded him now, although it had been a joy to behold.

He'd called Mike from Bletchley and invited him for supper. Martha had been thrilled. She was immensely fond of him and had skipped around for a full ten minutes when Harry had told her that Uncle Mike was coming. When he'd arrived he'd promised to read her a bedtime story, which was precisely what he was now doing, while Harry attended to the washing up.

While waiting for Mike to arrive, he'd taken a second call from Ellen. They were back at the hotel, having managed to book a third night. While they had been asked to remain in Scotland, Ellen had been relieved that they'd at least been allowed to return to the hotel, rather than spending the night at Inverness Police Station. It had also given them an opportunity to swap notes. Jane and Holly had, like Ellen, played their interviews straight down the line. Holly had even told them about the threats that she had received and the break-in at her flat, although as had been Ellen's experience, they hadn't seemed to be particularly interested, dismissing her suggestion that Micky Milburn might have been involved as pure speculation.

'Did she settle okay?' Harry asked, when Mike re-appeared.

'Of course.'

He had finished the washing up. 'Fancy a coffee?'

'Yup.'

Harry filled the kettle and put it on the hob to heat. 'Did you and Jane never think about children?'

'You're kidding, right,' Mike laughed. 'Jane? A mum? I don't think so. She hates kids.'

Harry could see his point. 'Well, she mothers you well enough.'

Mike pulled a face. 'Yeah, I guess she does. But I'm big enough to survive the experience.'

At six foot four, he was certainly that.

'Hey, guess what?' Mike said, changing the subject.

Harry let his expression ask the question.

'We're thinking about getting a dog.'

'A dog?'

'Yup.'

Harry thought about Jane. 'What, like a Doberman or something? Now I can see Jane with a Doberman. Or a Pit Bull.'

Mike grinned. 'No. A Cockerpoo.'

'A Cocker-what?' Harry said, laughing.

'A Cockerpoo. They're half Poodle and half Cocker Spaniel. Jane looked at a puppy last week. We're going to make a decision in the next few days. I was thinking about calling her Yaesu. You know, after the radio manufacturer?'

Harry laughed again.

'It was either that or Kenwood, but Jane wanted a bitch.'

'No comment. Mind you, the name will go down well at the radio club.'

Mike nodded. 'She can be our mascot.'

He finished making the coffee.

Mike followed him into the living room. They seated themselves at opposite ends of the sofa.

Harry was silent.

'You're worrying about Ellen, right?' Mike said at last.

'Should I be?'

'Not according to Jane.'

Harry raised an eyebrow.

'It was suicide. They're waiting for the Procurator's report. And then they'll be on their way. What's to worry about?'

'What if Lynette Bell didn't top herself? What if somebody followed them up there, waited for them to leave and then killed her?'

'Hey, you been watching Poirot again?'

Mike was one of those rare people who always seemed to assume the positive. Even when he was being negative, he always seemed able to turn it into a joke. 'Yeah, yeah, yeah. But come on, humour me. Suppose she was murdered.'

'Then the police are going to discover it. With forensics as good as they are nowadays, any murderer hoping to go undetected would have needed a plastic boiler suit. Who's gonna answer the door to someone looking like an extra from Porton Down?'

'You reckon?'

'Sure.'

He wasn't convinced. 'All right, but then why did she top herself?'

'Jane says that she knew a lot more than she was letting on.'

'Yes, but what did she know?'

Mike shrugged. 'Your guess is a good as mine and, let's face it, Bell's in no position to tell us now that she's making like a decoration on a Christmas tree,' he said, grinning.

Harry winced. Mike's inappropriate sense of humour was legendary. It had lost him several friends. Between the two of them; Jane with her acid tongue and Mike with his one good foot almost constantly in his mouth, it was a wonder that they had any. Thinking about it, with the exception of him and Ellen, Harry wasn't altogether sure that they did have any. 'Do you ever actually worry about anything?'

Mike looked serious. 'Only about the things I can change. You should try it Harry. You'd be amazed how good it feels.'

'What, free myself from all that negative energy?'

'Sure. Try living in Tromsø, where it's minus twenty and dark from November to January. You gotta do something to keep the seasonal affective disorder at bay.'

Harry smiled. Mike's philosophy had a certain attraction. 'All right, so with Bell out of the equation, who's going to tell us what the hell happened between the three of them?'

'I guess that depends.'

'On what?'

'On whether Gina Lawrence survived the experience. Or, if not, on finding the hole they buried her in.'

Harry took a mouthful of coffee. 'According to Ellen,' he said once he'd swallowed, 'Holgate's more convinced than ever that Micky Milburn killed her. Either by feeding her too many pills or maybe, the rough sex thing went too far.'

'Could be,' Mike agreed. 'Though I can't see how you're going to prove it.'

Harry shook his head. 'I knew we should have stayed out of it.'

'Hey, you're the one who's off to Soho tomorrow, or so Jane tells me. And no ropes. What, so they are showing you around?'

'Oh, God. Do you know I'd actually forgotten about that?' With all the drama, he'd shoved it to the back of his mind. 'Perhaps I should cancel. Ellen might not be back. Who's going to have Martha? And anyway, I might need to pick Ellen up from the station. I don't want her walking back on her own.'

'There you go again.'

'What?'

'Worrying. I can have Martha. If they get back while you're out, Jane can come back to Leighton Buzzard with Ellen, and Martha and I will pick them up from the station.'

'Hmm... I don't know. Are you sure?'

'Why not? It's no big deal.'

'Actually, I ought to check my email. See if I've had anything else from Des Munroe.'

Mike gestured for him to proceed.

He got up, walked out into the office, sat in his office chair and woke up the computer. There was nothing in his inbox but junk and an email from British Gas telling them that their latest bill was ready. As an afterthought, he opened Messenger. He was vaguely aware of footsteps on the stairs and assumed that Mike was going up to the bathroom.

There was nothing from Munroe either. But there was a message from Lester Pilkington. He clicked on the link and opened the message. Pilkington had sent a black and white picture of a young woman. Harry read the message, though he didn't need to read it to know that the picture was of Gina Lawrence. He full-screened the image. The picture lost none of its definition, making it likely that Lester Pilkington had scanned it from an original. It was a professional shot, he guessed. As though she'd been posing for an audition. Only her shoulders upwards were visible. She was wearing a plain white top with a low neckline. Her straightened hair was up in a beehive. Her lips slightly parted. Black eyeliner. Around her neck was a pendant. Harry found myself drawn to it. It was difficult to make out. Perhaps a St Christopher. He was about to click on the magnify icon when he heard movement and Mike's voice. He turned. Mike and Martha, in her pyjamas, were both staring at the computer screen.

He reached instinctively for the monitor's power button. Until he remembered why he'd asked whether anyone on the Facebook page had a picture of Gina Lawrence. He pushed his chair sideways so that they could both see the screen. They looked at the image together.

'That's her,' Martha said, without hesitation.

'Who, Love?' He needed to be sure.

'The lady I saw at the door the other night.'

'Are you sure?'

Martha nodded.

'You're absolutely certain?'

Martha nodded again.

Which settled it. He'd been half-hoping that she wouldn't recognise her. That it had all been a mistake. And that he'd be able to re-insert his head well and truly back in the sand.

'Who is she?' Martha asked.

But that wasn't going to happen. Not only had she seen them. But she'd seen them clearly enough to recognise her. 'She's called Gina.'

Martha hadn't taken her eyes from the picture. 'It looks kind of old.'

'Yes it is. It was taken a long time ago.'

'Before you and Mum were even born?'

He smiled. 'Yes, even before that.'

'She looks pretty in that picture. Was she on television?'

'No, I don't think she ever was. I think she was a dancer in London.'

'London? Have I been there?' Martha said, looking away from the computer screen and meeting his eyes for the first time.

'Yes, we took you to see Aladdin at the theatre there. When you were little. Do you remember?'

Martha wrinkled her nose. 'I think so. Is that where she liked dancing? At the theatre?'

'No, love. She liked to dance at a place called The Scene Club.'

Martha's expression became thoughtful. 'I think we should go there,' she said at last.

He glanced at Mike.

Mike shrugged.

'Why do you think we should go there?' Harry asked, looking back at his daughter. She was looking at him like he was missing the obvious.

'Because she wants us to, silly.'

CHAPTER EIGHTEEN

Monday, 16 May 2016

Spencer Milburn stared at the name flashing on the screen of his mobile phone. He toyed with the idea of letting the call ring out. It wasn't just their distant past that had driven a wedge between them, though it certainly had. For years, he had blamed his brother for Gina's disappearance. Ultimately, he still did, although it was ancient history now and Spencer had tried, on many occasions, to bury the hatchet. The trouble was that their enmity hadn't ended there. After The Monks had called it a day, which itself had been in large part due to the rumours that had continued to dog them, Micky's solo career had taken him to The States. He'd become resident there over forty years ago. An acrimonious battle had ensued between them over rights to the band's name. Micky had demanded exclusivity, even though his new band had featured none of the other original members. Whereas Spencer had continued to work with Pete Lumley and had eventually re-united the original band, minus Micky. It was due to Micky and the lawsuit launched by his management company, that Spencer had settled on calling his re-incarnation of the band "The Bad Habits". Since then, their relationship had remained distant, despite the many years that had passed. On the rare occasions that Micky made contact, it usually meant trouble of one kind or another. He braced himself and pressed the answer button. 'Micky. How are you?'

'I'm champion. Have you had any further contact with that reporter?'

His brother's reaction to being tricked into an interview by the reporter had troubled Spencer. While Micky never liked being outwitted by anyone, least of all a female reporter, his reaction had seemed disproportionate, even for Micky. So she had been working on the Gina Lawrence story but was the story really still a big deal, fifty years after the event? Micky might still be a name in the States but the reality, whether he cared to acknowledge it or not, was that Micky Milburn was no more than a minor celebrity in Britain and Spencer had long since ceased to be a household name, if indeed he ever had been. Who was going to be interested in a story about them now, as salacious as the story might have been back in '64?

'Which reporter?'

His brother said nothing.

'You mean the reporter who door stepped me?'

'Yes, the reporter who door stepped you.'

Micky had always sworn that he knew nothing about Gina's disappearance. Publicly, they had all denied that Micky had ever been in her flat. Even Spencer had been persuaded to take that line. Privately, Micky had maintained that he and Lynette Bell had left the flat in the early hours of the following morning, that Gina had been fine and given no indication at all that she was planning on leaving. He'd been adamant that he could not explain why, at some point in the hours that followed, she had simply packed a bag and slipped away unnoticed.

As much as he had blamed his brother and probably always would, Spencer had held to the view that Micky was family. Plus, of course, the band had just hit the big time. 'No, I've heard nothing more from her. I told you that if we ignored her, she'd lose interest.'

There had, though, always been doubt, nagging away at the back of his mind. If anything, it had increased with the passage of time. Her child had made her disappearance all the more inexplicable. Giving up the child had been tearing her apart. He'd never been able to understand why, if she'd wanted the child back so badly, she had chosen to leave. But Micky knew nothing about the child. Or if he did, he'd never given the slightest indication of it. Even if he did know, that wouldn't explain his reaction to the reporter.

Micky laughed. 'Yeah? Well, she hasn't.'

'What do you mean she hasn't?'

'I mean, that despite the frighteners being put on her, Holgate hasn't lost interest.'

Ultimately, however many years had passed, Gina's disappearance had been down to Micky. Whatever had happened, it had been Micky who had initiated it. Micky who had destroyed any prospect he'd had of a relationship with her. Micky who had mocked him on the stairs up to her flat. Micky was an arrogant bastard. 'For God's sake, Micky. What did I tell you? You just can't leave it alone can you?'

'I told you that we should have shut her down.'

Spencer sighed. Shutting the reporter down was Micky's way of describing the intimidation tactics he'd employed on reporters in the States when they came sniffing around his private life, which they had on plenty of occasions, and usually with good reason. He'd used the tactics to great effect by all accounts.

'I told you that all you would do was confirm whatever story she thinks she has. It's an old story, Micky. Who the hell cares anymore? She doesn't have anything solid. She can't have anything solid. If you'd just ignored her...'

'Wrong again,' Micky interrupted.

'Wrong again, how?'

'Holgate traced Lynette Bell.'

Lynette Bell. The young woman who had been present with Micky and Gina on the stairs up to Gina's flat. The young woman who had spent the hours that had followed in the flat with them. The only other witness to whatever had happened between them. Unofficially she had confirmed Micky's account. Officially, like Micky, she'd never been there. None of them had. And then she too had moved away, albeit that in Bell's case she had made no secret of her departure. Although he'd never discovered her destination.

'Lynette? Holgate traced Lynette Bell?'

'Yup. Holgate managed to trace her to Scotland. As a matter of fact, Holly Holgate; the reporter who you said that we should ignore because there was nothing for her to find, not only found Lynette Bell but is sitting in a police station in Scotland right now, telling them all about it. And do you know why she's sitting in a police station in Scotland?'

Spencer swallowed. 'No.'

'Because shortly after Holly Holgate visited her, Lynette Bell topped herself.'

'She what?' Spencer gasped.

'And that's not all. We've got another problem. Holly Holgate is no longer working alone. There are two women with her. One of which is the wife of Harry Stammers.'

It was a name that he vaguely recognised. 'Harry Stammers?'

'The investigator who, about ten years ago, made the newspapers, even over here, for toppling Max Banks. Remember Banks? The MP?'

He remembered. Stammers had been on the front cover of all the nationals. The coverage had been huge.

'Don't you think it is time you started taking this seriously, Spence?'

He was still reeling from the news of Lynette Bell's death. He didn't remember much about her. She'd been just another of the dancers at The Scene Club. 'What do you mean, I should I take it seriously? Why?'

Micky laughed. 'Do I really need to spell it out? If Bell spilled the beans to Holgate and the Stammers woman, and they're now spilling the beans to the police, how long do you reckon it will be before they're knocking on your door?'

'So what? I've got nothing to hide. I sure as hell don't have much to lose.'

'Really. So you told the police the truth back in sixty-four, did you?'

Spencer hesitated.

'Man, I can hear the penny dropping from over here. You lied, just like the rest of us.'

'I did that to protect you.' He was being defensive, which wasn't going to wash. He knew that as soon as he said it.

'Bullshit. You blamed me then and you've blamed me ever since. You lied for your own benefit. Same as me. What do you think the police are going to make of that? Think about it.'

He was thinking about it. They had lied to keep the link between Micky's propensity for drug fuelled sex parties with multiple young girls and the disappearance of Gina Lawrence from being linked to the band. Given that they'd just gone to Number One, the newspapers would have had a field day. But fifty years later and if it came to it, the revelation that they had lied to protect their reputation was hardly likely to make the front pages. It was hardly crime of the century and, in any case, how were they going be able to prove anything if Lynette Bell was dead? Unless... 'Oh, I'm thinking about it Micky. I'm thinking about what she might have told them that has got you so worried.' He'd said it and now he couldn't take it back.

'Meaning?'

'Meaning, what did happen that night? What did Lynette Bell witness that you're so afraid of? What did she tell Holgate that was so impossible to live with that, having told them, she could no longer live with herself?' Which was the point. So they'd covered up the fact that Micky and Lynette Bell had been in her flat, doing God knows what. At the time, lying about it had been necessary. Why was it so vital now to continue with the pretence?

'Get a grip, Spencer,' Micky replied, avoiding the question entirely.

'You know what? You're a bloody liar. You always were. Right from when we were kids.'

His brother said nothing.

'So come on Micky, what did happen? It was fifty years ago. I can take it.'

'Get a grip. I called you to give you the heads up, not to offer some fucking confession.'

'Yeah? Well, thanks for that. Now if we're done, I've got stuff to be getting on with.'

'Just shut the fuck up and listen Spence, will you? You might not give a monkey's about your reputation. Hell, you don't really have a reputation nowadays, do you? But Phelps does.'

'Phelps? What's this got to do with Marty?'

'It was Marty who got Lynette Bell out of the way back in '64. Told her that if she moved to Scotland and kept her mouth shut, he'd pay her off.'

'He what?'

This was news to Spencer. Bell had decided to move away. That was all he knew. Maybe a week or two after Gina's disappearance.

'You heard me. She was the weak link. She was there, in case you've forgotten. One word to the press and the shit would have hit the fan.'

'How much did he pay her?'

'Enough.'

'How much?'

'Five hundred notes.'

'Five hundred? How much is that in today's money?'

'How the hell should I know?'

'About ten grand?'

'The point is that as well as lying, just like the rest of us, Phelps went out of his way to cover up the truth, including paying off Bell. You should thank him for it the next time you see him.'

'Ten grand. That's just insane.' As he said it, he realised that it had been Phelps who had suggested that they should lie about it. He'd been adamant. Spencer had always accepted that Phelps had been acting to protect his commercial interests in the band but to go as far as paying Lynette Bell to leave?

'Like I said, you might not care about your reputation but Phelps is a pillar of the British fucking Establishment. He reckons that he's got a ticket to the House of Lords coming in the post any day now. Do you think he'll get his peerage if this goes off?'

As Spencer made one connection, so he made another. Marty Phelps had another reason for making sure that the shit, as Micky had so prosaically put it, never hit the fan. Gina's child. Though she had never confirmed it, Spencer had always assumed that it had been Phelps who had fathered the child and then passed her off as being born to his wife. Building and then maintaining a relationship with the child had been Spencer's one reason for staying under Phelps' management and for maintaining a friendship with the family. The older that Ronnie Phelps had got, the closer she had resembled Gina Lawrence, so much so that by the time that she was twenty, there had been no doubt at all in his mind. Though he had never consciously acknowledged it, unconsciously he had held onto the vague hope, over the years, that Gina might one day make contact with Ronnie. 'Isn't it a bit late to be worrying about that now, if Holgate is already talking to the police?'

'Marty's legal people are all over that already. They're going to discredit Lynette Bell whether or not anything comes from Holgate's conversation with the police. Make out that she was a fruit cake. That she'd sent him a string of crazy letters and emails, none of which could possibly be true, trying to extort money from him. In fact they've already set the wheels in motion.'

Neither Marty, nor his wife Barbara had ever suspected that Spencer knew about Ronnie. They'd seemed happy for him to befriend the little girl and Spencer had gone out of his way to do so, fetching her small gifts and lavishing her with attention whenever he visited the house. That he was able to do so relatively frequently was entirely down to Marty's management, initially of The Monks and later, of The Bad Habits. As a child and into adulthood, Ronnie had called him 'Uncle Spence'. Then, when she left home and had her own family, Ronnie's children, now in their twenties, had called him the same. It was something that had given him much pleasure but always with the taint of regret. Though he'd come close, he'd never told Ronnie, and as far as he knew, she'd never suspected that she'd been adopted. If adoption was what it had been. 'Marty can do that?'

It was a stupid question. Phelps might be older than them by some years. Spencer realised that he didn't actually know how old Phelps was. But unlike most men in their late seventies or early eighties, he hadn't truly retired. Sure, he had stepped back from his management company, but Phelps had establishment connections and he'd made no secret of using them to further his ambitions.

Micky laughed. 'Sure he can. But he expects us to stick absolutely to the story. I was never in Gina Lawrence's flat. Lynette Bell was never there. It never happened. Marty never knew Lynette Bell, personally. She was a pill head even then. As flaky as shit. Besides, they can't prove a damn thing. Just stick to the story. Got it?'

'What about Holgate, Stammers and this other woman?'

'Don't be worrying about them. Holly Holgate's reputation is going to take a nose dive. By the time I've finished with her, Mr and Mrs Stammers will want to distance themselves about as far away from Holgate as it is possible to get.'

'Micky, for God's sake.'

'Shit happens. Remember, stick to the story.'

The phone went dead. Micky Milburn had ended the call.

CHAPTER NINETEEN

Monday 16th May 2016

The black Ford Galaxy pulled into the pick up point outside the entrance to the film studios. The driver flicked the windscreen wipers to clear his view, tooted the car's horn and waited. After a few minutes, a woman emerged from the double doors and hurried towards the car, one hand raised to a scarf, which she'd thrown over her head to shelter her hair from the rain, the other clutching several bulging bags.

The driver was already on the pavement and had thrown open one of the rear doors by the time she had reached the car. 'Good evening Miss Phelps. Let me take your bags.'

Ronnie Phelps peered at him from under the headscarf. Beneath it he could see her trademark shock of dark, tightly curled hair.

She grimaced. 'Not the best of evenings,' she replied, handing him her bag and clambering into the back of the Galaxy.

The driver stowed the bags in the car's boot, walked around to the driver's door, opened it and got in. 'Earls Court Square, Miss Phelps?' he asked, adjusting the rear view mirror. She had removed the headscarf and was using it to pat her face dry.

It was the first time he'd driven Ronnie Phelps. She was certainly as good looking in person as she was on screen. Actresses rarely were without their screen makeup, the driver observed.

She flashed his reflection a perfunctory smile. 'Please. And as quick as you like. It's been a long day.'

He nodded. 'Very good, Miss Phelps.'

She had chosen to stay in London, as she usually did when filming in or around the city. The third floor flat, in the stuccoed terrace that ran around three sides of Earls Court Square, was comfortable enough. While staying with her parents ought to have been an option, she had her reasons for avoiding the house in Great Gaddesden. Certainly, travelling back to her own house in Padstow each day would have been impractical, no matter how badly she missed the tranquility of her cottage beside the sea.

She had closed her eyes and was imagining herself, drifting along the beach at St George's, when the sound of her mobile phone snapped her back to the present. She fished around awkwardly in her coat pockets. 'Uncle Spence,' she said, grappling with the phone once she'd found it, 'What a lovely surprise.'

As she spoke, her free hand had slipped involuntarily to the silver chain around her neck. He'd given her the St Christopher on her eighteenth birthday. She'd worn it almost continuously ever since. Even on set she was always reluctant to remove it. She had no idea why. It was nothing particularly special to look at and certainly not valuable, though she'd never seen another one quite like it. It made her feel safe somehow, which she supposed was really rather the point with St Christophers.

'Ronnie. How are you?'

She had always loved the sound of his voice. He'd managed to retain his accent, despite living much of his life away from the North East. 'Tired,' she replied honestly.

'David and Skye?'

'No idea. I hardly see David now that he's at Uni. Skye's at home at the moment but I'm in London.'

'London?'

'Yes, I'm filming at Elstree. It's a third rate film, to be honest. I cannot wait to finish it and get back to Cornwall. But, enough of me. How are you?'

'Me? Well, I'm champion.'

There was a pause.

'I was thinking about coming down to Cornwall soon, if it's convenient. It seems like ages since I saw the three of you.'

'That would be wonderful,' she said, wondering what he really wanted. 'David won't be around but Skye will be and she'd love to see you. We both would. When were you thinking of coming?'

'When do you get back?'

'On Wednesday, I hope. We're due to finish tomorrow but I thought I'd stay over in Earls Court and catch the early train back to Cornwall on Wednesday morning. Come whenever you want.'

'You'll need a week or so to recover.'

There was something in the tone of his voice that suggested he had some other motive for wanting to see her. 'Nonsense. A bath, a walk on the beach and a night in my own bed and I'll be as good as new.' She hesitated. 'There's nothing wrong is there?'

'No. No, of course not. I could just do with the break.'

She'd known the ageing musician for as long as she could remember. He'd never married and had spent most of his life on the road. His music had been his life. It still was. But his age and endless touring had seemed to take their toll these last few years and he had at last begun to slow down. While she was relieved that he was spending more time at home in Newcastle, she regretted the distance between them and increasingly found herself worrying about him. Spencer Milburn, like many people of his generation, had a habit of insisting that he was fine, even when he wasn't. In fact, particularly when he wasn't. If she challenged him about it, he'd say that he didn't want to worry her. What he didn't seem to understand was that not telling her made her worry even more. Or maybe he did. Maybe he wanted her to worry about him. Maybe he didn't have anybody else to worry about him. 'Are you sure you're

OK? I could come up to Newcastle if you're not well enough to travel.'

'Don't be daft, man. I'm 74, not 94. I can catch the train. I'll enjoy the journey.'

It was, perhaps, an unusual relationship. While they were not related in fact, he'd always been a stable, father-like figure to her. She couldn't imagine a time when he wouldn't be there. He'd certainly been more of a parent to her than either of her biological parents. Her father had been all but absent from her early life, travelling around the world with the many acts that he'd managed. A stint on a major television talent show in the 1970's had turned him into a household name but by then it had seemed to her that his audience knew him better than she did.

'Well, if you're sure.'

'Of course I'm sure.'

If her father had been absent, it was her mother who had driven her away. She had left home, in favour of acting school and a grotty flat in Ealing at her earliest opportunity. 'Are you coming for a week? I'd love...'

'No, no. I wouldn't want to put you out for a whole week.'

She had never understood her parents' marriage. She had witnessed little evidence, as a child, of any love between them. And yet they had remained married and, since his retirement, they were in fact spending more time at home together. In the same house that they'd bought before she'd been born, with the proceeds, apparently, from his first couple of big money deals. 'Uncle Spence, you never put me out. You know that.'

'Well, if you're sure.'

'I told you. I'm sure. Why don't you come on Friday and stay for a long weekend, at least? Travel back when you like?'

'That would be champion.'

'Wonderful. Give me a ring as soon as you know the train times. Will you come up to Roche? Or I can pick you up from Par if you like?'

'No, Roche will be fine. I'll send you a text once I've booked my ticket.'

'Can't wait. And Uncle Spence, you're sure you're all right?'

'Yes, I'm sure.'

They'd ended the call. But he had been hiding something, she was certain of it.

CHAPTER TWENTY

Tuesday, 17 May 2016

He had made up his mind. He'd been weighing up the issue all morning, considering the pros and cons but in the end he'd decided to go with his instinct. The likelihood of Ellen agreeing was another matter. The three women had been given the all-clear by the police and were due to catch the 14:47 from Inverness. It would get Ellen and Jane back into Leighton Buzzard at 23.24. By which time he'd be back. Ellen had sent him a text confirming their travel arrangements and was due to call him at one-thirty. He looked at his watch. It was one-fifteen.

They'd spent several hours on the phone since his conversation with Martha on Sunday and had discussed, at some length, her more recent reaction to seeing the picture of Gina Lawrence, although he'd downplayed Martha's suggestion that they should visit The Scene Club together. But having initially dismissed it out of hand, he'd gradually come round to the idea that taking her with him might be the right thing to do. Martha was involved. He and Ellen had both agreed, albeit with reluctance, that there was a connection. The nature of that connection was, as yet, unclear to them but it had been strong enough to awaken her sensitivity and that made it significant.

Perhaps it was because she was a child, free from at least some of the baggage that had made him so resistant to the very idea, that she had been able, not simply to accept her experiences so matter-of-factly, but to begin to interpret them. The more he had thought about her assertion that they should go to Ham Yard because "she wants us to" the more remarkable it had seemed. He would never be ready to accept that Gina Lawrence might be passing his daughter messages. But taken at face value, Martha had apparently been able to interpret the sensations she was feeling in a way that he never had. He had come around to the idea that it might have been his rational adult mind, all along, that had prevented him.

If his own experiences were anything to go by, Martha was never going to be able to wholly block her sensitivity and indeed, trying to do so would be likely to give her the kind of hang up that it had given him. Perhaps Mike had been right that trying not to worry about the things you cannot change was a philosophy more likely to lead to happiness. Perhaps acceptance would be healthier for Martha than suppression had been for him. The question he had ultimately asked himself was whether leaving her at home with Mike was in Martha's best interest or theirs. His instinct was that if acceptance was Martha's key to happiness, then they needed to show her the way, rather than trying to block it.

He looked at his watch. Five minutes to go. And then his phone rang. Five minutes early.

They emerged from the underground station at Piccadilly, hand-in-hand. The Circus, with its statue of Anteros atop a bronze fountain, was full of people; mostly tourists by the look of them and a scattering of shoppers, weaving their way through the crowd, to and from the shops in Regent Street and Shaftesbury Avenue. Harry took a moment to get his bearings.

He had collected Martha from school and they'd gone straight to the train station. As a consequence, she was still in her uniform; a green checked dress and a dark green cardigan. Harry had a bag over his shoulder in which, as well as his camera, he'd stashed his jacket. It had been hot on the tube and, with the sun still shining brightly, it was almost as warm above ground; unusually so for mid-May.

He squeezed Martha's hand. 'If we can find somewhere a bit quieter, shall we give Mum a ring? Tell her that we've arrived safely?'

Martha nodded. 'Yes, all right.'

Hourly telephone calls had been a precondition of Ellen's agreement to Martha joining him. She had taken less convincing than he had anticipated that she might, agreeing that while Martha appeared undisturbed by her experiences, and so long as there was no reason to think that her safety might be in any way at risk, it was probably in her interest that they should accept Martha's connection to events and include her. After all, she had reasoned, they were simply visiting a hotel in London. All that they were likely to find was that the basement had been converted to kitchens or something similar.

If there was any threat at all, then it arose from the harassment that Holly Holgate had told them she'd experienced and events in Balnakeil. Holly was over 500 miles away, about to board a London-bound train from Inverness Station. As for events in Balnakeil, Lynette Bell's death had undoubtedly shocked them all but there remained no evidence to substantiate Holly Holgate's suspicion that Micky Milburn was in any way connected. According to Ellen, the police in Inverness had been satisfied by the initial pathologist's report that suicide was the likely cause of death. They'd certainly given no indication at all that they were taking either Holly's reported harassment or any connection to the disappearance of Gina Lawrence seriously. Neither was there any reason to suspect that Harry's interest in The Scene Club had come to anyone's attention, and even if it had, that there was any threat.

'Hi Love. We've arrived.' He had to strain to hear her reply. 'Yes, she's absolutely fine. Just a minute.' He handed the mobile phone to Martha.

They had walked a short distance along Shaftesbury Avenue, away from the crowds at Piccadilly Circus, but it was noisy still. A London bus thundered past. Harry waited for Martha to hand the phone back to him. 'I'll give you a call when we get to Des Munroe's place. Don't worry, it'll be fine.' He ended the call and stashed the phone in his bag. 'Come on then,' he said to Martha, taking her hand again.

The walk to Des Munroe's flat in Great Windmill Street took them no more than ten minutes. They found it easily. A plain blue door, beside the entrance to a small fashion boutique. Harry buzzed the intercom on a panel beside the door. After a few moments a woman with an American accent answered.

'Hello. My name is Harry Stammers. I have an appointment with Des Munroe?'

'Yes, Des is expecting you. He's still filming. But someone will be down for you shortly.'

They waited. After five minutes he buzzed the intercom again. The same woman answered.

'If Des is still tied up I thought I might go and get a coffee or something. There's a cafe over the road. Would you let him know that we're over there when he's ready?'

She hesitated, as though about to ask a question and then said: 'No need. We're just about finished. I'll come down and get you.'

A few moments later, the door was opened by an attractive young woman who Harry guessed to be in her late twenties. 'Hi. You must be Harry.'

'Yes,' he agreed, holding out his hand. 'And this is my daughter, Martha.'

The young woman stared at Martha like she'd never clapped eyes on a child before. 'Oh. I don't think Des was expecting anyone else.'

'Well, if it's a problem…'

'No, I'm sure it will be fine,' the young woman said doubtfully. 'It's just that there isn't much space upstairs with all the cameras and recording equipment. You might have to wait on the landing.'

'Would you mind waiting on the landing?' Harry said, glancing down at Martha.

'No.' She shook her head. 'I wouldn't mind a bit.'

As it happened, they didn't have to wait on the landing for very long. Having led them up several flights of narrow, carpeted stairs, the woman had disappeared into the flat. She had re-emerged after a couple of minutes. 'Come in. Des would like you to wait in there.' She gestured towards a door to their left. 'He won't keep you long. Please make yourself at home.'

Harry opened the door and he and Martha stepped into the room. The woman closed the door behind them.

'Make yourself at home?' he whispered to Martha. 'In here?'

Martha had found the only available chair and sat down. 'Why don't you sit over there?' she giggled.

He did as Martha had suggested. Then he pulled his mobile phone from his bag and dialled Ellen's number. When she answered he said, 'If you can guess where I'm sitting right now, we'll take you out to dinner tomorrow night. No expense spared.'

He listened to Ellen's guess. 'Wrong. Try again.' He winked at Martha. She grinned.

He listened to Ellen's second guess. 'Wrong again. I tell you what, I'll let Martha explain where we are and what I'm sitting on. He got up, handed Martha the phone and returned to his seat.

'Hi Mum. We're waiting for Mr Munroe. In his bathroom.'

Harry pinched his nose and pulled a face.

Martha giggled. 'Yes. And Dad is sitting on Mr Munroe's toilet. It's green.'

CHAPTER TWENTY-ONE

Des Munroe was a tall, slim man in his late sixties, Harry observed, with short, neatly styled greying hair. He was wearing a vertically striped shirt with a buttoned down collar, jeans and an expensive looking three buttoned, tailored jacket. 'I'm sorry about making you wait in my bathroom. I hope you didn't mind?'

They had walked almost the length of Great Windmill Street and had just turned into Ham Yard. 'No, of course not,' Harry replied, honestly. It had been worth it just to hear Ellen's reaction. He'd be dining out on the story for months to come.

'We bought the flat to use as our London base while I was working but it is rather cramped.'

'You don't live there then?'

Munroe smiled. 'Good grief, no. My wife and I have a house in Cobham. When I retired, it made sense to keep the flat on so that we'd have somewhere to stay when we're in London.'

'I can imagine,' he agreed. He was trying to work out how wealthy a person would need to be to own both a house in Surrey and a flat in Soho. 'You didn't mind me bringing Martha, did you?'

'Not at all.'

'Only,' he hesitated, 'she's as keen as I am to see if we can locate The Scene Club, aren't you Love?'

Martha nodded. 'Yes. Did you go to The Scene Club to dance Mr Munroe, like Gina Lawrence?'

'Gina Lawrence?' Munroe said, flashing Harry a raised eyebrow.

'She's just someone who used to attend the club,' he replied vaguely, hoping to avoid a conversation about the missing dancer.

Munroe eyed him like he knew exactly who Gina Lawrence was. 'As a matter of fact, Martha, I did. I came to the club several times in 1966, just before it closed.'

'Were you a mod? Did you have a scooter like Daddy's?'

Munroe smiled. 'You have a scooter, Harry?'

'I do. A Lambretta TV175.'

'An excellent choice. No, I never did,' Munroe replied, addressing Martha. 'I preferred cars. I had a E-Type Jaguar at the time, actually.'

Harry added the price of an E-Type Jaguar to his assessment of Munroe's wealth and decided that even as a young man Munroe had almost certainly been very wealthy indeed.

They had approached the hotel entrance.

Harry recognised the doorman. A week before, he had been showing people from a Bentley Mulsanne into the hotel. The doorman held open the hotel door. 'Good afternoon.'

This time, Harry noted, his presence in the yard and at the hotel was entirely valid. He nodded as condescendingly as he could, suppressing a satisfied smirk.

The hotel's interior had what he imagined the brochure might have described as a "contemporary urban feel, with an ethnic twist". A series of carefully placed oversized vases were arranged on a low shelf in front of a gigantic full height window that fronted the reception area. It was at least twenty feet tall. Munroe approached the female receptionist.

'Good afternoon, Sir. How can I help you?'

Harry thought that she had smiled the kind of patronising smile that only hotel receptionists do. It was probably part of their training.

'We have an appointment with Jet Travers. My name is Munroe.'

'Ah, yes Mr Munroe. Welcome to Ham Yard.'

The smile had changed to the more normal kind, Harry noted.

'Miss Travers asked me to show you into the library. She will meet you there shortly.'

The library was really quite something. It was decorated in a modern regency style. Books lined the entire wall to their left and the alcoves either side of a wide chimney breast. A large Impressionist painting had been hung above the fire place. Harry felt awkwardly out of place but Martha seemed entirely at home. She let go of his hand, strode purposefully across the room and arranged herself neatly on the edge of one of three elegant sofas.

Within minutes a young woman appeared. She was wearing a pair of bright red shorts, a pink tee shirt with a fluffy heart design on the front and trainers.

'Jet, how lovely to see you,' Munroe said with evident sincerity. He kissed her on both cheeks.

'Hello Des. How are you?'

'I'm well, thank you.'

'And Susan?'

'Yes, Sue is on fine form. She's just back from St Lucia, actually.'

'St Lucia? How lovely. Mother was telling me that you want to see our basement?'

Harry had taken a seat beside Martha. He got to his feet.

'Yes, that's right. Jet this is Harry and Martha Stammers,' Munroe said, introducing them in turn.

Jet Travers smiled and shook their hands.

'Mr Stammers is a historian at Bletchley Park,' Munroe added.

It crossed Harry's mind to correct him, but he decided to let it lie.

'Bletchley Park? The code breaking centre?'

'Yes, that's right,' he agreed.

'Harry is researching the history of Ham Yard. Did Millie tell you that we're hoping to discover the whereabouts of a club that was here during the 1960's?'

'Yes, she told me about The Scene Club. It would be great if we had a famous night club in the basement. The Rolling Stones played there, I gather?'

'They did. And several others. The Monks, for example,' Munroe added meaningfully, giving Harry a sideways glance.

'Do you have any idea where exactly the club was? Most of our basement has been turned into a bowling alley, so there may be nothing left to see.'

'As a matter of fact we do.'

Jet Travers raised an eyebrow.

'Perhaps, if we show you?'

'Oh, yes. Please lead the way.'

They followed Munroe out into the yard, across the forecourt and approached the green metal doors. Harry held back. He had no wish to repeat his experience of a week earlier.

'This was the entrance,' Munroe said, standing in front of the doors. 'Do you think you can get us inside?'

Jet Travers hesitated. 'Ah. The trouble is, I'm afraid they're not ours.'

'Really?'

'No. Our boundary is there,' she said pointing to the new build that ended a few feet from the doors. 'I think these belong to Grace, the bar in Great Windmill Street. I'm terribly sorry but I rather think that you may have had a wasted journey.'

Harry felt his heart sink.

'Well in that case,' Munroe said, turning towards Harry. 'Perhaps we should go and see the people at Grace?'

Harry couldn't imagine how they were going to convince the staff at Grace to let them go poking about their basement. 'Do you think they will let us take a look?'

'Of course they will,' Munroe replied, like he was not about to be refused. He turned to Jet Travers. 'Would you like to come with us?'

'No. I'll leave you to it but please do come and see me when you've finished. I can show you our new roof garden. We've just had a tree craned up there. Mother's rather proud of it. She'd never forgive me if I let you leave without seeing it.'

Harry and Martha followed Munroe out of Ham Yard, into Great Windmill Street. Grace was several doors along.

'Do you think they'll allow Martha inside?' Harry said, as Munroe approached the doors. 'It is a bar after all.'

'They will if I have anything to do with it,' Munroe said, like a man who was used to getting his own way.

They entered Grace and approached the bar. 'We'd like to see the owner please young man,' Munroe said, addressing a startled-looking barman, who looked to Harry to be in his teens or early twenties.

'The owner?'

'Yes,' Munroe replied.

'The owner's not here, mate.'

'Well then, we will see whoever is in charge. I take it that somebody is?'

The young barman stared at him, then at Harry, then at Munroe again. 'I can get the duty manager, if you like?'

'Thank you. That would be splendid.'

Harry scanned the bar. A scattering of tourists were huddled around bar tables, mainly drinking garishly decorated cocktails from tall glasses.

'Leave this to me,' Munroe said, keeping his voice low. 'I'll tell them that you're a well known historian and that you're making a documentary. They'll be much more likely to cooperate if they think there might be some publicity in it.'

'You do know that I'm not actually a historian?' Harry offered.

'You work at Bletchley Park, don't you?'

'Yes.'

'Well, then take it from me. You're a historian.'

Harry smiled. He had to hand it to Munroe. Here was a man who knew how to make friends and influence people.

Within a few minutes the barman had returned with the duty manager, who lifted the bar gate and stepped forward. He didn't look to Harry to be much older than the barman.

While Munroe was explaining their request, Harry's phone rang. He answered it. 'No, we're in a bar on Great Windmill Street,' he said, in answer to Ellen's question. 'It looks like the doors in Ham Yard might lead down to the basement below the bar.' He listened. 'Yes, she's fine. We're both fine. There might not be a signal down there, so I'll call you as soon as we're above ground again.'

Munroe was trying to catch his eye.

'We're on,' Munroe whispered, as soon as Harry had ended the call. 'Apparently, there's an area downstairs called *The Milk Bar*. It's mainly used for private functions. He thinks that there is a fire escape at the rear, leading up to the doors out into Ham Yard. He's gone to get the keys.'

The duty manager returned and led them down a wide flight of stairs that terminated in a small foyer with two sets of doors. He unlocked the doors to their right and switched on the lights. They followed him through the doorway, into a large open space with a marble floor, punctuated by several pillars, presumably supporting the floor above. At the rear of the space was a garish mirrored drinks bar. It was reflecting pink light, thrown by a series of coloured spotlights suspended from the ceiling. *Tasteful*, Harry thought.

Along the back of the room was a series of small crescent-shaped alcoves, each fitted with white, faux leather padded seats and stubby round tables.

Harry felt his arms prickle. 'What do you think?' he asked, glancing at Munroe.

'I'm not sure. It certainly doesn't look like I remember it, but then it's probably been re-fitted several times since the sixties.'

'It has,' the duty manager broke in. 'We had the whole place re-fitted when we took on the lease.'

'Are those alcoves new?' Munroe asked.

'No. They were here when we came.'

Harry was thinking about the pictures taken at The Scene Club he'd seen on *Original Modernists*. They had shown a series of booths, with narrow arched entrances, arranged along one side of the dance floor. If, as seemed possible, these were the alcoves then the arches had been removed. He took his camera from the bag slung over his shoulder and took several photographs.

'The whole space was much larger than this,' the duty manager continued. 'We divided it when we came here. The only part of the building that might be original is the fire escape and corridor at the back. That's where the stair case is, up to Ham Yard. Through those doors over there,' he said, pointing to the rear.

Martha tugged at Harry's hand.

'Shall we go and take a look?' he said, observing her carefully.

Martha nodded eagerly. She led him across the floor and through the doors.

The contrast between the spaces on either side of the doors was startling. Whereas The Milk Bar had been garishly modern and scrupulously clean, the corridor into which they had stepped was anything but. The rendered walls, which had been painted white at some stage during their lifetime, were yellowing and there were signs of damp leaching up from the dully polished concrete floor.

Munroe had followed them out into the corridor. Harry turned and caught his eye. 'This is more like I remember it. It smells the same too. The entrance is along there,' he said, pointing to a flight of concrete stairs at the far end of the corridor. 'There used to be a cloakroom somewhere down here, I think,' he added, walking towards the stair way.

Harry stopped and snapped several more photographs.

'Yes, that's right.' The duty manager had followed them. 'We put in a partition and changed the layout. But there's still a small storage area where the cloakroom used to be. Up there on the right.'

Munroe went first, followed by the duty manager. Harry hung back. Martha was tugging at his hand.

'Here,' the duty manager said, looking to his right. 'Look, do you mind if I leave you to it? I've got to get on. If you go up the stairs, please don't try to open the doors out into Ham Yard. You'll set off the alarms. Otherwise, take as much time as you like.'

Harry thanked him, watched him retreat back along the corridor and then turned towards Munroe who was motionless and staring into the storage space.

'Dad, can we go that way?' Martha was saying, pulling at his hand.

'In a minute, Love. Let's see what Mr Munroe is looking at.'

'But Dad...'

'In a minute,' he said, pulling her along the corridor towards Munroe. When they reached him, Harry followed his eyes.

'Have you seen those pictures on Original Modernists, posted by that chap in the States?'

He had. They were a series of black and white photographs discovered in New York on a roll of un-developed Kodak film. How it had found its way to New York was anybody's guess. The prints, when the film had been developed, showed the members of The Monks playing at The Scene Club, presumably in 1964, to a dance floor full of kids in their teens and early twenties.

Monroe was staring upward. Above him was a patch of original ceiling. It was made of arched corrugated iron. It looked exactly like the ceiling in the photographs.

'What do you reckon?' Munroe said, glancing at Harry over his shoulder.

'Incredible,' Harry said, grinning broadly. 'I'd say that we are there or thereabouts.'

'Dad?' Martha was tugging at his hand.

Harry tore his eyes away. 'What, Love?'

'I want to go that way,' she said pointing back along the corridor, the way they had come. The look on her face told him that it was time he listened to her.

'All right, Love. Des?' he said turning back to Munroe, 'We'll be back in a minute.'

Munroe was still staring at the ceiling as if transfixed. Harry could feel his excitement, though Munroe was doing his best to mask it.

Martha led him back the way they had come, past the doors into The Milk Bar. They took a bend, mounted a short flight of steps and then Martha stopped. She was rooted to the spot, in front of a set of double doors. The hair on the back of Harry's neck prickled again. 'Through here?' he said, trying to mask his apprehension.

Martha nodded slowly.

He swallowed, reached out and gingerly touched one of the doors. He would later describe the sensation to Ellen as being like a faint echo, but instead of simply sounds there was a jumble of emotions: desire; anger; sadness; urgency. It was like a half-recalled memory. Or a phrase that was on the tip of his tongue. The sensation passed quickly. When it was gone he took a breath and looked at Martha.

She was watching him.

He pushed the doors with both hands. They swung open. They walked through the doorway together.

The space into which they had stepped was a stair well. Harry peered around for a light switch, found one and turned on the lights. They buzzed as they came on, illuminating a set of wide concrete steps.

'Come on,' Martha said.

They climbed four flights of stairs and came to a landing with another set of double doors, which Harry guessed led back to the main bar area at Grace. Martha dragged him onward, up another four flights of stairs that culminated in a landing and another set of doors.

'Through here?' Harry said, to make sure that she was certain.

Martha nodded.

'You're sure?'

She nodded again.

Harry braced himself, reached for the doors and pushed. This time there was no sensation. The doors opened into a short hallway. It looked to Harry like it had been disused for some time. A number of wooden tea chests were dotted along its length. A roll of old carpet was propped against the wall to their right. Harry again found a light switch but nothing happened when he tried the lights. Fortunately a single window at the end of the hallway allowed in enough natural light for them to make their way along. The hallway had bare floor boards that occasionally creaked as they stepped on them, but they appeared sound enough.

'Are you sure you want to do this, Martha?' But he knew that she was and he knew where they were headed.

Martha stopped again outside a half open door. He reached out and pushed it. As his hand found the wooden surface he was hit by an overwhelming sense of grief. The sensation was colossal. He felt the air being sucked from his lungs. He stumbled forward and sank to his knees, his vision blurring. 'Martha,' he gasped. The door had swung inwards. Martha had stepped past him. 'Martha, wait!' He stared into the space, trying desperately to hold onto consciousness. Martha had turned. For a moment he thought he was seeing double because beside her was another child. Slightly shorter. She was wearing a pink terry towelling robe. But then another figure appeared behind them. The sense of grief emanating from her slammed into him, taking the light from his eyes and sucking out what little air was left in his lungs. He toppled, face down onto the wooden floor and was gone.

CHAPTER TWENTY-TWO

He groaned. For a moment he wasn't sure where he was or why he was flat on the floor, his face pressed against the boards. And then he remembered. He hauled himself up onto his elbows and immediately saw her. Ahead of him, Martha was seated, crossed legged in the middle of a wide wooden floor. There was a scattering of objects in front of her. 'Martha?' He clambered to his feet, brushed the dust from his arms and took two unsteady steps towards her. She was holding what looked like a small woollen teddy bear. 'Are you all right?'

Martha looked up. 'Yes,' she said simply.

His eyes scanned the room into which he had stepped, in one wide sweep. Other than the two of them and the objects that Martha had arranged in front of her, it was empty. 'Are you sure?' he said, his eyes returning to his daughter.

She nodded.

Light was flooding into the room through a grimy sash window. 'Where did you find these?' he said, kneeling in front of her.

Martha pointed to the corner of the room. He followed the gesture. A short piece of wooden floor board, no more than a foot or so in length had been lifted and placed to one side.

He examined the objects, each in turn. There was a pair of tiny woollen booties and a pink knitted baby's cardigan, a plastic rattle, a black and white photograph of a tiny baby, perhaps only a few days old, and a yellowing envelope containing a birthday card with a teddy bear design. He opened the card and read the message out loud. 'To Veronica on your first birthday. My darling baby girl. I miss you so much. I will love you always.' The card had been signed "MUMMY XXX" in large capital letters.

He stood up, walked across to the corner of the room and stared into the gap in the floor where the discarded piece of floor board had been removed. 'Did you find it like this?' He glanced back at Martha.

She shook her head.

'How did you know that it was here?'

She shrugged.

He walked back and knelt in front of his daughter. 'Martha. Remember what you promised me when we spoke about this on Sunday?'

She nodded. She was still holding the woollen teddy bear.

'So how did you know?'

'They showed me. Well kind of.'

'What do you mean?'

Martha frowned. 'Well, they didn't exactly show me. Not really. I just knew to look.'

He reached out and placed a hand on her shoulder. 'Are you sure you're all right, Love?'

She nodded. 'Yes.'

'Tell me how are you feeling?'

She looked at him. 'I don't really know. Sort of happy and sad all jumbled together.'

'Well that's good I suppose. The happy bit, anyway.'

She nodded.

'Did you see them?'

'Yes.'

'Both of them?'

'Yes.'

'Were you scared?'

She shook her head. 'No. Not a bit. Were you? Is that why you fell over?'

He thought about it. 'No. Not really scared. It's difficult to explain, isn't it?'

Martha nodded. 'I think they were happy that we were here. I think they wanted us to have this,' she said, holding out the bear. 'And these other things.'

He took the bear.

'This was where Gina lived, wasn't it? Before she got lost.'

'Yes, I think so.'

'Are we going to try to find her?'

He hesitated. 'I don't know. I'm really not sure what to do next, Love.'

'Well, I think we should.'

He stared at his daughter. 'When I fainted it was because it felt like something very bad happened here, Martha. Something that hurt Gina very much. Something that made her very sad.'

Martha was staring at him.

When she said nothing, he continued. 'Sometimes, bad people do horrible things. We can't always make them right again. No matter how much we might want to.'

'But we have to try though. We have to do our best. Don't we?'

'Yes. Always. But it's not easy. We have to think about the bad things that might happen if we decide to do something, along with the good things. We have to weigh them up together and decide what do for the best.'

She was thinking hard. He could see the effort of it in her face.

'You're growing up. So fast, I can hardly keep up with you,' he smiled. 'Come here,' he said, holding out his hands.

She threw her arms around his chest.

'God, I am so lucky to have such a wonderful daughter,' he said, hugging her. 'Do you know how much I love you Martha Stammers?'

'A million miles,' she whispered.

He laughed. 'No. A million, billion miles. Now come on,' he said releasing her. 'Let's pick up all these things and get out of here. Des will be wondering where we've got to and we'd better give Mum a call too.'

Martha picked up each of the items in turn and handed them to him. He stowed them carefully in his bag. She had left the card until last. 'Do you think that's the little girl's name?' she said, handing it to him. 'Veronica, I mean.'

Harry stood up. 'Do you?' he said, holding out his hand.

Martha nodded. 'Yes, I do,' she said firmly. 'I think that's Veronica in the photograph too.' She took his hand.

'Do you know,' Harry said, squeezing her hand. 'I think you might be right.'

CHAPTER TWENTY-THREE

They had seated themselves around his office conference table. In front of them, Harry had arranged the items from the flat above The Scene Club. They had examined them, one at a time, exchanging only muted comments. Now they were seated in thoughtful silence.

It was Holly who spoke first. 'I'm sorry to be the one to state the obvious but who's to say these items were placed there by Gina Lawrence? It could have been anyone, at any time. Surely, if Gina had a child, June Lawrence would have mentioned it.'

He caught Jane's eye.

'Unless, of course, she didn't know,' Jane challenged.

He had been considering that possibility. Gina Lawrence would hardly have been the first young woman to have hidden an unwanted pregnancy. He reached for his coffee cup.

Holly hesitated. 'What are you suggesting?'

'June Lawrence told you Gina went missing for several months in 1961.'

'So?'

'For how many months, exactly?'

Holly frowned. 'I don't think she said.'

'So, maybe it was seven or eight months.'

Holly stared at her. 'Maybe,' she said at last. 'But it's a bit of a leap, isn't it?'

Jane shrugged. 'Maybe.'

Harry put his coffee cup down on the table. 'Could you talk to June Lawrence again and find out exactly when Gina went missing?'

'Sure,' Holly agreed. 'But I'm really not sure where are we going with this? Let's say that Gina did have a child. That she didn't tell June Lawrence and that the child was put up for adoption. So what?'

They were all silent.

'It's about building a picture, Holly,' Harry said at last. 'Who knows where it will take us? Maybe nowhere. But, if there was a child then it is just possible that there was contact between them after Gina left.'

'If she left alive,' Holly challenged. 'Which from where I am sitting looks unlikely, to say the least. I still say that she died that night and that Milburn and Phelps covered it up.'

'Maybe. But we need to keep an open mind.'

Holly shook her head. 'Oh come on. Bell told us that when she regained consciousness Phelps and Milburn were arguing. What were they arguing about, if Gina was alive and well?'

Which was a perfectly reasonable point, to which he had no immediate answer.

'Bell had a guilty secret. A very guilty secret. Why else did she top herself?'

He didn't have an answer to that, either.

'She told us that the two of them were close friends,' the reporter continued. 'And yet we're supposed to believe that, with Gina unconscious on the floor, Bell walked away from that flat without checking.' She shook her head like she didn't believe it for a second. 'Some friend that would be.'

He couldn't disagree with any of it. No matter how afraid Lynette Bell had been of Milburn and Phelps, or how confused she'd been as a result of the drugs, she could have checked and surely any kind of friend would have checked.

189

'I'm sorry but I just don't buy it. Bell didn't check because she knew that Gina was dead. That's why she so readily accepted the bribe from Phelps. She was terrified of finding herself in the middle of a police inquiry. That's why, when we turned up, threatening to rake the whole thing up again, she couldn't hack it. And that's why I've had all this shit thrown at me since I started poking around. Gina Lawrence didn't run away and she sure as hell didn't just vanish into thin air.'

Nobody spoke.

It was a perfectly reasonable hypothesis. In fact, he couldn't immediately see a flaw.

'Lets say you're right, Holly,' Ellen interjected. 'How are we going to prove it? Lynette Bell was our only witness.'

'Exactly,' Harry agreed. 'Which is precisely why we need to keep an open mind and build as big a picture as we can. That includes establishing whether Gina had a child and, if she did, tracing the child if we possibly can.'

Holly shook her head.

He couldn't quite figure her out. Being convinced that Micky Milburn was the villain was one thing. Maybe he was. But to dismiss any other possibility at this early stage just wasn't sensible. To have no interest in establishing whether Gina Lawrence had a child, when her original motive had supposedly been the discovery of a branch of her family tree, wasn't rational at all. 'Surely you're interested in finding a child who, if we're right, would be related to you?'

Holly stared at him. 'Of course I am. But it's a diversion.'

It was Harry's turn to shake his head.

'We could spend months trying to establish it and even longer trying to find the child if there was one. And then what? It's a red herring.'

The argument was getting them nowhere. Harry decided to side step it. 'Let's just keep an open mind. That's all I'm suggesting. I'd like us to stay with trying to tie these items to Gina Lawrence. It might come to nothing, but right now they're all we've got.'

Ellen nodded, 'Agreed.'

'Jane?'

'Agreed.'

He smiled, trying to ease some of the tension that had gathered around them. 'We're never going to date that photograph, but what about the card?'

Jane shook her head. 'The manufacturer went out of business in 1975. I'm still looking, but I have found nothing to date the design.'

'And the other items?'

She shook her head again. 'Nothing. Sorry.'

'What about the adoption records? If Gina Lawrence had a child called Veronica and put her up for adoption, what are the chances of finding any record of it?'

Holly sighed.

He ignored her.

'I'm working on it,' Jane replied. 'But don't hold your breath. Holly, as a potential relative you could add your details and Gina's to the Adoption Contact Register. If there's a match to someone on the register, or to someone who subsequently registers, then you might get notified. But it's a long shot because we have so few details.'

He turned to Holly and waited.

She stared at him.

'Are you willing to try?'

She hesitated and then shook her head. 'We're wasting our time.'

Her intransigence was beginning to irritate him. 'Okay, so what do you suggest?'

'I suggest that instead of chasing our tails, we focus on the most likely scenario. Which is that Gina's death was down to Milburn, one way or another. I suggest that we focus on drawing the bastard out.'

'And how do you propose to do that?'

'Publish,' she said, simply.

He stared at her.

'There's enough of a story here. *The Monks & The Missing Teen.* That was the headline back in '64. We've got The Milburns, Phelps, Lynette Bell's death, questions about Micky's violent past, the intimidation tactics he has employed in the States, the tactics he's employed on me. We get the story into the press and create as much of a stink about it as possible. Micky Milburn will have a fit. He'll make a mistake. He's his own worst enemy. And if half of the stories about him are true, others are bound to come out of the woodwork.'

It was, as far as Harry was concerned, the worst possible strategy. 'But Holly, we've got no evidence.'

'We don't need evidence. We just need to make enough noise.'

He shook his head. 'Even if you find someone willing to print it,' he continued, 'all you'll succeed in doing is turn the whole thing into a media circus. If it generates anything like the kind of interest you think it will, there will be press all over the place. Milburn and Phelps will close ranks, nobody will take us seriously and any chance of discreetly going about the business of investigation will be lost.'

Holly laughed. 'You don't have much faith in the power of journalism, do you Harry?'

'That's not fair,' Ellen interjected. 'Harry and I have been on the receiving end of your so-called journalism. The papers just want a story. If there's no story to be had, they just make one up. Twist facts around to make whatever point they want to make. Without any evidence, that is exactly what we'd be doing. Making it up. Trial by media.'

It was a solid defence. He flashed Ellen an appreciative smile. 'The press will stomp all over it for five minutes,' he added, turning back to Holly, 'wreck any chance we have of making progress and move onto the next story, leaving us where, exactly?'

'They might,' Holly agreed. 'But not if you put your name to it. Harry Stammers - the man who brought down Max Banks. David versus Goliath, Part Two. Or is it three?'

It was the final straw. 'You have got to be kidding.'

Ellen reached out, took hold of his hand and gave it a reassuring squeeze. 'Easy, soldier,' she said, under her breath.

'Sorry,' he continued, 'but if you think I'm going to have my name splashed across all the headlines, you can think again. This is precisely why I was reluctant to get involved in the first place. Forget it.'

'No, I'm not kidding,' Holly said, apparently unmoved. 'Look, this male violence among the rich and famous thing is a massive story waiting to break. Powerful men in the entertainment industry have been abusing women for decades. There are all sorts of rumours buzzing around Hollywood right now. Did you know that?'

'I don't care.' Though, in truth, he didn't know it.

'When it breaks,' she continued, 'it's going to make headlines, worldwide. If we present this in the right way, it could be the spark to set the whole thing off. Milburn can huff and puff all he likes. He'll find himself at the centre of a shitstorm. He'll make a mistake. I guarantee it. And when he does, we'll be waiting for him.'

Harry stared at her. 'Yeah? Well I won't. Because I'm not interested. Seriously, Holly. You publish and that's the end of my involvement. I will not be used to front some sort of media crusade. Yours or anyone else's.'

Holly snorted derisively. 'And there I was thinking that you might be committed to protecting women from monsters like

Micky Milburn. My mistake. So tell me Harry, what is your interest in this exactly?'

Harry opened his mouth to speak and then closed it again. The truth was that it had been the vision of the two figures beside the tree out in the courtyard, and especially Martha's experiences, that had prompted their involvement. But he was certainly not going there with Holly. The last thing he needed was that coming out in some story in the Daily Mirror.

Oddly, Jane had her head buried in her smart phone.

He took a breath and willed himself to calm down. 'Look,' he said trying to bridge build, 'we're trying to help you, here. Somewhat against my better judgement, Ellen and Jane agreed to go with you to Scotland. Whatever happened up there, a woman is dead. If that isn't tragedy enough, we lost our only witness. That's what happens when you go stomping about an issue like this with size ten boots. The thing spins out of control. Set another bomb off in the middle of it all and the thing is going to blow up in our faces.'

Holly said nothing.

'Think about it. You clearly believe that Micky Milburn is behind the threats you've received and the break-in at your flat. Maybe he was. Maybe he wasn't.'

'Of course he was,' the journalist interjected.

Harry held up his hand. 'Either way,' he continued, 'somebody is on your case. They decide to come after you and you're in serious trouble. We can try to help you find out what happened to Gina Lawrence. But we're not a bloody protection agency. Piss them off any more than you already have and you'll be putting yourself at risk. Serious risk.'

She said nothing.

Which Harry took as a good sign. 'If you want us to continue helping you, then here's the deal,' he pressed. 'We tread carefully. No bombshell articles in the papers. You want to splash this all over the press and you can do it without us. One whiff of my name being associated with this in the media and I'm out of here. I'm sorry, but that's the offer.'

She stared at him.

'It's not up for negotiation, Holly,' he repeated. 'Take it or leave it.'

Jane had looked up from her mobile phone and caught his eye. She was trying to tell him something.

'All right. Have it your way,' Holly said at last. 'But I am writing my piece.'

He began to object.

She held up her hand. 'I won't publish until and unless we are all agreed.'

He wasn't at all sure that he trusted her, but at least she appeared to have accepted his terms. 'You give us your word?' he said, meeting her eyes and holding them.

'Yes.'

It was risky. She was risky. But there seemed nowhere else to go. He nodded.

Jane had returned her attention to her phone. He was watching her from the corner of his eye. 'So for now we've got some things to be doing,' he said, trying to stay focussed. 'Will you try June Lawrence again? Maybe sign up with the adoption register?'

Holly nodded. 'Yes.'

'Shall we meet up again in a few days time? Say at the weekend?'

'Yes.'

'Ellen?'

'Agreed.'

'Jane?'

Jane was still staring at her phone.

'Jane?'

'Oh sorry, yes that's fine,' she said, slightly absently.

'Good. Let's call it a day then.'

They all stood up. Harry noticed Jane glance at Ellen and the two exchange a silent message.

'I'll walk Holly out to her car,' Ellen said, casually.

The two women left.

He waited for the door to close behind them.

Jane glanced up at him.

'Are you going to tell me what you've found?'

Jane got up. 'No, I'm going to show you.' She walked across to his desk and hit the space bar on his computer keyboard. 'Password?'

He had followed her. 'What?'

'Your password. What is it?'

He hesitated. 'Building41,' he said eventually. 'Capital B, no space.'

She looked at him over her shoulder. 'A bit obvious.'

Harry shrugged.

She turned back to the computer, typed the password, opened Internet Explorer and initiated a Google search. She clicked on an image and enlarged it.

It was a picture of a woman.

Jane straightened, turned and looked at him as though expecting a response.

There was something about the face. Something familiar. He raised an eyebrow.

'Recognise her?'

'Vaguely. She an actress isn't she?'

'Correct. Name?'

He thought about it. 'Can't remember.'

'Try.'

'I am trying.'

'Try harder.'

Harry wracked his brains. The more he tried to think of actresses, the more his initial impression faded. And then he remembered. 'Ronnie Phelps?' he said, relieved that he had passed the test but still not sure where Jane was heading.

'Correct. Daughter of Marty Phelps.'

'So?'

'Think about it.'

'I am thinking about it.'

'And?'

He thought about it some more.

Jane folded her arms.

Harry stared at the picture, then at her and shrugged 'Pass.'

Jane shook her head in disapproval. 'All that education and still no bloody common sense.'

'All right Magnus Magnusson, I passed, so give me the bloody answer.'

'The hypocoristic for Veronica is?'

'The what?'

'Dear God, I work with an idiot. The hypocoristic. The diminutive.'

'You mean the nickname?'

She stared at him. 'Hallelujah. Praise the Lord. Yes, the fucking nickname.'

He thought about it. And then the light came on. Followed, a second later, by a connection. 'Shit.'

'Shit indeed. Ronnie Phelps. Veronica Phelps. That any plainer for you?'

But he was no longer listening. The connections were firing like it was the fifth of November.

'Date of birth?' Jane continued.

'What?' he said, still making connections.

'Ronnie Phelps. What's her date of birth?'

He ran his hand through his hair. 'How the hell should I know?'

'February 8th 1962. Smack, bang in the middle of our window.'

CHAPTER TWENTY-FOUR

The American Airlines Boeing 777-300 taxied to the stand at London Heathrow's Terminal Three. Inside the plane, a male passenger with short grey hair and a goatee beard adjusted his sunglasses, unfastened his seatbelt and slipped an iPhone from the breast pocket of his shirt. The phone had been in airplane mode for the duration of the long-haul flight. The passenger made the necessary change and waited, while the other passengers in First Class began to disembark. The phone vibrated several times. He read each of the text messages in turn and then stored the phone back in his shirt pocket.

'Thank you for flying with American, Mr Stevenson. Do you need any further assistance?'

The passenger glanced at the stewardess. She was pretty. The kind of pretty, he reflected, that most stewardesses were. 'Just my bag and jacket from the overhead locker.'

He stood up. She hadn't recognised him. As far as he knew, none of the flight attendants had. Which was fortuitous, if not a little disappointing.

'Certainly, Sir.' The stewardess reached for the overhead locker, retrieved the jacket and held it out to him.

He slid his arms into the jacket and watched her stretch again to reach the bag. She was, on reflection, prettier than most.

'Will there be anything else, Sir?' she said, handing him his bag.

'No.' He smiled. 'Thank you,' he added as an afterthought.

'My pleasure Mr Stevenson. Enjoy the rest of your trip.'

He nodded and made his way to the exit.

Forty minutes later, and having collected his luggage, cleared customs and been greeted in Arrivals by a uniformed driver, Micky Milburn was sitting in the back of a silver Mercedes E-Class on the westbound carriageway of the M4. He slipped the iPhone from the breast pocket of his shirt, selected a name from the contact list and waited. 'It's Micky,' he said, when the call was answered.

'Good flight?'

'I've had worse.'

'Were you recognised.'

'No. What's the latest?'

'Everything is under control.'

'What does that mean? Have you heard from the police?'

'Not directly. My people are handling it.'

'Handling it, how?'

'We're assisting them with their enquiries. Bell was unbalanced and we've provided the emails and letters to prove it.'

'Did they swallow it?'

'Relax, Micky. I told you. Everything is going to plan.'

He laughed. 'Sure it is.'

'We dealt with it.'

'You should have dealt with it when you had the chance.'

'We were unlucky, that's all.'

'What did Bell tell them? Do you know?'

'Bell was mentally ill. Delusional. Why else would you live under a false name, in a God forsaken shit hole like that? Holgate pushed her over the edge. Just the kind of intrusive tabloid journalism we've come to expect from the gutter press. Holgate's finished. We'll be making sure of that.'

'What about this Stammers guy?'

'We can talk about Stammers when you get here. You are coming straight here, I take it?'

'Sure.'

'What time do you expect to arrive?'

'Just a minute.' Micky tapped on the glass screen.

The driver opened the intercom. 'Yes, Mr Stevenson?'

'What's our E.T.A?'

'Shortly after five, Sir. Depending on the M25.'

'Did you hear that?' Micky Milburn said into his phone.

'Yes. Does Spencer know you're here?'

'My idiot brother thinks I'm still in Florida. He was never very quick off the mark.'

'You're sure he'll stick to the story, if they pull him in?'

'Why would they pull him in?'

'They won't. But if they do.'

'He'll stick to the story. Spence is stupid enough to imagine that being my brother counts for something. Besides, he's got just as much to lose as we have.'

There was a hesitation. 'Not quite as much.'

Micky smiled. 'And certainly not as much as you do, Marty. Just remember that.'

Bright sunlight and a light breeze combined to cast a myriad of sparkling reflections on the surface of the garden swimming pool. Marty Phelps watched them dance across the rippling blue water from his vantage point behind the French doors. His mind, though, was elsewhere. Dealing with Holgate was one thing. The journalist had plenty of skeletons in her personal cupboard. But Stammers was another, entirely.

He turned, walked the short distance to his office and sat down at his desk. Not only was Harry Stammers squeaky clean but it wasn't easy to understand his motive for involving himself in Holgate's little crusade. He'd been a reluctant hero when he'd taken on Max Banks and certainly hadn't courted the publicity that toppling Banks had earned him. Yet here he was, poking his nose into affairs that didn't, or oughtn't to have concerned him. For the life of him, Phelps could not understand why.

He woke up his PC and skimmed through the files in his documents folder until he found the report he was looking for. The difficulty with Stammers was going to be identifying a lever. As clean as Stammers appeared to be, there wasn't a man alive who didn't have one. Max Banks had opted for straightforward intimidation, albeit on a rather grand scale. But it had backfired. Phelps was not inclined to repeat the mistake.

The one potential chink they'd thus far discovered in the Stammers family armour didn't concern Harry Stammers directly. It concerned his elderly mother. It was public knowledge that in 1977 Elizabeth Stammers had played a pivotal role in countering a Far Right plot to bomb the Palace of Westminster. Given the involvement of the security services, it wasn't altogether surprising that the legal action that had followed had mostly taken place behind closed doors, or that those few records that had found their way into the public domain had been heavily redacted. But the same was true of the records from the inquest into the fire at Hordle in the New Forest in 2005, from which Harry Stammers had famously rescued his estranged mother. Which was intriguing.

Phelps leaned back in his office chair. It hadn't just been the authorities that had been determined to maintain a cloak of secrecy around both sets of events. The Stammers family had also gone to considerable lengths to prevent publication of anything that implied, let alone detailed, Elizabeth Stammers' involvement. Which could mean only one thing. When it came to skeletons, Harry's cupboard might be empty but his mother's was evidently rather well populated. The trouble was that the security services had locked the door and the Stammers family had the keys.

There was, however, a potential opening. The Stammers family had been unable to entirely silence rumours of a relationship between Elizabeth Stammers and Peter Owen, then leader of Nationalist Union of Great Britain. If the rumours were true then they might explain why, when Elizabeth Stammers disappeared, her husband Ted and their children didn't go with her. The

Stammers family had always refused to comment but, as far as Phelps was concerned, there was no smoke without fire. He picked up the telephone handset, punched out a number and waited.

'Chris? What's the latest on Elizabeth Stammers?' He listened to the lengthy reply. 'Interesting. Talk to anyone who nursed Ted Stammers while he was in hospital. Men on their death beds have a habit of spilling their secrets.' He listened again. 'Find Peter Owen. Pull out all the stops.' He hesitated. 'And tell the team to be subtle about it, Chris. I don't want the security services breathing down our necks. Any hint of that, let me know immediately, okay?' The reply was short. 'Thank you.' He ended the call.

Phelps stared at the report on the computer screen. The Elizabeth Stammers angle had potential but, for now, they needed to focus on the more pressing issue. Holly Holgate had thus far resisted their rather muted attempts at intimidation. It was time that they turned up the heat on the wayward journalist and Phelps was in no mood for moderation.

CHAPTER TWENTY-FIVE

'You are kidding,' Ellen said, glancing from Harry to Jane and back again.

Harry was still staring at the picture of the actress on his computer screen. 'I had no idea that she was Marty Phelps' daughter,' he said, still trying to figure all the implications. 'To be honest, I didn't even know that Phelps had a daughter.'

Ellen had accompanied Holly Holgate to her car and returned within minutes of leaving. 'But hang on,' she said, shaking her head. 'Just because she's called Ronnie, doesn't make her the Veronica mentioned in the card.'

Harry ran his hand through his hair. So far as he was concerned, the card wasn't really the point.

'No, of course not,' Jane agreed. 'But there is also the date of birth.'

There was something else. Something that he had recognised as soon as Jane had bought the image up on the screen.

'Right,' Ellen said, like she was still uncertain of the connection.

'Think about it Ellen,' Jane continued. 'Gina Lawrence went missing at the end of April '64. We know that she moved into the flat no later than May 1962, when June Lawrence says she visited her there. So that gives us a window from May '62 to April '64 when she could have written the card. We know it was written shortly before the child's first birthday. If that child was Ronnie Phelps, then the card would have been written, probably in January

1963, right in the middle of our window. Gina Lawrence lasted another year at the flat before she vanished. It's either one hell of a coincidence or Ronnie and Veronica are one and the same.'

Ellen stepped away from the desk and walked across to the office window. He watched her staring out towards the tree where he'd first seen them. A woman and a young child. A young child whose face had been clearer each time he'd seen her.

'I don't know,' she said, like she was still trying to make the connections.

Harry cleared his throat.

The two women turned to face him.

He focussed on Ellen. He didn't much fancy seeing Jane's reaction.

'What?' both women said in unison.

He ran his hand through his hair again. 'I mean, I can't be certain, of course. It's just that…' He stopped and stared at Ellen, waiting for her to come to his rescue.

'How sure are you?' she said, without breaking eye contact.

How sure could he be? Certainty came from evidence. Or it was meant to. 'Please don't ask me how, because I don't have the slightest idea. I've given up trying to work that one out. But I'm as sure as I can be. It's her.'

Surprisingly, Jane hadn't said a word. He chanced a glance in her direction. She'd perched herself on the corner of his desk like a vulture on a telegraph pole, waiting for the kill.

'I know. It's crazy,' he acknowledged.

She grinned. 'You said it.'

'Jane,' Ellen reprimanded her.

Jane shrugged. 'Hey, I'm convinced. And I'd be saying that even if old Russell Grant here, hadn't made a connection to the *other side*,' she added spookily.

'Fuck off,' Harry retorted. Her reference to the television psychic reminded him why he had always regarded those who claimed a sixth sense to be mumbo-jumbo spouting frauds. 'And anyway, she's not on the *other side*, is she?' he mimicked. 'Whatever I'm seeing, it is not the ghost of Ronnie Phelps, that's for damn sure.'

'All right, you two' Ellen broke in. 'Can I just point out that Harry's intuition has never once been wrong.'

He appreciated the defence.

Jane held up her hand. 'No argument from me on that point.'

'So let's go over this,' Ellen said, demonstrating considerably more patience with Jane than Harry was feeling. 'Gina Lawrence gets pregnant in…' She hesitated, evidently trying to do the maths.

Jane beat her to it. 'May 1961.'

'Right. She doesn't want the Lawrences to know about the pregnancy. So, before it begins to show, she goes to stay with friends.'

Jane nodded. 'Yup.'

'Who?'

'No idea, but it's an angle to explore.'

'She has the child on 8th February 1962. The child is adopted by Marty Phelps and his wife,' Ellen continued.

'Keep going.'

'They name the child Veronica. Gina moves into the flat above The Scene Club.'

'Evidently.'

'She retains some keepsakes from Veronica's birth which she hides under the floor in her flat. They include a card that she writes but never sends. Why?'

'Maybe Mr and Mrs Phelps didn't want any contact,' Jane replied. 'Adoptive parents often don't.'

'Right. She meets Spencer and Micky Milburn at the beginning of 1964?'

'Correct,' Harry agreed. 'When The Monks come down to London from Newcastle.'

'Spencer Milburn falls for her but, for some reason, their relationship doesn't work out.'

'According to Holly,' Harry interrupted, 'Micky muscles in, leading to tension between them. Understandably, especially if Micky knew that Spencer had feelings for her,' he added.

'According to Lynette Bell,' Ellen continued. 'Gina goes along with Micky, not because she fancies him, but in order to make Spencer jealous. It works. After the party to celebrate the band's first Number One, there's an altercation between Micky and Spencer on the stairs going up to Gina's flat and Spencer leaves.'

'And Micky, Gina and Lynette Bell retire to the flat for a night of wit and repartee,' Jane cut in.

Harry grimaced.

'When Gina disappears, Micky denies ever having been there…'

'Don't forget Spencer,' Harry added. 'He said nothing to the press, or to the police, about any altercation with Micky. In fact, nobody did until Bell spilled the beans. It's as though it never happened.'

'Yes, that's right,' Jane agreed. 'And Lynette Bell leaves a few days later on a fifty year long holiday to the Highlands of Scotland, courtesy of…'

'Marty Phelps,' Harry completed the sentence for her.

'Why?' Ellen stared at each of them in turn. 'Why was Phelps so keen to see the back of Lynette Bell that he was willing to pay her what was a significant sum of money in 1964?'

'On the face off it, because he didn't want Micky's propensity for drug fuelled sex sessions with multiple young women splashed all over the press,' Jane replied. 'Which would have been a wise move. It would undoubtedly have damaged his reputation and the band's.'

Harry had been thinking. 'If that's all there is to it and Gina was fine, then why would she have left?'

'Who knows?' Jane replied. 'Maybe she was just too ashamed to stick around to face his brother.'

'I can understand that,' Ellen agreed. 'If she was in love with him, imagine how she would have felt about facing him. But what

I don't understand is why she left those things behind,' she said, gesturing towards the conference table. 'I mean, you just wouldn't, would you? They were surely among her most treasured possessions. All that she had left to remind her of her daughter. Why would you go to the trouble of stashing them under the floor boards and then leave them behind?'

'Which takes us back to Holly's view,' Jane replied, 'that she didn't leave. Not alive, anyway.'

They fell silent.

Harry ran his hand through his hair.

Ellen noticed the gesture. 'What?'

He wasn't at all sure that he wanted to voice what he'd been thinking. Not with Jane in the room. 'It's nothing.'

'Harry, what?'

He glanced at Jane.

She held up both hands. 'Ignore me. Make like I'm not here.'

He resisted the temptation to voice the obvious retort. 'Look, I don't understand this any more than you do, right?'

Jane tipped her head in acknowledgement.

'But, Ellen,' he said, turning back towards his wife, 'you've always said that instead of trying to rationalise things, I should run with them.'

'Yes, I have. I think you should.'

He took a breath. 'Okay. So let's assume that Ronnie Phelps is Gina Lawrence's daughter. It's not just my...,' he hesitated.

'Intuition,' Ellen completed the sentence for him.

He tipped his head in acknowledgement. 'Right. It's not just that. The evidence for it is beginning to stack up.'

Ellen nodded. 'Agreed.'

Now the difficult part. 'Let's just say that Ronnie is the little girl I've seen with Gina, first out there,' he nodded in the direction of the window, 'then at our place and twice in Soho, once in Ham Yard and again in the flat.'

Ellen nodded again.

'When I see them, I see Gina as an adult from around the time she went missing. When we have got very good reason to suspect that something bad happened to her in that flat. Either she died, or something that was bad enough to prompt her disappearance, leaving all that stuff behind,' he said, gesturing towards the conference table.

Ellen nodded again.

'That would explain why I get an overwhelming sense of sadness from her, which was strongest, by far, in her flat.' He stopped and glanced at Jane.

'I'm with you so far,' Jane agreed.

'Okay. So I've been thinking about Ronnie. Martha says...'

Ellen flinched.

He could understand why. 'I'm sorry, Love, but whether we like it or not...'

'It's all right. Go with it,' Ellen said, smiling weakly.

He stared at her for a moment longer and then continued. 'Martha says that the little girl feels different, somehow. For a while, I didn't know what she meant. But I've been thinking about what I felt when I saw them in that flat. Not what I saw. But how it felt. And I think Martha might be right. The overriding impression I get from the little girl isn't sadness. It's different. It's like she's...' he hesitated, searching for the right word. 'Stuck?' he said at last.

'Stuck? What do you mean?'

'I'm not sure.' He was thinking on his feet. Running with his gut feeling. It was unfamiliar territory. 'Maybe something happened to her. Some kind of trauma, perhaps. It's like she has been unable to move on. When I see the two of them, it feels like they're both frozen at different points in time. Like someone took a snapshot.' He ran his hand through his hair and glanced from Ellen to Jane, looking for reassurance that he wasn't talking gibberish. When he saw none in Jane's expression, he shook his head. 'This is bollocks, isn't it?'

'No, I don't think it is bollocks at all,' Ellen said, smiling weakly.

He looked at Jane.

'Hey, go with it Harry. At least you're owning it. It's about bloody time, to be honest. It just might take some getting used to, that's all.'

She was certainly right about that.

They were silent.

'Since we're engaging our inner voices,' Jane said, suddenly, 'want to hear mine?'

Harry raised an eyebrow.

'Supposing Gina changed her mind? Supposing she wanted Veronica back.'

They both stared at her.

Jane shrugged. 'Maybe Gina's disappearance wasn't down to Micky Milburn at all. Think about it. If she changed her mind and was hassling Phelps, then he would certainly have had a motive for wanting rid of her, wouldn't he?'

CHAPTER TWENTY-SIX

Sunday, 15 March 1964

Gina Lawrence was staring through the French doors, into the house. She'd caught the train to Berkhamstead from London, cadged a lift from a truck driver into the Hertfordshire village and walked the remaining distance to the house. By the time she'd located the gateway into the sprawling grounds that surrounded the house, it had been early evening and the daylight had been beginning to fade. She'd walked purposefully down the gravelled drive, as though on autopilot, in full view of the house and heedless of any risk that she might be observed. But as she'd neared the house, reality had begun to whisper to her. She would fail. They were not going to let her see her. He had made it clear that there could never be any contact. That was the deal they had struck and to which she had agreed. They had shaken on it and she'd made a solemn vow. Her hand had felt like it was not entirely hers for months afterwards. The hand that had given away her beautiful baby girl. It had felt numb and her chest, like she'd had her heart torn out and the cavity filled with concrete.

Those awful months had eventually passed and, for a time, she'd been sure that she'd done the right thing. What did she have to offer a child? One grimy bedsit after another, cared for by a neighbour trying to scratch out a living by looking after other people's kids, or fending for herself while her mother waitressed in restaurants and bars. She'd thought of all the single mothers she had known. Not a single one of them had been happy. She wanted a future. She was pretty and she could dance. She could even sing. Phelps had promised that he'd find her an opening and that they'd give Veronica a better life. What could she offer in comparison?

Then, shortly before Veronica's first birthday, when it had dawned on her that she couldn't even send her daughter the card she'd purchased from a shop on Oxford Street, the awful emptiness had returned. The terrible realisation that she'd never see her again. That she had handed over to Phelps the only thing that really mattered. It had begun as a feeling of creeping sadness. During the months that followed it was as though it had leached from the pit of her stomach, into her veins and then along her veins, into her arms and legs, until it had infected every part of her. She'd tried to ignore it. Dancing at the Scene Club had been her only real escape, along with the pills and the alcohol. The only way to banish the overwhelming sadness that, when she was alone and especially at night, threatened to engulf her entirely.

At the last moment, she had realised that if she approached the house from the front, in full view of the great bay windows into the living room, where Barbara and Marty Phelps usually spent their evenings, when Marty was at home at least, they would be sure to see her. She had skirted the front lawn and made her way to the back of the house.

Meeting Spencer Milburn ought to have been her chance. She'd seen something in him. She'd met many musicians, men who'd gone on to become recording stars and men like Spencer who surely would. But none of them quite like him. There had been a spark. She'd known it as soon as she had caught his eye. Like a spark of recognition that had leapt across the space between them. She had felt it immediately. He'd felt it too. She'd been sure of it. But after making love to him in Guy Steven's flat, he'd gone cold. And she knew why. She couldn't blame him. She didn't blame him. He'd looked into her eyes and seen her for what she was. A woman who had given up her child. Worse. A soulless bitch who had sold her baby for a shitty little flat above The Scene Club and the promise of becoming one of Marty's girls. He had seen it and rejected her. Who could blame him? Without her baby, she was worthless. An empty husk of a woman. Without Veronica she was nothing.

She'd been surprised to find the rear garden looking like a building site. A brooding mechanical digger had been abandoned a few yards from a deep rectangular pit, dug parallel to the house. Several spoil heaps from the pit, piles of bricks and other builders' paraphernalia were scattered about. She'd picked her way around them as carefully as she could.

Marty Phelps had talked about the possibility of building a pool, she remembered. Images of Veronica, as a child, laughing and splashing with her friends in the summer sunshine flashed across her mind. She banished them and stared into the oak panelled dining room, longing for a glimpse of her. Desperate to see her. To hold her. To never let her go.

The room was empty and in darkness but she could see light from the hallway beyond. She tried the door. It was unlocked. She opened it and slipped inside, closing it, as quietly as she could, behind her. She kicked off her shoes, so that her feet would make no sound on the wooden floor and crept across the room toward the doorway out into the hall. She stood at the doorway and listened. She could hear the sound of a television and occasional voices. Their voices. She held her breath and walked across to the stair case and made her way up the stairs. Veronica's room was the second on the right along the carpeted upstairs hallway. She made her way along, her heart in her mouth, desperately hoping that the floor boards wouldn't creak. The door into the bedroom was ajar. She pushed it open slowly and stepped into the room.

The first thing that she noticed was that they'd replaced Veronica's cot with a bed, but otherwise the room was exactly as she remembered it. Large and airy, the walls decorated with pink floral wallpaper with matching curtains obscuring the window. Veronica was asleep on the bed. She was wearing pink pyjamas and was laying on her back. She had kicked off her bed covers and was holding a little knitted teddy bear.

If she had imagined that seeing her daughter was going to help to ease the longing, she had been wrong. It was all that she could do to stop herself from snatching Veronica up from her bed and fleeing. Instead, she crept forward and sank to her knees beside the bed, tears filling her eyes. She had to wipe them away with her jacket sleeve so that she could see. Veronica had grown so big and her hair was longer. Gina watched her chest, as it rose and fell with her breath. She reached out, her hand shaking uncontrollably, smoothed Veronica's hair away from her face and stroked her cheek with a single finger. 'My darling girl,' she whispered and leant forward to brush the sleeping child's cheek with her lips. The familiarity of the child's smell flooded through her. It was like drinking wine on an empty stomach. It made her giddy and soon the tears had turned to sobbing. 'My gorgeous, wonderful princess. What have I done? What have I done?'

Veronica stirred. 'Mama?'

A stab of fear. 'Shh… Shh..'

'Mama?' Veronica opened her eyes.

Terror. They would hear. They would come. They would take her.

Veronica sat up and began to cry. 'Mama. Mama.'

'I am your Mama. I will always be your Mama. Always.'

Veronica began to wail.

She got up from the floor, picked up the now screaming child and sat down heavily on the bed, hugging her tightly. 'It's all right. It's all right. Mama won't hurt you. Mama would never ever hurt you. Shh. We'll be together.'

Urgent voices. Footsteps on the stairs.

Veronica dropped her teddy bear. Gina snatched it up and stuffed it into the front of her jacket.

Marty Phelps burst into the room, followed by his wife. 'Gina? What the hell are you doing?' he yelled.

'She's my baby. My baby.'

Barbara Phelps was yelling. She shoved past her husband and tore Veronica from Gina's arms. 'Get her out. Get her out.'

She had clambered to her feet. Marty grabbed her and dragged her from the room.

'She's mine, Marty. I've changed my mind. I want her back.'

'She is not yours,' he yelled, dragging her along the corridor, to the top of the stair case. 'She will never be yours.'

She kicked out and he let her go. 'I want her back,' she said, backing away from him. 'She's my baby. I gave birth to her. She's mine.'

Phelps stared at her. 'No. Barbara is her mother. Barbara will always be her mother. We've got the papers to prove it.'

'But I didn't sign any papers. I can change my mind.'

'No, you can't. Not now and not ever. It is Barbara's name on the birth certificate and we've got a signed statement, lodged with our solicitor, from the midwife who delivered her, that it was Barbara who gave birth.'

'What? You can't have.' She shook her head in denial. 'She's lying.'

'Oh, can't I? I'll have my solicitor make a copy for you if you wish.'

She stared at him. 'I'll go to the police.'

'And say what? That we stole your baby?' He laughed. 'Who do you imagine is going to believe that?'

She looked away. 'They'll be able to tell that I gave birth. I've got the fucking stretch marks.'

'Really. So where is your baby, Gina? What did you do with it?'

She was struggling to grasp his meaning. 'I was here. Veronica is…'

'No,' he interrupted her. 'You were never here.'

'But…'

'Name one other person who saw you here.'

She stared at him.

'You can't, can you?'

'I didn't want anybody to...' She fell silent as the reality of her situation began to settle on her. It was like a deadweight across her shoulder. She felt herself shrinking under the burden of it.

'You didn't want anybody to know. And nobody does know because it never happened. Whereas all of our friends knew about Barbara's pregnancy. We made sure of it.'

'You can't have. You can't...'

Phelps laughed again. 'Oh, we can and we did. You, on the other hand, don't have a single scrap of evidence to prove that Veronica is yours, do you?'

She stared at him. The emptiness inside her was so vast that breathing seemed almost pointless.

'Let me make this absolutely clear to you, Gina,' Phelps said, his expression deadly serious. 'Because I don't want there to be any doubt in your mind. If you go to the police, I'll make sure that someone testifies to witnessing you dumping a package in the Thames. A baby sized package. Do you understand what I'm saying?'

She nodded, woodenly.

'You will never come here, or anywhere near Veronica, ever again. Do you understand me?'

'Yes.'

'You can keep your flat. For now, I'd rather have you where I can see you. And I will be watching you, be assured of that. If you ever repeat these ridiculous claims to another living soul I will personally see you ruined. Have I made myself clear?'

She was beaten. She'd lost Veronica forever. There was no way back from this. There never would be any way back.

CHAPTER TWENTY-SEVEN

Friday, 20 May 2016

Holly Holgate slid into the blue Mazda MX5, clicked the central locking and stared at the car's offside wing mirror. The street outside was illuminated by a nearby lamp and the lights from the shop windows. In the mirror she watched a man open the door of a car three cars back, get in and close the door. She waited. Nothing. She waited a minute longer. Still nothing. She slid her key into the Mazda's ignition and started the engine. The headlights came on. She checked the mirror. The lights on the car three cars back came on. She waited for another minute. Nothing. 'Shit.'

He'd been following her for at least the last hour. A tall, stocky man who she estimated to be in his late thirties or early forties. Dark hair. Wearing jeans and a leather jacket. He'd made only rudimentary efforts to avoid detection. He was making little or no effort to avoid it now. Which she took to mean that he wanted her to know; that whoever he was working for wanted her to know. She pulled her smartphone from her pocket, took a breath and opened the car door. She slid out of the Mazda, with the engine still running and, holding her phone out in front of her, marched directly towards the car, three cars back.

It began to reverse, presumably to achieve the angle necessary to pull out. She stood directly in its path, still holding out the phone. 'See this?' she yelled. 'It's a camera phone. I'm streaming this live to *Mumsnet* and the last time I looked there were 575 viewers.'

The car had halted. She could see the driver's face behind the windscreen. It was nondescript and not a face that she recognised. It sure as hell was going to be one that she would remember. 'Do you wanna give them a wave? Maybe your wife is watching.'

He revved the engine and nudged the car forward. She stood her ground. 'Who are you working for?' she yelled.

A young man wearing a set of headphones, maybe twenty to twenty-five she reckoned, had stopped on the pavement beside the car. He called out. 'Hey, are you all right? Do you want me to call the police?'

'No,' she called back. 'Just film us, would you? This joker seems to like the limelight. We can combine our shots. Maybe even turn it into a feature film.' She returned her attention to the driver. 'I said, who are you working for?'

The young man on the pavement had pulled out his camera phone and was now pointing it at the car.

The car accelerated, nudging her backwards.

'Don't fuck with me,' she yelled, slamming her fists onto the car's bonnet. 'You think I'm intimidated by some scumbag in a Vauxhall Astra? Well think again.'

The car accelerated slowly. She stepped backwards and sideways between her car and the next. The Astra pulled away, its tyres squealing on the road surface. She sat on the bonnet of her Mazda, panting.

'Fuck. Are you all right? Do you know that guy?' The young man with the head phones had approached her. He was still holding out his phone. Several other passers by had stopped and were staring at her.

'I'm fine. And no, I've no idea who he was. But do me a favour?' she said, still panting.

'Sure.'

She reached into her inside pocket, pulled out a business card and handed it to him. 'Post that all over Facebook,' she said, glancing at his phone. 'If anyone recognises the car or the driver, let me know, would you?'

'But you were streaming to Mumsnet?'

She smiled. 'I was bluffing. My camera doesn't work.'

It was after eleven when she arrived back at the flat. There had been no further sign of the man in the Vauxhall Astra. She reckoned that he had achieved his objective, although if the kid with the headphones was good to his word, having his face splashed all over the internet probably hadn't been in the driver's plans. She'd managed to appear calm during the incident, although appearance was all that it was. The uncomfortable truth was that she was vulnerable. She knew it and presumably so did Milburn. That had been one of her reasons for approaching Harry Stammers and it was why he was wrong now about holding back. Milburn was not going to give up. He had too much to lose. Publishing might blow the whole thing wide open and Harry was right that faced with a media storm, Milburn's response was unpredictable. But doing nothing was going to leave her vulnerable. The evening's events had more than demonstrated just how vulnerable she was and she felt it. She climbed the stairs to her flat, used her key to open the front door and stepped into the hallway.

She was used to a level of intimidation. Nowadays, dealing with intimidation came with the job. Anyone with a modicum of knowledge could make anonymous threats via the internet and if they were skilled enough to hijack your Twitter and Facebook accounts, could wreak havoc with your social network, as Milburn had done in her case.

She ran her hand along the wall, found her target and switched on the hall lights. Except Milburn had supplemented intimidation with good, old fashioned, physical threats. She had to hand it to him, when it came to intimidating journalists, Milburn was a past master.

She knew, before she spotted him, that somebody was there. She stepped into the lounge and saw the movement out of the corner of her eye as he reached out to switch on the lamp on the stand beside the arm chair in which he was sitting. 'Good evening Holly.'

She recognised him instantly, although he looked older than he had in the most recent pictures she'd found of him. The same craggy features with deep wrinkles, short grey hair, and a stubby grey moustache and goatee but thinner faced. Like he'd recently lost weight. 'How the hell did you get in here?'

Another man had stepped out from the kitchen to her left and taken up a position behind her. She observed him over her shoulder. The man from the Vauxhall Astra.

'Johnnie here, used to be a locksmith, didn't you Johnnie?'

Johnnie grinned.

She turned back toward Milburn. 'What do you want?'

'Well, now. Your mobile phone would be a reasonable starting point. Personally, I'm not averse to publicity but, for some reason, Johnnie has a bit of an aversion to having his face splashed all over the internet.'

'It's a bit late for that. He's probably making it big on Facebook as we speak,' she said, hoping that the threat of publicity might work in her favour. But it was a hope that was soon dashed.

'Oh, I don't think so. Filming in stereo was a smart move. But Johnnie double backed and relieved the kid of his mobile phone, a couple of minutes after you drove away. He put up a struggle, so unfortunately for him, he's now on his way to hospital. Nothing too serious. Just two sets of broken fingers. It's Johnnie's trademark.' He hesitated. 'Well actually, it's only one of them. He's got a few, to be fair.'

It was an odd accent. A mixture of Geordie and lazy, East Coast American.

She hesitated.

'Your phone please?' he said, holding out his hand. 'Johnnie can take it from you if you'd prefer?'

She glanced back at Johnnie. He was still grinning. She reached into her pocket, pulled out the phone and tossed it to Milburn. He caught it.

'Thank you. On to business then. Would you like to take a seat?'

'I'd rather stand.'

Milburn shrugged. 'I'd like to congratulate you on finding Lynette Bell. That must have taken some digging. It had unfortunate consequences for Bell but hey, she was just another source, as far as you guys are concerned, right?'

She said nothing.

'How did you find her, by the way?'

She ignored his question.

'Hey, now look. The silent thing is not going to work here, okay? Johnnie is a man of many talents. I'm sure he is more than capable of giving you a little encouragement. In fact, he'd probably quite enjoy it. So how about you spoil his night?'

'You wouldn't dare. I've already told the police about your intimidation. Anything happens to me and they'll know you were responsible.'

He smiled. 'Ah. Well now, how's that even possible, with me back in the States? See, I flew over here on a false passport. Right now, I am at home in Florida and there are plenty of witnesses who will be more than happy to confirm it.'

He left a pause, presumably for his last statement to sink in. 'I didn't kill Lawrence you know. You've got me all wrong.'

Like hell, he didn't. She thought it but she remained silent.

'And this theory you've got that I'm behind all this; that I've been pulling the strings from 4000 miles away. I mean, come on. An ageing rock star goes to all that trouble because of what? Some chick who nobody has seen since 1964?' He laughed. 'Who's gonna believe all that shit, especially coming from somebody with your reputation?'

Her reputation. Which he'd been rubbishing ever since she'd first started digging.

'The police in Inverness certainly didn't.'

She said nothing.

'As far as they're concerned Bell was a fruitcake, with a history of mental illness, pushed over the edge by a two-bit hack with some crazy vendetta dressed up as a story. I'm surprised they didn't arrest you for wasting police time. In fact, I might have my people suggest it to them.'

He was evidently enjoying himself.

'What else have you got? Any reputation you once had for serious journalism died with Bell. There's not a newspaper editor out there who would touch a story with your name on it.'

She was thinking that they'd be sure to touch a story coming from Harry Stammers. They'd snap his hands off.

'Come on Sweetheart, you're all washed up. And who the hell cares? The story died in 1964.'

'I care,' she said tersely.

'Oh, that's right. The personal vendetta. What is Lawrence to you, for fuck's sake?'

'Gina Lawrence was my aunt.'

Surprise flashed across his features. 'Seriously?'

'Yes. Seriously.'

He recovered quickly. 'So what, you're investigating your family tree now?' He smiled broadly, like he was enjoying the joke.

She ignored him.

'So, how did you find Bell?'

She stared at him. Milburn had the upper hand and he knew it. 'Bell's name came up easily enough,' she said, eventually.

'But she was using an assumed name.'

'She had been using an assumed name. She couldn't use it to claim benefits. I've got a contact at the Benefits Agency. There aren't that many Lynette Bells claiming.' Which wasn't the whole truth but she wasn't about to drop Rickie Lambton in it. He might yet be useful.

He smiled. 'Impressive.'

She snorted.

'Let's cut to the chase, shall we? You think you're smart and finding Bell was clever, I'll give you that. But Sweetheart, you're small fry compared to some of the hacks that have crossed me in the States. Big names, with bigger news agencies behind them. Do the research. Most of them burned their careers for good and the others? Well, let's just say that it was fortunate for them that they had health insurance because they sure as hell needed it once my people were finished with them.'

She decided to fight back. It was a gamble but his arrogance was going to be his downfall. Besides, he was getting to her. 'I'm not afraid of you, Milburn. Money and fame might talk over there but this is Britain. If there's one thing we despise over here, it's bullies like you. People who throw their weight around and pick on the little guy. So you or your apeman here,' she said, nodding over her shoulder, 'trashed my flat. Big fucking deal. In fact, be my guest; trash it all over again. Knock me about a bit as well if you like. Because that's exactly the kind of material that I need.'

His smile had begun to fade.

'You think I need a newspaper editor to break this story?' She laughed. 'You're getting old, Micky. Losing your touch. I can post my story any time I like and have it all over the internet in twenty minutes. In fact, I've already got the first draft up there in The Cloud, just waiting to go. And enough people know it's there to press the button if I can't. So back off.' She was bluffing but there was no way he could know that.

His face had turned to stone. He nodded. Before she could move, there was an arm around her neck. Micky Milburn climbed to his feet and took a step towards her.

She struggled but the arm around her neck tightened.

'Bluff. It's all bluff,' he spat. 'You want to play dirty?'

He was now standing directly in front of her. He leant forward and sniffed. 'Smell that Johnnie? That is the smell of fear. It always turned me on. Even at seventy-two it puts a stiffy in my pants.'

He ran his hand slowly up the side of her torso.

'Nice.'

She kicked out wildly but missed her target. The arm around her neck tightened. She began to feel light headed.

'You ever taken drugs, Holly?' Milburn nodded.

The arm loosened. She gulped a lungful of air.

'Have you?'

She managed to shake her head.

'It's amazing what a girl will do if you stick enough pills down her throat. There's an art to it, you know. Too many and they lose consciousness altogether. Who wants that? It's like screwing a sack of potatoes. Too few and they're a little too...' He hesitated. 'Lively,' he finished the sentence. 'You know what I'm saying?'

She kicked out again but she was becoming weaker.

'We've been playing around until now, Holly. Giving you a chance to see the light and back off. But from here on in, it gets serious. You drop this now or I will take everything you have.'

He'd lowered his hand and slipped a finger between her legs. 'And I do mean everything.'

She had begun to lose consciousness but was conscious enough to hear his final words.

'And when we've finished with you, we'll find you a rope. Or maybe just throw you off Waterloo Bridge. I'll leave that to Johnnie. Faking suicide is one of his other specialities. Final warning.'

And then she passed out.

CHAPTER TWENTY-EIGHT

Tuesday, 28 April 1964

Spencer Milburn was panting from climbing the stairs so hurriedly. He had burst through the doors into the short corridor that led to her flat but now that he'd arrived outside the door, he was hesitating.

Micky had said nothing since the party, either about their altercation on the stairs, or about what had happened afterwards and, in truth, avoiding the subject entirely had been the only way that Spencer had been able to get through the seemingly endless photo-shoots and interviews with his brother and the rest of the band. But on arrival at The Scene Club for their regular Tuesday night gig, he'd noted her absence, asked a number of the regulars and discovered that Gina had not been seen by anyone since the party.

He had bounded up the stairs to her flat with no real idea of what he was going to say to her. Now that he was outside her door he was even less sure. He reached out hesitantly and wrapped his knuckles on the door. 'Gina?' There was no reply. He knocked, harder this time. 'Gina? It's Spencer. Are you there?' He tried the door. It was unlocked. He pushed it open and called out again. Still nothing. He stepped into the flat.

A short hallway, with doors to the left and right, led into a spacious bed-sitting room. As well as the bed, there was an old leatherette two-seater sofa along the back wall, a small chest of drawers, a television on a stand in one corner with a record player on the floor beside it. The room was in darkness, thick curtains obscuring most of the light from the street. He walked across to the window and pulled open the curtains. Light flooded the room.

He turned and scanned the room again. A well worn, patterned rug covered most of the wooden floor. There was a pile of 45's beside the record player. A Dansette, by the look of it, with the lid up. A record was still on the turntable. Various personal belongings were dotted about the room. But his eyes were drawn to the double bed and to the cabinet beside it, on the far side, atop which were two empty Champagne bottles and an open bottle of Gordon's Dry Gin. He stood and stared at the bed, unable to avoid the scene that his mind conjured for him. The bed was unmade and scattered with items of clothing. As though she had pulled them from the chest of drawers in haste, perhaps to pack an over night bag or suitcase.

He tore his eyes from the bed and checked both the rooms off the little hallway. A tiny kitchen and a bathroom. He checked the bathroom cabinet. There was no toothbrush and very few toiletries. His heart sank.

He returned to the main room and searched it for a note or any clue as to where she might have gone, but he could find none. On the floor beside the bed was a pile of worn clothes. He recognised them. She'd been wearing them the last time he'd seen her. On the stairs up to the flat. He reached down and picked up her blouse, beneath which was a pair of worn knickers. As he straightened, his eyes caught the glint of a silver chain. He reached down to retrieve it. The silver St Christopher, its' chain broken. She'd been wearing it the night they made love in the DJ's flat. He sat down heavily on the edge of the bed, staring at the St Christopher. *Gina.* Whatever had happened that night; whatever Micky had done, she had gone. He could not escape the feeling that he was never going to see her again.

CHAPTER TWENTY-NINE

Saturday, 21 May 2016

Ronnie Phelps bent down and picked up a seashell. 'The kids used to love collecting shells when they were little. They're all over the garden. We used to have contests for who could find the biggest one.'

They'd walked southwards from the beach at Padstow, along a wide sandbar, toward the creek that flowed down to Little Petherwick. There was water to their left and to their right but they were safe enough, she reckoned, with the tide still flowing out. The weather was glorious. Warm but with a slight onshore breeze. They'd both removed their shoes and had been paddling along the edges of the water, squeezing the soft, sandy mud between their toes.

'I thought Skye might have come with us.'

She smiled. 'You're joking. Skye doesn't do Saturday mornings, I'm afraid. Not if she can help it, anyway. Besides, I suspect that she thought we might want some time to ourselves.'

She'd been dropping hints; giving him an opening, on the presumption that he had something to tell her. That there was a reason for his visit. But if so, he had made no mention of it, despite her prompting.

He'd put on weight since she'd last seen him, she observed. Not so much as all that but enough so that she had noticed. But that was good, she supposed. He'd always been as skinny as a rake. Now that he wasn't touring as much, making only guest appearances rather than working with his own band, he was probably eating more regularly. As long as he was doing enough exercise to maintain his fitness. She couldn't imagine him being idle.

'It is beautiful out here isn't it?' he said, brightly. 'I don't get down to the sea as much as I'd like. Maybe I should take up fishing again.'

'You? Fishing?' she laughed. She couldn't imagine him fishing. She couldn't imagine him doing anything that didn't involve music and, more particularly, beating seven bells out of a set of drums.

'Well, sure. My dad used to take me and Micky to Tynemouth when we were kids, you know. We used to fish off the beach there. During the summer we'd sometimes camp overnight. Have a fire and all that. Cook whatever we'd caught for supper. Sausages for breakfast in the morning if we were lucky, like.'

'It sounds idyllic.'

She didn't know a great deal about his childhood, she realised. Spencer had been a war baby. She knew that much. And coming from a working class family in the North East of England, they'd have keenly felt the austerity of the time. Yet, on the rare occasions they had discussed his childhood, he'd spoken fondly both of his parents and of the period in general. 'You had a happy childhood, didn't you?'

'Me? Yes, I guess so. They were tough times, you know. We didn't really have a lot. Nobody did, back in those days. But my mum and dad always made the best of it. In spite of the hardships. It's a funny thing. We had nothing but we wanted for nothing.'

Which was in sharp contrast to her own childhood. She'd had everything but nothing that mattered. 'Tell me about your father.'

He paused, staring over toward the hills on the other side of the estuary. 'He was an optimist, my dad,' he said, at last. 'Mum used to say that he was a changed man when he got back from the war.

They'd been childhood sweethearts. Married before he went off to fight. Just in case he didn't come back, I guess. They were just kids. He sure wasn't a kid when he came back.'

'He was a good father, though?'

'He was. Nothing was ever too much trouble for him. That's how I got into music, you know. As soon as he realised that I had a thing for music, he started taking me along to the local colliery band. That's how I got my first trumpet. Somehow he scraped the money together and bought it from one of the band members.'

'I didn't know you played trumpet,' she said, smiling.

He looked at her, sheltering his eyes from the sun with a hand. 'Sure, I did.'

'Do you still play? Do you still have one?'

He grinned. 'I do. The same trumpet in fact. Me and that trumpet go back a long way.'

She stared at him. Unexpectedly, she found her eyes filling with tears.

His smile faded. 'What's wrong?'

She really wasn't sure that she wanted to go there. She wasn't sure that she could explain the way that she was feeling. 'Oh, it's nothing. Come on, let's head back. Maybe we can get a coffee and some breakfast up at the harbour.'

They turned and began the long walk back towards the town.

They walked on in silence. She knew that there was something bothering him and he now knew that there was something bothering her. But it was as though neither of them could speak it. After five minutes, he quite unexpectedly took hold of her hand. It was an unusual and intense gesture. She couldn't remember another time when he had held her hand. Certainly not since she'd been a child. They walked on. Occasionally she glanced at him. He seemed lost in thought.

'There's nothing wrong is there?' she said, suddenly. 'I mean with you?' If he wasn't going to volunteer it then asking him directly was her only option.

'Me? No. I'm fine.'

'You'd tell me, wouldn't you? If there was?'

'Sure, I would.'

'Do you promise? Because if there is, I'd rather know.'

'There's nothing wrong with me. I promise.'

They walked on in silence. After five more minutes, she stopped, quite suddenly and stared at him. 'My mother hated me. I never understood why.'

She saw the pained expression in his face.

'Do you know, I can't actually remember her saying a single loving thing to me. She was completely hateful.'

He blinked. 'I didn't know that.'

'You must have seen it. Surely that is why you came to see me as often as you did. Because my mother hated me and my father was hardly ever there.'

He shook his head. 'No. I never knew that she treated you badly.'

She broke eye contact and stared out towards the sea. How could he not have seen it? Her mother had hidden the excesses, from her father most especially. She had reserved her most hateful behaviour for the occasions when they were alone. But she'd been so unhappy. 'I could never understand why she was so hateful. I still can't. She used to say that I was a disappointment. Was I really such a terrible child?'

'No, of course not. You were a wonderful child. I used to love coming to see you.'

'Why? What was so special about me? Why did you bother?'

He was hesitating. As though there was something that he didn't want to say. 'Oh, I don't know. I had no children of my own and well, you were always so happy to see me. I suppose that you were like the daughter I never had. You still are,' he added, smiling and squeezing her hand.

'I was happy to see you because you were the only adult who ever showed me any love. I used to long for your visits, though I never mentioned it to my mother. I was afraid that she might stop you coming.'

They walked on.

'I have a recurring dream about my childhood, you know.'

'You never told me before.'

She smiled. 'No, I never did.'

'What is the dream?'

'I'm standing by that bloody pool in my swimsuit, or that horrible robe I used to wear. Do you remember it?'

His forehead had creased into a frown. 'I think so.'

'Mother is drunk. She's holding me by the hair and shaking me. Screaming abuse at me. And then I break free and I'm running. I run as fast and as far away from her as I can, with her words ringing in my ears. Into the woods behind the house. Running until I am completely lost. Until I trip and fall. And then I wake up.'

He said nothing.

'I've had that dream for fifty years. Not every night or even every week. Just once in a while. But it's always been exactly the same. Until two weeks ago when it changed. Just like that. For no reason at all.'

'Really? How did it change?'

'I'm running through the woods and suddenly, up ahead, there's somebody there. I slow down and stop. Straining to see. And then she is standing directly in front of me. A little girl with shining blond hair. She holds out her hand and I take it. She leads me out of the woods. We emerge from the trees, into the garden. And when I turn the girl is gone.'

'That's it?'

'That's it. I've dreamt that new ending three or four times in the last two weeks. Why? What the hell's that all about?'

'Who knows with dreams? Are you worrying about something?'

She smiled. 'Well, I have been worrying about you, for one thing. You've been more of a parent to me than either of my own. I'd be absolutely devastated if I lost you.'

'Lost me? Why would you lose me?'

'You're not getting any younger, Uncle Spence.'

He laughed. 'Stop worrying. There are plenty more years left in these old bones.'

'I know that. But when you said that you wanted to come and see me, I thought that you were going to tell me that you had cancer or something.'

He stopped, turned to face her and took hold of both of her hands. 'Ronnie, I don't have cancer.'

'But there is something you're not telling me. I know there is.'

He sighed.

'Tell me. Please.'

He let go of one of her hands. 'Come on, let's walk.'

They walked on.

'One of the reasons I took you under my wing,' he said eventually, 'was that you reminded me of someone.' He paused, as if selecting his words carefully. 'Even as a very small child, you were very much like her.'

'Who was she?'

'I met her when we first came down to London. She was a dancer, at the club in Soho where we first played. I was...' he hesitated, 'very fond of her.'

'You were in love with her?' It surprised her. He'd never mentioned there being anyone in his life. As far as she knew he'd always been single.

He hesitated. 'Yes,' he said simply. 'I guess so.'

She laughed. 'You guess so? Uncle Spence, I think you'd have known if you were.'

He smiled. 'I was young. You fall in love at the drop of a hat at that age. I didn't even really know what love was.'

They walked on.

'What happened to her?'

'She left suddenly. I never saw her again.'

'Why? Where did she go?'

'I don't know. I never found out.'

'Did you look for her?'

'I tried. I searched her flat for a note.' He hesitated. 'But there was nothing.'

'You must have been devastated.'

He smiled but she could see the sadness behind his eyes. 'I made a pig's ear of the whole thing. The band was on the brink of success and I was full of it. Within a few weeks of her leaving, we were jetting off to the States and, well, I just got caught up in everything that followed. And that was that. I never saw or heard from her again.'

This was ringing a bell. She trawled her memory. 'Wait a minute. This is the girl that went missing?' She'd read about it. 'The one that was in the papers? What was her name?'

He sighed again. 'Her name was Gina Lawrence.'

'Gina Lawrence. Yes, that's right. I remember reading about it.'

'There was a lot of stupid talk at the time. You know the papers.'

She did. Being an actress had put her in the public eye, with all the unwanted media attention that went with it. 'But that was all a long time ago. Why is it on your mind? Has something happened?'

'I made a mistake.' He paused. 'Actually, I made a number of them. But the biggest one was that I told a lie. And like most lies do, this one has come back to haunt me.'

'It's come back? What do you mean?'

'A reporter has been sniffing around. Asking questions. Micky is furious.'

Micky Milburn. She had seen him several times at the house, as a child. And once as an adult. He'd come over from the States for some event that her father had organised. She'd been maybe sixteen. 'You don't get along with your brother do you?'

'Not really, no.'

She was searching her memory, trying to recall the detail. 'Wasn't there something about the two of you falling out over her? Is that true?'

'Yes. I've never really forgiven him, to be honest.'

'Why? What did he do? What was the lie that you told?'

They had reached the edge of a sand dune and begun to make their way up its side, toward the sea wall.

He stopped and turned to face her. 'Ronnie, this must go no further. I don't want you getting caught up in this if it hits the newspapers again. You must promise me. Otherwise I can't talk to you about it.'

'Of course I promise. I'd never repeat anything you tell me. You know that.'

He nodded.

They continued climbing the dune. When they reached the top, they both stopped and turned to look out towards the sea. A small flock of seagulls wheeled above them, screeching out their calls. It was the sound she missed most when she was away.

'When Gina Lawrence went missing,' Spencer began, 'Micky lied to the Police. We all did. Micky had spent the night with her and another young woman. They were together in her flat.' He hesitated. 'In her bed, I expect. Micky had a taste for that kind of thing.'

'Oh.' She knew something of the rumours about Micky Milburn.

'He knew that I was fond of her. He did it to get one up on me. He's always been like that, ever since we were kids. I fancied a girl, he'd get her into bed if he possibly could.'

She said nothing.

'The thing is, with Gina it was different. I was crazy about her and I know she felt the same about me.'

Which begged an obvious question. She just wasn't sure that he was going to want to hear it. 'But it was her choice to spend the night with Micky,' she said gently.

He snorted. 'Choice had nothing to do with it. Micky had plied her with so many pills it was a wonder she was still standing. She was completely off her face. He made damn sure of it.'

She said nothing.

'I tried to stop her. I tried to stop them both. But Gina was too far gone. She had no idea what she was doing. When I spoke to her she barely even knew who I was.'

A gust of wind blew sand up into their faces. She held up her hand. When the gust had passed, she brushed the sand from her face and returned her hand to her side. 'Are you saying that Micky deliberately drugged her?'

Spencer nodded.

'To get her into bed?'

He stared at her. Then he nodded again. 'That's exactly what I'm saying. That's exactly how it was. Micky knew what he was doing.'

'You're saying that she would never have consented had he not drugged her?'

He stared at her.

'Because if that is what you're saying then it was rape. You do realise that?'

He looked suddenly confused. 'Well, I don't know about... I mean, it was different in those days...' he stammered.

'Different, how? You're saying that your brother set out to get her into bed by deliberately drugging her.'

He stared at her but said nothing.

'That she would not have gone along with it had she not taken the drugs?'

'That's the thing isn't it?' he said, his bitterness plain. 'I'll never really know what was going on in her head, will I? What she really wanted.'

He was back tracking. 'Well, I'm sorry, Uncle Spencer. But what you've just described is rape. By any measure.'

He said nothing.

'This is what you lied about?'

He faced her. 'I told the police that he was never there. That I knew nothing about it.'

'You covered for him? Why would you do that?'

'Micky is my brother, Ronnie. For all his faults, he's the only brother I have.'

She returned his stare. 'You've just told me that Micky raped the woman you loved. He knew that you loved her. Despite that, he deliberately drugged her to get her into bed. How could he do that and why the hell would you cover for him?' It sounded all the more incredible now that she had voiced it. She shook her head.

'If I'd told the truth. If we'd all told the truth, then...'

'Stop,' she interrupted him. 'Stop right there.' The magnitude of what he was saying was beginning to dawn on her. 'That was the last time that anyone saw her alive?'

'Yes.'

'She disappeared immediately afterwards?'

He nodded. 'The following morning.'

'She has never been found?'

'No.'

She stared at him. 'My God.'

'I should have told the truth. I know it now,' he blurted. 'And do you know the worst thing about it?'

She couldn't easily think of anything worse. She shook her head.

'I didn't really do it out of loyalty to Micky. I'm not going to stand here and pretend to you that I did. I was as angry with her as I was with him.'

She laughed. 'How the hell did you work that one out?'

He looked away. 'I thought she loved me, Ronnie. I was hurting.'

'I get that, Uncle Spence. I do. But to go as far as lying for him. That's what I'm struggling with.'

'We'd just achieved our first Number One. I let them convince me that if news broke that she'd been involved in some pilled up three-in-a-bed thing with Micky and then vanished, we were going to lose it all. That unless I stuck to the story, we'd be finished. It was a completely cowardly and selfish thing to do. Don't think that I don't see that now. But if I'd told the truth…'

'If you'd told the truth,' she interrupted, 'then Micky could have been suspected of a good deal more than her rape.'

'What do you mean?' he said, the colour beginning to drain from his face.

She hesitated. 'For God's sake, Uncle Spence, think about it. Micky drugs and rapes her, after which she vanishes, never to be seen again. Has it really not crossed your mind that he might have been suspected of her murder?'

He stumbled. For a moment, she thought that he was going to collapse. She threw her arms around him. 'It's all right. I've got you,' she soothed. She waited until he felt more steady on his feet. 'Are you all right?' she said, holding him at arms length. 'I'm sorry.'

'There's never been… I never…' he stammered. 'She went missing. I never saw her again. But I… Micky is my brother. He'd never have…' He left the sentence unfinished, his voice fading away.

But something else had dawned on her. 'You let *them* convince you,' she said, staring into his eyes.

He blinked.

'Who did you let convince you? Micky and who else?'

He said nothing.

'It was my father, wasn't it?'

He stared at her. Then he nodded. 'Yes. Your father knew. It was Marty who fabricated the story and who insisted that we stick to it.'

CHAPTER THIRTY

Sunday, 22 May 2016

Marty Phelps had been watching the elderly man who had seated himself on the bench, about a dozen or so metres from his vantage point in front of the cafe overlooking The Serpentine. He was wearing a knee-length rain coat and was holding a folded umbrella. A wise choice, given the weather. It had been overcast all morning and there were ominous, dark grey clouds overhead. He had short grey hair and a stubby grey beard but was otherwise nondescript. It was hard to imagine that forty years previously, not only had this man led a resurgent political party that had threatened the established Westminster order, but that he'd also planned the bombing and overthrow of parliament itself. It was a plot that had, of course, failed, and for which he had served over 25 years in prison. Though now in his mid eighties, the man had walked confidently and unaided to the bench and had taken his seat easily, which was all the more impressive given the privations he must have experienced whilst residing at Her Majesty's pleasure.

Phelps finished his coffee, put the cup and saucer on a nearby table and walked across to the bench, seating himself beside the elderly man without introduction or comment.

'You are aware that we are being watched?' the man said quietly and without shifting his gaze.

'Of course.' Phelps had spotted their watcher from the cafe. A young black man, in jeans and a casual jacket, reading a newspaper on the bench, across the road immediately behind them. He'd been following Owen and had taken his seat behind him. 'I take it that he cannot hear us.'

'Oh, I don't think so. They're vigilant but not as worried about me as they once were. How much trouble can an old man make?'

Phelps smiled. He was thinking about the trouble that the man might make, with a little assistance. 'It might have been easier had we done this over the telephone. Or perhaps by Skype.'

'You might think so. But they are still worried enough about me to occasionally monitor my telephone calls and I am prevented from using the internet as a condition of my licence. Not that I bother with all that. I never really understood computers.'

'Still it must be an inconvenience.'

'Not really. I have my liberty or the vestiges of it. We should be thankful for small mercies, I suppose.'

'I am grateful to you for agreeing to see me so readily,' Phelps said, watching a pair of swans on the lake in front of them. It had been the mention of Elizabeth Stammers that had prompted Owen's interest, as Phelps had anticipated that it would. 'I trust that our meeting has not prompted too many questions.'

'I have already dealt with that. I let it be known that you are an old acquaintance from my university days at Ealing. You managed a band that appeared there in 1966.'

Phelps thought about it. 'The Monks. Of course.'

'We have maintained casual contact over the years. Our relationship has nothing whatever to do with my political activities at the time. They approved, actually. I think they see it as part of my rehabilitation, that I should re-establish contact with old friends. With certain provisos, of course.'

'Of course.'

'Tell me, Mr Phelps, how did you locate me?'

Phelps smiled. 'The recent leak. The press may have been silenced but my office is not entirely without resource.'

'Ah, yes. Former Detective Inspector James. A publicity stunt apparently, for her forthcoming book. I understand that she is promising some interesting revelations though, to be frank, she was a minor player only.'

'Will she be allowed to publish?' Phelps asked, genuinely interested.

'I expect she will manage it. If not here in the UK then elsewhere. There are several administrations around the world that would, I imagine, be happy to facilitate another embarrassment for The Service.'

Phelps nodded. James's revelations would pale into insignificance in comparison with his own, especially with Owen's assistance.

'I must admit that I was intrigued by your communication,' Owen said, after a pause.

'I thought you might be.'

'Tell me, what is your interest in Elizabeth Stammers?'

Phelps chose his words carefully. 'I am having certain difficulties with her son. He is making something of a nuisance of himself. Poking his nose into my affairs. It seemed to me that I might poke my nose into his with a little more vigour than he is expecting.'

Owen smiled. 'Ah yes. Harry Stammers. He seems to have a habit of involving himself in matters that do not concern him. He has inherited that particular trait, I suspect.'

'Indeed,' Phelps said, knowingly.

'And how do you imagine that I might assist you?'

Phelps considered the question. 'While Harry and his mother do not court publicity; indeed they have gone to considerable lengths to prevent it, they nonetheless both enjoy an almost mythical reputation for their selfless defence of national values against overwhelming odds and, in Elizabeth Stammers' case, at great personal sacrifice.'

Phelps had been watching Owen's reaction to his words from the corner of his eye. At his mention of Elizabeth Stammers, Owen had so tightened his grip on the umbrella that his knuckles had whitened. 'I suspect that their motives are a little less noble,' he continued. 'Indeed, it strikes me that this might explain their aversion to further scrutiny. I have reason to suspect that they are not, as they appear happy to have us believe, driven solely by humility and a desire for personal privacy. Putting it frankly, Mr Owen, I have already discovered several skeletons that they might prefer remained in their family cupboard. I was rather hoping that you might be willing to help me amplify them a little. Or rather a lot, actually.'

'And why would I want to do that?'

Phelps glanced at him. 'I would have thought you'd be as keen as I am to see Elizabeth Stammers' reputation take a tumble.'

'That may very well be the case,' Owen countered. 'But unfortunately, that is a pleasure that has long since been denied to me. My position would not allow me to become involved, or indeed to be linked in any way to such an initiative, no matter how noble.'

'Understood. But I am under no such restriction. Armed with the right information, I intend to make their lives considerably less comfortable than they have become. And of course, it may very well be that your reputation might be somewhat enhanced, if not entirely restored of course, were certain matters which have been hidden to the public, to be revealed.'

Owen turned and stared at him. 'How much do you know? And how, exactly, do you know it?'

'I know,' Phelps said carefully, 'that Elizabeth Stammers is a consummate liar. That she lied to her husband and that, to his dying day, he never forgave her for it.'

Owen snorted and looked away. 'Lying was her stock-in-trade. I cannot see how revealing it is likely to damage her.'

Phelps hesitated. 'Let me ask you then, if I may; how much do you know about just how fundamentally she deceived you?'

Owen said nothing.

'Did you know, for example, that Edward Stammers was not Harry's father?'

Owen whipped his head around and stared at him.

Phelps had fixed his eyes on a couple walking along the bank, on the far side of the lake. He waited.

'What are you suggesting?' Owen said, after a pause.

'I am suggesting that Elizabeth Stammers lied to you as fundamentally as anyone could. Or more precisely she withheld from you completely the truth about your son.'

'My son? What are you talking about?'

'You are Harry's father, Mr Owen. She knows it and so does he.'

Owen laughed. 'And how did you discover that little gem?'

He had laughed but there was an edge of doubt in his tone. 'While he was in hospital, suffering from the effects of a stroke and just before he died from the effects of another, Ted Stammers briefly regained the power of speech. He was angry, Mr Owen, and full of bitterness. So angry and bitter that when Harry came to see him he would rant at him about the extent of his wife's deceptions. Sometimes, he became so agitated that he had to be sedated by the nursing staff. On more than one such occasion, the attending nurse overheard him telling Harry that he wasn't his father and that you are.'

'Nonsense. I don't believe it. It can't…'

'I can supply you with a copy of the transcript of our conversations with the nurse, if you wish. She was entirely certain. Perhaps, if you are having difficulty believing it, and I can well understand why you might, I could arrange to have the matter put to the two of them. It would be interesting to hear what they have to say about it, would it not?'

CHAPTER THIRTY-ONE

'I can't believe that Holly isn't here,' Harry said, making no effort at all to mask his irritation. 'Where the hell is she?'

They had seated themselves around the conference table in his office. Mike next to Jane, Ellen opposite them and Harry at the head of the table. They'd left Martha sitting at Jane's desk in the general office, playing Patience on Jane's office PC. Neither the office nor The Park had been busy. It had been pouring with rain since just before midday and most of the park's morning visitors had left early.

'Jane, you spoke to Holly. What did she say?'

'She said that something had come up.'

'That was all?'

'Just about.'

The rain was so heavy that it was hammering against Harry's office window. 'Jesus, it's bucketing down out there.'

'Did she sound all right?' Ellen asked.

Jane shrugged. 'What does all right sound like? She sounded like Holly.'

Harry reached for his cup. 'She drew a blank with the June Lawrence thing?'

Jane nodded. 'June Lawrence is in bed with a heavy cold. They were none too keen to allow another visit until the latter part of next week at the earliest.'

He swallowed a mouthful of coffee. 'Nothing from the adoption contact register, I take it?'

Jane shook her head. 'Nothing. It was always a long shot. It could be months before anything comes of it, if it ever does.'

'Which leaves us where?' Harry said, placing his cup back down on a coaster.

'Nowhere,' Ellen said, shaking her head.

'Not quite nowhere,' Jane said casually.

He knew that she had something up her sleeve. She'd been out of the office most of the day on Friday and tight lipped, when he'd asked on Friday morning, about where she was going. Even Mike had evidently been sworn to secrecy. He caught Ellen's eye and winked. 'So, come on Sherlock, let's have the big reveal.'

Mike sniggered.

The look that Jane gave him was priceless. Harry wanted to shake Mikkel Eglund by the hand.

Jane opened a pocket file she'd bought into the meeting with her, selected two sheets of paper and slid them across the table, one each to Harry and Ellen.

Harry examined the document. 'It's a birth certificate.'

'Sheer genius,' Jane said, acidly. 'And?'

'And it confirms that Ronnie's real name is Veronica. But we knew that already. You only have to google her to discover it.'

'What else?'

He looked again at the document. 'It gives Marty and Barbara Phelps as Veronica's birth parents. Nothing particularly unusual about that either. Birth certificates are amended when a child is adopted. That's right isn't it?' He looked at Jane and Ellen, each in turn, for confirmation.

'Not quite,' Jane answered him. 'When a child is born, they are registered in their original name, with both their parents recorded on the birth register. If the child is adopted an entry is made in the adopted children register and a new birth certificate is issued. But the original entry remains, usually with the word "adopted" added.'

Harry looked at Ellen, who shrugged.

'Anyone can search the adopted children register,' Jane continued. 'Although to get a certified copy of an entry you have to apply to the General Register Office, rather than a local office. But in Veronica's case, that wasn't necessary.'

'I'm not with you,' Harry said, now thoroughly confused. 'Why wasn't it necessary?'

'Because there is no entry for a child called "Veronica" or "Ronnie Phelps" in the adopted children register. Not on any day in 1962. Nor, as a matter of fact, in '61 or '63. The certificate you have in front of you is from the birth register. There is no mention or record of any adoption.'

Harry could see where she was going.

'How did you get it so quickly? I thought you had to order them,' Ellen challenged.

'True. And I have one on order. I got the copy you have in front of you online from an ancestry website. She's a celebrity. Plenty of people have researched the Phelps family tree. As Harry says, google it and up she pops.'

'Genius,' Harry said, mimicking her.

Jane folded her arms and stared at him. 'Tell me something I don't already know.'

He ignored her. 'So, you're saying that Ronnie Phelps wasn't adopted?'

'No. I'm not saying it. The register of adopted children is saying it. Ronnie Phelps was not adopted. Fact. Had she been, there'd have been an entry in the register. So far as the registers are concerned, Marty and Barbara Phelps are her natural parents.'

He was trying to work out what that meant.

'While we are on the subject of registers,' Jane continued, 'neither have I been able to find any entry for anyone named Gina Lawrence giving birth to any child on 8 February, 1962, nor in fact to the birth of any female child with the surname Lawrence on that date. It's a work in progress but there doesn't seem to be any evidence that Gina Lawrence ever gave birth to a child.'

'So maybe she didn't. Maybe we've got the whole thing wrong,' Ellen said, looking gloomy.

'I don't think so. But before we get to that, there is one other significant detail on the certificate.'

He'd been thinking and at her prompting, looked at the certificate again.

'The place of Ronnie's birth is given as Great Gaddesden,' Jane continued. There was and still is no hospital in Great Gaddesden. So assuming it's correct, she was almost certainly born at home at the Phelps' house.'

'Hang on,' Harry broke in, 'if that is right then Gina must have been staying at the Phelps' house while she was pregnant and gave birth there.'

'Correct. Give that man a medal.'

'In which case it must have been arranged,' Harry said, now thinking out loud. 'Gina didn't go to stay with friends to conceal her pregnancy and give birth, she went to stay with the Marty and Barbara Phelps.'

'Also correct.'

'Yet they didn't adopt the child.'

'No they didn't.'

He stared at her. 'Are you suggesting that they adopted the child unlawfully?'

Jane stared at him, then reached into the pocket file and passed them another sheet of paper.

It was a photocopy of a newspaper article. Harry noted the date and name. 'What's this got to do with it? Who is Gerald Phipps?'

'Marty's original name is Gerald Martin Phipps. He dropped the name Gerald and changed his surname to Phelps on his release from prison in 1953. He'd served 21 months for gross indecency with a minor. She was 14 years old. He was 21. Presumably, he wanted to avoid the conviction following him around like a bad smell.'

Mike grinned. 'Yup, you guessed it. Phelps is a paedo.'

'Mike for God's sake,' Ellen scolded him.

Harry suppressed a smile. He just loved Mikkel Eglund. Always had. Always would.

'Well, technically of course, Mike is right,' Jane said, unusually coming to her husband's defence. 'But the important point here is not so much the conviction itself as its effect. There were rather fewer offences in 1962 than there are today that barred you from adopting a child. But gross indecency with a child was one of them. It is possible that Marty Phelps didn't adopt Veronica lawfully because he couldn't adopt her lawfully. His conviction would have prevented it.'

There was silence in the room.

'I won't even ask how you managed to find this,' Harry said at last, still holding the article in his hand. He had to hand it to her. Jane was incredible.

'She has been at it all week,' Mike said. 'All night. Every night. And unfortunately not with me.'

'Not every night,' Jane said, blushing.

She was actually blushing. Harry didn't think he'd ever seen Jane Eglund blush. He was going to remember this moment for a very long time. 'Is that it? Or do you have something else up your sleeve?'

Jane grinned at him. Or possibly she was baring her teeth. Either way, it was disconcerting.

'Since you ask, there is another possibility.'

They all stared at her.

Jane hesitated.

Harry rolled his eyes. 'What are you waiting for, a drum roll?'

'Fuck off.'

'Ah, that's better. The Jane Eglund we know and love.'

'Do you want to hear this or not?'

'I want to hear it,' Harry admitted. He did.

'Good. Then shut up and listen.'

Harry held up his hands in mock surrender.

'Gina Lawrence was born on August 5th, 1945, right?'

He guessed so. He couldn't remember whether they'd already established it. 'Right.'

'She's on the index of adopted children register and, as Gina Bettis, on the birth register. Bettis was her mother's maiden name.'

Which he didn't already know. He glanced at Ellen who looked like she didn't know it either.

'Ronnie was born on February 8th, 1962.'

They all knew that. 'So?'

'So if the pregnancy ran full term, then Ronnie was conceived in May 1961, when Gina would have been fifteen. It looks like she had the baby at the Phelps' house and gave the baby to Mr and Mrs Phelps who entered into a private arrangement with Gina and passed baby Veronica off as their own.'

'I'm with you so far.' But he was still thinking.

'Good. So why Phelps and why Gina? What was the relationship between them?'

'Relationship?' He stared at her.

'Think about it, Harry.'

'Wait a minute,' he said, suddenly. 'Are you suggesting that Marty was actually the father? I mean, the biological father?'

Jane looked entirely pleased with herself. 'Well, why not? Perhaps Phelps has more than a passing penchant for underage girls.'

Mike sat back in his seat and folded his arms. 'What did I tell you?'

Jane glowered at him.

There was silence in the room, which once again, Harry broke. 'But if that's right,' he said, carefully, 'then this really starts to stack up. Particularly if Gina Lawrence did start making noises about wanting Veronica back and let's say was threatening to go for custody. That would have given Marty Phelps more than a sufficient motive for wanting her silenced permanently.'

'Or at very least,' Jane added, 'to conceal her death if, as Holly suspects, Micky Milburn did the actual deed. One thing's for sure. It means that Phelps would not have wanted the authorities poking their noses into Gina's or his own personal affairs.'

Harry nodded his agreement. 'He could have lost his daughter, been prosecuted for falsifying her birth records and, to cap it all, have faced a second charge of gross indecency with a minor and ended up back inside.' He reached for his cup and drained it, wincing slightly as the lukewarm coffee went down.

Ellen had been examining both the documents Jane had passed her. 'The trouble with all this is that we still haven't actually established that she died.'

'Not with certainty, no,' Jane agreed. 'But if Phelps was the father then it makes her death much more likely.'

Ellen stared at her. 'Why?'

'If Gina was alive, then she must have left either of her own volition or as a result of Phelps paying her off and sending her away as he did with Lynette Bell. You said yourself, Ellen, that if that had been the case then she'd have taken the photograph of Veronica and the other items she'd hidden under the floor with her. I'm sure you're right. If you also factor in his motive, and if she'd just been subjected to God knows what by Micky Milburn, would Phelps have been sufficiently confident in Gina to just pay her off and send her away?'

Harry shook his head. 'I doubt it.'

'So do I. She could have changed her mind, at any time, and gone to the authorities about both of them.'

'So could Lynette Bell,' Ellen challenged. 'Yet Phelps was confident enough in Bell to pay her off.'

'That's as maybe but far as we know Bell had nothing tying her to Phelps or to her former life in London. Gina certainly did. Gina had Veronica. Or more to the point, she didn't have her. Phelps did.'

Ellen nodded. 'True.'

'All of which suggests that she died in her room that night. Until now we've assumed that could either have been as a result of an overdose of drugs and alcohol, or that Micky's tendency to violent sex went too far.'

'Or a combination of the two,' Harry added.

'Indeed,' Jane agreed. 'And that could be right. But Phelps' motive presents a third possibility. That, whether by design or chance, Marty Phelps entered the room and killed her. He could have accused or implicated Milburn and Bell, and used it to intimidate Lynette Bell into agreeing to exile in Scotland. Maybe it was the guilt that she felt and the possibility that we might expose her supposed part in Gina's death, that ultimately led her to take her own life.'

They were silent again.

'The difficulty is going to be proving it,' Jane continued after a pause. 'If I'm right, there were four people in that room. Neither Marty Phelps or Micky Milburn are going to admit it, and Gina and Lynette are in no position to tell us.'

She was right. While she had been speaking, Harry's thoughts had turned to Ronnie Phelps. Both he and Martha had imagined her, not as an adult but as a young child. There was something significant about that. There had to be. It had been niggling away at the back of his mind.

This time it was Ellen who broke the silence. 'What about Spencer Milburn?'

Harry looked at her and held her gaze.

'He might not have been in the room but he was there at The Scene Club that night,' she continued. 'He must have known more than he let on.'

Harry tilted his head to one side. 'If he does, he's never given it away.'

Ellen was thinking. He could see it written in big letters across her face. 'The relationship between Micky and Spencer never really recovered did it?' she said at last. 'By all accounts, it so soured it that within a few years the band had split and the two brothers had gone their separate ways. Spencer must have blamed his brother, at least in part.'

Harry couldn't disagree with that analysis. 'Spencer Milburn stayed with the Phelps stable, you know. Micky didn't but Spencer did. He may very well still be with Phelps.'

'Which all feels a bit odd, doesn't it?' Ellen said, still holding his gaze. 'According to Lynette Bell, it was Phelps who was adamant that they cover up the fact that Micky had spent the night in Gina's room. And yet Spencer stayed loyal to both his brother and to Marty Phelps. Why?'

Harry heard a sound from behind him. He turned.

Jane evidently hadn't noticed. 'Hang on a minute. I'm sure I saw a picture somewhere of Spencer Milburn and Ronnie Phelps together. At her wedding or something?'

Ellen stifled a cough. 'Really?'

But Harry was only half listening. Martha was standing in the doorway.

'Just a minute, I'll try to find it...' Jane continued.

He stood up, scraping his chair backwards. 'Hello, Love. Are you all right?'

They all turned. Except Jane who was tapping away on her smartphone.

'Yes. I got tired of the card game. I wanted to know what you were all talking about.'

Harry smiled. 'Come on in then,' he said, approaching her and taking hold of her hand. He led her back to the table.

Ellen gestured for her to sit. Martha walked around the table and sat beside her on the chair that would have been occupied by Holly.

'Got it,' Jane announced suddenly. 'Look, there they are at Ronnie's wedding.' She held out her phone to Ellen who took it, examined the picture and then passed it to Harry. Spencer Milburn was standing next to the newly married couple. 'Yup. That's definitely Spencer Milburn.' He was trying to think about the implications as he handed the phone back to Jane.

'Have you been talking the whole time about Gina and Ronnie?' Martha asked.

'Yes, Love,' Harry replied. 'Pretty much.'

'Shit,' Jane said suddenly. She looked up. 'Oh Sorry,' she said, acknowledging Martha's presence for the first time.

There was an awkward silence.

It was Mike who offered a solution. 'Come on Martha. How about you and I go and make us all a drink?'

'I'd rather stay here,' Martha replied like she meant it.

Ellen caught Harry's eye.

'I am big enough, you know. I am ten years old. I'm not a child.'

He suppressed a smile. Mike was openly grinning and even Ellen was struggling to mask her amusement. 'Go ahead Jane,' Harry said in answer to Ellen's silent question.

'I can't believe I missed this,' Jane said, shaking her head.

They waited.

'Spencer didn't just maintain a relationship with Marty Phelps. He built one with Ronnie. The two of them are described here as "close friends". Apparently he's the godparent to both her children.'

Harry was thinking about the implications of that too. But it was Ellen who voiced them.

'He knows.'

Jane said nothing.

'I mean, that Ronnie is Gina's daughter. Why else would he have built and maintained the relationship?'

'Why else, indeed?' Jane agreed. 'It is, of course, possible that Ronnie knows too.'

Harry glanced at them each in turn. Something was telling him that while Spencer might know, Ronnie almost certainly didn't. He was about to say so when Martha broke in.

'I think Ronnie is in a muddle and…' she hesitated.

They all stared at her.

'Go on,' Ellen said, nodding her encouragement. 'What else do you think, Martha?'

'I think,' Martha said, carefully, 'that she has been all muddled up for a very, very long time. Since she was a little girl. Smaller than me. Like when we see her.'

Martha had turned towards him, as if seeking his confirmation. Harry felt the hair on the back of his neck prickle. 'Like she is stuck?' he said quietly, facing his daughter, but feeling their eyes on him. 'Like something happened when she was little. Something that she couldn't deal with. That she still hasn't dealt with.'

Martha nodded. 'It makes me sad. We should help her. That's what she wants. That's why she comes to see us.'

It was a child's view. He'd never be able to truly accept that Ronnie Phelps had somehow been sending them telepathic messages. That was gobbledegook and it was always going to be gobbledegook. But, incredibly, he and Martha had come to the same view. 'I think you're right, Love. I think finding Ronnie; the real Ronnie Phelps, is really what this is all about, don't you?'

Martha nodded again.

There was silence in the room.

It was Jane who broke it. 'You know Martha, when it comes to understanding the important things in life, like feelings, us girls are usually right, aren't we?'

Martha nodded, archly. 'Boys are like dogs. They run around, barking their heads off all day.'

'Amen to that,' Jane said, grinning.

'But girls are like cats. Cats know what you're feeling. They just sit there and look at you and they know. Everything. That's why cats are my favourite animal.'

When they had all finished laughing, Jane summed up what Harry had been thinking. 'Perhaps it is time,' she said to them all, 'that we made contact with Ronnie Phelps.'

CHAPTER THIRTY-TWO

He'd turned in early. They'd had an enjoyable enough day on the face of it, the highlight of which had been supper together. Ronnie and Skye had spent hours in the kitchen preparing it. But as much as he had enjoyed both the meal and their company, their conversation on the beach and the burden of the knowledge that he was carrying had become almost intolerable. In the end, he had made his excuses and had retreated to the sanctuary of the bedroom. Away from them, he had time to think. The trouble was that the more he thought about it, the more afraid he had become of Ronnie's likely reaction were he to take further the conversation that they'd begun on the beach but had since both been studiously avoiding.

He was laying on his back on the double bed, watching a moth, fluttering back and forth, confused by the light from the lamp on the wall above his head.

It had been one thing while she was a child. Then, it had been easy enough to justify both his inaction and his complicity in covering up the circumstances surrounding her mother's disappearance. Ronnie had, or so he had believed, enjoyed a stable and happy childhood. Even that, he now knew, had been an illusion. There had been many times, into her adulthood, when he had considered telling her, but the more their relationship had deepened, the more fearful he had become of her reaction. With the exception of Micky, Ronnie and her children were the closest thing he had to a family and he loved them like they were his own.

He turned and faced the window. He had left it ajar and the curtains open, so that he could hear the sound of the sea. He felt the cool brush of the sea breeze on his face.

Their conversation on the beach had presented him with the opportunity that, by coming to Cornwall, he had hoped to engineer. But it had taken a turn that he had not engineered, nor been expecting. Not only had she been appalled that he had lied about events and the actions of his brother, but she had named the demon that he had been holding at bay for fifty years. While he had blamed Micky for Gina's disappearance and on occasion, thoughts had crept into his mind about the events in her room that night, he had never been willing or able to contemplate the possibility that Micky might have killed her. Even now, with the demon named and the door to his thoughts thrown wide open, he was unable to truly face that possibility. Micky was capable of many things, but not that. They were brothers. Not even Micky was capable of that.

But as much as he could deny the possibility, she was thinking it. She was blaming them all and rightly so. However he might attempt to justify it now, he had, by his silence, lied. Not only about Gina's disappearance and the actions of his brother, which were despicable at the very least. But more particularly he had lied to her. That was the truth of it. Since the day he had first clapped eyes on her. Just as Marty and Barbara Phelps had lied to her. And that was by no means the worst of it. He hadn't simply withheld the truth from her. He had actively conspired, with her father, to conceal the rape and loss of her mother. It was unforgivable and he had little doubt now that were she to discover it, she would indeed never forgive him. If he told her now, she would see him for the selfish liar that he was. That he had always been. His only hope, he realised with a sinking knot of disgust taking up residence in the pit of his stomach, was to continue the pretence. He had already shared too much. Now, his only hope, if she ever discovered that

Gina Lawrence was her mother, would be to tell her that he didn't know. That he had never had reason to even suspect it.

The moth, unable to resist the allure of the light bulb, finally made contact, fizzed and fell on to pillow beside his face. He shivered and flicked the moth away onto the floor with his hand, the acrid smell of burning moth wings in his nostrils. Then he reached out for the switch beside his bed and turned off the light. But, for Spencer Milburn, sleep was a long time coming.

CHAPTER THIRTY-THREE

Who the hell was playing music? Where the hell was he? He hauled his eyes open, recognised The Jam's '*Girl on The Phone*' as his ring tone and reached for his smartphone, still only half awake. 'Hello?' he croaked, his voice hoarse.

'Harry?'

'Lizzie?' He scanned the room, his eyes focussing on the digital clock beside his bed.

'Harry? Is that you?'

The voice sounded like his mother's. But there was an edge to it that he hardly recognised.

'Who is it?' Ellen mumbled, coming awake beside him.

'Of course it's me.' He turned to Ellen 'It's Lizzie,' he mouthed, silently. 'Are you all right? Is something wrong?' It was obvious that there was. Even half awake, he could tell.

'He knows. I'm so sorry. Don't ask me how, but he knows.'

He was trying to pull his scattered thoughts into some sort of order. 'Who knows what?'

Ellen sat bolt upright and stared at him.

'I don't know how. But he knows, Harry. I know it's him.'

She was struggling to contain her emotions. He could hear it in her tone. 'Lizzie, slow down,' he said, trying to keep his voice level. 'Just tell me what's happened.'

'It was on the door mat when I got up.'

'What was on the door mat?' He caught Ellen's eyes and held them.

'A letter, Harry. And there's no stamp, so it was delivered by hand. Which means that he knows where I am.'

There was only one man alive who could have the effect that this letter had obviously had on his mother. He took a breath. 'What does it say?'

She hesitated. 'I don't know. I haven't opened it.'

He pulled back the duvet, pivoted and clambered to his feet. 'Then how…?'

'Because of the name on the envelope.'

'The name?' He glanced back at Ellen.

'It's addressed to you Harry. It's addressed to Harry Owen.'

He was holding the letter in his hand. A plain white envelope. The name and address in type. No stamp, as Lizzie had said. He had thrown on some clothes and jumped in the car, straight after her telephone call, leaving Martha with Ellen. 'This was on the mat when you got up this morning?'

Lizzie was ashen faced. She nodded. 'About twenty minutes before I called you. I don't know how long it had been there.'

They were sitting in her lounge, Lizzie still wearing a dressing gown, both of them staring at the letter in his hand.

'Why didn't you open it?'

'I couldn't.'

He glanced up at her.

'I just couldn't.'

He nodded his understanding. 'There was no sign of anyone outside?'

She shook her head.

He inserted a finger and tore open the envelope. Inside was a single sheet of paper. He opened it. Printed on the sheet of paper was a mobile telephone number and the text "Call me at 10am". He looked at his watch. He held out the sheet of paper.

She stared at him and then took it.

He waited.

'What are you going to do?' she asked, without raising her eyes from the letter.

'I haven't the faintest idea. We've got two hours and fifteen minutes to decide.'

She said nothing.

'What do you think I should do?'

She looked up at him. 'I don't know. I need time to think.'

'Have you spoken to Millbank?'

'No.'

'Don't you think you should?'

'I don't know, Harry,' she blurted. 'I just don't know what to do.'

They were silent.

'I know you think it is from him,' Harry said at last, 'but we don't know that. It could be from anyone.'

'I'm sorry but when I saw that name, I just panicked.'

'It's okay.' He gave her what he hoped was a reassuring smile.

'I won't speak to him, Harry. I can't.' She shook her head vehemently.

'You won't have to. The letter is addressed to me. It's me they're expecting to dial that number.'

She stared at him but said nothing.

'The question is, who's behind this and what do they want?'

'And how do they know?'

'Perhaps they don't. Perhaps it's just a fishing exercise.' It was a possibility. If he made the call, he might confirm their guess work. But if he didn't...

'If you don't make the call, he won't leave it there,' she said, finishing the thought for him. 'Believe me. I know him. I know what he is capable of.'

He said nothing.

'I always feared that he would try to contact me. Ever since the day that I learned of his release. But I never thought that he would discover this. I'm so sorry, Harry.'

'Sorry? What have you got to be sorry for?'

She smiled but there was no joy in it. 'You need to ask?'

'We settled this a long time ago. You did what you did. It is in the past.'

'Is it?' she said, almost in a whisper. 'It is with me, every day. The things I did. The lies I told. The people I hurt.'

He started to speak.

'Please don't tell me that I did it for your benefit,' she interrupted him. 'Or that I had no choice. We always have a choice.'

He bowed his head. 'You know what?' he said, looking up at her. 'I don't care what you did.'

She stared at him, her eyes brimming with tears.

'It makes not the slightest difference to me. You're my mother. I have you in my life, thank God. We have you in our lives. What you did, all those years ago? The choices you made? I don't care. Who am I to judge? I've made some pretty shitty choices in my life too, you know. People have suffered. My responsibility. Just the same as you. Just the same as everyone. I can't change any of it and neither can you. I live with my mistakes, just as you live with yours.'

He got up, walked across to her, sat beside her and put an arm around her shoulders. 'I don't care what you did, Mum.' He rarely used that word. It still seemed alien to him somehow. He'd spent so many years without her. 'I love you. Ellen and Martha love you. We couldn't love you any more than we do. None of it matters to us.'

'But he's your father…'

'No. He isn't. My father is gone. Like you and me, Ted made his choices. He lived and sadly for him; sadly for all of us, died with them. Perhaps he should have chosen differently. If he'd taken us into hiding with you; if we'd started a new life together, things would have been different. Who knows whether they would have been better or worse? I don't. I'm not going to judge him. He was my dad. He did his best.'

'But you have another father.'

He shook his head. 'No. I really don't. Owen is part of your story, not mine. I don't know what he hopes to achieve by this, if he is behind it,' he said, holding out the letter, 'but I have nothing to say to him. My only interest in this is you. I will not let him hurt you, Lizzie.'

'He's had good reason to want to hurt me, all these years. If he now knows that he is your father and that I have kept that from him, he will have a good deal more.'

'Maybe, but I don't really see where he wants to go with this.'

'Don't you?'

He stared at her.

'Hatred, Harry. He will want to hurt me. In any way he can and simply for the sake of it.'

Harry ran his free hand through his hair. 'And if he isn't behind it?'

'Who else could be?'

'I don't know. A journalist, fishing for a story?'

'Then they will almost certainly have approached him and he will know about you. If so, there will be a great deal of detail that he could put into the public domain. He will manipulate the story so that he is cast in the best possible light and me in the worst. He will want, not simply to paint me as the callous liar that I was, the woman who lied to her husband and to her children and then abandoned them to their fate, but to destroy my reputation entirely. Make me the public pariah that I deserve to be.'

He shook his head. 'Stop it. You don't deserve anything of the sort. By foiling Owen's plot, you saved the lives of countless people and the country from a fascist coup, for God's sake. You're a national bloody heroine, if only people knew it. He can say what he likes. People will never believe him.'

'Won't they? Who is going to tell them any different? I have never spoken in public about any of it and I don't intend to start now. I live here, quietly and away from the public eye, trying to do right by my family,' she said, reaching out and taking hold of his hand. 'I will not justify myself to him, nor to anyone else but you and Ellen. I will not be made to go through it all over again. I couldn't.'

He feared that she was right. She had been reasonably stable, these last few years, suffering only from occasional bouts of depression. But her obsession with Peter Owen, the events leading to her self-imposed exile in the New Forest and the trauma of her rescue had left their mark. Beneath the thin shell of normality that she had managed to construct, was a fragile and uncertain soul. He'd always had the sense that it would take very little to tip her over the edge. 'Whatever this means, whatever it brings, we will face it together. You ceased to be alone the day we welcomed you back into our lives. That's what family means. There is nothing that Owen could reveal that would alter that.'

'I know,' she said, tears now streaming down her cheeks. 'I am so blessed to have you all. But I'm afraid. You don't understand what he did to me. I don't think anyone ever could truly understand it,' she said, letting go of his hand, to wipe her eyes on the cuff of her dressing gown.

'Here,' he said, producing a tissue from his pocket. 'It is in the past and that is where it is going to stay, if I have anything to do with it.' He looked at his watch. 'Now, I'm going to call Ellen. She'll be worried sick. Then I'm going to dial the number and we will deal with this. Together.'

CHAPTER THIRTY-FOUR

He was packing his bag. She was watching him from the doorway, lining up his clothes on the bed and folding them neatly before putting them into the battered overnight suitcase. 'What time is your train?'

He glanced at her over his shoulder. '10.05.'

'You're sure you don't want to stay longer? You can, you know. As long as you like.'

'I know and thank you. But I really should be getting back. I'm guesting at a gig on Thursday. I said that I would be available for rehearsals tomorrow or on Wednesday.'

She knew that he was making excuses. There had been an awkwardness between them since their conversation on the beach. It had saddened her, but his revelations about the missing woman and the involvement of her father had shocked her and she had needed some space. Maybe he did too. Still, she didn't want him to leave on a sour note. 'I'm sorry. I over-reacted on Saturday,' she said, choosing her words carefully. 'You do know that I don't think any less of you? If anything comes of it in the papers, I'll be here for you Uncle Spence. I'll always be here for you.'

He stopped and straightened. 'It was a long time ago, Ronnie,' he said, turning towards her. 'Fifty years long. What we did, Micky, your father and I, was wrong. We should have told the truth. We made the wrong decision.'

She felt a stab of sympathy for him. Who hadn't made a decision in their lives that they now regretted?

'You were right about what Micky did,' he continued. 'At the time, I guess I was thinking about it from my own, selfish perspective. I was incredibly hurt. And angry, too. When she went, I blamed them both but especially Micky. He'd taken her from me. I was determined that he wasn't going to take the rest. I allowed that to become my be-all and end-all. That was my mistake.'

She nodded.

'You were also right that I should have been thinking about Gina. Seen it for what it was. However you look at it, it was rape. They might have been different times and we were just kids. But rape is what it was. I should have seen it that way from the outset. I will always regret that I didn't.'

She walked across the room and hugged him. His embrace was awkward at first but then she felt him relax.

'I'm sorry. I shouldn't have burdened you with all of this,' he said when they had finally released each other.

'Yes, you should. You can't deal with this on your own. You mustn't. Everybody makes mistakes, Uncle Spence. For most people, those mistakes don't get paraded in public but, as far as the media is concerned, fame makes us fair game, doesn't it?'

He nodded. 'You can say that again. I just didn't want you reading about it in the papers. If it all takes off again, you know?'

She frowned. 'Do you think it will?'

'I think it might. Micky just won't leave it alone.'

'What do you mean?'

'I mean that he's going after the reporter, big time. The more noise he makes, the more determined she becomes. No smoke without fire, you know? I've tried to tell him to back off but he is having none of it.'

She hesitated. She wasn't sure that she wanted to re-open the issue that had been on her mind, more than any other. But she spoke it anyway. She couldn't help herself. 'What about my father?' she said, gently.

He sighed, turned and sat down on the edge of the bed.

He looked weary and older, somehow. She waited.

'Are you sure you want to hear this? It's not good,' he said, looking up at her.

She stared at him and then nodded.

'I haven't spoken to your father about it. Not for many years, actually. But there was an incident up in Scotland. The reporter managed to get hold of a witness called Lynette Bell. I barely remember her, to be perfectly honest, but she was the other girl in the room with Micky and Gina that night. I don't know what she said to the reporter but if she told the truth, she might very well have implicated your father.'

She felt her stomach flip. 'Implicated him? You mean that she might have told this reporter that he knew about Micky being with Gina Lawrence the night she went missing?'

He nodded. 'And that's not all. I had absolutely no idea about it at the time. In fact, I only found out from Micky, a few days ago. But after Gina went missing, your father paid Lynette Bell to leave.'

She wasn't entirely sure that she knew what he meant. 'He did what?'

'According to Micky, Marty thought that she might talk to the press. So he gave her some money and set her up with a place in Scotland. Micky says that she went voluntarily. As far as we knew at the time, she had simply decided to move away. But apparently, it was your father who had paid her to go. He wanted her out of the way.'

She sat down on the bed beside him. 'He paid her off?'

Spencer nodded. 'That's about the size of it.'

'Dear God, what a mess.'

'It gets worse.'

She stared at him.

'Much worse, Ronnie.'

'Tell me.'

He took hold of her hand. 'After the reporter left, Lynette Bell committed suicide.'

She gasped and pulled her hand away. 'What?'

'She was found, hanging in her living room.'

'Oh, My God.'

Spencer said nothing.

'Why? Why would she have done that?'

'Who knows? She was with Gina and Micky that night. God knows what they got up to. It upsets me, even now, to think about it. But whatever happened led Gina to pack a bag and leave and, a few days later, Lynette Bell to accept your father's offer and move to Scotland. Maybe the prospect of having it splashed all over the newspapers again was too much for her.'

She thought about it. 'Do you know what, if anything, she told the reporter?'

He shook his head. 'Not yet, but I guess that it's only a matter of time before I find out.'

'Have the police spoken to my father?'

'I don't know.'

'Have they spoken to you?'

He shook his head.

'When did this happen?'

'Two weeks ago.'

'God Almighty. What are you going to do?'

'I'm going to have it out with Micky. If I have to fly out to Florida to see him, I will. This has gone on too long. I've been lying, Ronnie. For fifty years. I need to know what I've been lying about. I need to hear it from him.'

'And then what?'

He hesitated. 'I don't know. I guess I'll have to decide whether I'm prepared to go on lying.'

'You'll have the same dilemma. Carry on lying and you'll be covering up a rape. Tell the truth and you could all be in difficulty. Micky, you and my father.'

He smiled. But there was only bitterness in it. 'Well, exactly. But at least I'll know why. I need to know what happened. I need to know why Gina left.'

She wanted to say "if she left" but she didn't. She couldn't say it to him again. 'Be careful. I know I said what I said, and I'm sorry…'

'You really don't need to apologise.'

'Yes, I do. I was too quick to judge. Nothing is ever that simple.'

'This certainly isn't simple.'

'Be careful, Uncle Spencer. Go easy on yourself. I'm worried about you.'

He stood up. 'I'll deal with it. I don't really have any choice. Now we'd best be going. Or I'll miss my train.'

They hugged each other again and then made their way downstairs. He found his coat, while she collected her keys from a hook on the kitchen wall. As they were leaving, the telephone in the hall rang. She glanced at him.

He looked at his watch. 'Go on, we've got twenty five minutes.'

She walked across the hall to the phone and picked up the handset. 'Hello? Brian?'

She met Spencer Milbrun's eyes. 'It's my agent,' she mouthed. 'What? Who the hell is Jane Eglund?' She listened. 'She can't be serious?' She listened again. 'Look, I've got to go, I'm dropping someone off at the station. Email it to me would you? I'll look at it when I get back. All right. Thanks.' She put the phone back on its cradle.

'Is everything all right?'

She stared at him. She was trying to process two sets of thoughts at once and getting nowhere.

'Ronnie?'

On top of which, he had a train to catch. 'It's nothing,' she said, doing her best to focus on the here and now. 'Just some crank email. Fans, eh? Can't live with them. Can't make a living without them.' She reached for her coat. 'Its fine. Come on. Let's get going. God, what a crazy day.'

CHAPTER THIRTY-FIVE

Harry had his mobile phone in his hand. He was gazing from the kitchen window into the garden where, a few days earlier, Lizzie had been pushing Martha on the swing. He was thinking about the call he was about to make. Ellen had agreed that he should make it. Lizzie too. The note, they had all agreed, had been sent for a reason. It was undoubtedly in their interest to discover it now, rather than to provoke the sender to make another move, whatever it might be. He checked his watch. In the absence of any clear indication of the writer's motive, it was impossible to anticipate the conversation. There was nothing for it. He dialled the number. The call was answered within three ring tones.

'Mr Stammers, I assume.'

It was an older male voice. Well spoken. No identifiable accent. Not a voice that he recognised. 'Who are you? What do you want?'

'My name, unlike yours, is unimportant.'

Unlike yours. The implication was clear and obviously intended.

'It is an honour to speak with you, Harry. It is acceptable that I call you Harry? I have learned so much about you and your family, it is as though I already know you all.'

Harry tried to keep his tone neutral. 'I said, what do you want?'

'Yes, let's get straight to the point, shall we? You have been poking your nose into affairs which do not concern you.'

'What affairs? What are you talking about?'

'Oh, come now, Harry. You know exactly what I am talking about. Let us not play games. You, Miss Holgate and your merry little band of amateur investigators have made quite a nuisance of yourselves. It has not gone unnoticed. Did you really think that it would?'

It had occurred to him, vaguely, that the two might be linked, but the lack of any obvious connection had led him to all but discount the possibility. He was struggling now to make a connection. 'What I do with my time is my business,' he said, somewhat lamely and playing for time.

'Ah, yes. Your business. You see, this is where you and I apparently differ. The way I see it is that a man's affairs are a private matter. Not something that any of us would, I imagine, wish to have splashed all over the media, exposed, as they would be, to the vagaries of public opinion.'

The connection meant that he was evidently talking to someone whose primary interest was the Gina Lawrence story rather than Peter Owen. It was unlikely to be either of the Milburn brothers. There was no trace of any accent, either Geordie or American. Which made it more likely that he was talking to Marty Phelps. But if so, then what was Phelps' interest in Peter Owen?

'I value my privacy, Harry, and I assure you that I have the utmost respect for yours. Which is why I find your actions so perplexing. You and Miss Holgate do seem rather determined to interfere in the affairs of others, without any regard to their privacy and the damage that you do in the process. I am thinking of poor Lynette Bell, for example. A harmless and obviously vulnerable woman who, until just a few weeks ago, was living peacefully in The Highlands of Scotland but who, thanks to your entirely unwarranted and thoughtless intervention, now lies on a mortuary slab.'

Whoever he was, he was obviously well informed. Lynette Bell's suicide had not, so far as Harry was aware, attracted any particular media attention, at least this side of the border. 'That was none of my doing,' he said, still playing for time.

'Really. Do you think that she would be dead now, had Miss Holgate, your wife, and I gather one of your staff, not crashed headlong into her private affairs, without any regard to the impact that it might have on the poor woman?'

Trying to second guess the speaker's motive was getting him nowhere. 'Look, what's your point?'

'My point is that when one interferes in the private affairs of others, there are consequences for the individuals concerned. I, for example, am in possession of a good deal of information concerning you and your mother, which I imagine neither of you would wish to find its way into the public domain. The identity of your father, for example, and the circumstances surrounding your birth. As a matter of fact, I have the major part of your mother's life story, which I must say, rather contradicts the accounts we have of her in the public record. Indeed, I have a team of people working, right now, on filling in the blanks. It is already a most intriguing story and one which would be read avidly, I'm sure, were we to have it serialised in one of the Sunday newspapers.'

Harry said nothing. But he was thinking. It was, at least, becoming clear where this part of the conversation was heading.

'I would imagine that were we to do so, your mother's reputation would take quite a tumble. She does seem to rather prefer anonymity or, at least, the somewhat sanitised version of events that has thus far found its way onto the public record. I would imagine that she might find the light of scrutiny, were the full story to be made public, rather disturbing. It would be tragic indeed, were she to be as disturbed by the publicity as poor Lynette Bell was disturbed by the mere prospect of it. Being reminded of one's past misdemeanours can have quite devastating consequences to a person's fortunes, to say nothing of their mental state.'

Whether he was talking to Phelps, or perhaps someone working for Phelps, they couldn't possibly have any real idea of Lizzie's mental state. In any other circumstance Harry would have dismissed the threat and called their bluff. Except that he was obviously in possession of information of which even Peter Owen had been unaware. Which meant that the threat was at least credible. 'What makes you think that my mother cares?' he ventured.

The man laughed. 'Oh, I think she cares. Ultimately, I suppose, the question is how much she cares. And, of course, whether you wish to put that to the test.'

'Are you threatening us?'

'Not at all. I am simply offering you an alternative. Putting it simply, Harry, you stand your team down and I will stand down mine. Neither of these stories need ever see the light of day.'

So that was the deal. But there was a flaw in his strategy. 'Which might work if it was my team or my story. It is neither.'

'Ah yes, the reporter. I must say that I am rather surprised that you have allied yourself with Holly Holgate, given her history. She is really quite unbalanced, you know. Did you know, for example, that there is still an injunction in force against her, instigated by her ex-partner? He has custody of their child, apparently.'

A child. Holgate had given no indication that she was a parent and the suggestion momentarily wrong footed him. 'What?'

'You didn't know? It is a rather sad story. Holgate has a history of quite serious mental illness, I'm afraid. When they split up and he won custody, she stalked them obsessively and made all sorts of spurious allegations against him. She told the police, for example, that he'd broken into her flat, trashed the place and threatened her. She staged the whole thing herself. Ring any bells?'

Could it be true or was he simply trying to sow the seeds of doubt in his mind? Harry said nothing.

'According to the reports she was entirely incoherent when she was sectioned. Ask her. She had a lengthy stay in a psychiatric hospital. I am no expert when it comes to mental illness, but it is a well known fact that these patterns of obsessive behaviour do seem to repeat themselves.'

He was clever, Harry had to give him that. 'Like I said, not my team and not my story. Holgate's mental health is irrelevant.'

'A very noble attitude to take toward the mentally ill, I must say. Still, I would have thought that the personal risks that come from associating yourself with such a person, especially given your own family's rather colourful history, might suggest that a certain amount of caution would be wise. Were your family history, your association with Holly Holgate and her history all to become public knowledge at the same time, it might rather dent your own reputation, don't you think?'

'You seem to think that I am able to influence her. What Holly does is a matter for Holly. I am not her keeper.'

'True, and if you are unable to prevent her, then we will. But you could, were you so minded, decide to withdraw your support and cease your involvement in this matter. It is, after all, based entirely on supposition. There is not a shred of evidence to support any of Holgate's ridiculous theories. I hope I have adequately explained why disassociating yourself from Holgate and ending your involvement in this matter would rather be in your best interests and, in particular, those of your mother.'

Harry hesitated. 'And if I agreed to this?'

'Did I not make myself clear? It is really rather simple. Desist and we will reciprocate. You have my word. Although there is one more condition, concerning which my hands are, I am afraid, entirely tied.'

The sting in the tail. Harry had been waiting for it. 'And that is?'

'Your father wishes to see you and your mother. In fact, he insists on it.'

His heart sank. 'My father is dead. I don't have a father.'

The voice on the end of the line turned to laughter. 'You do now, Harry.'

CHAPTER THIRTY-SIX

It was a nice house in a smart street. Nothing particularly special. Detached but with houses nearby on both sides. Built, she guessed, in the sixties. In the days when Newcastle still had a vibrant industrial base.

She'd been sitting in her car for the best part of an hour, watching the house for any sign of life but if Spencer Milburn was at home, she'd seen nothing to indicate it and little activity in either of the neighbouring properties. His absence was a disappointment but it might also be an opportunity. She was no house breaker but neither was she about to go back to London with nothing to show for the long drive northwards. She needed a place in which to lie low. Somewhere she could finish the piece she had begun to write, without any risk that Micky Milburn might find her. And this place was just about the last place on Earth Milburn was likely to look for her. She had made damn sure that she hadn't been followed to Newcastle.

She opened the car door, climbed out, retrieved her laptop bag from the back seat and slung it over her shoulder. She locked the car doors and walked across to the house. She rang the door bell and waited. Nothing. She walked around the side of the house and tried the gate. It was unlocked. She glanced over her shoulder, saw nobody, opened the gate and closed it behind her.

It was a largish garden. Unremarkable but well tended, with another, smaller building at the bottom of a winding garden path. A studio, perhaps. She made her way around to the back of the house and tried the half-glazed back door. It was locked. She peered in through the window. Inside, the house was tidy, the decoration a little dated perhaps, in keeping with the age of its' occupant. There was nothing obviously out of place; certainly nothing to indicate that there was anyone at home.

To one side of the door was a small window. She looked around for something with which to break it and found it in the form of a concrete garden ornament. A small gnome, of all things. She hadn't really had Spencer Milburn down as a gnome sort of man. She walked back to the window, weighed the gnome in her hand, and gave the window a single, sharp tap. The glass shattered. She reached in, undid the latch and opened the window, removing the shards of glass on the inside ledge carefully, to avoid injury. Climbing in was going to be awkward. She removed the laptop bag from her shoulder, lifted it through the opening and lowered it cautiously to the floor. Then she heaved herself up and managed to manoeuvre herself through the opening without mishap. Once inside, she turned and closed the broken window. It was going to be obvious to anyone looking at it that there had been a break-in but the back of the house was not overlooked, so her chances of remaining undetected seemed reasonably good.

The small room into which she had clambered housed a washing machine, a tumble drier, a sink and not much else. She picked up her laptop bag and made her way into the house. As she had observed from the garden, it was tidy and scrupulously clean. Not at all the chaotic bachelor pad she had been expecting. In the hall, there were several framed gold discs on the walls. Albums by The Monks. Five in all. Impressive. In the kitchen, she checked the fridge and found a plastic bottle of milk. She opened it and sniffed. It smelt okay. She filled the electric kettle from the kitchen tap and set it to boil. She found a tin of teabags and cups in a kitchen cupboard and when the kettle had boiled, made herself tea. She took several mouthfuls, left her laptop bag on the kitchen table and set about searching the house, avoiding the main lounge, with its wide bay window overlooking the street.

Upstairs, were three bedrooms but only one had a bed. A double. It had been neatly made and was covered by an ochre coloured bed spread. She reached down and tried the mattress. It was hard. She yawned.

The second bedroom housed a drum kit. She had an urge to try it out but thought better of it. The third bedroom, which overlooked the back garden, had been converted to an office. There was a large desk, an office chair and a filing cabinet. She tried its top drawer. It slid open easily. Either he had nothing to hide, or he was not expecting a break-in. It was at that moment that she realised that she hadn't given any thought to the presence of a burglar alarm. She froze, realised that had there been an alarm it would certainly have sounded by now, and smiled.

Over the space of the next hour, she searched the filing cabinet, his desk drawers and just about every other place she could find, ensuring as she did that she replaced everything, exactly as she had found it. Among the more interesting of her discoveries was a box containing a collection of photographs. Many were of The Monks at various stages of their career. One of them was a small black and white photograph, showing a sea of dancers and the band playing on a low stage. Among the dancers was Gina Lawrence. There was no mistaking her. Slim, dark skinned and wearing a pale coloured mini-dress, her hair up in a beehive. Beside her was another face that Holly recognised, initially with a little less certainty but, on closer inspection, without any doubt. Lynette Bell. On the back was a date: "19th April 1964". One week before Gina Lawrence went missing. She studied their faces, uncertain of what she was hoping to see but willing them to speak to her. But they didn't. Not a word.

The box also contained a collection of photos of the actress Ronnie Phelps, many of them showing Spencer and Ronnie together. She had not, until that moment, realised that the actress was Marty Phelps' daughter but now that she did, it seemed obvious. The scale of the collection revealed that Ronnie Phelps and Spencer Milburn had shared more than a passing association. He had been there at her birthdays, her wedding, at the christening of her children and, by the look of it, at just about every other key event in the actress's life. Unlike the pictures of the band, each of the pictures of Phelps had been meticulously dated on the back in, she assumed, Spencer's hand writing. The earliest was dated February 1966. A birthday party probably taken at the Phelps' house. Without really thinking about why she did it, she stuffed it into the back pocket of her jeans, returned the other photographs to the box and returned the box to the cupboard in which she'd found it.

Then she picked up her now empty tea cup and returned to the kitchen. She booted her laptop, found Spencer Milburn's broadband router on a shelf beside his front door, connected her laptop to the internet, returned to the kitchen table and began to write the piece that she had told Micky Milburn was already in The Cloud. It wasn't but it soon would be, whether Micky Milburn or, indeed, Harry Stammers, liked it or not.

CHAPTER THIRTY-SEVEN

'What are you going to do?'

It was lunchtime. But he wasn't hungry. After making the call, he'd waited with Lizzie until Ellen had arrived and then driven home, had a shave, changed into his work clothes and driven to Bletchley. 'I wish people would stop asking me that. I don't know what I'm going to do.'

Jane had pulled up a chair and seated herself on the opposite side of his desk. 'Did he give you a deadline?'

'Twenty-four hours.'

'Or?'

'Or he will send everything he's got to the Daily Mail.'

Jane's expression was thoughtful. 'How did Lizzie take it?'

'How do you think she took it?'

Jane shrugged.

'I've never seen her in such a state. Facing Peter Owen would be her worst nightmare. I really don't know that she could handle it.'

'Poor Lizzie. Is Ellen staying with her?'

He nodded. 'Until I get back.'

'I don't know why you came in.'

Which was a perfectly reasonable point. The truth was that he wanted Jane's view. With Lizzie within earshot at the house, he'd managed only a brief conversation with Ellen. 'Believe it or not, I value your opinion.'

Jane looked surprised. 'Sorry? Well, there's a first.'

He smiled. 'So?'

'So what?'

'So what is your opinion?'

Jane had been chewing the end of a pen. 'I think,' she said, after a pause, 'that you should agree to his demands.'

He didn't know what he'd been expecting but he hadn't been expecting surrender. 'What?'

'You heard me. Tell him that we're dropping the whole thing. Agree to his demands. It will buy us some time, while we take stock and plan our next move.'

Which might have been a good idea if they had one. 'Remind me. What is our next move?'

'One step at a time. He's put the ball in your court. So bat it back.'

He looked at her doubtfully.

'Owen won't be able to see you straight away. He'll be under restriction. It'll take some time to set up a covert meeting between the three of you. Appear to play ball and Phelps won't want to put your cooperation in jeopardy.'

Which was all very well but then what? If they continued, sooner or later Phelps was going to find out.

'If he finds out,' Jane said, as if reading his thoughts, 'then we'll threaten to go public with everything we've got, including our suspicions about Ronnie Phelps. That will put the cat amongst the pigeons. The question is, will Phelps find publicity any more palatable than you and Lizzie would find it.'

He thought about it. 'There is, of course, another alternative.'

She stared at him. 'You could, could you?'

'Drop the whole thing? If it comes down to a choice between Lizzie's wellbeing and discovering the truth about Gina Lawrence, sure I could.' But as he was saying it, he was wondering how sure he really was.

'Have you asked her?'

'Asked who?'

'Lizzie, you idiot. Have you asked your mother about how she wants to handle this?'

'No, of course not.'

'Why of course not?'

'Because this is my shout. It's down to me.'

She shook her head. 'You see, there you go again. What is it with you men?'

He knew what was coming. He'd heard it all before.

'I know you think you were put on this Earth to protect us, Harry. But women are actually capable of making decisions, you know. Maybe you should think about tackling this one with your mother, rather than for your mother.'

She was right. He'd told Lizzie that they would face it together.

'Let her get over the shock and then ask her. Who knows? Maybe she'll surprise you.'

He stared at her and then nodded.

'Good.'

But he wasn't feeling good. He was feeling anything but good. 'What about Holly? Have you managed to track her down?'

'Nope.'

'You have tried?'

The look she gave him told him that he was on dangerous ground. 'Of course I've tried. She is not answering her phone and her mobile is switched off.'

'Where the hell is she?'

'Don't ask me. I'm not the fucking clairvoyant.'

She had said it deadpan but he knew Jane well enough to know that there was a sense of humour lurking there somewhere. 'Don't even go there.'

Her expression looked like butter wouldn't melt.

'I told you that Holgate was trouble,' he said, shaking his head.

She crossed her arms. 'Don't tell me that you fell for all that shit about Holly?'

He decided to take her on. 'What, so you're saying that it's nonsense, are you?'

'No. I'm saying that it doesn't make the slightest difference. So maybe Holly got herself into a mess with her ex, fell off the deep end and spent some time in hospital. So what?'

'Mental hospital,' he corrected her.

She stared at him. 'Hospital,' she repeated. 'Where people go when they are ill and need treatment,' she said, with an emphasis on the final word. 'That's what they do in hospitals.'

'All right. But if I'd known that when she turned up here…'

'You'd have what?' Jane interrupted. 'Dismissed her as a fruit cake? Oh, wait a minute,' she put the pen to her chin. 'But you did that anyway.'

He shrugged.

'Look,' Jane said, after a pause, 'maybe Holly is fixated on Micky Milburn.'

'Maybe?' Harry interjected. 'There's no *maybe* about it. She's not remotely interested in anything else.'

'Maybe,' Jane repeated. 'That doesn't make our hypothesis any less likely.'

'No,' he conceded. It didn't.

'Something happened in Gina Lawrence's flat, right?'

He nodded.

'After which she disappeared. The Milburn brothers and Marty Phelps covered up their involvement and Phelps paid Lynette Bell what would have been a considerable sum of money in 1964 to take a life-long holiday to the Highlands of Scotland. Does Holly's mental state change any of that?'

'No, it doesn't,' he conceded.

'We've got good reason to believe that a couple of years prior to her disappearance, Gina Lawrence had a child, very possibly fathered by Marty Phelps. We think that child may very well be Ronnie Phelps.'

He didn't think it. He knew it.

'Had he acknowledged the child as his, Phelps would have been admitting to sleeping with a minor, which given his earlier conviction, would have landed him a whole heap of trouble. He couldn't risk it. Neither could he legally adopt her, for the same reason, so they staged Barbara's pregnancy and, when Ronnie was born, pretended that she was theirs. Does Holly's mental state change that?'

'No, it doesn't but...'

'It is likely,' she interrupted him again, 'that Gina hid the keepsakes from Ronnie's birth that you found under the floor in her flat. If the kid in that photograph does prove to be Ronnie Phelps, then what other explanation could there be?'

He ignored the question and, instead, asked another. 'Did you email Ronnie Phelps?'

'Yes, I did. First thing this morning.'

'Great. She takes it to her father and I'm screwed.'

'She won't.'

'She might.'

'She won't, Harry. She'll call me. She's a woman. Trust me.'

He raised an eyebrow.

'The point is that Holly Holgate's mental state doesn't make the slightest difference to any of this. It's bullshit, Harry. Designed to make you doubt her. Because he thinks that apart from what Lynette Bell told us, Holly's all we've got. It's his big mistake. He's underestimating just how far we've got with this. The truth is, he's not half as good at this as he thinks he is.'

Harry smiled weakly, despite the anxiety he was feeling.

'You asked for my opinion. You've got it. Play along with Phelps. Tell him that you'll do whatever it takes to protect your mother. Make him believe it. Stall on that date with Owen if you have to. But convince him that he's got the upper hand. While we wait to hear from Ronnie. If she confirms that the photograph is her, then there'll be a tsunami coming his way and we won't be riding the wave, Ronnie Phelps will.'

'What about Holly?'

'Leave Holly to me. I don't know how, yet. But I'll find her.'

CHAPTER THIRTY-EIGHT

Email from: **Jane Eglund at Bletchley Park**
Date: Monday, 23 May 2016
Re: Strictly confidential
To: Ronnie Phelps

Dear Miss Phelps,

I am sorry to contact you by email but I had no other means to do so. My name is Jane Eglund. I work for Harry Stammers, Chief Officer at Bletchley Park Museum, in Buckinghamshire. We believe that the attached photograph was taken a few days after your birth. There is no easy way to explain, in an email, why we think the photograph may be deeply significant to you. I'm sure you receive many emails from people whose motives are questionable but please be assured that we are genuine and sincere in wishing to pass on to you, in complete confidence of course, some information and items which have come into our possession that we believe may be of considerable personal relevance to you. We would rather talk to you directly, to avoid any risk of compromising your confidentiality and would wish to do so reasonably urgently. I wonder if you would give me a call at your earliest convenience please?

Sincerely and with kind regards,

Jane Eglund

Head of Administration

Bletchley Park Museum

T: +44 (0) 1908 640404

She had read the email several times, made herself a coffee, returned to her desk and was staring at the photograph. After a few moments she got up, walked across to a row of bookshelves in the small room that, when she was at home, functioned as an office and selected a large, intricately bound, photograph album. She walked back to her desk, opened the album, found the photograph she was looking for and glanced, back and forth, between it and the image on the screen. The resemblance was clear, although the photograph in the album, which had been taken at her christening in the church of St John The Baptist, at Great Gaddesden, appeared to be the more recent of the two. Probably by no more than a few weeks.

'Who is that?'

She had been only vaguely aware of Skye's presence in the room. 'It's me. I think,' she said, without turning.

'Aw, that's cute,' Skye said, bending down to peer at the image. 'I'm going into town,' she said, straightening. 'Do you need anything?'

'No, I…' She was wondering what other items might have come into Jane Eglund's possession and how they had found their way to Bletchley Park. She was unaware of any link between her family and Bletchley. And what did Eglund mean by "information of considerable personal relevance"?

'Where did it come from?'

'What?' She looked over her shoulder. Skye was the spitting image of her father. For a split second she imagined him standing there. Which thankfully he wasn't.

'The picture. Where did it come from?'

'Oh, somebody emailed it.'

'Somebody?'

She hesitated. 'Look, take a look at this would you?' She clicked on the email. 'Then tell me what you think.'

Skye read the email. 'Intriguing,' she said after a few moments.

'So what do you think? I can't make up my mind.'

'I think you should call her. What have you got to lose?'

'She could be a crank.'

'She doesn't sound like a crank. Have you looked her up?'

She stared blankly at her daughter.

'All right. Move over,' Skye said, reaching for the spare chair. 'There,' she said after a few seconds of searching. 'Doesn't look like a crank to me.'

Jane Eglund's profile was on Bletchley Park's website. She scanned it. 'No, she doesn't.'

'Well, there you go,' Skye said, getting to her feet. 'Call her, Mum. You can tell me all about it when I get back,' she added, over her shoulder. 'You won't know, unless you do,' she called out as she left the room.

Ronnie Phelps hesitated, heard the sound of the front door closing, sighed and reached for the telephone.

CHAPTER THIRTY-NINE

The mini cab turned onto Eastern Way. The balding driver glanced over his shoulder.

'Over there on the right. Pull up anywhere you like. What do I owe you?'

'Eighteen pounds.'

He fumbled with his wallet and pulled out a twenty. 'Keep the change.'

Both he and the driver got out of the car.

The driver retrieved his bag from the boot. 'I thought I recognised you,' he said, suddenly wagging his finger. 'I've been trying to figure it. Spencer Milburn, right? The Monks?'

'Right.' It had been a while since he'd been recognised. A long while.

The driver held out his hand, 'Brian. Brian McAuley. I was a big fan, back in the day. Saw you play a couple of gigs. Sixty-six, I think it was. I was just a kid, you know?'

Spencer shook his hand. He did know. They'd all been just kids.

'I can't wait to tell the wife. Spencer Milburn. Fancy that,' the driver said, shaking his head and grinning.

Spencer nodded, wearily.

'I've still got all your records, you know.'

It was nice to be recognised but it had been a long journey and, right now, he just wanted to sink into an arm chair.

'Do you still play?'

'Sure, I do.'

'Well, it's an honour, man.'

'Thanks,' he said, turning away and taking several paces toward the house.

'How's Micky?' the driver called out. 'What a voice, eh?'

He'd been waiting for that. It had always been the same. 'Champion,' he said, under his breath and without stopping.

He fumbled in his pockets for the house keys, almost missing the faint glow of a light as he pushed open the door. But as the door swung inward and he stepped into the hallway, the light from the kitchen at the rear of the house became more obvious. Which was odd. He let the door close behind him and put down his bag. The faint sound of tapping. He glanced at the telephone on the shelf beside the door and then at the broadband router next to it. The router's lights were blinking. They only did that when the network was busy. 'Hello?' he called out, expecting a familiar voice, though he couldn't immediately imagine whose voice.

The tapping paused, for seconds only, and then resumed.

The only computer in the house was upstairs in his office. He took a breath and walked the short distance to the kitchen.

As the kitchen came into view, the woman who was seated at the oval table, looked up and smiled at him. 'Hello. I hope you don't mind, but I've been getting on with the piece while I waited for you. I'm almost done.'

The reporter. He recognised her from their last encounter. It had only been brief but he had a good memory for faces.

'Can I get you some tea or coffee? You look shattered,' she said, smiling at him like she had every right to be there.

'What the hell are you doing here? How did you get in?'

'Ah,' she said, glancing toward the door at the kitchen's rear. 'I'm afraid I had to break a window. In there,' she added, nodding toward the utility room. 'Just the small one. Don't worry. I've already booked a glazier. He's coming tomorrow. It's all paid for. I was rather hoping that you'd be away for another day or so and that it would all be done by the time you got back.' She smiled again. 'Nice place, by the way.'

'What are you talking about?'

'Look, why don't I make us a drink? You really do look tired,' she said, getting to her feet.

He took a precautionary step backwards.

'Then maybe I can talk you through the piece I've written.'

He glanced at the laptop.

'Just to make sure I've got the finer details right.'

'You're crazy. What are you doing here?'

'I needed a place to hide for a few days. From Micky and that apeman he has working for him. Just while I finish the piece. The two of them broke into my flat on Friday. They were really quite threatening. When you were not at home, well, I thought that since they broke into mine, I'd break into yours. An eye for an eye and all that.' She'd walked across to the kettle and was filling it from the tap. 'Seemed only fair,' she said over her shoulder.

'Micky is in Florida.'

She'd put the kettle on to boil and had found two cups. 'Er, I don't think so. Unless he has a remarkably good double. Tea or coffee?'

He stared at her. 'Coffee.' What was he doing? He ought to be telling her to get out. He ought to be calling the police. Micky was in Florida. She was nuts.

She flashed him another smile.

'If he was coming to the UK, he'd have told me.'

'Evidently not. Black or white?'

'White. No sugar. You're saying that he broke into your flat?'

'Yes. He was there when I got home. He had The Apeman hold me, while he fingered me. You know, between the legs. He's a bit of a perv, your brother, isn't he? No offence intended. Then he threatened to drug me, introduce me to the stiffy he said he had in his pants and afterwards have The Apeman throw me off Waterloo Bridge if I don't pack it in. What a charmer, eh? So I needed somewhere to hide and when you weren't here, I thought, why not? After all, it's probably about the last place on Earth Micky will think to look for me, when I publish the piece. Do you see?'

He'd pulled out the chair opposite hers and sat down heavily. He was tired of this. Tired of carrying it around with him. Tired of the mental gymnastics. Tired of the whole damn business.

'Here,' she said, handing him the hot cup. 'That all right for you? Not too strong?'

'It's fine,' he answered without checking.

She sat down opposite him.

He drank in silence, watching her. 'Why are you doing this?' he said, at last. 'Why don't you just give it up?'

She didn't answer him immediately. Instead, she stared at him.

He held her eyes.

'Before I answer that, can I ask you something?' she said, like they were old friends, having a conversation over breakfast.

He let out a long sigh. This was insane. He nodded wearily.

'Doesn't what happened to Gina Lawrence bother you?'

Of course it bothered him. It bothered him a very great deal.

'I mean, sure it was a long time ago,' she continued, without waiting for his reply. 'But an innocent young woman lost her life. Doesn't that bother you at all?'

'Who says she lost her life?' he shot back.

She raised an eyebrow. 'Because it sure as hell bothers me. And I'll tell you what else bothers me.'

He didn't want to hear it.

'It bothers me that three men; three now wealthy and successful men, know exactly what happened to her. It bothers me, not just that they have remained silent, but that they have persistently lied about it. Worse, it bothers me that they have actively sought to intimidate anyone who even tries to discover the truth.'

'That's not true. I don't know what happened to her. I never did. And I haven't tried to intimidate you or anybody else.'

She smiled. 'Maybe not. But you have lied. Covered up for your brother. And you're still covering for him. Why is that, Spencer? Doesn't your brother's behaviour bother you at all?'

He said nothing.

'I understand your loyalty to Micky. Really, I do. But you must know, better than anyone, the kind of man he is. That he uses his wealth and power to abuse women and then to silence them. Maybe Gina was the first, but she sure as hell wasn't the last. I can personally vouch for that. He left me in no doubt at all that he means what he says.'

He said nothing.

'Did you know he killed Lynette Bell?'

'What? Don't be ridiculous.' She was crazy. Micky had been in the States when Lynette Bell had hung herself.

'Well all right. Micky didn't actually do the deed. But The Apeman did. According to Micky, faking suicide is one of his specialities.'

'You're insane.'

'He'll keep on doing it, you know. Don't you think it's time he was stopped? Time you stood up to him?'

'Micky is my brother.'

'All the more reason that it should be you. We all tolerate crap from our families that we'd never tolerate from anyone else. But Micky is something else.'

He said nothing.

'Did you know, at the time, that Micky killed Gina Lawrence?'

'Killed her? Look, I've had enough of this. There's not one shred of evidence....' he said, pushing the chair back and beginning to rise.

She interrupted him. 'So where is she?'

He hesitated. 'What?'

'Where is she? Where did she go? There has been no trace of her in fifty years. And I have looked. I've looked damned hard. Nothing.'

He sat back down. 'I don't know where she went,' he said, honestly, 'I never knew.' The expression on her face told him that she didn't believe it. 'People go missing all the time,' he said, dismissively.

'Not if they've got a child, they don't.'

His heart felt like it had stopped beating. She couldn't know about Ronnie. It wasn't possible. 'A child? What are you talking about?'

She was watching him, trying to gauge his reaction, he was sure of it.

'Did you know that somebody hid a photograph of a newborn baby under the floor boards in Gina's flat at The Scene Club? Along with a teddy bear and a birthday card?'

He didn't know that.

'Want to know what was written in the card?'

He met and held her eyes.

'To Veronica. My darling baby girl. Mummy loves you. Mummy will always love you.'

Veronica. He bowed his head. Ronnie had never used her birth name. Even as a tiny child, she'd been known as Ronnie.

The reporter was waiting. He could feel her eyes boring into him. She hadn't made the link to Ronnie Phelps. Had she made it, she'd have been pressing him. He felt a short-lived surge of relief. When he raised his head she was staring at him. 'I don't know anything about a child,' he said woodenly.

She smiled, shaking her head. 'You know, for someone who has been lying for fifty years, you're really not very good at it.'

His short lived sense of relief was immediately replaced by the realisation that if she hadn't made the link, she almost certainly soon would.

'Whoever wrote that card doesn't sound to me like a woman who would have just walked away.'

She was so close.

'You loved Gina, didn't you?'

It was not a question he'd been expecting and he was not prepared for it. Neither was he prepared for the surge of raw emotion that constricted his chest and brought tears welling into his eyes, try as he might to prevent them. 'I was fond of her,' he whispered.

'Oh come on. It was more than that. All these years later and it still gets to you, doesn't it?'

There was no point denying it.

She reached across the table and took his hand. He flinched, but let her, his eyes fixed at a random point on the table's surface.

'Lynette Bell told me that Gina was in love with you.'

He looked up at her. 'She told you that?'

'Yes, she did. She told me that the only reason that Gina strung Micky along that night, was to make you jealous.'

He let go of her hand and wiped his eyes on the back of his jacket sleeve.

'Micky must have known how you felt about her.'

'Of course he knew,' he said, his voice hoarse.

'Fancy doing that to your own brother. What a bastard.'

'We were just kids.' But it was an excuse. He'd been making excuses for his brother since the two of them had been children.

'Micky knew exactly what he was doing. He went out of his way to get her into bed, Spencer.'

'Stop it.'

'By feeding her pills, for God's sake. Lynette Bell said that they were completely off their faces by the time he got them up to her flat.'

He didn't want to hear it.

'Which would be bad enough if that was the one and only time. But he's done it since. In fact, according to Micky, he's perfected the technique.'

'Stop it. I don't want to hear any more.'

'I know that you tried to stop them,' the journalist persisted. 'Lynette told me that you pleaded with them on the stairs up to her flat.'

Tears were now trickling down his cheeks. 'Please…'

'But Micky just laughed in your face.'

It was a scene that he had tried to forget. Because it wasn't just Micky who had laughed at him.

'Some brother you've got there,' she said, shaking her head.

She was toying with his emotions. Playing him for stupid. 'Enough,' he barked, slapping the table, hard with the flat of his hand.

She said nothing.

'Where are we going with this? Gina has gone. Whatever I felt for her, she went a very long time ago and she isn't coming back. I don't know what happened to her. I don't…'

'You don't want to know,' she finished the sentence for him.

'I didn't say that,' he snapped.

'But you were going to. If you don't pull that head of yours out of the sand soon, you're going to suffocate.'

He let out a long breath. 'Look,' he said, trying to regain his composure. 'You think you understand this, but it's not that simple. You journalists see everything in black and white. Real life isn't like that. There are real people at stake here. Real lives. You haven't got a clue.'

'Then tell me.'

He shook his head. 'Then what? You publish that article of yours?' he said, glancing at the laptop.

'It's the only way to stop him, Spencer.'

'Stop him? Are you crazy? Publishing that article won't stop him. All it will do is put you in danger.'

'I'm already in danger.'

'Then stop it. Maybe you're right that someone needs to stand up to Micky. Maybe I will. When I'm ready.'

She smiled. 'You've had fifty years to stand up to your brother. If you were going to stand up to him, you'd have done it a long time ago. Gina was more than enough reason, or should have been,' she added pointedly.

His anger flared again. 'Gina. Who the hell is Gina to you?' he snapped.

'She was my aunt.'

He stared at her, open mouthed. 'What?' he said, at last.

'Gina Lawrence was my aunt. My father's half-sister.'

He shook his head. 'I don't believe you.'

'Gina's father was a black American airman, stationed over here during the war. My grandmother was white. They had a brief affair and the resulting kid was mixed race. It was 1945. Think about it.'

It dawned on him suddenly that if she was telling the truth then Ronnie was her cousin.

'He never knew. My grandmother hid the pregnancy from him, ended their relationship and gave the child up for adoption. She regretted it until the day she died. But before she did, she asked me to find her. Family. That's what Gina Lawrence is to me.'

Family. Ultimately it had been family loyalty that led him to tolerate his brother's behaviour, and to cover for Micky all these years. It had been the desire for a family of their own that had led Marty and Barbara Phelps to adopt baby Veronica. It had been the loss of her daughter that Gina had been so unable to bear. It was his own desire to hold onto the surrogate family that Ronnie Phelps and her children had become, that made the prospect of losing them now so unthinkable. 'I didn't know.'

'No? Well you do now. Your brother is the reason why neither of us have Gina Lawrence in our lives. That's the truth of it. And that is why I'm going to blow this whole fucking thing wide open. Whether Micky likes it or not. He can go to hell.'

He stared at her. She was so close to discovering Ronnie. Sooner or later she was going to make the link. 'I need to think about this. I need time.'

'You've had long enough,' she said firmly. 'I'm giving you an opportunity here. To give your side of the story. To set the record straight.'

He wasn't ready.

'Help me to finish the piece.'

'What?'

'You heard me. Help me finish it.'

It was out of the question. His cooperation would make no difference. If she published now, events were going to run out of control. He needed to stall her while he thought about how to stop her. 'Look, let me think about it. Please. Stay here tonight. You're right. Micky will never think to look for you here. You're safe. Give me until the morning.'

'To do what?'

'To do what?' his anger flared again. 'For God's sake. You break into my home and, out of the blue, announce that you're going to turn my life; the lives of us all, upside down. And you expect me to agree to help you? Just like that?'

She hesitated.

He was watching her reaction. Her hunger for the story was written all over her face. 'There is so much more to this, Holly,' he offered. 'So much more I could tell you.'

She said nothing.

He felt a flicker of hope. 'Give me until the morning. That's all I'm asking. There are people I need to think about. People who will be hurt.'

She smiled. 'You're damn right about that.'

And then he made a mistake. 'Innocent people, Holly. People who know nothing about any of this.' He knew, as the words left his lips, that he had gone too far.

It took only seconds for the light to come on. He watched it illuminate her features. 'You know, don't you?' she said, a smile spreading across her features.

Panic. 'Know? Know what?' he said, trying to evade the accusation.

She stared at him. 'Veronica.'

Despair. He was going to lose her. Just like he had lost Gina. Micky had taken her from him. He was not going to lose Ronnie.

'I don't believe it. You've found Veronica Lawrence.'

CHAPTER FORTY

Harry was watching them through the kitchen window, kicking a ball back and forth. It was an everyday scene. A grandmother and her granddaughter, playing on the lawn in the early summer sunshine. But he could see the tension in her gestures; the worried expression behind her smiles, masked but present nonetheless. 'How has she been?' he said, without turning away from his view of them.

'Putting on a brave face, for Martha's sake,' Ellen answered. 'Having her here has helped. It's given her something else to focus on. But she's scared, Harry. What the hell did Owen do to her?'

He turned towards Ellen. She was standing by the sink, drying the dishes. 'I don't think we'll ever really know, do you?'

Ellen shook her head. 'Are you going to talk to her?'

He nodded. 'Yes. I said that we'd deal with this together and we will. If Lizzie is going to get through this, she needs to have some semblance of control. And if we're going to play along with Phelps and Owen, then we need her to hold it together. Not fall apart if there is further contact from them.'

Ellen had approached the window and was staring out into the garden with him. 'She might be scared, but your mother is a strong woman. Think about her career. What she has been through. She wouldn't have made it this far if she wasn't.'

'I just worry about her, that's all.'

Ellen smiled sympathetically. 'I know you do. Me too. But we need to stop seeing as her as a victim.'

Harry nodded. 'I doubt that we'll need to maintain the pretence with Phelps and Owen for very long. When Ronnie Phelps discovers the truth, my guess is that she will confront her father, at which point Marty Phelps is going to have a lot more to worry about than any trouble we may make for him.'

'If she believes us.'

He frowned. 'You think she might not?'

'I don't know. Would you?'

He raised an eyebrow and watched the irony of the question dawn on her.

'Well, all right. But agreeing to meet with us is one thing. There's really no telling how she'll react when we tell her that she isn't who she thinks she is. You know how difficult that is likely to be for her.'

He tipped his head in acknowledgement. 'I guess we will find that out on Wednesday. Until then, we need to convince Phelps and Owen.'

'Unless, Ronnie tells him about our meeting.'

'She won't,' he said confidently.

'You're sure?'

He thought about it. 'No. But Jane was. And, let's face it, Jane is usually a pretty good judge of character.'

'Are you going to tell Lizzie about the meeting with Ronnie?' Ellen said, turning her attention back to the window and the garden beyond.

'I wasn't going to, but the more I think about it, the more I think we should give her the full story. In any case, unless Phelps is bluffing, Owen already knows that he's my father. That bridge has already been crossed. Sooner or later and regardless of what happens with Phelps, we're going to have to deal with it. Lizzie. You. Me. All of us. I just hope that she's got the strength.'

Ellen slipped an arm around his waist and pulled him towards her. 'Perhaps it will be for the best, in the end, Love. She's avoided it all these years. But avoiding it doesn't mean that it isn't there. Sometimes, I look at her and I think I can see him hovering over her shoulder like some kind of phantom.'

Harry smiled. 'Now don't go letting your imagination run away with you. That's my department.' He turned, held her eyes and kissed her.

There was a sudden loud thud that made them both jump backwards.

'Jesus, what the hell was…' Harry hesitated, instinctively glancing out into the garden. There was a neat, football-shaped print on the window glass. Beyond it, Martha was stood with her hand over her mouth and Lizzie was laughing. 'Well, I'm glad somebody finds this funny.'

CHAPTER FORTY-ONE

She'd managed to fall asleep, but now she was wide awake again. She glanced at the digital clock on Spencer Milburn's bedside cabinet. It was 3.17am. He'd insisted that she have the bedroom, opting to sleep on the sofa. He'd denied that he'd found Veronica Lawrence but she was in no doubt at all that he had. It was the look of sheer panic on his face and the vehemence with which he had denied it that had both revealed the lie and so puzzled her. She'd been over and over it in her mind. What was he afraid of? If Veronica had been given up for adoption at birth, what could her discovery add to the story that she didn't already know? There was something she was missing. Something that put Veronica Lawrence at the centre of it all. Why else had Spencer been so obviously panic stricken?

She turned over onto her back and stared up at the ceiling. Protecting Micky Milburn and, undoubtedly, his own career. Those had been Spencer's aims all along. No matter what his feelings had been for Gina Lawrence or how extreme his brother's behaviour. Their parents had died, within a few years of each other, early in the brothers' careers and Spencer had never married or built a family of his own, meaning that Micky was the only family that Spencer had. Which probably explained his attachment to his manager's daughter. It was evident from the photographs she'd discovered in the box in his office that the attachment, formed when she had been a young child, had developed into a life-long friendship. Ronnie Phelps. She stopped breathing and sat bolt upright. *Ronnie Phelps*. Marty Phelps' daughter.

She got out of the bed, located her jeans and retrieved the photograph. She turned and was about to switch on the bedroom light when she heard the sound of a car pull up outside. She froze, walked to the window, slid a finger between the curtains and peered cautiously out onto the street below. 'Fuck.'

A figure had got out of the car. She recognised him instantly. 'Fuck.'

She threw on her jeans, hopping from one foot to the other in her haste and slid her feet into her trainers. She glanced toward the place where she had left her laptop bag. It was gone. 'Fuck it,' she cursed out loud. She grabbed her jacket, wrenched open the bedroom door and tore down the stairs. Spencer Milburn was in the hall, blocking her way. 'Bastard. You fucking bastard.'

He was rooted to the spot, his eyes flicking from hers and over her shoulder, towards the door.

She glared at him. 'Get out of my way.'

'I'm sorry, Holly. I couldn't let you publish your piece. You were right about Micky being in the UK. I called him. I told him I had your laptop. That's all he wants. Promise us that you'll drop this and Micky has given me his word that you'll come to no harm.'

'Micky's word? Are you mad?'

'And my word.'

'I said, get out of my way,' she yelled. And then she charged him.

She hit him hard, tipping her shoulder against his upper chest as she made contact. The impact knocked him sideways. She registered the sound of what she imagined was his head hitting the hallway wall. She did not stop. She flew to the back door, found the key in the lock and, now with voices at the front door, wrenched open the door and charged out into the back garden. She stood panting for a moment. Discounting the possibility of exiting by the side gate, she slid her arms into her jacket and then she ran down the pathway that led to the small building at the garden's rear.

By now, she was not alone. She'd heard the sound of running footsteps. The Apeman.

As she approached the little building, she scanned the garden's rear fence for a gate or other means of escape but she could see none. Six foot high, larch lap panels bordered the garden on all sides. And then she saw her only chance. She vaulted onto a wooden rain butt and hauled herself onto the building's roof, hoping to God that it would hold her weight.

Her pursuer had gained on her. As she stood and turned, he too had clambered onto the rain barrel. The moonlight illuminated his face. The Apeman was grinning. She returned his smile, took aim for his jawline and kicked him in the face, as hard as she could without falling. Her foot made contact with his mouth with a satisfying thud and what she hoped was the crunch of smashing teeth. He went down with a howl and a hollow thud as he hit the grass.

She walked gingerly, for fear of the roof giving way, to the building's edge and jumped into the neighbour's garden, rolling as she hit the grass lawn and coming to a stop in a breathless heap. She waited to catch her breath for a moment only, hauled herself to her feet and ran up the neighbouring garden, skirting the house and exiting through a side gate onto the street.

It only took her a moment to get her bearings. She reached into her jacket pocket as she ran, found her keys, but as she neared her car, there was a commotion behind her. She glanced over her shoulder and saw The Apeman stagger out from Spencer Milburn's house. He was clutching his face.

She pipped the central locking, ran towards the car, hauled open the door and leapt into the seat, panting breathlessly. Then she started and revved the engine and accelerated away, making no effort to avoid The Apeman as he leapt out of the way, missing him by only a few inches. She checked her rear view mirror and saw the lights of the Mercedes pull out behind her. She had to hand it to him. Micky Milburn's Apeman didn't give up easily.

He was also an excellent driver and the Mercedes was certainly a more powerful car than her Ford. He was rapidly gaining on her despite being hampered, she hoped fervently, by the distraction of a broken jaw.

She hurtled on through the largely deserted streets of suburban Newcastle, with hope of escape slowly fading. Pending a miracle, she was simply not going to be able to outrun him. She cast her eyes left and right, hoping beyond hope for the sight of a police car. Disappointed, she fumbled in her jacket pocket for her smartphone but it was not there. 'Fuck.' She checked her rear view mirror. She estimated that the Mercedes was perhaps fifty metres behind her, no more.

Up ahead, she saw a sign for the city centre. Bracing herself, she heaved a sudden and sharp left, fighting to retain control of the car, as it rolled, its' tyres screeching in complaint. There were traffic lights up ahead. Red traffic lights. 'In for a penny, in for a pound,' she muttered under her breath. She gritted her teeth and floored the accelerator. As she neared the junction she noted the approaching articulated lorry, its' headlights dazzling her as she entered the junction. The sound of the lorry's hooter blared like the fog horn from The Titanic. She held her nerve and her breath, bracing herself for impact. The lorry driver had slammed on his brakes. The lorry began to jack-knife, smoke billowing from its tyres.

She made it with what seemed like only inches to spare but as she exited the junction, her car caught the wing of a parked van. There was a colossal bang and the car ricocheted to the right, narrowly avoiding a crossing island. She gripped the steering wheel, regained some semblance of control and checked her rear view mirror. The lorry had blocked the junction but, to its side, she saw a pair of headlights mount the pavement. She took another sharp left, but the Mondeo was not steering correctly, she guessed due to a burst tyre, damage to the steering or both. She looked to her left and right and, without further thought, veered into an entrance way, between what appeared to be an empty department store and a neighbouring shoe shop, and drew the car to an untidy halt. She turned off the engine and, for a moment, sat in silence. Then she got out of the car, scanning the car park for an exit or for somewhere to hide.

The entrance through which she had driven, evidently doubled as the exit. She could see no other. Her eyes strayed, in desperation, to a large, steel paladin bin, one of several arranged in a row beside high steel shutters that presumably hid the old store's loading bay. But the bins were too obvious and too enclosed. If he found her there would be zero chance of escape. She was fast running out of time.

Her eyes followed the line of a flight of steel stairs up the back of the former department store. At the top was a landing, a door into the building and a small window. She peered upward, straining to make it out, because the window appeared to be ajar. It was a gamble. If her eyes were deceiving her, then it would be a dead end. Possibly literally. 'Fuck it.'

She ran for the stairs and begun to climb, zig-zagging back and forth as the metal steps changed direction. One flight from the top, she could see that the window was indeed ajar by just a few inches. Reaching it at last, she extended a hand through the gap, lifted the latch and hauled it open. Then she climbed through.

Inside, the building was in darkness. She turned, intending to close the window behind her, but as she did so, the loading area behind the store was flooded with light and the Mercedes came into view. The car drew to a halt and The Apeman emerged. She ducked and reached upward to ease the window slowly closed. She hoped to God that he hadn't caught sight of the movement. Then she turned and waited, allowing her eyes to adjust to the darkness.

The room into which she had climbed was one of the building's toilets. Then she heard him. Footsteps clanking in rapid succession on the metal steps below. She ran for the interior door, hauled it open and emerged, via a lobby, onto the old shop floor. Evidently the womenswear department. It was dully lit by the building's emergency lighting system which was thankfully still operational. The vast space was littered with rows of clothes racks in disarray, discarded boxes and packing materials. Behind her, the unmistakable sound of breaking glass.

She ran in what she hoped was the direction of the stairs, dodging her way between the detritus left behind when the store had been vacated. She had made it to the middle of the space, crouching as low as she could to minimise the risk of detection. But the reality was that if she continued moving he was going to spot her easily. She glanced around frantically for a hiding space. She found it in the form of the floor's pay station. Dropping down onto all-fours she made her way to the rear of the station, crawled into a space beneath the counter and waited, trying desperately to slow her breathing so that he would not hear her.

It was dark beneath the pay station but, as her eyes adjusted, she caught a glimpse of stainless steel. She reached out and froze. He was nearby but motionless, presumably listening. She held her breath.

The events of the next few seconds happened in a blur. The Apeman had obviously heard something. He had circumnavigated the pay station, his legs and crotch coming into view in front of her. At any moment, he might bend down to check the space below the counter. She reached out for the glint of steel, closed her hand around the pair of scissors and then, holding them in her fist, stabbed The Apeman with as much force as she could manage, given the confined space.

She had meant to stab him in the crotch, but he had moved at the last minute. The scissors penetrated his upper thigh. He roared in pain and staggered backwards. She burst from her hiding space and shoulder-barged him. He staggered backwards, but as she turned to flee, he caught hold of her hair. 'Bastard,' she bellowed, spinning around to face him. He grinned and, with his right fist, punched her in the face. Once. Twice. Until she lost count.

CHAPTER FORTY-TWO

Harry and Ellen were seated on a bench, overlooking the lake at Bletchley Park. The fountain was sending plumes of water into the air, the droplets twinkling in the early summer sunshine as they fell back to the lake's rippling surface.

Ellen sighed. 'I wonder what Gran would have made of all this, had she still been here with us. She was a big fan of Ronnie Phelps, you know.'

'Was she? I didn't know that.'

'She was. She especially loved that film she starred in with Bill Nighy. The one about the writer.'

Harry turned his head and looked at her blankly.

'You know the one.'

He didn't.

'Oh God, what was it called?'

'Don't ask me. I'm hopeless with films.'

'Martha,' Ellen called out a warning. 'Come away from the water.'

Martha turned and waved at them.

Harry looked at his watch. 'Half an hour.'

'Are you nervous?'

Harry pulled a face. 'Why would I be nervous?'

'Oh, I don't know. How is she going to react? It's a big deal, telling someone that their mother isn't their mother. Do you think she has any idea at all?'

Harry shrugged. 'I didn't, when Dad told me that he wasn't my dad.'

'No idea at all? Not even an inkling?'

He thought about it. 'No. I can honestly say that the possibility had never crossed my mind.'

'Well, I guess we're about to find out whether it's ever crossed Ronnie's.'

Harry nodded. 'At least Phelps seemed to swallow it when I told him that we were standing down. And I reckon Jane was right that it'll take them a while to line up a meeting with Owen.'

Ellen smiled weakly. 'Let's hope so.'

They were silent.

'I'm getting increasingly worried about Holly, though,' Ellen said at last. 'Jane has still not managed to contact her.'

Harry snorted. 'Holly's a loose cannon. She was using us, Ellen. All she wanted was to use my name to give her story validity.'

'Do you really think so?'

'Why else have we seen neither hide nor hair of her since the day I told her I wasn't interested?'

Ellen sighed. 'Do you think that any of that stuff that Phelps said about her was true?'

'I wouldn't be surprised. Sorry, but we're well shot of her, as far as I'm concerned.'

'A little harsh.'

Harry shrugged. 'Perhaps.'

'Still, I'd rather we knew that she is safe.'

Martha had made her way back towards them. 'Is Ronnie going to be here soon?' she asked, plonking herself down on the bench beside them.

Harry smiled. 'Yes, Love. In fact, we should be getting back to the office. I want to make sure we've got everything ready.'

'I can't wait to meet her,' Martha said brightly.

'Now, Martha,' Ellen asserted, 'I don't want you getting in the way. While we're talking to Ronnie, you're to wait in the office. You can use Jane's computer. I'm sure she won't mind.'

'But, Mum…'

'No buts,' Ellen interrupted. 'We don't know how Ronnie is going to react. She might not believe us. She could become upset or even angry. It's going to be a conversation for grown ups, Martha.'

'Well, I don't think she's going to be cross at all,' Martha said with confidence.

Ellen smiled. 'I hope you're right but we can't be sure.'

'She's going to be happy that we're helping her.'

Harry and Ellen exchanged glances.

'Remember what we all agreed,' Ellen continued. 'You are not to mention seeing them. Ronnie won't understand.'

'You mean she'll think we're weird.'

'Yes, she might very well think that. She'd be wrong. You and your dad are not weird.' She hesitated. 'Mind you,' she said, glancing at Harry, 'your dad's a bit weird at times, let's face it.'

Harry grinned and got to his feet. 'Come on weirdos. Our destiny awaits.'

The three of them made their way along the pathway that led toward the mansion and across the car park, to the bungalow that housed Harry's office.

They had been sitting at the conference desk in his office, both deep in thought. There was a knock at the door. They both stood. Jane entered followed by Ronnie Phelps.

He was immediately struck by her resemblance to Gina Lawrence, albeit that her complexion was a shade fairer. She was wearing blue jeans and a suede jacket and was taller than he had been expecting. She looked nervous and oddly distracted. As though something had already surprised her. He caught Jane's eye and asked the silent question.

Jane shook her head, almost imperceptibly.

'Miss Phelps.' He held out his hand.

'Ronnie, please.'

It was a firm, though slightly hesitant handshake. 'I'm Harry. This is my wife, Ellen.'

Ellen shook her hand.

'No doubt, Jane has already introduced herself.'

'Yes, indeed.'

'Are you sure I can't get you a drink?' Jane offered.

'No. Thank you.'

'Please, take a seat,' Harry added, indicating a chair at the conference table.

Ronnie Phelps removed her jacket, hung it over the back of her chair and they seated themselves, Harry opposite the actress, Ellen next to her and Jane nearest the door.

'Thank you for coming to see us,' Harry began. 'I gather that you live in Cornwall. It must have been quite a journey.'

'I came up last night. I have a flat in Earls Court. I use it mainly when I'm filming in and around London.'

Harry smiled. 'I hope we haven't put you to too much inconvenience?'

'That rather depends on what you have to tell me.'

'Indeed,' Harry acknowledged, uncertain of quite where to begin.

'You said, in your email,' the actress said, glancing at Jane, 'that as well as the photograph you sent me, certain items have come into your possession. May I see them?'

'Of course.' Harry removed the lid from a small box that he'd positioned, along with a folder, on the table in front of him. He passed it across to the actress. 'Please take your time.'

She removed the items from the box, one at a time, examining each carefully and placed them on the table in front of her. The last of the items was the birthday card which she opened and read.

Harry glanced at Ellen but her eyes were glued to the actress.

'You obviously believe that the Veronica mentioned in the card refers to me,' the actress said, still staring at the card.

Harry hesitated. 'Yes, we do,' he said at last.

'Because of the photograph that was found with it?' she answered, glancing up at him and searching his face.

Harry held her eyes. Her expression was an odd one. Like she knew that something was coming. Like perhaps she had known for a very long time that something was coming. 'Yes, in part. But by no means only that.'

'Then what?'

He swallowed.

'Before Harry answers that, can I ask you a question?' Ellen broke in.

The actress turned her attention to Ellen, tipping her head in agreement.

'Do you recognise the child in the photograph?'

The actress reached for the photograph and studied it again. 'It is difficult to be entirely certain. I don't have many photographs of me as a small baby. My mother was not...' she hesitated. 'It doesn't matter.'

'But you think it might be you?'

Harry was watching her. There was no doubt that she recognised the child in the photograph. Why else had she come? But there was an internal argument taking place behind her features. She was masking it, but it was showing. The actress cleared her throat. 'I'm sorry, could I have a glass of water after all, perhaps?'

'Yes, of course,' Ellen said, pouring her a glass from a jug on the table and handing it to her. 'I'm sorry, I didn't mean to press you.'

The actress took a sip of water. 'It certainly looks like me.'

Ellen glanced at Harry and nodded.

'We found these items in a bag hidden under the floor, in a flat above a former dance club in Central London. We believe that the bag was placed there by a young woman called Gina Lawrence.'

'Gina Lawrence?'

The actress had shot back the question without hesitation, which Harry took to mean that she knew the name. But his reference to it had evidently caught her by surprise.

'You know of her?'

She hesitated, clearly struggling to regain her composure. 'You said *we*. Who found them, exactly?'

He glanced at Ellen for reassurance.

Ellen nodded.

'It was our daughter, Martha, actually. I was there with her but it was Martha who found them.'

'Your daughter?' Her eyes darted from his to Ellen's and back again. 'The little girl sitting in the office outside?'

'Yes.'

She tilted her head to one side. 'It may seem like an odd question, but have we ever met?'

It was an entirely odd question and for a moment it wrong-footed him. 'I'm sorry?'

'I mean, your daughter Martha and I? Perhaps we met at an event? I thought I recognised her, that's all.'

He looked first at Ellen, then at Jane and back at the actress. 'No, I don't believe so.'

She was staring at him. 'No matter. I interrupted. I'm sorry. Please continue.'

Harry ran his hand through his hair. 'We believe that Gina Lawrence moved into the flat shortly after your birth. She was certainly there by the time of your first birthday, when the card was written.' He waited. When the actress said nothing, he continued. 'We believe that Gina wrote it.'

The actress had reached for the card. 'To Veronica on your first birthday. My darling baby girl. I miss you so much. I will love you always,' she read out loud.

Harry said nothing.

'What are you saying?'

He had rehearsed his answer to that question but, now that she had posed it, he couldn't quite find the words.

'Are you saying that she thought she was my mother?'

Which was another question he didn't know how to answer.

'But that's preposterous. If she wrote it, then she was deluded.'

He studied her face. 'We don't think so. I'm sorry but there is no other way of saying this, Ronnie. We've got good reason to believe that Gina Lawrence was your mother. Your birth mother, that is.'

The actress stifled an uncertain laugh, turning briefly to each of them and then back to Harry. Then she laughed out loud. 'You can't be serious.'

'We believe that having given birth, Gina gave you up,' he continued.

'But that's ridiculous.'

'It must seem ridiculous. But I can assure you that we wouldn't be saying it if we didn't believe it to be true.'

The smile was still there but her discomfort was obvious. He was struck again by the internal argument he imagined being played out behind her features. She had his sympathy. He remembered the feeling only too well.

'And who do you believe is my father?' the actress said, like the idea was a bad joke. 'It appears that I may have a whole family that I know nothing about.'

It was an understandable response. 'As far as we know, Marty Phelps is your father. We have no reason to believe otherwise.'

'Well, thank goodness for that,' the actress said, leaning back in her seat.

He continued. 'We believe that he and Gina Lawrence had,' he hesitated, 'a relationship. We believe that Gina gave birth to you at the house in Great Gaddesden, by arrangement with your father and Barbara Phelps. That photograph was taken shortly afterwards.'

He noticed that her smile had faded completely at the mention of Barbara Phelps. She was shaking her head but her eyes were averted, as though, once again, she was arguing with herself. 'Let me get this straight. You're saying that my father,' she hesitated, 'what exactly? Had an illegitimate daughter by this Gina Lawrence and won custody?'

'Not exactly. We believe that they entered into a private arrangement with Gina Lawrence and thereafter that Barbara pretended to be your birth mother.'

'Oh come on. That is completely ridiculous,' she said, shaking her head. 'I'm sorry to disprove your theory, but I've seen photographs of my mother looking very pregnant indeed.'

He braced himself. 'We believe that she feigned the pregnancy.'

The actress shook her head. 'I'm sorry,' she said, pushing her chair backwards and getting to her feet.

Harry and Ellen followed suit.

'Ronnie, I'm so sorry,' Ellen broke in. 'I can't even imagine how difficult this must be.'

But Harry's eye had been drawn to a charm that the actress was wearing on a chain around her neck. As she had stood, it had slipped out from beneath her blouse.

'I think I've heard all I need to hear.'

'Wait,' Harry blurted with such force that they all fell silent. 'Wait,' he said more softly. 'Just a moment. I want to show you something. Before you dismiss this entirely.'

The actress was staring at him as if weighing up her options.

'Please.'

She sighed, which he took as a signal to proceed. He walked around the desk, reached for the folder and withdrew a sheet of paper. He handed it to the actress. 'This is Gina Lawrence.'

Ronnie Phelps glanced at the picture briefly and apparently unmoved, looked up at him and then back at the picture. Then her eyes widened.

He watched the colour drain from her face. 'The pendant,' he said, softly.

The actress had raised her hand involuntarily to the silver St Christopher around her neck.

'Can I ask where you got it?'

Ronnie Phelps appeared so shaken that Harry wondered whether she was about to pass out. Ellen was immediately at her side.

They both helped her to a seat. Ellen picked up the glass of water and handed it to her. 'Are you all right?'

'It's a coincidence. It can't be,' she stammered, taking a mouthful of water.

It was no coincidence. Harry had recognised it immediately.

'We're so sorry, Ronnie,' Ellen said. 'This must be terribly difficult to take in.'

'It can't be,' the actress repeated, shaking her head. 'He gave it to me. He can't have... He wouldn't...' her voice trailed away. Tears had formed in her eyes. Harry watched them roll down her cheeks.

He ran his hand through his hair. 'Who gave it to you, Ronnie?'

She stared at him. 'My uncle. It was a gift on my eighteenth birthday.'

He glanced at Ellen. Her face told him that she was as surprised as he was. 'Your uncle?'

'He's not my real uncle. But I've always called him that.'

Harry waited.

'Uncle Spence.'

'Spencer Milburn?'

The actress nodded.

Connections. They were firing in his head. If Spencer Milburn had given her the St Christopher then he had done so for a reason. There could be only one.

Ronnie Phelps had begun to weep. Ellen had knelt in front of her and taken hold of the actress's hand. Jane had re-filled her glass. At that moment, it felt like an intrusion to be an observer to the actress's distress.

He found himself drawn to the window in his office, only vaguely aware of the hushed voices continuing behind him. If Spencer Milburn had given her the St Christopher then he knew. He had always known. Harry stared out into the sunshine, toward the Horse Chestnut tree. Quite without warning, his vision began to narrow to the space beside the tree. As before, it was a space occupied by Gina Lawrence. She was far clearer than he had ever seen her. Her face, no longer out of focus. This time she was alone and the intense sense sadness had been replaced by one of longing. It clawed at him. Beseeching him to act. At that moment, he knew that whatever had been done with her body, she wanted him to find it. He felt a hand on his shoulder.

'Harry?'

'What?' His vision widened suddenly and the apparition faded and was gone.

'Are you all right?'

Ellen. He held her eyes. 'Yes.' He took a breath. 'Yes, I'm fine.'

She took his hand.

He turned. Martha was standing in the office doorway. Jane was beside her. Martha stepped into the room. She walked purposefully toward the actress and stood in front of her. 'Hello, Ronnie,' she said, confidently.

Ronnie Phelps stared at her, apparently lost for words.

'You look different.'

'I know you,' the actress said, hesitantly.

The hair on the back of Harry's neck was standing on end.

Martha smiled. 'I know you too. Do you feel better, now that we have found you?'

'I don't know. I... ' the actress stammered. 'I don't understand,' she said, glancing towards Harry. 'Will somebody please tell me what is happening here?'

Harry wasn't altogether sure that he could.

'It's all right,' Martha replied, confidently. 'We don't really understand it either. But that's OK. It's not weird or anything. It's just our brains.' And with that, she stepped forward and threw her arms around the stunned actress.

Ronnie Phelps glanced over Martha's shoulder, first toward Ellen and then at Harry, her arms splayed out like she didn't quite know what to do with them.

Harry held her eyes.

Slowly the actress folded her arms around his daughter and, sniffling a sob, hugged her like they were two long lost friends.

'It's all right,' Martha said. 'We're going to find her, you know.'

'Who are we going to find?' the actress said, weakly.

Martha untangled herself from the actress's embrace. 'Your mummy, of course. My dad is going to find her. Aren't you Daddy?'

They all looked at him.

He stared at Ronnie Phelps. 'You need to understand something, Ronnie.'

She said nothing.

'I'm sorry, but we believe that Gina Lawrence is dead.'

'Dead?'

'We think that she was killed. We're not certain whether it was accidental or intended. But we believe that whatever the cause, her death was concealed and her body disposed of.'

'Who?' she croaked.

'We're not certain. But we think that there were three people in the room with her when she died. Micky Milburn, a woman called Lynette Bell and one other.'

She bowed her head. When she raised it again, her face was ashen. 'My father.'

Harry stared at her. 'Yes. I'm sorry. Your father and Micky Milburn almost certainly disposed of the body.'

She nodded. And then she surprised them all. She looked at them each in turn and then she said. 'I think I might know where.'

CHAPTER FORTY-THREE

She came-to in the darkness. That she was in the boot of a car was self-evident. The Mercedes, presumably. Though she had no idea how long she'd been there or where The Apeman was taking her. She pulled an arm out from beneath her and gingerly explored her face with her free hand. The bridge of her nose was throbbing and her face was encrusted with blood. 'Bastard,' she muttered under her breath.

She turned over onto her back, placed her feet against the boot lid and pushed, as hard as she could. But the effort was in vain. The boot lid wouldn't and wasn't going to budge, making further exertion entirely pointless. She tried to relax, slowing her breathing, willing the pain in her face to abate and focussing her thoughts on the detail of her plight.

So, Spencer Milburn had made his choice. He had betrayed her to his brother. He had waited for her to fall asleep, taken her laptop and probably her phone too, and called Micky Milburn who had, true to form, dispatched The Apeman.

But the Milburn brothers now had a problem. The car chase through Newcastle would have featured on several street cameras. There was every possibility that The Apeman's face would be all over the footage. The police would, in any case, be able to identify her from her car's number plate, both from the street camera footage and when they found the car parked up behind the old department store. Which they undoubtedly would and hopefully already had. If he killed her, she reasoned silently, he would be the one and only suspect. Even if the plates on the Mercedes were false, the blood from the stab wound she had inflicted on him would, thanks to modern forensics, identify him. There would have been traces of his blood left behind on the scissors and probably spattered all over the former pay station. Sooner or later, they were going to catch him.

If he released her then she would go straight to the police. If he kept her captive, there'd be a search. Her abduction might well make the national headlines. Micky Milburn would surely be in the frame, given the information she'd provided to the police in Scotland.

The car came to a slow halt. She heard and felt the gravel or stones beneath the car's tyres; the sound of the doors opening and muffled voices. 'Let me out, you bastard,' she yelled, kicking the boot lid. 'Let me out!'

She waited. Nothing. Except the faint, but recognisable sound of a burbling engine. A light aircraft engine. 'Shit.'

The boot lid was sprung, filling the space in which she had been confined with light. She held up her hand to shield her eyes.

'Come on, darling. You've got a plane to catch.'

It was Micky Milburn's voice. His grinning face slowly came into focus.

'Fuck off,' she spat back at him.

And The Apeman. He stepped forward, grabbed her arm and hauled her out of the boot.

She found her feet, noticing as she steadied herself and with some satisfaction, the deep red blood stain on The Apeman's right thigh.

'You'll be flying economy, I'm afraid,' Milburn said, still smiling at her. 'A romantic break will do the two of you no end of good. A chance to settle your differences and get to know each other a little more intimately. You know what I'm saying?'

The Apeman had hold of her arm.

She turned towards him and spat in his face.

He raised a clenched fist.

She braced herself.

Milburn placed a restraining hand on The Apeman's arm. 'Save it for later. In three or four hours time you'll have her all to yourself. Now won't that be something?'

'Bullshit,' she said, between clenched teeth. 'They'll have run that number plate,' she said, glancing back at the Mercedes, 'and mine, through the PNC. Right now, every force in the country will out be looking for me. I'm amazed you got this far.'

'Possibly,' Milburn said, like the suggestion was of little consequence. 'Which is the reason for your little excursion. You did bring your passport, I take it?'

She stared at him but said nothing.

'You didn't? Too bad. We'll just have to avoid customs. You won't be needing it for the return journey. Because, in your case, darling, there ain't gonna be any return journey.'

She scowled. 'You don't scare me, Milburn. It's on the record that you've been threatening me. It'll take the police five minutes to work out who is behind this.'

He scratched his chin. 'Which might work if I was here. But see, it's like this; I'm not here. I was never here. Right now, as far as the authorities are concerned, I'm back home, sunning myself by the pool. Which is precisely where I will be in,' he said, looking at his watch, 'about twelve hours time.'

'Yeah? And how is your brother going to explain away the fact that my DNA will be all over his house?'

Milburn shook his head. 'You just don't get it, do you? You're a serial stalker, right? You stalked your ex and now you're stalking Spence, on the back of a crazy obsession with some missing kid from fifty years ago. It's gold plated bullshit. But he feels sorry for you. You give him some sob story about needing a place to lay low and the idiot lets you stay. He always was a bit of a pushover. Then, in the middle of the night, some guy in a balaclava rolls up, out for your blood. You must have pissed off some other victim of your rubbish brand of journalism. Poor old Spence does his best to fight the guy off, but he's built like a brick shithouse. Spence has the bruises to prove it, which I gather you supplied. In the middle of the struggle, you escape and the guy gives chase. Spence has no idea what's gone down but he's shit scared. He's 74, for fuck's sake. The victim of some crazy, washed up journalist, who cons her way into the homes of the elderly and pisses people off for a living.'

She laughed. 'You seriously believe that's how they will see it?'

Milburn shrugged. 'Who's gonna tell them any different?'

She stared at him. 'Harry and Ellen Stammers might.'

Milburn laughed. 'I wouldn't bank on it, darling. The Stammers family have their reasons for wanting nothing more to do with you.'

'What do you mean?'

'Let's just say that the chances of Stammers staging a late cavalry charge are somewhere between zero and zero. Now if you don't mind, I've got people to see and places to go.' He hesitated. 'I'm travelling business class. You, on the other hand are going to be slumming it in economy. Bon voyage, sweetheart,' he said, turning away.

CHAPTER FORTY-FOUR

Spencer Milburn pounded his fist against the wide, wooden door. He'd driven almost the entire length of the A1, flat out and with only a brief stop in a lay-by, when Micky had finally answered his phone. Spencer had been in no mood for niceties. 'You gave me your fucking word, Micky,' he'd yelled down the phone. 'You said that she would come to no harm.'

'Wrong. I gave you my word that if she agreed to drop it, she'd come to no harm. She didn't. So no deal. But hey, relax. Johnnie hasn't done any lasting damage. Yet.'

'It was all over the local fucking news. He chased her half way across Newcastle.'

'She's alive isn't she? The deal was…'

'Deal? This is not some fucking game, Micky. Where is she?'

'Look, Johnnie is taking care of her. Mind you, he's pretty pissed with her, actually. As well as knocking several of his teeth out, the bitch stabbed him in the thigh. That was not her best move.'

'She what?'

Micky had laughed. 'The chick has got some spunk, I'll give her that.'

'What are you going to do with her?'

'Me? I'm doing nothing with her, man. Johnnie, on the other hand, has big plans for your pet journalist.'

'Where, Micky? Where is he taking her?'

'Why? Fancy joining the party?'

If he could have, he later reflected, he'd have done what he should have done years ago and punched the fucker in the face. Instead, he'd gripped the steering wheel with his free hand so tightly it had made his knuckles burn. 'For fuck's sake, where?'

'Out of harm's way. Depending on your perspective. Now, if you don't mind…'

'The Phelps place,' he'd interrupted. 'I'm about forty minutes away. Be there. Or God help me, I will spill the whole fucking thing to the police. I've had enough of this, Micky.'

Micky had laughed. 'Police? I don't think so. You're in this up to your neck, just like the rest of us.'

'I don't care. If it's a game, then the game's up. I've been lying for you for fifty years. If you won't see reason, then perhaps Phelps will.'

'Phelps? You're off your rocker, man. You think Phelps is going to roll over? He's got too much to lose.'

'Be there Micky. I mean it.'

'Maybe.'

'Micky?'

The line had gone dead.

He pounded his fist on the door again. It opened. Marty Phelps took a step backwards.

'Where's Micky?' He shoved his way past him into the house. 'I said, where is he?'

Phelps faced him. 'He's not here. In fact, he was never here. Ring any bells? You're too late, Spencer. Fifty years too late.'

CHAPTER FORTY-FIVE

Harry turned the car onto the gravel drive that led toward the house. It was a grand, Georgian-styled double fronted building, he observed, with a pillared porch and wide bay windows. There were three cars parked outside. A silver-grey BMW, a blue Volvo and a Jaguar in what looked to Harry like British Racing Green. He pulled up beside them. They each stared at the house and then, without exchanging a word, got out of the car. When they had gathered beside the car, Harry glanced down at Martha who had taken hold of Ronnie's hand and then up at the actress. 'Are you ready for this?'

Ronnie Phelps grimaced. 'As ready as I'll ever be.'

He nodded.

They approached the house. Ronnie went first and rang the door bell.

To say that Phelps looked startled when he opened the door would be an understatement. Otherwise Phelps appeared, pretty much, as Harry had been expecting. Elegantly dressed, smartly presented and with underpinning air of arrogance about him.

'Father,' Ronnie said formally. 'These are my friends, Harry and Ellen Stammers and their daughter, Martha.'

Phelps swept their faces. 'I know who they are,' he said tersely. 'What are they doing here? What are you doing here?'

'We have come to see you and Mother.'

Phelps stared at her. For a moment, Harry thought that he was going to turn them away. But then he stood aside. Ronnie and Martha entered first.

They had stepped into a wood panelled hallway. Ahead of them, was a grand wooden staircase. Harry might have admired it in any other circumstance.

'She is at home, I take it?' the actress said, giving nothing away.

'What is this, Ronnie?'

'This, Father, is something I should have done a long time ago. You are both going to listen to what I have to say and then, for once, you are going to tell me the truth.'

Phelps was adjusting to the prevailing circumstances. Harry watched him calculating his options. 'Why are Mr and Mrs Stammers here, Ronnie, to say nothing of their daughter?' Phelps said calmly. 'If we are going to discuss our private affairs than I would rather that we did so in private.'

'I really don't care what you would prefer,' the actress said like she really didn't. 'They are here because I want them here.'

Phelps gave Harry a look of pure acid. 'You are going to regret this intrusion, Mr Stammers.'

Harry shrugged and managed something approaching a smile. 'Perhaps. But like Ronnie said, we are here because she wants us here.'

Phelps stared at him. 'Very well,' he said, turning back to his daughter. 'I will ask your mother to join us. Go through. We have another guest. You'll find him waiting in the conservatory.'

'Who?' the actress shot back.

Phelps smiled for the first time. 'I will let you discover that for yourself.' He turned away from them and began to climb the stairs.

Ronnie led them down the hallway toward a set of French doors. They opened into an impressive, glass conservatory. As they entered, a man who had been seated on a sofa stood up and turned towards them.

'Ronnie? What are you doing here?'

Harry recognised him. Spencer Milburn. It was slightly surreal to see him in the flesh. The Monks had been almost as famous as John, Paul, George and Ringo in their day, and yet here he was. He had smiled but Harry had noted his expression. If there had been any colour in his face, it was rapidly draining.

Ronnie Phelps released Martha's hand and marched across the conservatory, towards him. 'How could you? You knew, didn't you? You've known all along.'

'Known?' he said, looking, at that moment, like he wanted the floor beneath his feet to open and swallow him.

'Fifty years, Spencer. Fifty years.'

He stared at her, like a rabbit caught in headlights.

'You could have told me at any time. Those things you said at the weekend. You could have told me then. Why in God's name didn't you?'

'What I said... it was the truth...' he stammered. 'I didn't...'

'Don't you dare,' she interrupted him. 'If you didn't know, what the hell is this?' she added, taking hold of the St Christopher on the chain around her neck.

He stared at it, ashen faced.

'That's right. Take a long, hard look. You gave it to me. The only link I had to my mother. You knew all along.'

He said nothing.

'Did she give it to you?' Ronnie continued. She let the St Christopher slip from her hand.

'I found it,' he blurted. 'In her room. I wanted you to have it.'

She ignored him. 'You've been like a father to me. Ever since I was a little girl. I trusted you. But it was all a lie, wasn't it? You let me believe that I was hers,' she said, gesturing over her shoulder toward the doorway back into the house. 'Even when I told you how abysmally she treated me.'

He shook his head in denial. 'I had no idea, Ronnie. You don't understand.'

'Really? Then tell me. Tell me now, why you've kept the identity of my real mother from me…'

'Your mother, was nothing.'

Harry turned. They all did. All except Martha. After the actress had let go of her hand, she had drifted away toward the conservatory door, where she was standing, staring out into the garden.

Barbara Phelps had entered the conservatory, followed by her husband. She was an elderly, glamorous but severe looking woman, Harry observed, with a dark complexion and short grey hair. 'She was nothing, Ronnie. If we hadn't taken you in, you'd have lived your life in poverty. You'd have had nothing. You'd have been nothing.'

Harry noted her accent. It might have mellowed somewhat over the years but still revealed her African origin.

'I'd have been loved,' Ronnie Phelps said in a small voice.

'Loved?' The scorn in the elderly woman's tone rippled around the room.

'Yes, loved,' Ronnie said more forcefully. 'You never really did, did you? Have you ever actually loved anyone?'

Barbara Phelps expression hardened. 'You were always such a rude and ungrateful child.'

Ronnie shook her head, like she didn't quite believe what she was hearing. 'Ungrateful? I was an unhappy child. Did you even notice?'

The elderly woman scowled.

'I never understood why you hated me. I used to think that there was something wrong with me. Do you know that? For years I thought that I must be so detestable that my own mother hated me. Except that you were not my mother, were you?'

'We gave you everything.'

'And nothing that mattered.' Ronnie turned to her father. 'What did you do with Gina Lawrence?'

'Ronnie, I don't know what nonsense these people have been telling you,' Marty Phelps pleaded, gesturing towards Harry and Ellen. 'You're going to pay for this, Stammers. My lawyers will take you to the cleaners. When we have finished with you…'

'Stop it,' Ronnie interrupted him. 'Just stop it. All you've ever done is lie. Tell me the truth. What happened to my mother? My real mother.'

'Nobody knows what happened to Gina Lawrence, least of all us,' Phelps began.

Harry noted how easily he switched between threatening them and appealing to his daughter. If he had doubted it before meeting the man, he certainly didn't now. Phelps was a contemptible slime bag of a man.

'She disappeared in 1964,' Phelps continued. 'She was never found. Mr and Mrs Stammers have, I am afraid, been rather taken in by a very persistent, but entirely unbalanced journalist, with an equally unbalanced story, very little of which has any basis in reality. She's a fantasist, Ronnie. All I have done is try to protect you; to protect all of us from this,' he said spreading his hands. 'This madness,' he said for emphasis.

Harry glanced at Ellen. She shook her head. He took the gesture as a request to say nothing.

'We took you in because Barbara couldn't have children of our own,' Phelps continued. 'As soon as you were old enough, we should have told you. That was our mistake. I'm sorry. Truly I am. We thought it better that you didn't know. We have always tried to act in your best interest.'

Harry grimaced. Evidently, acting ran in the family. It was a fine, if uncomfortable performance.

'So where are the adoption papers?' Ronnie challenged.

Phelps stared at her. 'What?'

'If I am adopted, show me the papers.'

He said nothing.

She smiled, bitterly. 'You can't, can you? Because there are none. There was no adoption. You,' she said, gesturing towards her mother, 'even pretended to be pregnant. What did you do, shove a pillow under your jumper?'

'How dare you talk to me like that. If…'

'How did you convince her to give me up? Did you pay her? Buy me like some calf at a cattle market?'

Harry was watching Marty Phelps. The speed with which he was able to adapt his approach to Ronnie's accusations was impressive, Harry had to give him that.

'Tell me, why didn't you adopt me formally?'

'We would have adopted you. But…' Phelps hesitated.

'You couldn't, could you?'

Phelps dismissed the question with a wave of his hand. 'Really, I am not prepared to have any more of my personal affairs discussed in front of Mr and Mrs Stammers. Do you really want this splashed all over tomorrow's newspapers?'

'It's a little late for that. Harry and Ellen are well aware of why you could not adopt.'

As slick as he was, Phelps was beginning to sweat.

'It was a trivial matter,' Barbara Phelps interrupted. 'A minor financial misdemeanour. In those days, such a conviction prevented perfectly good people from adoption. Completely ridiculous and blatantly discriminatory.'

Ronnie Phelps laughed. 'Is that what he told you?'

'That's enough…' Marty Phelps tried to interrupt her. To stop the revelation that was coming.

'He told me,' Barbara Phelps continued, 'the truth.'

'The truth?' Ronnie Phelps spat. 'My Father has been lying for so long, he has forgotten the meaning of the word. Did he tell you that his real name is Gerald Phipps? Did he tell you that he changed his name to Phelps on his release from prison?'

'Yes, of course he did,' Barbara snapped, apparently unfazed.

'Did he tell you that he'd served 21 months for gross indecency with a minor?'

'Nonsense,' the old lady spat. 'Who has been telling you all this?'

'She was fourteen years old. Fourteen.'

'Rubbish.'

But Harry noticed a flash of uncertainty pass across Barbara Phelps' features.

'No, it isn't rubbish.' Ronnie Phelps took a folded sheet of paper from her inside pocket. 'Here,' she said, holding out her hand.

'What is this?' Barbara Phelps said, snatching the paper from Ronnie's hand.

'Read it.'

She unfolded it and read.

'He lied to you. Like he lied to me. Like he lied to the police about Gina Lawrence. Like they all lied,' she said, glancing towards Spencer Milburn. 'Like they're still lying.'

Barbara Phelps said nothing.

Ronnie turned to her father. 'In any case, you didn't need to adopt me, did you?'

He stared at her.

'How old was Gina Lawrence when you slept with her?'

'Now, wait just a moment...'

'I'll tell you how old she was. She was 15. A child, for God's sake. You slept with her, got her pregnant and took her baby. What did you do when she told you that she wanted me back?'

'Wanted you back?' Barbara Phelps broke in. She laughed. 'She never wanted you and I can't say that I blame...'

'That is not true,' Spencer Milburn interrupted, stepping forward.

Harry had been watching him, shifting uncomfortably from one foot to the other.

'Gina loved you, Ronnie,' he continued. 'Never doubt that for a moment. She regretted what she had done. I saw the toll that losing you took on her. The agony in her eyes. I watched it, played out in front of me.'

Ronnie had turned to face him. 'Then why in God's name didn't you help her?'

He bowed his head. 'Because I was afraid,' he said, looking up and holding her eyes. 'It was like I told you. We were just kids. We had our first record deal. We'd just gone to Number One. Everything we'd been working for. If I'd sided with Gina against Marty, we'd have been finished.'

'Bingo.'

They all turned.

Micky Milburn was standing in the conservatory doorway.

'And there you have it,' he said, grinning. 'The big admission. St Fucking Spencer of Monkchester. Not so saintly after all. Played along with it, just like the rest of us.'

'No. Not like the rest of you,' Spencer Milburn challenged his brother. 'There was a difference. I cared for her. You never did. You used her. Like you use everyone.'

'Sure you cared. You cared about protecting your own ass. Just like the rest of us,' Micky shot back. He glanced towards the garden. 'Hey, you might want to watch your kid.'

They turned. Martha was outside. Standing beside the pool.

'It's all right, I'll go,' Ellen said, walking across to the gap Martha had made in the sliding door.

'What have you done with Holly Holgate?' Spencer said, taking a step toward his brother.

'I told you, Johnnie is taking care of her.'

'Where Micky? If any harm comes to her, I'll…'

'Hey,' Micky said, holding up his hands. 'If you really want to know, right now,' he said, glancing at his watch, 'I'd say she's probably 1500 feet over the French coast, heading south.'

Spencer stared at him.

'What, so you've got the hots for her or something?' Micky said grinning.

Spencer took another step forward.

Harry stepped into his path, caught his eyes and slowly shook his head.

'You've got me all wrong, Spence,' Micky continued. 'You always did. Just like you got me wrong back in '64.'

'Yeah? So tell me, Micky,' Spencer shot back. 'Tell me how I got you wrong back in '64. Tell us all.'

'Me?' Micky replied, holding his arms wide. 'So what, you want the graphic details?'

'I want to know what you did to Gina,' Spencer Milburn said, icily.

Harry could see the tension mounting in Spencer Milburn's features.

'Fine. I screwed her brains out. Then I screwed that other bitch too. Then I did it all over again. And you know what? They enjoyed it.'

'You fucking bastard,' Spencer yelled, suddenly charging his brother.

Harry had been waiting for it. He grabbed him around his chest and held him. The struggle went out of him easily enough. Harry thought that he felt like a beaten man.

'Do you want to know something else, Spencer? Watch my lips. I. Didn't. Kill her,' his brother mouthed.

'Bullshit,' his brother managed between gritted teeth.

'All along, you've blamed me. And all along you were wrong. It wasn't me. You want the truth? That is the truth.'

'Liar. You're a liar.'

'Oh yeah? Tell him, Marty.'

'Micky...' For the first time, Marty Phelps sounded truly menacing. 'I am warning you. Stop this, right now.'

'Has my brother not told you?' Micky continued. 'He's had enough. He wants to know exactly what we've been lying about all these years. So tell him. Tell us all, Marty. Let's get this over and done with.' Micky glanced again at his watch. 'I've got a plane to catch.'

'Micky, I'm warning you.'

'Tell him. Tell him who killed her. Then tell him who had the only witness strung up like a kipper. You know what, Spencer is not the only one who is sick of this pretence. And don't even think about threatening me, Marty. I've got one hell of a legal team back home and the Yanks sure know how to fight a lawsuit, believe me. If we're all putting our cards on the table it won't be me doing time in Wormwood Scrubs.'

'You?' Spencer said, facing Marty Phelps. 'You killed her?'

Harry watched as Marty Phelps' composure began to crumble but he wasn't entirely beaten. He turned to his daughter. 'Gina Lawrence vanished,' he pleaded. 'We tried to find her. We did everything that we could.'

'I don't believe you,' the actress replied coldly.

Phelps scanned their faces. 'Where's the evidence that she is dead? No body. No murder. This is all nonsense. Don't be taken in by it, Ronnie,' he said, appealing to his daughter once again. 'If you want to blame anyone for her disappearance, blame them,' he said, gesturing towards the two brothers. 'It was Micky who instigated it and Spencer who didn't have the courage to stop him.'

It was the desperation in his tone that revealed the lie, as far as Harry was concerned, and Spencer Milburn had clearly reached the same conclusion.

'You killed Gina? All this time. It was you?' he said, his voice breaking.

Micky Milburn laughed out loud. 'God All Mighty, Spencer. Do I really have to spell it out? Not him. Her.'

They all turned and stared. Micky was pointing his finger at Barbara Phelps.

CHAPTER FORTY-SIX

Monday, 27 April 1964

It was as though her thoughts had been scattered, like pebbles on a beach, tumbling back and forth with the ebb and flow of the tide. She'd been nowhere and everywhere. Flitting from one semi-coherent thought and sensation to another. Rhythmic music and colour. The movement of bodies. Dancers. Faces. Some that she recognised. Others that she didn't. Coming to her in slow-motion waves.

She stirred, her eyelids heavy; her arms and legs like lead weights.

Her thoughts began to coalesce around a single sensation. Nakedness. She opened her eyes. She was laying, flat on her back, the space around her familiar, yet unfamiliar. The patterned wallpaper. The shade on the light, high up on the ceiling above her. Her room. She glanced at the familiar sheets on the bed beside her and up, into the face of a woman. An unconscious woman. Her forehead covered in sweat and hanging over the edge of the bed. And a hand. A male hand. His hand. She remembered. And as she remembered, she became aware of another presence. Movement to her right. Still unable to move her arms, she managed to tilt her head.

She caught a glimpse of her for a split second only. A woman, her face contorted in an expression of rage and pure loathing. Then darkness. Pressure. Panic. She began to fight it. Twisting her head wildly, from side to side, willing her arms and legs to move. In the struggle, she caught a glimpse of her friend, lying on the bed above her. Her eyes had flickered and opened, and there was a flash of recognition. And then darkness, renewed pressure and a burning sensation in her lungs. It quickly sapped what little strength she'd been able to summon.

In the last few moments of conscious thought, she knew what was happening. She knew the identity of her assailant and what she intended. And she knew why. Veronica. She had given away her daughter. Surrendered her to the woman who was kneeling on her chest, suffocating her. On the edge of consciousness, all her physical strength spent, Gina Lawrence swore a silent oath, made with every ounce of will that her soul possessed. She screamed it silently into the feather pillow covering her face. Whatever death might bring, she would deny it. No matter how long it took. She would never rest until Veronica found her.

CHAPTER FORTY-SEVEN

Thursday, 26 May 2016

If looks could kill, Harry reflected, Micky Milburn would have been a dead man. But, as well as fury, there was something else in Barbara Phelps' expression and Harry recognised it. It was fear.

Micky was staring at his brother. 'When Marty brought me round, Gina was already dead. He told me that it was the drugs. That her death was down to me. That if news of it got out, I'd be finished. That we'd all be finished. And, you know what? I fell for it. Hook, line and sinker. That's why I lied to the police. Just like you lied to them.'

Spencer Milburn said nothing.

'But he was lying, Spence. I had no idea. I swear.' He turned towards Phelps. 'Tell them.'

Marty Phelps said nothing.

Micky Milburn, shook his head. 'No, I didn't really think you would.' He turned back to his brother. 'I was unconscious. But Lynette came around. She saw Barbara enter the room and she saw what she did. I knew absolutely nothing about it.'

They turned towards Barbara Phelps.

She was staring at Micky in stony-faced silence.

Micky smiled. 'Well? Are you going to tell them or shall I?'

'You can't prove a damn thing,' the old woman said, narrowing her eyes.

'No? But I can,' Ronnie Phelps said, her voice as cold as ice.

CHAPTER FORTY-EIGHT

'It was the summer time. 1970, I think. It was hot and the sun was shining. I remember it so clearly. I said, "Mother, can I stop now? I have swum five lengths. I don't want to swim anymore." But she wasn't listening. She rarely listened to me. Not when she had been drinking and especially not when she was entertaining.

My mother was laying on a sun lounger, beside the pool. She was wearing sun glasses and a one-piece swim suit. It had black and white stripes. I remember it clearly. She had a cigarette in one hand and a glass in the other. There was a man, laying on another sun lounger beside her. I think his name was Daniel but I really cannot remember. He had long blonde hair and a tattoo of a snake on his shoulder. I do remember that. Nowadays you see tattoos like that on men all the time but in those days it was unusual.

I didn't like any of the men who came to our house. Apart from Uncle Spencer who came to see my father when he was at home and who always bought me small gifts and sometimes read to me at bedtime. The men who came to our house when my father was away were different. My mother called them her "man friends". They rarely paid me much attention. I don't think she liked it when they did. Which, I suppose, is why they didn't.

Daniel heard me. I know he did, because I saw him glance in my direction and say something to her, though I couldn't hear what. She waved her hand in my direction, dismissively.

'I don't want to swim any more. I'm tired.' I called out. Louder this time.

'You can get out when I tell you to get out and not before,' I saw her turn back to Daniel and the two of them exchange words. They were laughing at me. Or that is what I thought; what I felt.

Mother made me swim every day during the summer holidays and at the weekends, unless Father was at home, which he rarely was. I detested swimming and I hated that pool. She knew that I hated it. But the more I complained the more she would insist. I knew that if I complained too much or worse, refused, she would fly into a temper and send me to my room. I only ever did so if she had company, because I knew that she didn't like them to see her behave badly towards me. Sometimes she would hit me, but only when we were alone or when she was very drunk.

I swam across to the ladder and climbed out of the pool. I stood there for a moment, staring at them. Sometimes I hated her. Sometimes I didn't care if I made her angry. Sometimes I wanted to make her angry. I walked across to the cast iron table and chairs that were a few yards from their loungers. I collected my terry towelling robe from the back of a chair, put it on and began to walk towards the house.

I heard Mother call out. 'Stop right there.'

I stopped, turned and faced her. Mother always tried to mask her accent, especially when she had company. She tried to make herself sound like an American but she was born in South Africa. When she had been drinking, her accent became stronger. I never liked that accent. I still don't. Especially when a woman speaks with it. It makes my stomach turn.

She said 'Did I tell you that you could get out of the pool?'

I stared at her.

'Answer me.'

'I don't want to swim. I'm tired and I'm cold.'

She looked at me like she hated me. 'Get back into the pool. Right now. You can get out when I say you can get out.'

But I stood my ground.

She turned to Daniel. 'She does this deliberately,' she said, like I wasn't there. Like I didn't count. 'She just has to make a scene in front of my friends.'

I was feeling defiant. She had made me feel like that. 'No, I don't. I just don't want to swim any more. Why should I, if I don't want to?'

She placed her glass down on the floor and stubbed out her cigarette in the ash tray on a stand beside her. 'Are you defying me?'

I was beginning to shake. Perhaps it was in anger or fear. I don't know which. Perhaps it was both. 'I am not going back in the pool. I hate swimming and I hate you. I am going to my room,' I said, turning away from them and marching towards the house.

I didn't get more than a few paces before I felt Mother grasp my upper arm. She dragged me into the house through the French doors that led into our dining room. She let go of my arm, turned and slammed the doors behind us. 'What is wrong with you? Why must you always create a scene in front of my friends?' she yelled, making no effort now to mask her true accent.

I had backed away from her but I wasn't ready to back down. I could feel the hurt burning in my chest. 'They're not your friends. They're your *boyfriends*.' I spat that word like I knew exactly what it meant. 'You wait till I tell Father that you have boyfriends come to the house when he is away.'

'You ungrateful little bitch,' she screamed, hurling herself towards me. She grabbed me by the hair. 'Don't you ever speak to me like that again. After everything I have done for you. Is this how you repay me?'

She was shaking me by the hair. I felt my knees buckling and tears welling in my eyes. 'I'm sorry,' I cried out. 'I'm sorry.'

'Do you think your Father will listen to your lies, you evil little vixen? Do you think he will believe you when I tell him how nasty you are to me? When I tell him how you speak to me? How you treat me? Well do you?' she yelled.

'No. No. I'm sorry. I didn't mean it. I won't say anything. I won't.'

'I wouldn't have dared speak to my mother the way you speak to me. She'd have thrashed me until I begged her to stop. Is that what you want?'

'No, Mother. No,' I sobbed.

'Mother? You're no daughter of mine.' She laughed in my face. 'I wanted a real daughter. Do you know that? A little girl who would show me the respect I am due. Instead, your father gave me you,' she spat. 'The child of a worthless whore. She wanted you, though God knows why. So he put her where she can see you. Every day. Now go to your room and stay there,' she hurled, shoving me toward the door. 'Go on, get out of my sight. If I hear one peep out of you, Veronica Phelps,' she said, spitting my surname like it disgusted her, 'God help me, but I will thrash you beyond reason.'

I fled then. Out of the room, up the stairs, along the hallway and into my bedroom, throwing myself on my bed and bawling into the blankets. When I finally fell asleep, still sobbing gently and catching my breath, I dreamt that I was running. Away from her. Away from that pool and the house. Into the woods. Searching, always searching. Until I was utterly lost.

Something changed for me that day. Something switched off in my head. I blanked her words and her ill treatment. I blanked her. I have had that dream countless times since. It was always the same. Until a few weeks ago. I dreamt that somebody else was there with me. In the woods. A little girl, with shining blonde hair. She took my hand and led me back to the place where I think my mother may be buried. Will you and Martha come with me to find her?'

Harry Stammers looked from Ellen, to their daughter. She was seated beside Ronnie Phelps, holding the actress's hand, her expression serious, but untroubled. His head was telling him that it would be madness to take Martha there. But his instinct was telling him that it was always meant to happen that way. That to deny it would be to deny her. That part of her that she was only now just discovering. Ellen had said that their instinct always led them to the truth. A truth that was unavoidable. It would find them by the long route or by the short. But it would find them in the end. 'Martha?' he said at last. 'Think seriously now. What is that special part of your brain telling you would be the right thing to do?'

Martha's face wrinkled. 'I think everyone deserves to know where their mummy is. I think Gina has been trying to tell us. I think we should go with Ronnie to find her.'

'Are you scared?'

'A bit. But we have to be brave and do the right thing.'

Harry nodded. 'Martha is right,' he said addressing the actress. 'We will go with you to find your mother.'

CHAPTER FORTY-NINE

Ronnie had taken a pace towards Barbara Phelps so that they were facing each other. The enmity between them was almost palpable. The thought crossed Harry's mind that the two women might come to blows. He braced himself to intervene.

'I can prove it, because you told me,' Ronnie said, her voice level but steely.

'Told you? What are you talking about?'

'The day you dragged me into the house by the hair. Do you even remember?'

The old woman snorted.

'I was seven years old. Seven,' she said with a mixture of horror and disgust. 'I didn't understand who you were referring to or what you meant. But I understand it now. Was is it your idea to put her there? Where she could see me.'

Barbara Phelps stared at her daughter.

'Was it?' the actress yelled suddenly. 'Was it you who killed her? You evil bitch!'

Harry instinctively reached out and placed a restraining hand on Ronnie's shoulder. And then he saw the older woman's fury overcome her.

'Yes, I killed her,' she spat. 'She deserved it.'

Ronnie Phelps recoiled.

'Had she gone to the police, she'd have ruined us. Ruined everything.'

'She was little more than a child,' Ronnie said quietly.

'She was a filthy slut. A slut who slept with my husband. She had nothing to offer you. We gave you everything. A home. A life. You wanted for nothing. She would have taken that from you. From us. She had no right.'

'She was my mother.'

'Your mother,' Barbara Phelps mocked. 'She wasn't fit to be a mother. When I went up to her flat that night to confront her, I found her on the floor, still out of her head. Scratch marks all over her. Her and that other slut. With him,' she spat in Micky Milburn's direction. 'All three of them unconscious and naked, like pigs after rutting. The stink of it made me feel sick. Is that a woman who is fit to be a mother?'

There was a heavy silence in the room.

Harry put his arm around Ronnie Phelps and the actress turned towards him. Her expression was one that he would never forget. It was a mixture of loathing and realisation.

'So I picked up a pillow,' the old woman continued. 'It was filthy with their vomit. And I smothered her with it. That should have been the end of it. It would have been the end of it had that other bitch not seen me. I should have finished her too and I would have, had you not stopped me,' she said, turning to her husband.

Harry had been watching Marty Phelps out of the corner of his eye. He looked like his life was imploding.

'All you ever cared about was that fucking band and the money they were going to make,' Barbara Phelps continued. 'We could have killed them both, blamed him, and ditched them. But no. You had to send her away to Scotland.'

'Where I found her in 1967,' Micky broke in.

Spencer, who had also taken a step towards Ronnie, but backed away when Harry had shaken his head, stared at his brother. 'You found Lynette Bell?'

'Sure I did. Barbara is right. Sending her to Scotland was their big mistake. Australia and maybe I'd never have found her. But,

Scotland?' He shook his head. 'Now that was plain stupid. I spotted her in a photograph taken at some festival up there. Which got me kinda thinking. I don't know, call it a hunch. Something just never sat right with me. So Gina was pilled up. We all were. But the more I thought about it, the more it just didn't seem likely that she had overdosed. So I looked for her. Asked about. And when I found her in that shit hole she called home, she soon spilled the beans. With a little encouragement, it has to be said. I was pretty pissed about it, actually. All that time, taking the can, you know? But good things come to those who wait, eh Marty?'

'What are you talking about?' Spencer Milburn said, addressing his brother.

'Where else do you think I got the money to set myself up in the States? Certainly not from The Monks. They'd screwed us for every penny. So hey, I thought I'd return the favour.'

'You blackmailed them?'

'I wouldn't call it blackmail, exactly. Let's just say that we came to a working arrangement.'

'Dear God,' Spencer said, shaking his head.

'Shake your head all you like, Spence. But like I've always told you, it wasn't me. I didn't kill Gina and, while I might have scared Bell shitless.' He hesitated. 'All right, I did scare her shitless, but I didn't kill her. Now if you folks want to decide where you're going with all this, that's fine by me,' Micky said, looking at his watch. 'I need to be on my way.'

Harry took a deep breath. 'Except for one small detail,' he said, releasing the actress. He reached into his jacket pocket and pulled out the radio transmitter.

They all stared at him.

'Did you get all of that?' he said into the device.

Mike's response was clearly audible. 'Sure thing. It's all on the record. Listen up guys.'

The faint sound of sirens in the distance.

'The police are on their way.'

Harry smiled.

'Oh, and Harry?'

He keyed the PTT, 'Roger?'

'Jane says that the police told her that French air traffic control are tracking Holly's plane. When they land, there's going to be quite a welcoming party.'

CHAPTER FIFTY

They were standing in silence, at the pool's edge, staring at the water.

'Do you think you'll ever recover your relationship with Spencer?' Ellen said at last.

Ronnie Phelps sighed. 'I don't know. Right now, it feels too raw. I trusted him, but he let me down, Ellen. Terribly. I'm not at all sure that I'll be able to trust him again.'

'I hope you will. He doesn't strike me as a bad man. A weak man, perhaps. But not a bad one.'

The actress tipped her head in acknowledgment. 'Maybe.'

'To think that, knowing what she knew, Barbara Phelps made you swim in that pool every day,' Ellen said, shaking her head.

'Barbara told me that he had put her where she could see me. I never really understood what she meant, until I spoke to the three of you at Bletchley.'

'It is hardly surprising,' Ellen said, her voice solemn. 'To do that to a child. It was pure evil.'

'For years, I think I just blanked it. I just couldn't face it.'

'I told Daddy you were stuck,' Martha spoke up. 'I knew you were.'

Ronnie Phelps smiled. 'And you were right, Martha Stammers.' She took hold of the little girl's hand. 'Is she really down there, do you think?' she said, after a short pause.

'Oh yes,' Martha replied, with conviction. 'She's been down there all along. Right there,' she said pointing with her free hand, to the middle of the pool.

'How do you know?'

Martha looked up at her. 'Daddy said, I should never tell anyone else. In case they thought I was weird. Even though I'm not really weird at all.'

Harry smiled. 'It's all right, Love. You can tell Ronnie.'

Martha nodded. 'I know because I saw her. She was lying on her back. Looking up at the sky.'

'Can you still see her?' the actress asked.

Martha shook her head. 'No. When you came out, she turned her head and smiled. I think she was very happy to see you, Ronnie. Then she went all fuzzy and now she's gone. I don't think I'll be able to see her anymore.'

Ronnie Phelps squeezed Martha's hand. 'But you will be able to see me Martha. You can come and see me whenever you want. In fact, I hope you will come to see me in Cornwall.'

'Do you still have a pink dressing gown?'

Ronnie frowned and looked from Martha, to Ellen and then to Harry.

Harry shrugged.

'A pink dressing gown?' the actress repeated.

Martha nodded. 'Like the one you used to wear when you were little.'

Harry smiled, in spite of himself. 'Ok, so maybe we are just a bit weird.'

Ellen reached out and pinched him. 'Speak for yourself, soldier.'

'But in a good way,' he added, hastily.

'You know the one I mean,' Martha insisted. 'It looked like a big towel.'

Her expression told Harry that Ronnie knew.

'No, I don't still have one,' she managed.

'Good. Because pink doesn't suit you at all.'

Harry laughed. He just couldn't help himself. 'You'll get used to us. Eventually.'

Ronnie shook her head. 'I can try,' she said, flashing them a crooked smile. 'Perhaps you can come for a holiday. I think we can accommodate you all. Just about.'

'What do you think, Martha? Would you like that?' Ellen asked.

'I wouldn't mind,' Mike said grinning.

Jane gave him a look like daggers.

Martha wrinkled her nose. 'Ronnie, can I ask you something? It's important.'

'You can ask me anything, Martha. Anything at all.'

'Do you have a cat?'

'I do. As a matter of fact I have two cats. They're called Abbott and Costello.'

'Good. Because in that case, I think I would like to come to your house. I think I would like it very much.'

EPILOGUE

Saturday, 9 July 2016

Harry Stammers approached the bench overlooking the Serpentine and sat down beside the man with short grey hair and a stubby grey beard. The sun was shining. Harry had removed his jacket. He had folded it and laid it across his knees.

'It is unfortunate that your mother was unwilling to join us,' the man said after a few moments.

'She has nothing to say to you, Owen.'

Owen snorted. 'But evidently, you do.'

Harry said nothing.

'You were under no compulsion to come here. The arrest of Mr and Mrs Phelps and the exposure of our little ploy went down rather badly with the authorities. Mine was a minor part only, of course, but it was nonetheless a breach of my licence. I have been assured that any further,' he hesitated, 'unauthorised contact with you or your mother would see me back in prison.'

'Keep going. I'm all ears,' Harry said, sourly.

'Prison would almost be a price worth paying in order to see the truth about your mother made public. But not quite. So for now, at least, your secrets are safe with me and you can continue to enjoy your reputation. I see that you have made the headlines once again.'

'We're not interested in the headlines.'

'No, of course you're not. You're just interested in fighting the good fight. Exposing Mr and Mrs Phelps and locating the body of someone who had been missing for fifty years was a good fight indeed and a job very well done, I must say.'

Harry said nothing, but his irritation was rising. He hadn't come to listen to this.

'Tell me, how did you know that they had buried her beneath their swimming pool. I haven't yet managed to work it out.'

'Intuition,' Harry replied. Which was the truth.

'Impressive. You're a chip off the old block. I'm proud of you.'

Owen's remark was the final straw. 'You're proud of me?' he said, laughing sarcastically. 'Seriously?'

'You're amused that I might feel a sense of pride in the achievements of my son?'

'Amused? I think it's fucking hilarious.'

Owen appeared stung by the remark.

'My achievements have nothing whatsoever to do with you, Owen. You may have been present at my conception and, as a consequence, we might share some of our genes, but that is the extent of what we have in common. I am not your son. I will never be your son.'

'The truth, Harry. I can well understand why you might wish to deny it, but it is seldom good for one's mental health to live one's life in denial. That was your mother's big mistake.'

'My mother? You know nothing about my mother.'

Peter Owen laughed. 'Ah, but I do, Harry. I suspect that I know a good deal more about your mother than she has told you. Perhaps, more than you will ever know. Unless, of course...'

Owen had left the comment hanging. Harry shook his head. 'Wrong. You know about my mother's past. Or rather that small part of it that you shared. But it is exactly that. The past.'

Owen said nothing.

'My mother has a life with us. In the present. What she did, twenty, thirty, forty years ago? What she was, or pretended to be? It is not important to us. Do you know why?'

Owen tilted his head. 'Tell me.'

'Because we know the woman that she is. She is my mother and our daughter's grandmother. Lizzie, Martha, Ellen and me. We're family. We love each other unconditionally. Nothing that you or anyone else could say will ever change that.'

'How touching,' Owen said, with barely concealed acidity. 'But I wonder whether the public would love her if they knew what I know.'

Harry shook his head. 'You just don't get it, do you?' He turned to face him but Owen stared resolutely out toward the lake, refusing to meet his eyes. 'Do you honestly think we care what the public think?'

Owen laughed. 'There you go again. Denial. Anybody who has gone to the lengths that your mother has gone to conceal her history obviously cares very much about what people would think were they to discover it. Aren't you just ever so slightly curious to know what I know, Harry? Isn't that why you are here?'

Owen was trying to play games with him. Trying his damnedest to sow the seeds of doubt. 'If you're talking denial then perhaps you might try looking a little closer to home. Do you know, I actually feel sorry for you. Where has your life got you? Does anyone love you unconditionally, Owen? Do you have anyone? Other than your hatred of my mother, does your life have any meaning at all?'

Owen said nothing. But Harry saw the tension in his jawline.

'Did you seriously imagine that I was going to ask you for the lowdown on my mother? And then what? Having listened to it, abandon my mother, ally myself to a man like you, just because you're my biological father? Well, think again. You're nothing to me. You'll always be nothing to me. You're wasting your time.'

'Then why exactly are you here, Harry?' Owen spat, his composure suddenly slipping.

Harry thought about it. 'I'm here because I wanted to see for myself the kind of man you are. And now I've seen it, I know that my mother was right. You're a man consumed by hatred.'

But Owen wasn't giving up. Harry watched him calculating his next move.

'Is that what she told you? She's been manipulating you, Harry. Remember, she had years of practice. Manipulation was her stock-in-trade. She did it to me. She did it to her husband and now she's doing it to you and your family. If your mother is so unconcerned about what I might reveal, tell me, why, when Phelps had that note dropped through her letter box did she not just say publish and be damned. Because my guess is that she didn't. My guess is that she was panic stricken.'

It was a clever ploy but Harry was tiring of the game that Owen was playing. 'Of course she was panic stricken. You knew that she would be. You and Phelps were banking on it.'

Owen snorted. 'Because of the damage that she knew I could do to her reputation. To the cosy little family she has created for herself.'

Harry let out a long sigh. 'No,' he said, shaking his head. 'You really don't get it, do you? Lizzie wasn't afraid of you. She was afraid of herself. She loved you once, Owen. God knows why, because I'm damned if I can see it. And loving you certainly never did her any favours. On the contrary, it wrecked her life and the lives of everyone around her. But the point is that she was afraid that she might still love you.'

Owen turned and stared at him. And then he laughed. 'Is that what she told you?'

It was pointless. Owen was too far gone. 'No, it isn't what she told me. She didn't need to tell me.'

'She's taking you all for fools. Your mother is afraid that if the pubic knew the truth....'

'Enough,' Harry barked. 'The public will know soon enough.'

'What?'

He hadn't actually intended to go there, but now that he had made reference to it, there seemed little point in trying to double back. 'Something good at least has come from all of this. That note and your poorly conceived attempt at blackmailing us, prompted Lizzie to reflect on the silence she has maintained all these years. She was silent because she felt that she should not have to justify herself. But on reflection, she has come to a view that I share. She has nothing to justify. We all make mistakes, Owen. I've made them and Lizzie has made them. She did what she did. Lizzie, just like the rest of us, is human. And so she has decided to publish her story.'

Owen looked like he had swallowed a fish.

'She's writing it as a novel, rather than a straight biography, actually. I've seen her outline plot and it is going to be one hell of a book.'

'But she can't. They won't let her,' Owen choked.

'Oh, I think they will. She might have to skirt around certain matters, of course. Change certain names. National security and all that. But that's the advantage of writing it as a novel. She's a resourceful woman and a lot stronger than we all give her credit for. And what a story it is. A sure-fire best seller, I reckon and I'm not the only one. There are already several publishers wanting a piece of the action.'

Owen stared at him.

'She's calling it "The Battle of Wood Green", by the way. I'll reserve you a copy if you like. I'm sure you'll find it gripping.'

POSTSCRIPT

The starting point for 'The Scene Club' was an interview I did in May 2006 with John Steel, drummer with The Animals, for an internet radio station called 'SFR'. While running SFR I interviewed several musicians whose bands had, like Steel's, become household names in the early sixties. But it wasn't the fact that I was interviewing the drummer from such a well known band that stood out for me, it was that he spoke so candidly and engagingly about his experiences. The Animal's second single, *House of The Rising Sun,* had been a huge hit on both sides of the Atlantic, catapulting the band, in the space of little more than a few months, from the relative obscurity of the northern clubs where they had been playing, to international superstardom. In no time at all they were being escorted by police outriders from the airport at JFK, into New York and appearing on the Ed Sullivan Show.

While the interview, recorded on a MiniDisc recorder (remember them?), had sat in a cupboard for over ten years, Steel's description of the impact that sudden fame had on him and on the other members of the band, made a lasting impression and I had often thought about it. A much altered version of the interview appears in Chapter One of *The Scene Club*, although Steel is replaced by the wholly fictional character, Spencer Milburn and his fictional band, *The Monks*. The characters and, of course, all of the events in the book are entirely fictional and no association with Steel, The Animals or any real person is intended or implied.

Something else that stood out for me from that interview was mention of The Scene Club, a small dance club and music venue, where the band played when they first came to London. Located in a basement below Ham Yard in London's Soho, off Great Windmill Street, the premises had previously been occupied at night by Cy Laurie's Jazz Club and, during the day, by Mac's Rehearsal Rooms. By late 1963 The Scene Club's DJs, most notably Guy Stevens, who went on to work with Island Records and produced The Clash's acclaimed album, *London Calling,* had begun to play rhythm and blues and soul records imported from the United States; recordings by artists like Jimmy Reed, Bo Diddley, Howlin' Wolf, Big Joe Turner and Chuck Berry. While many went on to be big names, in 1963 their music was new to Britain and, in particular, to British youth.

As a jazz club, The Scene had already been the venue of choice for an emerging youth subculture, the members of which became known as modernists or 'mods'. The subculture had its roots in a small group of London-based stylish young men. They were labelled 'mods' mainly because they listened to modern jazz but they readily embraced the new brand of music played by Guy Stevens and the other DJs at The Scene and elsewhere, at clubs like the Whisky a Go Go, La Discotheque, and The Flamingo Club on Wardour Street.

The mods were by no means the first such youth subculture in Britain. They were preceded by the teddy boys of the 1950's, with their draped long coats and crepe-soled shoes, and later, by rockers and ton up boys who wore jeans, leather jackets and rode motor cycles. It has been suggested that modernism was, in part, a reaction against the fashion, aggressive stance and perceived 'dirtiness' of the rockers by the more style-conscious, clean-living London mods.

Undeniably, the scenes portrayed in the British press, through their coverage of several violent seaside confrontations between marauding mods and rockers in 1964, gives evidence to the rivalry that developed between the two subcultures. But in 1963 these rivalries were less pronounced, if not entirely non-existent. Many of the bands emerging in London and elsewhere, adopted subsequently by the mods, had their roots in rock and roll. Some, like The Animals from Newcastle, who played at The Scene Club in 1963, had never even heard of modernism. Speaking to me in 2006, John Steel, the drummer of The Animals, said:

"We couldn't really understand it. We were just a bunch of northern rockers. The fact is that we didn't even know what a mod was until we arrived at The Scene Club. It was purely a London phenomenon at that time. When we arrived at our first gig [at The Scene Club], the yard outside was absolutely packed with Lambrettas and Vespas, you know. Loads and loads of chrome. Lights. Long aerials with foxtails. And guys in suits and parkas. We'd never seen anything like it. It just wasn't anywhere else in the country at that time."

The Scene Club was a tiny and, by all accounts, rather dingy venue. The entrance was via a doorway in a corner of Ham Yard and access to it was via a flight of concrete steps down to the basement.

"You went down a staircase, paid your money, had your hand stamped... and went into a rectangular room. As I recall the DJ was in a little box to the right of the entrance, but it was flush to the wall. In the right hand corner opposite the DJ was a bar, that only sold soft drinks (I remember cola that was made from powder and water, really horrible). A bit further to the left of the entrance was a passage to the cloakroom. Along the far wall to the left were booths, I think the first few times I went there you couldn't see what was going on, but later they were opened up, I think this happened after a raid for drugs. And I think on the right hand wall between the bar and DJ booth were benches. The rest was a dance floor (I seem to remember a pillar or two, but again I could be wrong). People stood around or danced. A lot of the time it was a case of being seen at the right place."[1]

The mod subculture expanded rapidly and by the mid sixties was driving mainstream 'swinging London' fashion, popular music and the pop art movement. To the original mods mainstream popularity was anathema and by late 1966 many were moving on and The Scene Club had closed. Some mods embraced psychedelia and the later hippie movement. Harder elements adopted reggae, ska and the rude boy look that was popular in and around the black communities of South London, becoming suede-heads and later, skinheads. In northern towns like Wigan, others danced to the more obscure soul music of sixties and seventies America known as Northern Soul, or became scooter boys, a cross over sub-culture that included mod, skinhead, soul boy and later, punk elements. The mod sub-culture was revived, more directly, during the late 1970's by bands such as The Jam and Secret Affair, again splintering into different streams that included the 2-Tone Ska music genre and bands like The Specials, The Beat and Madness. In the 1990's, the Britpop scene embraced many mod references with bands like Oasis, Blur and The Verve. Today, mod music and fashion remains influential, in bands like The Spitfires and illustrated by clothing brands such as Ben Sherman, Lambretta and Pretty Green.

Each generation, it seems, finds its own expression of *modism* but for all of them, one place encapsulates the original mod subculture, arguably above all others: - The Scene Club in Ham Yard. Perhaps it is because it was there at the beginning, albeit as Cy Laurie's, that the venue has an almost mythical reputation among mods the world over. Perhaps it is because, having been at the centre of the subculture in 1964, it had closed by late 1966, and disappeared without a trace soon afterwards. That was my stand-out thought in early 2016 as I listened again to my interview with John Steel, considered part-setting my next book at The Scene Club, circa 1964, and wondered what had become of the little venue.

As Harry Stammers does in Chapter 9, my first step was to visit Ham Yard, to discover whether any trace still existed of the entrance to The Scene Club. I travelled there on Friday, May 13 2016, whereas Harry was there a few days before me on May 10. There is no significance in that. It was just how the plot worked out. I arrived in London early that morning for a business meeting in Victoria and like Harry, felt compelled to visit Ham Yard, which is a few minutes walk from Piccadilly Circus. The early commute into London was typically unpleasant. All twelve carriages on the train from Leighton Buzzard, where, also like Harry, I was living at the time, were packed and, with the warm weather refusing to entirely give way, the London Underground heaving as usual, and with a little less than an hour to spare, I very nearly gave up the idea at Green Park and stayed on the Victoria Line.

I persevered, however, and arrived at the junction of Ham Yard and Great Windmill Street, feeling rather pessimistic about the possibility of finding the basement formerly occupied by the little club that had played host, in 1964, to the likes of The High Numbers (later The Who), Georgie Fame and The Blue Flames, Chris Farlowe and The Thunderbirds and, of course, The Animals. Ham Yard, it quickly became apparent, had been almost entirely reshaped by the building of the new and impressive Ham Yard Hotel.

Incredibly, however, as I entered Ham Yard and turned left, to the rear of The Lyric public house, there it was. Tucked away in the far corner behind a wheelie bin and not exactly picturesque, although I don't think it was ever really that, were the doors leading, presumably, to a stairway down into the basement and the old Scene Club, minus the sign announcing its presence, but certainly one and the same. Later that day, I wrote in my blog: "Of course, I've no idea what is down there now or whether any sign of the former club still exists. It has been fifty years since The Scene closed its doors for the last time, to the dancers, bands and faces of sixties mod London. But I'd very much like to find out."

In Chapter 11, Harry posts his request to the members of *'Original Modernists 1959-1966'*, one of the Facebook groups of which he is a fictional member (the group is not fictional and if you'd like to join it, please do look it up). In fact I did exactly that, a few days after visiting Ham Yard, and like Harry, shortly thereafter, had my reply. I'd like to thank again, a gentleman called Craig Sams, for his response. As Des Munroe did for Harry, so did Mr Sams do for me, including keeping me waiting in his bathroom. I'm still dining out and writing books on the back of that story.

While the events surrounding Harry and Martha's visit to Ham Yard in Chapters 20-22 are entirely fictional, the description of what they found, until the point at which they climb the stairs to Gina Lawrence's former flat (neither the stairs nor the flat exist) paints a reasonably accurate picture of what we found. The basement below what was then the bar called 'Grace', in Great Windmill Street, is divided into several areas. Having descended the stairs, doors lead to the left, into the original basement at Grace and to the right, into what is (or was) an area called the 'Milk Bar', apparently occupying the space beneath 41 Great Windmill Street. We found the Milk Bar to be all beige leather seats and pink lighting, not at all reminiscent of The Scene Club, although a series of half circular alcoves might feasibly have originally been booths, rather like those I'd seen in pictures from The Scene and described in the book. To the back of the bar area was a door, behind which was a passage. It was when we passed though it that we knew we were in roughly the right place. We had entered a corridor, at the end of which was a flight of concrete steps up to the doors that led out into Ham Yard. This was, we were confident, the entrance to The Scene Club from the inside. It was a genuinely thrilling moment.

So far as we could make out, the area behind the Milk Bar had been divided to form a fire escape, with new walls erected with extensive re-modelling. Having worked that out, we were beginning to wonder whether there was going to be much more to see, when I happened to look up. In all the pictures I'd seen of the 1960's Scene Club's interior, the club's ceiling has a particularly distinctive, corrugated appearance. There above our heads, in a small patch of uncovered ceiling was the same ridged design. We found patches of the same ceiling elsewhere. It was quite a moment. Like Harry sometimes experiences, I found the hairs on my arms standing on end, though I am pleased to report the absence of any apparitions.

It has since been suggested that we might not have been in exactly the right spot and, in all truth, it is impossible to be entirely certain. The basements below Ham Yard and the adjoining properties have been extensively remodelled since the 1960's, in part to accommodate the redevelopment of Ham Yard and its new hotel.

From my selfish point of view, it doesn't really matter. Whether or not I stood, that day, in exactly the same spot that the dancers of The Scene Club had stood, I was able to feel a connection. I have adopted this method of research for all of my books to date and it has worked for me every time. Unlike Harry and Martha Stammers, I certainly don't claim to have any kind of sixth sense. However, much as Harry does, I have concluded, albeit with a certain amount of natural scepticism, that with a little imagination and an open mind, spaces can be encouraged to speak. Some places, I find, need a little encouragement, but others do so without any invitation at all. You walk into them, or even find yourself drawn to them, and as you step over the threshold, Pow! - an impression hits you right between the shoulder blades. This has happened to me on many occasions, often when I'm least expecting it. It did in G-block and in Building 41 at Bletchley Park (the result being my first and third books) and it certainly did that day, in the basement below Ham Yard, staring up at those ceilings. If this ever happens to you, don't be like Harry and dismiss it as mumbo jumbo. Take a breath, close your eyes and let the space tell you a story. There might just be a book in it.

(1) Geoff Green, Alice Fowkes and Chris H, 'London: The Scene Club and Soho', http://jackthatcatwasclean.blogspot.co.uk

THE SHELTER

THE HARRY STAMMERS SERIES, BOOK ONE
ANDY MELLETT BROWN

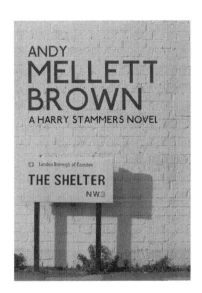

It is 10 November 1944 and a young woman in a woollen coat steps off a trolley bus into the darkness of wartime London and vanishes. Sixty years later, museum curator Harry Stammers receives an intriguing invitation from Bletchley Park veteran Elsie Sidthorpe. Aided by Ellen Carmichael, Elsie's great niece, Stammers sets out to discover the truth about what happened to Martha Watts.

THE BATTLE OF
WOOD GREEN

THE HARRY STAMMERS SERIES, BOOK TWO
ANDY MELLETT BROWN

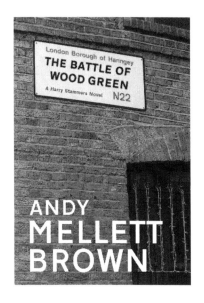

1970'S North London provides the backdrop to part two of the thrilling Harry Stammers series. School teacher and mother Liz Muir believes that she has put her life as an MI5 agent behind her, but when an ex-pupil is brutally murdered at an anti-Nazi rally and the mysterious 'Smith' reappears, Muir is forced back into service and a life built on secrets and lies begins to unravel.

BUILDING 41

THE HARRY STAMMERS SERIES, BOOK THREE
ANDY MELLETT BROWN

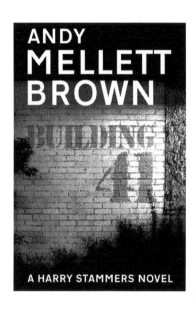

Taking the codebook from the petty officer's kitbag had been like tossing a stone into the ocean. The ripples of it seemed endless. Now some sixty years later, time and tide finally catch up with Bletchley Park veteran Elsie Sidthorpe, as she is tested once again by Günther Möller, the renegade German with his own hidden past. This time Elsie has an insurance policy. Or two, in fact. When the first of them fails, Bletchley Park curator Harry Stammers is thrust into a desperate race to unravel their secrets and the truth about a mother who has been missing since his childhood. With the mysterious 'Smith' manipulating events for his own covert ends and Möller preparing his final move, Stammers and the acid-tongued Jane Mears must accomplish the impossible. But not before they have deciphered the secrets of BUILDING 41.

ANDY MELLETT BROWN was born in Harringay, North London and lived there until he was sixteen. He joined Haringey Social Services Department in 1982 and presently works for the Care Quality Commission. He was President of the resident Radio Society at Bletchley Park until 2016, whose members campaigned to save The Park from demolition.

Published in June 2013, Andy's first novel, *The Shelter,* has earned him an ever growing and enthusiastic following. *The Battle of Wood Green* is the second in his *Harry Stammers Series.* The third, entitled *Building 41* is the thrilling finale to the initial series. Happily for Stammers fans, Harry is back in a new novel and Andy's fourth, entitled *The Scene Club.*

Andy now lives in Heckington, Lincolnshire with his wife, Patricia, Yaesu, their Cockerpoo, and an aged black cat without spots, called Spotty.

Meet the author at www.andymellettbrown.com

* Photograph by Janice Issitt

Printed in Great Britain
by Amazon